Hazel Graves is an Australian author based in sunny Southern California. The author of more than two dozen titles under various pseudonyms, Hazel loves finding the morbid in the romantic and the romantic in the morbid. And of course, the humour in both. When not ruining her characters' lives, she can be found walking her Jack Russell terrier, sampling French pastries, and eavesdropping on juicy café conversations. *Four Weddings and a Funeral Director* follows in the strange footsteps of *The Little Coffee Shop of Terrors*.

Also by Hazel Graves:

The Little Coffee Shop of Terrors

FOUR WEDDINGS

AND A

FUNERAL DIRECTOR

HAZEL GRAVES

avon.

Published by AVON
A division of HarperCollins*Publishers* Ltd
1 London Bridge Street
London SE1 9GF

www.harpercollins.co.uk

HarperCollins*Publishers*
Macken House, 39/40 Mayor Street Upper
Dublin 1, D01 C9W8, Ireland

A Paperback Original 2025
1

First published in Great Britain by HarperCollins*Publishers* 2025
Copyright © Stephanie Campisi 2025

Stephanie Campisi asserts the moral right to be identified as the author of this work.

A catalogue record for this book is available from the British Library.

ISBN: 978-0-00-877047-1

Set in Birka by HarperCollins*Publishers* India

Printed and bound in the UK using 100% Renewable
Electricity at CPI Group (UK) Ltd

This book contains FSC™ certified paper and other controlled
sources to ensure responsible forest management.

For more information visit: www.harpercollins.co.uk/green

For Linda – here's to champers and shenanigans!

Contents

Died and Gone to Heaven

Lily

Gosh, this place was romantic.

Not that Lily had romance on the brain. She'd set that part of herself aside somewhere between the warning klaxon of her mom's disastrous post-divorce relationships and the approximately seven hundred weddings Lily had attended last year as a maid of honour. A job she'd finally – after a viral Instagram moment and much prodding from her friends and her Uncle Roger (a CPA) – agreed to monetise in the form of her new wedding planning business.

There was no denying that Mirage-by-the-Sea, a fairy-tale destination a few hours north of San Diego, was the ideal spot to hang out her hot-pink shingle. Beloved by influencers of the West Coast, it regularly trended on social media under the hashtags #quaint and #bougainvillea and #cottagecoregoals. Home to a pedestrian-only promenade that wound around storybook cottages and quirky businesses propped up by intergenerational wealth rather than actual business plans, it was the sort of place that should've stopped existing sometime back in the Seventies, before the hyper-capitalism of the Eighties took over. And yet, thanks to state grants and a large cash infusion from an anonymous lottery winner, the dream paraded on.

Lily had visited several times as a child with her mom and whomever her mom had been dating at the time, and had fond memories of it: eating giant scoops of gelato up on the grassy hills as the wind whipped her hair into her face; sitting cross-legged on a picnic blanket in the amphitheatre as a swing band played; reading battered books from the antique shop with the huge gumball machine that, in the childhood jackpot Lily would never forget, dispensed multiple gumballs at once.

The town had many charms, but not least was the initiative from the Chamber of Commerce that enticed quirky new businesses by offering them a massive discount on their rent should they take over an empty shopfront. Lily's friend Annika, who was constantly sharing pictures of unfairly cheap houses in Sardinia and Sweden and extremely beautiful but terrifyingly rural parts of the US, had sent the post about it to Lily along with several heart-eye emojis.

Lily, a few glasses of wine and several Instagram pages deep into the beginnings of a quarter-life crisis, had immediately applied.

Business Type? Wedding planner.

Business Name? Eternal Elegance.

Years of Experience? None. No wait. When had the first of her friends got married? Because her expertise started then, with the first of her many unpaid (and unappreciated) internships.

That had been a mere month ago. And now, here she was, hot-pink, keyring-decorated duffel bag at her feet, ready to bestow matrimonial bliss upon the sleepy village.

Lily hoisted her duffel bag over her shoulder, carrying it from the parking area behind the shops and down Moonkissed Alley, a plant-filled cobblestone laneway dotted with tiny shops (Made-to-order taffy! Absurdly expensive wine! Artisanal windchimes!) and cosy rocking chairs covered with plush macramé-edged cushions and rhinestone-dotted folk art. The laneway opened out to a larger promenade, home to a winding array of larger two-storey shops with thatched roofs and arched windows and individual patios draped with wisteria and astonishingly vivid flower baskets. You could follow the promenade downhill (to arrive at the Hot Pot, the internet-famous tea and coffee house), or up (to arrive at Rerunning Up That Hill, the local second-run theatre, which made most of its money off its monthly fun runs). From the top of the hill you could see the spread of homes reaching towards the ocean, with its foggy fingers and sharp winds and happily splashing sea lions.

And for the next year – for that was how long the discounted lease ran – it was home. Lily hugged her duffel, drinking in the perfection of it all as she waited for her realtor, Angela, to arrive with the key.

Her new space was even more beautiful than in the post Annika had shared, and in the photos she'd spent hours browsing online. Art, it seemed, had failed to imitate life, but in the best possible way. The shop was a whitewashed building with gingerbreading all over and clematis climbing up every wall and pillar in a fragrant explosion of pinks and purples.

Just imagine all the cake tastings and stationery craft sessions she could host here! All the happy couples smiling mushily over their carefully selected bonbonniere and boutonniere! All the photo albums and guest books they'd leave hugging under their arms, filled with some of the most important, magical memories of their lives!

Lily took a deep breath, bespelled by the shop and her new upstairs apartment, which had its own plant-filled terrace and hanging array of hummingbird feeders – all of which were busy with the flitting of the tiny green-breasted birds. Sheer chiffon curtains draped the floor-to-ceiling windows, hiding the living space behind the multi-paned glass.

It was perfect.

Well, except for one thing.

The red flag that was the eye-gouging reality of the building next door.

'What's with the circus tent?' she asked, as Angela – a striking dark-eyed woman whose three-quarter black culottes perfectly matched her severe bob – breezed up, giant handbag and giant earrings swinging.

Neither the online listing nor Lily's endless ground-level digital wandering in Google Street View had shown the massive yellow and red striped tent over the building next door. It looked as though a jumping castle had fled a particularly abusive set of jumpers and had taken a leap of faith, resulting in it being upended upon Lily's neighbour. Unless, she fretted, the building always looked like that.

'Just a fumigation tent,' said Angela airily. 'They should be done in a day or so.'

'Just as long as I'm not working alongside a troupe of clowns.'

Angela, who was digging about in her enormous bag for Lily's keys, snorted. 'Definitely not clowns. More like . . . the opposite of clowns.'

Lily nodded, hoping Angela was telling the truth.

'Aha!' Angela flourished a pink key with a strip of cloth attached. She gestured to the wrought-iron frame hanging above an art deco sconce light. 'All it needs is your sign, and you're ready to go. Are you ready to do the honours?'

Lily had never been more ready for anything in her life. This cute building was about to be hers! Well, sort of hers – it still belonged to whoever actually owned it. But it was Lily's for all intents and purposes, and those intents and purposes were to help bring people together in a manner as over the top as she could possibly manage. And also a little bit to avoid her newly coupled-up friends and the awkwardness of being the single solo person at the table. Not that she was being invited to many dinner parties these days. The whole dinner invitation thing started to drop off when you weren't part of a couple.

('It's the odd number of seats that throws me off,' her friend Kennedy had explained. 'Things just work in pairs. No one has seven bowls or nine portions of dessert. And then you start to wonder . . . why are they single, you know?' Lily had left that party early, although not before eating an extra slice of cake and stowing a bottle of wine in her handbag.)

After unlocking the door – which was white and with a charming slot for letters, something that Lily had always longed for in a building – Angela gestured for Lily to lead the way.

Lily didn't need to be told twice. She lugged her duffel past the patterned exterior tiles, then over the threshold, dropping it on the astonishingly beautiful parquetry flooring, which boasted ornamental flowers and sunbursts every few feet. A fireplace claimed one section of the wall, just begging for Lily to finally purchase the decorative brass peacock fireguard she'd had on her vision board for years.

'It's so beautiful,' breathed Lily.

'Isn't it? You were lucky to get it. We had five hundred applicants for this space – including one from a scientist stationed in Antarctica. But sometimes the stars align.'

'The scientist couldn't make it back from Antarctica in time, huh?'

'I said what I said,' said Angela, with a grin.

Overhead, vintage floral light fixtures straight out of Murano gently spotlighted the vintage furniture and hanging artwork. Lily just wanted to stand on the magical spot where sunlight met lamplight met firelight, feeling their communal warmth and staring out at the lush greenery outside. This must be what it felt like to be a cat: always seeking the sun.

'What was it before this?'

'A tailoring business. Janessa Hodges?' Angela cocked her head as though Lily might have heard of her. The name rang a bell, but Lily couldn't place it.

'She made the most exquisite over-the-top outfits you've ever seen, mostly for celebrities and socialites. And Burning Man. Not for the faint of heart, or faint of pocket. Before that, we had a watchmaker, a glitter bomb delivery business and a luxury pet rock store. They peddled mostly in geodes. Before that, I believe it was actually part of the business next door.' Angela gestured at the brick wall that separated the two buildings. 'But that was before my time.'

Lily nodded, her eye catching on a decorative grille set about eye-height in the wall the realtor had pointed out. (Well, eye-height for a person of average height – tiptoe-height for Lily, who had stopped growing somewhere around sixth grade, in defiance of the height potions she'd mixed with her cousin Tessa. Or perhaps because of them, when she considered the ingredients.) She wondered what was going on over there, beneath the striped tent. At least they'd patched up the other side so that whatever poison they were using to zap the vermin they were waging war on wasn't blasting through to her side of the wall. Especially since that wall was home to a gorgeous (and likely irreplaceable) antique desk and a fat leather chair. And, weirdly, a sledgehammer.

'Nothing like stepping into a furnished place,' said Angela. 'Makes life so much easier. So does wine,' she added, spinning the desk chair to reveal a welcome basket filled with wine and chocolate and bath bombs.

'Oh, I like you,' said Lily.

'There are a bunch of gift cards in there for the village businesses as well. And a small business treasure hunt map. Get a stamp at each one, and come to the Chamber of Commerce to collect your prize. Do you have help to deal with those?'

She was referring to the stacks of packing boxes up against the far wall. These contained all sorts of knick-knacks and swatches and stationery samples, which Lily was looking forward to unpacking and setting out in a colourful array. Lily was a maximalist by nature, and there was no reason her shop should be any different.

'I have a pocket knife and a bottle of wine,' said Lily. 'I'm all set.'

'Oh, I should give you my wife's card as well.' Angela produced a card die cut in the shape of a typewriter. *Tink Nowak. Type Upsetter.* 'She does letterpress everything – cards, invitations, whatever your imagination can spin up. She has a studio higher up the hill, near the cinema. Might come in handy in your line of work.'

'It absolutely would.' Lily pocketed the card, noticing Angela clocking her ringless ring finger as she did so. That's right, she'd committed the sin of being an unmarried wedding planner. 'How's the cinema?'

'Amazing. Single screen, second-run movies, and the best popcorn you'll ever eat. And they host book club, trivia night, you name it. You should come down tonight – it's Tightass Tuesday, and there's live piano music and everything.'

'Sold. I'll be there as soon as I'm done with all of this.' Lily gestured at the boxes waiting for her attention.

Angela's phone was buzzing. 'Ugh, that'll be my 11 a.m., this investor bro who's got his eye on this sweet old man's house for a shitty flip. Thank God I've got the ear of the town planning commission – I'll get him so bogged down in permits he'll run back to Silicon Valley with his slimy tail between his legs.'

Lily grinned. She couldn't wait to unpack her decor and get to work. She already felt at home in her charming shop, with its equally charming upstairs apartment overlooking the pedestrian-filled promenade. Now *that* was her dream commute. She could roll out of bed, head downstairs, and be right at her antique, soon-to-be-painted-pink desk. Not too shabby at all.

As Angela strode out on her stacked wooden heels, Lily snapped a pic of the space and sent it to Mom, who could do with the pick-me-up after her latest breakup.

Like mother, like daughter, texted back Mom. *I knew you had my sharp business mind. And itinerant spirit.*

Lily was texting back when a ringing sound shattered the peace: the yellow rotary phone on the desk was absolutely going off. Who knew those old phones were anything other than decorative?

'Eternal Elegance, Lily speaking,' she said, feeling very businesslike. Her first call at her new location! This was a champagne moment. Luckily in addition to Angela's wine she had a whole carton of mini bottles of bubbly somewhere in the stack of boxes. In theory they were to taste-test with clients, but a girl deserved to celebrate her wins.

'My husband's dead. I need to make preparations,' came a scratchy voice over the line. 'Do you do that? And about the price . . .'

Lily blanched. 'I don't . . . I don't think I can plan a wedding if one of the parties is dead.'

'Isn't this Eternal Elegance? Emphasis on *eternal*?'

'Yes, but not like . . .'

'Bah. I'll try Coffins 'R' Us down in Bayside. Ridiculous.'

The caller hung up, leaving Lily in a state of icky bafflement.

Sure, her whole thing as a wedding planner was slightly kooky, off-kilter, inclusive weddings, but arranging a marriage to someone dead was pushing the decorative envelope a bit. Maybe the caller had been trying some sort of tax-evasion thing. Or some teenagers were hosting a pizza and prank-call party.

Oh well. Lily couldn't spend too much time worrying about it – she had unpacking to do. But first, a soak in her new clawfoot tub.

All's Fair in Love and Mortuary Studies

Mort

Mort's week was off to a lousy start. Literally. No one wants to learn that the family business is overrun by termites, especially within just a few months of taking it over. It would have been nice for Gramps to mention the whole persistent woodlouse invasion thing, but then, he couldn't really fault the old guy – he should have retired twenty years ago. He probably would have, if he'd been able to find anyone to take over the business, and damn had Gramps tried. But it takes a special kind of person to become a funeral director. Or in Mort's case, a special kind of failure. Mort had given himself until age thirty to make his dream of becoming a concert pianist reality, but life had a habit of running the clock down. So now, here he was, doing his bit to help Gramps out by sending off grizzled old gents and smart-mouthed widows and a worrying number of motorcyclists into the Sweet Hereafter. Or wherever it was that people went once they closed their eyes that final time. Mort had spent a good deal of time considering the whole thing, but still hadn't come up with an answer he was happy with.

'At least you gave yourself time to pursue your dream,'

Gramps had said. 'Not everyone gets that. And there's still the organ.'

The organ Gramps had been referring to was the one inside the funeral home upon which a young Mort had belted out his early efforts at Mendelssohn, Mozart and Beethoven. (Funeral attendance numbers had, thankfully, improved as he had.) Mort still played it – in fact, even more so these days, now that he was living in the drab apartment above the funeral home and had ready access to it. Gramps, on the other hand, insisted on remaining in the huge, dark house that he'd raised Mort in. Mort loved the house as much as Gramps did, even though it was a death trap (to be fair, everything in a funeral director's eyes was a death trap), and the maintenance was becoming too much for Gramps to handle. And for Mort to handle. Every spare day that Mort had was now spent hammering at loose boards or dealing with dodgy wiring or righting a tree felled by a savage gust of ocean wind.

He'd been trying to get Gramps out of the house and into somewhere more manageable, like one of the townhouses in the village, but Gramps was as stubborn as, well, Mort was. But Angela was savvy – she'd use her realtor's wiles to entice Gramps away from the house and into somewhere he wasn't likely to fall down the carpeted stairs or get squashed by a crystal chandelier or suffocate while trying to draw the extremely thick velvet blinds, all of which were very real possibilities. (Mort judiciously read each and every coroner's report, and had a deep awareness of all the ways a house might try to kill you.)

Mort's phone pinged, almost giving him a heart attack. *Just a mild panic response, Mort,* he told himself. After all, he was at low risk for heart attacks, and the body-weight exercises he did every morning were designed to ward off an early death.

Delivered, flashed an app on his screen. *Signed for by . . .* a squiggle.

Mort frowned. That squiggle should have been made by *his* hand, but it was decidedly not. He'd absolutely not signed for the package, because right now he was sitting at The Hot Pot reading over the sheet music for the silent movie showing at Rerunning Up That Hill later tonight. Unless Mort had a doppelganger running around the village, either someone had forged his signature, or Roddy, the village's delivery guy, had slipped up. (This was not unheard of, given that Roddy was well into his eighties. But Roddy was a nice guy, and people gave him the benefit of the doubt. Especially when he brought treats for their dogs, which was often.)

'All done there, hon?' Dierdre, the owner of The Hot Pot, was swinging by with a moon-shaped teapot and a stack of clattering half-moon teacups. Dierdre was a town treasure, known for her colourful tattoos, her colourful language, and her colourful crockery collection, which she'd inherited from some distant hoarder aunt.

Mort gathered up his plate and teacup, setting them into the yellow tub atop the heavily decoupaged credenza along the far wall. Dierdre's decor was entirely too bright for Mort, but she did make the best tea and the fanciest croissants in town. 'Business calls.'

'*Another* death?'

'Worse: a misdelivery.'

Dierdre made a face. 'At least it's not solar sales.'

Mort snorted. 'If they come to the door again, we *will* be talking about a death.'

'I, for one, would be happy to give you an alibi, hon!' Dierdre waved as Mort headed out the door, stopping briefly to give a belly rub to Jenkins, the café's resident terrier. Then he hurried up the wide promenade towards the funeral home, dashing through tourists' vacation selfies and interrupting a game of pathway Connect Four – something that the town advertised as a charming diversion that could result in a surprise dinner voucher discount, and which Mort personally thought was a public menace.

'Hey!' A dad with a sweater knotted around his neck scowled through expensive glasses. 'You made me lose concentration.'

'Sorry, I didn't realise you were playing a critical game of chess against Garry Kasparov,' muttered Mort.

'What was that?'

'Nothing, nothing. Enjoy your stay.' Mort, who hadn't slowed one iota, waved vaguely as he hustled up the promenade. Thankfully he was no stranger to the journey, and was barely winded by the time the funeral home was in sight.

Well, not the funeral home precisely, but rather the red-and-blue stripes of the fumigation tenting covering the funeral home. He shook his head – they couldn't have gone with a stately black? After all, fumigation was a death-related business, too.

'Almost done here, bud,' said Franco, the fumigation worker sitting on a bougainvillea-drenched rock wall, Ninja Turtle lunchbox in hand. 'We should be able to take this off tomorrow, get you back in business.' He took a bite of a peanut butter and honey sandwich with the crusts cut off. 'Accidentally grabbed my kid's lunch. Not bad. Lunchable?'

He held out a package of cheese and chopped ham. Mort shook his head.

'Grape juice?'

Mort shook his head again. Vehemently.

With a shrug, Franco popped open the juice box, draining it in one sip.

'Did you receive any deliveries today?'

'What, through that?' Franco nodded at the massive tent, which was wafting up and down in the breeze. A few pigeons had taken up residence on top and were enjoying the ride. 'Maybe they went next door. There's a new gal.'

Ah, next door. The yin to the funeral home's yang. Where the funeral home was an all-black affair that dripped with velvet and obsidian and had an entrance marked by two black marble greyhound statues (which were, annoyingly, a favourite photo op of the tourists), the building next door was an extravaganza of colour. Sure, the exterior paint was mostly white, but there were pops of bright pink and yellow everywhere you turned, and more wildflowers than seemed acceptable in the planters out the front.

As Mort steeled himself to approach whatever perky creature would inhabit the building for the next twelve months, the front door swung, and a tiny woman with springy hair and a springy step emerged. She was wearing what Mort could only describe as the outfit of a recently landed skydiver, and carried a wooden sign under one arm. An orange-handled screwdriver poked out from one ear.

She was alarmingly bright, and alarmingly attractive. Mort's heart was stuck somewhere between sinking with foreboding and ballooning with joy. He gulped, trying to get his sudden arrhythmia in order. *No heart attacks, Mort,* he chastised himself. *Don't be a statistical outlier!*

'Hey there!' she said, in a voice that perfectly matched the crinkle of her bright blue eyes. 'Looking to get married?'

'What?' Mort coughed, then thumped his chest. He was making an excellent impression here.

'Guess not. I'm Lily, the town's new wedding planner.' She gestured at the shop that had until recently been home to Janessa Hodges, who after a brutal bout with influenza had moved instead to a small six-by-one subterranean abode at the Mirage-by-the-Sea Cemetery. Mort had helped her move in. (The town had advertised none of this on the small business application FAQs.)

'Are you local?' she asked, her brow wrinkling slightly. She gave him a very thorough once-over. Then a twice-over. 'You don't . . . seem like a tourist.'

Mort glanced down at his all-black attire. What, the gleaming black Oxfords and the black pocket square didn't scream beachgoer? 'Mort. I work . . . around here. I was just wondering, did you collect a package earlier? For Eternal Elegance?'

Lily cocked her head. 'Are you some kind of delivery quality assurance guy? Because this lovely old man *did* drop off a package – he even came in for a cup of coffee and a chitchat about his granddaughter's wedding last September.'

Ah. Amelia May's wedding. Mort had been invited, but he'd spent the day dealing with a funeral emergency instead. Who knew it would be so hard to find an on-call archaeologist to deal with some potential dinosaur bones in a funeral plot? At least Roddy had come by after with some sugared almonds to thank Mort for his gift of a customisable casket cap panel.

'That would be Roddy,' said Mort.

'But there was some kind of mix-up.' Lily paused to point out a hummingbird in a burst of hot-pink bougainvillea. 'Don't you love hummingbirds? Anyway, the business name was right, but they got the address wrong. I didn't realise until after I opened it and found this vase inside.'

Mort grimaced. Ah yes, a vase. For flowers. Definitely not for the ashes of Meryl Halston, who was booked in for a date with the crematorium.

Then he frowned. 'Wait. What do you mean the business name was right?'

Lily flashed the pink-and-white sign she'd been preparing to hang up outside her new building. *Eternal Elegance – Wedding*

Planner, it read, in a carefully hand-painted script surrounded by folk-art-style flowers and birds.

'On top of that, I've been getting phone calls from *beyond the grave*. Well, their loved ones, I suppose. I think there's a crossed-line situation going on.'

Oh shit, thought Mort. Oh *shit*.

Just then, there was an incredible swishing sound as Franco and his workers hauled the striped tent down from the funeral home . . . revealing the black and gold hanging sign that perfectly matched Lily's, right down to the name.

Eternal Elegance – Funeral Director.

'There ya go, boss!' called Franco. 'Ain't nothing alive in there now. Not even a cockroach could've survived that.'

It didn't take a glance in the newly revealed windows to know that the look on Lily's face mirrored the one on Mort's.

'I'll . . . go get your urn,' said Lily.

(Burial) Plot Twist

Lily

Lily sipped an emergency prosecco from the bar fridge in her shop, giving thanks to Janessa Hodges for including such an important appliance in her workplace decor.

Everything had very quickly turned topsy-turvy. When the tent had whipped off from the building next door, revealing a building straight out of *The Munsters*, Lily had felt as though she'd stepped through a mirror. (A bad one.) All black gingerbreading and stern gargoyles and black planters filled with midnight petunias, it was the evil twin of Lily's new shop. Although the black greyhound sculptures out the front did have some charm. As did the wild-haired, dark-eyed, black-clad man who'd come hurrying up to the shop asking about a misdelivered parcel. A wild-haired, dark-eyed, black-clad man she hoped hadn't noticed how she'd almost swooned when their gazes had clashed that first time. If she'd been one of her myriad recently married friends, she might have described it in romantic terms. Love at first sight. Lust at first sight. Hiccup at first sight. Some sort of very real visceral reaction to an incredibly hot man who'd come hurrying up . . . and whom she'd immediately pressed about his interest in marriage.

Lily groaned. *Looking to get married* indeed. What an

impression she must have made. The man probably thought she was a stalker. Especially after she'd cleverly, and entirely accidentally, given her business the very same name as his. What were the odds? Lily stared ruefully at the vinyl decal she'd stuck on the front door, and the decorative flower-board she'd put up on an interior wall – the one where pink rosebuds spelled out *Eternal Elegance* against a gerbera backdrop.

Well, it explained all those strange phone calls. And the pretty vase that had turned out not to be a vessel for flowers at all, but a vessel for . . . well, Lily didn't know exactly for whom, but she assumed it was someone of the human variety, not the floral variety.

At least her new business cards hadn't arrived yet. Maybe she could tell the print shop to put a hold on those until she thought of a new business name. And new branding, and new decor . . .

No, absolutely not. She'd promised herself she was going to stick with something for once in her life, and she was going to see it through, no matter what. *Think of the cheap rent, Lily.*

She sighed, leaning back in her leather swivel chair (which was now topped with a freshly unpacked pink shag throw pillow) and sipping urgently at her prosecco. Maybe it wouldn't be so bad. Perhaps they could send each other business. And at least they were next door to each other, so it was just a matter of Lily escorting a bereaved widow a few steps, and Mort scooting a happy couple away from a coffin or a burial plot.

Would Mort do that, though? Would he send them her way, or would he just warn them sternly that all love ended in death, and that they might as well save themselves the hassle – and the bill – and put that money towards funeral insurance instead?

Lily sighed. It seemed unfair that someone so deathly handsome could be so . . . deathly inclined.

Her phone buzzed. Annika.

Well??? How is it???

Lily snapped a photo of the shop and texted it back. *It's perfect.*

Make sure you stay long enough that I can come visit!!!

(Annika was not one for restraint when it came to punctuation. Or emojis. Or anything in life, really.)

Promise, texted back Lily. But before she could hit send, her phone rang.

'Eternal Elegance,' said Lily, a smile brushing her lips as she said the new business name aloud.

'Lily! It's Rina Morgan and Emmett Smiley. We're the Christmas in July wedding.'

'In July,' added Emmett helpfully.

'Believe me, I'm as excited as you are,' said Lily. She eyed the stack of cardboard boxes filled with props and decor ideas. This particular wedding was one of two she'd inherited from a friend of a friend, herself a wedding planner who'd needed to take a leave of absence in order to plan her own wedding. After seeing Lily's viral post, she'd slid into Lily's DMs asking her to take over the planning honours. And so a clientele and a profitable P&L was born.

Thankfully the big pieces – the venue and catering – had already been put in place by the previous planner, and Lily just had the details to work on. Like finding a suitable Santa. And sending out 'nice list' invitations to their formidable guest list. Which reminded Lily that she needed to call Tink the printmaker.

'We can't wait!' Rina's voice buzzed with eagerness, and perhaps some seasonally inappropriate eggnog. 'Did you see the inflatable candy cane pictures we sent you? They'd look amazing lining the aisle.'

'They really would,' agreed Lily, pulling up the wedding mood board on her laptop and adding it to her inspiration collage. Wow, she could almost smell the peppermint spilling off the screen.

'Oh, and we were thinking maybe that one of us could jump out of a snowdome? Probably Emmett. He was a high jumper in college.'

'Love it,' said Lily, adding a note about a sexy snowdome in the margins of the mood board.

'So, there is one thing,' said Rina.

Oh good. Just one thing. The thing was that when it came to weddings, the *just one thing* was never something small. It was the sort of thing you needed a PhD in International Relations to successfully navigate. Or some expertise in bomb defusing.

But Lily could do this. She had her cute new shop and her cute new sign, and business cards on the way. There was no turning back now.

'Absolutely!' she said brightly.

'It's . . . the seating plan. We have some, I suppose you'd say complicated family dynamics. Some people have a family tree; I have a family boa constrictor. Is it okay if I send over my notes to you? I think maybe an impartial third party might be the way to go.'

'If there's one thing I'm good at, it's musical chairs,' lied Lily. (She actually had a highly complicated relationship with musical chairs, having been taught from an early age to always give up her chair to someone else who needed it.) 'Send them over whenever you're ready.'

There was the distinct sound of sleigh bells ringing in the background as Rina clapped her hands, then rang off. Then, oddly, the jingling sound of sleigh bells switched to the sharp tones of an organ.

Lily checked her phone just in case the Addams family was calling – nope. She glanced around. Where was that coming from? Was someone pranking her? She paused, trying to triangulate the source of the music. Turning, she realised it was coming through the grille above her head.

'Hello? Mort?' she said uncertainly.

'This is he. You're not a ghost, I hope?' came Mort's muffled voice.

Lily knelt on her chair, leaning against its upholstered back. 'I was going to ask the same thing. It's just Lily from next door. We share a grille.'

'I hope I'm not bothering you.'

Not at all. In fact, Lily was utterly intrigued. 'No, it's lovely. What are you playing?'

'Schumann. It sounds better on a piano, but, you know. The clients have expectations.'

Lily hummed a few bars of the 'Funeral March' through the grille.

'Precisely,' came Mort's disembodied voice. 'Are you . . . coming to the theatre tonight?'

'Sure. Angela invited me. Apparently it's the place to be, and the town's most eligible bachelor is in charge of the music.'

A discordant few notes rang out through the grille as Mort fumbled the keys.

Lily straightened up in her chair. Had he fallen off his piano stool? Mort didn't seem like the falling-off-things type – that was more Lily's jam. (Lily's friends had banned her from roller skating ever again after The Great Mangled Toe Incident.) 'Everything okay?'

'Just a work call.'

'Ah. Death at the door, I see.'

'Something like that.' There came the sound of furniture

scraping as Mort apparently hurried off to deal with the Grim Reaper. Lily wasn't sure what the rush was: Mort was a funeral director, not a paramedic. Presumably he dealt with clients who had decisively tumbled off the mortal coil.

But maybe the whole mortuary sciences thing was like Lily's work – big emotions and life-changing moments were at play, and *everything* became an emergency. Everything, like napkin colours and RSVP rates and table arrangements and trying to ignore her own fear of commitment.

Swivelling her chair around to face her desk, Lily pulled up the seating chart notes that Rina had sent her and set to work.

A few hours later, brain addled from the endless scandals of Rina's family and the subsequent inability of anyone to sit together for fear of reprising said scandals, Lily shut her laptop. And not a moment too soon: Angela was texting to confirm she was coming to the evening's showing of *Vice Versa* (the 1916 silent version, not the 1988 Fred Savage version, the realtor made sure to reiterate).

I'll be there, she replied, adding a dancing emoji for good measure.

A moment, and then Angela responded with: *Just arrive before sunset. Trust me.*

Lily rummaged through her duffel for a suitable outfit. She hung up her more wrinkle-prone outfits as she went, throwing the other items on her bed until she had time to properly sort through her things. Like the shop, the upstairs apartment had come furnished, which meant she didn't have to haul a box of flat-pack furniture up the stairs or go begging for a replacement for an Allen key that would inevitably disappear. Sure, the walls could use some paintings – or at least a mural – and she was definitely going to pop down some extra rugs and cushions (you could never have too many), but Lily had lived in places with worse vibes. There was even a rocking chair that overlooked the meandering promenade – and a balcony bordered with dramatic flower baskets whose rainbow spoils spilled almost down to the ground outside.

As if called by Lily's gaze, a beautiful black-and-white cat with a plaintive expression appeared on said balcony.

'How'd you get there, kitty?' Lily opened the patio door – which was trimmed with the most beautiful floral lead lights – letting in her new furry friend. The cat leapt primly onto the rocking chair, then regarded Lily with what her mom had always called *hungry eyes*. Well-fed pets always had the expectation of more food.

She opened the narrow pantry next to her fridge. Aha, a Leaning Tower of Pisa lovingly crafted from tins of cat food. So this kitty was a known visitor.

Lily cracked open the can. As the cat daintily fed, a gleaming crystal bauble dangling from its collar caught the light. Tiny rainbows spangled the air.

'Pretty,' said Lily, approvingly. 'What's your name?'

She bent to reach for the tag that sat behind the bauble: *Esmeralda*. A fitting name for a kitty with such hypnotic eyes – one blue and one brown.

'I hope you don't mind watching me get ready,' Lily told Esmeralda as she considered a taffeta dress she'd picked up from a thrift store back in La Jolla. It was a creamy colour that felt a bit too bridal for a movie outing, and given the whole new-wedding-planner-in-town thing, she didn't want to give off Miss Havisham vibes. Maybe she could dye it purple. Did she have time?

There was always time to look fabulous.

She popped a few dashes of dye into a water-filled bucket

and swished the dress around in it until the cream fabric had turned the rich purple of a moonlit night. Then she pulled out the dress, wringing the excess water from it, and threw it into the ancient dryer that lived in a cupboard in the bathroom.

While it bumped and spun around, the dye setting, Lily carefully applied her makeup and pinned up her hair. The very second she'd popped in a pair of moon-shaped amethyst earrings, the dryer buzzed.

Esmeralda purred, impressed.

'I'm really good at time management,' explained Lily to the fluffy cat. 'There's a reason I got promoted from perpetual bridesmaid to perpetual wedding planner. Well, my excellent time management skills and the whole being perennially single thing.'

Esmeralda made a noise that was either pitying or in solidarity – Lily wasn't quite sure which.

'Are you all right to stay here, friend?' Lily cracked open the window for the cat. 'Here, just in case you need to go out and about.'

She locked the door to Eternal Elegance (Wedding Edition) behind her, feeling a sense of pride as she did so. Her own business, in her own building. And what a building. She couldn't think of a more perfect location to help people plan one of the most special days of their lives. After all, Mirage-by-the-Sea was one of the most romantic places she'd ever set foot in. The tiny storybook buildings, the hot pink clouds of bougainvillea, the tiny brook that twined its way beneath the promenade, gleaming with wishing coins and delicate glass beads. If she were a fairy godmother, this was precisely the type of place she'd magic a beloved godchild off to.

Lily joined a chatty trickle of people heading uphill towards the theatre, which was a stately blue and white art deco building with a scalloped façade and a bold marquee sign that showed the movie of the day on one side, and personalised notes on the other. (Today's read *Happy Smurfday, Charlie*, which was a bit confusing, but the world was a diverse place, after all.)

A small crowd had gathered out the front, sipping on giant ice-cream-topped drinks and watching the sun slink down over the distant bluffs and into the spangled ocean. Digital camera shutters clicked over and over, with Lily's among them. She was completely taken with how the setting sun played across the sky, creating an astonishing contrast with the village's fairy-tale buildings, which grew somehow even more magical as the shadows stretched and the fairy lights, twined around the bougainvillea hedges and over the garden arches, glimmered to life.

Angela waved with her free arm – her other arm was looped through the arm of a svelte woman in an incredible polka dot gown. 'You made it!'

'I was never going to miss it. I mean, I haven't seen *Vice Versa*, but I *have* seen *Freaky Friday*, which seems like it's in the same vein, and I'm a fan.'

'I *do* love a switcheroo,' said Angela. 'Misery. Confusion. It's what I strive to leave in my wake.'

'She fails miserably,' said the woman in the polka dot gown. She had a low, warm voice – perhaps that of a singer.

'I bet.' Lily held out a hand to her. 'I'm Lily, by the way. Great dress.'

'I'm Martinka. I mostly go by Tink. And thanks, I got it on sale at Pat's Consignments. It has pockets.' Tink showed off the bag of M&Ms she was smuggling into the theatre in said pockets. 'I hear you've set up shop next to the funeral home. Lucky you. Great space, though.'

Lily grinned. 'It is. If you two are planning a wedding, let me know.'

Tink chuckled. 'And not shy on the sales front, I see.'

'I just know true love when I see it.'

'Speaking of . . .' Angela nodded at a slimy-looking guy in tight trousers and a half-unbuttoned shirt chatting on the phone. A gold chain gleamed around his neck. (Lily had dated enough to know the dangers of guys who wore gold chains.) 'He just had a whole conversation with someone called Amber in which he dropped the words "baby" and "sweets" and "hot tub" a lot. But he's here with another girl.'

'Ooh, putting the "mess" into "mezzanine seats".' Tink rubbed her hands together.

Angela groaned. 'No. Babe. That was bad.'

Triumphant in her terrible humour, Tink pulled open the bag of M&Ms and picked out a handful of blue ones. She pointed. 'There's the other girl.'

A tall, curvy brunette in a gorgeous satin skirt was waving at Slimy Guy, urging him to come into the theatre. 'Nate! Show's about to start!' she called.

Slimy Guy/Nate held up a finger. 'Just on a work call.'

Lily shot the brunette an urgent look, trying in one glance to communicate everything she'd overheard. But apparently all she managed was a solid dose of crazy eyes, because the brunette blinked and turned away.

'You tried.' Angela patted her arm. She passed Lily a small paper ticket shaped like the retro movie tickets of old, but with some lovely embossing. 'Our treat. We're going in!'

'Cute ticket.' Lily thumbed the embossed projector image on the ticket as she queued up.

'Thanks,' said Tink, popping another M&M. 'Want one?'

Lily did indeed.

'The ticket is one of Tink's designs,' explained Angela.

Lily was impressed. She wiped M&M stickiness off her hands so that she could examine the ticket against the light of the art deco chandelier overhead. 'Oh, I *need* you as a vendor.'

'You should stop by the studio.' Tink took a flyer for the month's theatre showings from the student worker handing them out. 'It's just around the corner: Estellita Lane, off the bit of the promenade with the bodega and the thrift store. It should be on the treasure map that Angela gave you.'

With a flourish, Lily pulled the treasure map from her handbag.

'That's the one.' Tink was impressed.

'The Chamber of Commerce works overtime here, huh?'

'We look after our own,' said Angela, with a grin.

The cosy crowd pressed into the theatre, which was a riot of floral carpet and plush, impossibly oversized couches banded with gold. The concessions stand queue was almost as long as the line for the women's bathroom: dozens of people crowded around ordering giant boxes of popcorn and equally generous pours of beer. The warm aroma of popcorn and freshly baked cookies buttered the air.

'This place is gorgeous,' breathed Lily, imagining the type of wedding she could host here. What a stunning event space! And well intentioned, too, given the signs noting that profits from the showing would be donated to a local animal shelter.

'That's Aunt Dot over there,' said Angela, pointing out a vivacious woman in a dramatic muumuu and turban combination. 'Hey, Dot! Come meet Lily!'

Dot waggled her fingers at Angela. Shoving up a half-door on the counter, she came over to greet them.

'Lily! You're in Janessa's space, next to the funeral home! That's where I got this.' She tapped the swan-shaped jewel in the middle of her turban proudly. 'We're going to love having you here in Mirage-by-the-Sea. There's a small business owners meeting at the library next week. Join us! You can meet the giant goldfish in the library fish tank. Jaws.'

'Sure.' Lily never passed up an opportunity to meet someone new, and Dot looked like a hoot. 'I'll bring wedding cake samples. And decorative napkins.'

'Sounds like a date.'

'Aunt Dot, do you have your stamp handy?'

'Do I ever!' Pulling a stick of wax from her bra, she heated it up with a gold cigarette lighter, waiting for the dollop of wax to drop on Lily's treasure map. This she jabbed with the giant ring on her index finger, leaving an ornate seal. 'How's that.'

'That's . . . remarkable,' said Lily.

'I aim to surprise. Well, this popcorn isn't going to serve itself.' Dot waved, then returned to dispensing popcorn and beer to the hungry crowd.

'In we go!' Tink guided Angela and Lily towards the theatre door. 'Oh, I love this theatre so much. And the fact that everyone gets so dressed up, like we're a town of old-school glitterati.'

The trio pressed into the theatre, which was a dazzling space crafted from endless red velvet and elaborately painted rosettes. Heavy curtains draped the sides of the room and the screen in front, and tiered, geometric lights glinted like glass wedding cakes.

Lily was so focused on contemplating how a cake maker might actually reproduce these that she required a nudge from Angela to turn her attention to the tall, broad-shouldered guy in a very well-fitting tuxedo – with tails! – stalking down the dimly lit aisle towards the front of the theatre. Poor thing must have arrived too late for any of the decent seats.

Lily blinked as the guy passed them, his head turning, briefly, just long enough to catch her eye. She blanched – Mort? Mort was here? And in a top hat and tails, no less.

Then Mort took a seat at the piano on the stage.

Lily sloshed her drink. *Mort* was playing the film score?

'Are you all right?' whispered Angela, passing Lily a crumpled tissue from her handbag. 'You look like you've seen—'

'The love of your life,' whispered Tink. 'I'd know that double take anywhere.'

'Shh!' whispered an old guy behind them. Turning sheepishly, Lily recognised him as Roddy, the village's bicycle delivery guy. She offered him an M&M in apology, receiving a wink of forgiveness in return.

The theatre lights softened until only the faintest light glowed along the aisles and over the doors.

There was a hum of microphone feedback as Aunt Dot swanned out on stage.

'Thank you, all, for coming out on this beautiful Thursday evening! Rerunning Up That Hill is one of the many jewels of Mirage-by-the-Sea, and I'm honoured that you chose my dinky theatre over all the other options. Like The Hot Pot. Or the ocean. Or the funeral home.'

A light laugh rose up as Mort waved awkwardly and tinkled out a quick few improvised notes.

'Tonight's showing is *Vice Versa*, an amazing British science fantasy film where a schoolboy swaps places with his father. If you love *Freaky Friday* – and who doesn't – you'll love this one. Especially with Mort Vesper on the ivories.'

With a creaking sound, the curtain rose, and the wobbly sounds of the world's ricketiest piano filled the air.

Of course, the muffled tone of the piano, together with the

slight ringing sound that overhung it, could have been due to Lily's slightly-too-fast breathing.

Ahem. Lily chowed down on her popcorn and tried to focus on the movie – and not the moody soundtrack played by the pianist with the dark, beautiful eyes.

Fatal Attraction

Mort

Mort could feel his pulse in his temple, which did not seem like a good sign. He was also hyper-aware of his heart bouncing around in his chest, which similarly felt alarming. But he'd had such experiences before. Many times before. After he'd expressed his concern to Dr Rubenstein for the umpteenth time, she'd sent Mort away with a lollipop and an admonition that he not return unless he started bleeding from the eyeballs or somehow lost a limb in a freak accident.

Was it so odd that Mort was in touch with his own mortality given that day in, day out, all he dealt with was death? When you grew up around the funeral business, you became intimately acquainted with all the ways that people could die, and it became increasingly difficult not to think about the same happening to you. Everything became a threat, a risk. You became painfully aware that you were a soft-skinned bag of meat walking around courting death at every turn.

And ever since he'd met Lily, his body had been on high alert. Heart pounding, hands clammy, the whole lot. It did not seem healthy in the least.

Ordinarily, Mort didn't get nerves when playing piano. Especially here at Rerunning Up That Hill, where he'd played for as long as he could remember, and knew all of the emergency exits and safety protocols. But as he'd stalked down the aisle to the piano, his gaze had brushed over a tiny, chirpy figure sitting next to Angela and Tink. Lily, wearing a dramatic purple gown of chiffon and lace, along with long, sleek earrings that shimmered as she turned her head. Mort's heart had threatened to go into palpitations. And now here he was, sitting on the piano stool, fingers on the keys, preparing to score *Vice Versa* live . . . as Lily watched on.

His nerves were such that he barely heard Dot introducing him. He managed a belated wave and an improvised ditty to set the mood. The crowd broke into applause – and a disturbing number of wolf whistles.

Dot stepped back, gesturing for the projectionist (her nephew Bastien) to let the movie roll. Fortunately the whole thing did not go up in flames – Bastien was not known for his attention to detail, and at least once a week the audience had to bellow at him to change out the reel.

The audience chuckled as a series of local ads played. Mort hammed it up, banging out the jingles he'd worked with the local businesses to compose. The audience played along, whistling when Dierdre from The Hot Pot came on, writing her address on a teapot-steamed window, and whooping lewdly when Len from the Elephant Car Wash showed up in nothing but his signature trunks.

Mort bit back a grin as he saw Lily clapping her hands over her mouth.

When Eternal Elegance (Funeral Edition) came on the screen, he launched into Mendelssohn's 'Funeral March', to some smattered applause. And then when, to his surprise, Eternal Elegance (Wedding Edition) followed it, he launched into Mendelssohn's 'Wedding March', feeling grateful that one composer could do it all.

Honestly, he was impressed that Lily had figured out that the cinema even did local advertising – let alone that she'd put an ad together so quickly. Perhaps the Chamber of Commerce had helped, in which case they'd be sending out updated treasure hunt maps with the new business added any day now. Which meant more treasure hunters banging on his door and angling for a stamp. (Mort's was the hardest stamp to get, something he was secretly rather proud of.)

As Mort played the 'Wedding March', he became aware of a couple in the front row having a Very Bad Time™. The man kept texting, holding his phone at an angle so that the woman couldn't see what he was typing. Meanwhile, she was reaching for their shared popcorn in a very peculiar neck-craning kind of way. Mort wanted to advise her against it. He'd seen more than one person who'd died of a severed artery after some ill-advised neck manoeuvres. There'd been the woman addicted to neck massages, the guy who'd tried chiropractic techniques on himself, and the rugby player who'd tackled a brick wall on a dare.

Finally, the ads wrapped up, and Mort played a few jazz bars while Bastien changed over the reel.

'It's nothing to worry about, babe,' said the guy in the front row. 'She's like a sister to me.'

The girl nodded, reaching for another handful of popcorn. 'We'll talk about it later.'

'C'mon. Don't be like that. The jealous type. It's just a work thing . . .'

The film reel started, and a series of shushes went around the theatre. The time for heckling local businesses and their owners' questionable swimwear was over. The time for oohing and aahing and constructive commentary was here. Dot had always been vocal about movies being a participatory thing.

If you came to a Rerunning Up That Hill screening, you were expected to chime in. And also to roll orange chocolate balls down the theatre floor, which was part of some longstanding tradition that Mort couldn't quite grasp.

Mort focused on the keys as the film began, ignoring the choc oranges finding their way under his damper pedal. But then, right as the on-screen father and son swapped bodies, someone shrieked in the manner of an extremely excited terrier who has spotted a feline nemesis on a wall.

Mort fumbled his score. Was the person particularly enamoured of the body-swapping subgenre? Or was something amiss?

'Is there a doctor in the house?' someone screamed from the row in front of where Lily, Angela and Tink were sitting. 'Fran just keeled over!'

The chandeliers and aisle lighting abruptly brightened, leaving the audience in a confused, blinking state.

'Is this part of the movie?' stage-whispered Karo, the local fitness guru who ran Spinning Out, the spin studio next to The Hot Pot. (Karo was not known for adhering to the norms of Inside Voice.) 'It was that other time.'

'Only on Halloween,' replied an older guy with a valiant comb-over whom Mort recognised as Stribley, of Stribley's Plumbing fame. He was well known at the funeral home – people in mourning tended to flush a lot of tissues. 'It's May.'

The theatre hummed with consternation as the patrons tried to check each other's medical credentials.

'I only *played* a doctor,' said a handsome guy who looked exactly like someone who might play a TV doctor. He pulled out a stethoscope from his pocket and frowned becomingly. 'See? Fake.'

'Don't look at me,' the fake doctor's date was saying as Mort hurried down the aisle. 'Mine's just a lowly doctorate in literal philosophy. Ask me about rhetoric, not about resuscitation.'

Mort squeezed between the seats to see if he could help. Although not a doctor himself, he did hold an up-to-date CPR certification, and had successfully performed the Heimlich manoeuvre twice. (Gramps had a thing for eating salted caramels faster than he could chew.) He spent enough time with death to want to avoid it at all costs.

'Is she going to be okay?' asked Lily, who'd climbed out of her seat to donate her handbag for use as a pillow for Fran. 'She seems . . .'

Mort nodded. 'We'll do what we can.'

'She just loves movies so,' said the screamer, an old guy in a flat cap better known as Derrick, owner of the local bodega. 'We're celebrating our anniversary. Fifty years! Our golden one. But she gets so worked up when the pictures come on. She's been out of sorts, but I couldn't say no, could I? Do you think . . .'

Shooting Mort a please-help-me look, Lily wrapped Derrick in a hug. 'Let's just wait for the doctor. She's on her way.'

'*Paging Dr Rubenstein*,' came Dot's voice over the PA system. '*Dr Rubenstein, your expertise is needed in the main theatre.*'

'Oh damn it, really? It's my night off,' muttered a woman in a dramatic silk gown clutching a beer in each hand. Then, composing herself: 'I'm here, I'm here. Sorry, had to pee, and you know what the queues at the ladies' are like. What's going on?'

Mort gestured to Fran, whose pallid expression and immobile state said it all.

Trying to be charitable even in the face of the obvious, Dr Rubenstein gently took Fran's wrist, listening for a pulse. Momentarily, she grimaced up at Mort. At least it wasn't a scowl and an admonition for him to stop overreacting and go take a stroll around the block instead.

Although Fran probably didn't feel that way.

Although honestly, Fran probably didn't feel any particular way right now.

'Mort,' Doctor Rubenstein said, 'I'm afraid we've crossed into your area of expertise.'

Mort sighed. Goddamn it, he thought, trying to ignore Lily's stricken face as she presumably visualised what life living next to a funeral parlour might entail. Was there *anything* that didn't kill you?

'She's dead!' screamed Derrick, then, clutching his heart, promptly keeled over himself.

Double damn it.

Love at First Plight

Lily

Sure, the line *till death do us part* is a core component of any wedding vow, but Lily hadn't expected the death part to arrive before she'd even presided over an actual wedding. She couldn't shake the faces of Fran and Derrick – nor the fact that her favourite handbag had become the resting place for a corpse's head. (She hoped this wouldn't preclude her from listing it on Poshmark, but she'd have to check the terms and conditions. And maybe lie a little.)

As she always did when she was dealing with stress – for example trying to talk her serial monogamist mother through yet another one of her disastrous relationship breakdowns or accepting that the perfect shoes she'd bought off Etsy were too narrow or having two people abruptly die in front of her at the cinema – Lily threw herself into her work. This was probably a good thing, as her phone had been ringing off the hook with people enquiring about her services (and on a couple of occasions, about the funeral parlour's services, but she was getting good at forwarding those).

Speaking of the phone, it was ringing again.

'Hi, this is Venus,' came a smooth woman's voice over the phone. It was the voice of someone who spent a good deal of their life livestreaming their every thought to a captive audience. Which of course Venus, as the sole heiress to one of the nation's largest toothpaste empires, absolutely did.

Lily tried to modulate her voice so that she sounded cool, calm and professional, and not like she'd secretly been following Venus's relationship exploits across every fashion blog, podcast and dental office magazine for as long as she could remember. There was the Greek mouthwash heir, then the co-founder of the mail-order orthodontics start-up that had mysteriously shuttered in the night, and most recently the DIY fluoridation entrepreneur. (Venus tended to stick within a particular niche when it came to her dating life.)

'Venus!' Lily exclaimed, her voice breaking and coming out in a squeak.

Oh well, she'd tried.

'Lily, I'm so glad we connected. I knew that Honour Nivola would come through with the backup wedding planner goods after I showed up on her doorstep that night – she just has good karmic juju like that, wouldn't you say?'

Lily didn't know the specifics of how this had happened, but Honour Nivola was somehow tangentially connected to Annika, who had a job in PR and therefore was about two degrees of Kevin Bacon away from most people in the world. Lily had had no personal contact with Honour, although she *did* love Effanie, the villain she played in the daytime soap *Time After Time*, which was second only to *Passions* in its narrative brilliance. Who could have guessed that Brooks Masters had a secret twin called Masters Brooks? Or that Ainsley Harlow would somehow return from her coma after three years to drive her pink Cadillac into the living room of her cheating husband's mansion?

'Absolutely, she's fab.' Lily couldn't wait to share the details of this call with Annika.

'I'm sure you've been given the basic rundown, but the energy is flowing today, and I thought I'd give you a call to send it out your way. Put it out there, you know?'

'Can't argue with the energy,' said Lily.

'So as you've probably gleaned from the fact that we've rented a fifty-acre space on a microgreens farm – friends of the family, they're such darlings, *so* down to earth – we're looking for something earthy, green, a boho vibe. Very low-key, rustic. Please, spend whatever you need to make it look rustic.'

'I . . . can absolutely manage that,' said Lily, who in fact was a bit alarmed by the statement. She'd never had a blank cheque to work with before, and the responsibility was worrying. But surely Venus hadn't meant *whatever* whatever. Everyone had a budget, didn't they?

They were interrupted by a hammering at the door. Or rather, given the hulking, black-clad figure she'd caught a glimpse of through the front windows, less a hammering and more of a Poe-esque rapping, rapping at her chamber door. Mort. Lily wondered how he was doing after last night, although maybe he wasn't fazed at all. Perhaps it was completely normal for him to scoop up a couple of corpses as part of a night out.

'Let's get a meeting on the books, Venus,' she said, getting out her planner and a glittery highlighter. (Lily had a weak spot for stationery, but who didn't.) 'How's Friday, 10 a.m.?'

'Oh. Well, I don't actually believe in linear time, you know? I find it awfully restrictive. How about I have my assistant handle that for you. She's wonderful at her work. Much better than the last three. Anyway. Toodles.'

Venus rang off to wash her hair in a sensory-deprivation chamber, or whatever it was that toothpaste heiresses who don't believe in time did in their spare moments, and Lily hurried – no wait, walked leisurely – no wait, walked at a normal pace – no wait, oh, whatever, she was doing her best – to the front door.

The bell above the door tinkled as she let Mort in, ignoring the flop of her heart as she drank in the way his black shirt, which he wore with the sleeves rolled back, hung on his muscular arms, just so. Did Mort . . . *work out*? She couldn't picture him skating on the spot on an elliptical or grunting over a barbell. Maybe lugging bodies around built muscles. Did funeral directors lug bodies?

If so, had he lugged the bodies of Derrick and Fran back down the hill last night? No, she couldn't be thinking like that. The village's dead were her new neighbours. And Mort was their mayor. In a manner of speaking. She had to get used to it, or she'd end up with bodies permanently on the brain, and that did not bode well for her wedding planning ambitions.

Squaring her shoulders, she mentally swept the bodies of Derrick and Fran under the rug. (A metaphorical rug, but a big metaphorical rug.)

'What can I do for you, Lurch?' she said cheerily to Mort.

'You could update your mailing address.' Mort handed over a small box. 'These were misdelivered to me. Business cards. You should use Tink next time. She's great, and will even hand-deliver them to the right address.'

'Oh go on, Roddy's doing his best. Ah, you opened them, I see.' Lily pulled open the box, admiring the cards. The printer, one she'd used often back in La Jolla, had done a fabulous job – all that foiling and debossing, and the way the cards folded together in a kiss! Glorious. She demonstrated, and Mort nodded brusquely.

'They were addressed to Eternal Elegance. Easy mistake to make. Although . . .' Arms folded, he took in the very cheerful, very bright decor of Lily's shop.

Lily grinned as she spun a quick circle, gesturing at the

library catalogue cabinets she'd repurposed for stationery, the balloon corner, and her favourite bit: the flower wall, which ran amok with a rainbow of gerberas and sunflowers and ranunculi. She hadn't got around to painting the desk, but she had a hot pink tub of paint on standby. 'Our businesses couldn't be more different, could they?'

'My clients are certainly easier to manage.'

'Grim. But probably accurate,' she agreed.

Mort browsed through the display of wedding favours adorning a bright yellow table: vintage-looking matchbooks, stained-glass granola jars, gold records, little bags of potpourri. Did he linger on the hacky sacks?

'What on earth are these . . . doodads?' he asked, appalled. He prodded a pyramid made from tiny jars of honey with decorative bees on top.

'Wedding favours. The couple gives them to guests as gifts.'

'Ah, because they're doing said couple a favour by attending?'

Rude. So rude. But not entirely wrong.

Was there a touch of a smile there? Lily suspected he was teasing more than judging.

'Sometimes they are indeed. It's probably the same at your funerals, though.' Lily accordioned the kissing business card in and out. 'You should get Tink to make you some of these. The punters would come running.'

Mort shook his head. 'And what do you propose the design would consist of? A body being plopped into a casket? A casket being lowered into the ground?'

'You could get some nice texturing if you added grass,' Lily said thoughtfully. 'Maybe some hands, and a dove.'

'I'll let my marketing manager know,' Mort noted wryly.

'You should definitely have them reconsider your uniform. It's very . . . Gomez Addams.'

'Next time I'll wear my orange boiler suit,' said Mort, now peering through a disposable camera wrapped with a cardboard sleeve that could be personalised with a couple's preferred design. (Even better, every photo came out watermarked with a bespoke romantic message.) 'I bought it for an OSHA-related funeral.'

Lily folded her arms. 'You didn't.'

'I didn't. I look terrible in orange. Washes out my complexion.'

Lily could see how this could be true. Was he simply afraid of the sun, or had he not seen a steak in a solid ten years? He had the porcelain skin of, well, the porcelain dolls that Lily's terrifying step-cousin Pomona collected. Oh well, for all her faults, Pomona and her dolls were keeping climate-controlled storage units in business. 'At least you have the makeup for that. Hey, was everything . . . all right last night? With Fran and Derrick?'

Okay, so not mentioning Fran and Derrick wasn't going so well. But she was a novice to this whole death thing. She was entitled to at least one question.

Mort sniffed a custom candle (tailorable to your unique couple's scent). 'As all right as it could be. They were definitely dead.'

Lily couldn't imagine being so sanguine about multiple deaths. She'd spent the previous night staring at the pink chiffon canopy over her bed, wondering how it felt to have your partner die beside you. And at the good part of the movie, no less.

Thankfully Lily, who'd never dated anyone for more than three months, would presumably never be in that situation. (Unless something went *terribly* wrong.)

'At least it was a nice way to go, I suppose. An anniversary night, in their finest clothes, with a great movie playing . . .'

'Yes, other than the carking-it bit, it was a perfect night.' Mort was testing Lily's extensive fountain pen collection on the sample guest book she'd set out on a table dolled up with crockery ideas and elaborately folded napkins in every colour of the rainbow.

Lily raised an eyebrow. 'Wow, you really were aptly named, aren't you. Mr Morbid over here.'

Mort doodled some curlicues with a black marbled pen with a stylised bird on the top. 'I was a baby. I doubt my infant personality was established enough for nominative determinism.'

'Ah. So you're morbid *because* you're named Mort. You grew into it.'

'Nice of you to admit it.'

Lily didn't humour him with a laugh, but she did have to fight it. For all of his gloomy, grumpy appearance, Mort was . . . rather hilarious. Lily found him easy to chat with, and their humour shared a particular cadence.

Outside, the standard low-level hubbub from tourists strolling around, eating gelato and taking selfies with the greyhound statues outside the funeral parlour, had grown into more of a ruckus. Lily turned, squinting into the mid-morning sun to see what was going on. Mort peered through a set of pink feathered opera glasses from Lily's prop wall.

'Is The Hot Pot doing its custard croissants again? The queue does make it this far up the hill sometimes.'

'They were sold out by the time I got my coffee three hours ago.' Lily was a bit sore about that, but at least she'd got her stamp from Dierdre (a cute block cut of an alien cat riding in a teacup). And a promise of a chocolate torsade tomorrow. 'Look, it's that couple from the cinema. The slimy guy – Nate – and the poor girl with him.'

Mort joined Lily by the front window, setting down his opera glasses and raising a hand to his eyes to block the sun. The brunette from last night was pretending to browse the shelves of The Naked Bookshop as she hissed insults at her cheating boyfriend, who was spending a good half of the argument dodging flying paperbacks, and the other half checking his phone. Frankly, Lily thought the girl was doing a good job of modulating her voice – she reached shouting volume only a couple of times per minute.

'I remember them,' said Mort, sounding not particularly overjoyed by the fact. 'They were seated in the front row. He has some sort of high-flying job and kept making business calls and texts. If I played a smaller instrument I would've thrown it at him.'

'You should've trundled the piano over his foot.' Lily jabbed an accusing finger towards Nate, who was jumping up and down in agony after the corner of a hardcover had hit his toe just so. His girlfriend had a good throwing arm. 'He does not, in fact, have a high-flying job. He's a sleazeball. That whole time, he was on the phone to another girl.'

'No.' Mort looked shocked. Well, not that shocked.

'Yep.'

'What a shithead.'

'A shithead who wants it all.' Lily folded her arms as she watched Nate turn his attention to the most romantic spot in the whole village: The Grand Gazebo. His eyes lit up as he contemplated a possible out from the current couple's tiff. 'Cue the love bombing.'

Mort pointed out a cube-shaped bump in Nate's back pocket. 'I think he's going a step further than that.'

'Oh, please let that be a dad wallet and not what I think it is.' Lily grimaced. She'd seen this before, when her friend Christine's boyfriend had half-heartedly proposed as a way to get her to come with him to Nashville, where he'd been offered a job. How was he supposed to do his laundry on his own? Christine had accepted, because what else were you meant to do when someone got down on one knee? What else could you do when you were that far along in a relationship?

Lily only ever heard from Christine via social media now. (Christine was all about the heart and prayer-hands emojis.) But she *had* scrubbed her social media of all evidence of Lachlan, and *was* posting a lot of thirsty selfies from Honky Tonk Highway these days, so hopefully she'd made the smart decision eventually.

Mort raised an eyebrow. 'Are you saying you don't want it to be a ring? Doesn't your whole business rely on young people making misguided, expensive choices?'

'I wouldn't take those jobs. Unless the theme was *really* good.'

'Any standouts so far?'

'The *Succession*-themed one with the Kendall Roy rap was pretty good.'

'What the fuck?'

Lily lightly whacked Mort's hand as punishment for his guile. 'Okay, I made that up. But you'd attend, right?'

'I would arrive with the world's most expensive waffle maker as a gift if it meant seeing that.'

'I'll add that to my registry recommendations. Should we step outside for a better look?'

'I think it's very important that we have a good vantage point. For posterity. After you.'

Mort swung the door open, gesturing for Lily to go ahead of him.

'Should we stick with the patio?' whispered Lily. 'Or get closer? Like David Attenborough reporting on the secret lives of meerkats?'

'I appreciate the anthropological angle, but you should be ready and waiting to offer your services,' said Mort, with a light

45

touch at Lily's lower back. Lily bit her lip as she tried to ignore the flicker of attraction that sparkled through her.

'I hadn't taken you for such a gossip.' They strolled surreptitiously along the promenade, pretending to admire the purple and pink phlox that spilled over the size of the planters lining its edges. (All right, so the phlox *was* worth admiring.)

'Death is my sphere of interest.' Mort's dark eyes twinkled. 'And that includes social death.'

'Babe, over here.' Nate grabbed his girlfriend's hand, dragging her over to the wisteria-draped gazebo, shoving various selfie-snappers out of the way. (Lily felt for them – the spot was so picturesque that she'd already had to upgrade her cloud storage plan, and she'd barely lived here a full day.) Then he pulled her up the bright Spanish-tiled steps, until they were poised like the figurines atop a wedding cake. *No, not like that, Lily. Think of a different simile, one that doesn't lead to this poor girl getting engaged to this jerk.*

The poor brunette looked more uncomfortable than Lily had after she'd licked the stamps and envelopes for a thousand save the dates to go out for a friend's wedding last year. By the end she'd been hallucinating from eating far more adhesive than the FDA recommended.

'My Veronica loves being the centre of attention,' Nate assured a gang of teenagers in fluffy outfits sharing an enormous bottle of Fanta between them.

Veronica smiled hesitantly.

'He's doing it publicly, to coerce her into it,' whispered Lily to Mort.

'Bullying someone into loving you really doesn't seem like the way to do it.'

Drawn like a seagull to a carton of French fries, a photographer emerged from between two planters. (Presumably he'd been sleeping there, because he had leaf refuse on his head.) Catching Nate's eye, he screwed a disposable bulb into his old-school camera, then ducked his head beneath the tent that covered his tripod.

'Whenever you're ready, boss!' he called, sounding exactly like a gangster out of a 1930s movie.

'Almost,' said Nate. He clapped his hands, and the husky tones of an accordion coloured the air. The player of said accordion strutted forward, a rose clenched between his teeth.

'Oh wow, this is a whole pre-planned thing.' Lily was aghast.

'You can buy a proposal package at the Chamber of Commerce,' said Mort, deadpan.

'I'm . . . honestly not sure if you're joking.'

Mort winked.

Lily flushed. Oh, but he was doing a number on her.

Fortunately there was plenty going on to give her an excuse to look away. As if the strains of an itinerant accordion player weren't enough, the promenade was suddenly abuzz with the combination of flip-flops slapping and high heels clacking as a group of young people hurried up in excitement.

'Hey, Nate-Nate!' A girl with legs so long that surely there were stilts involved waggled manicured fingers at the stricken brunette. 'Veronica! Over here!'

'We're all here!' Two bros with baseball caps propped defiantly high on their heads – was there a *Ratatouille* rat in there holding them on? – chugged beers as they waited for the moment. 'We're missing some sick surf for this, dude. She'd better say . . . *ow*.'

Stilts had grabbed a handful of the bro's forearm hair and twisted.

Veronica narrowed her eyes. She was struggling to hold the flowers and chocolates that the slimy Nate had abruptly dumped in her arms from a roller-skating Grubhub delivery guy (roller skates were a permissible form of wheeled transportation along the promenade). 'Say what, exactly?'

'Oh shit, she's figured it out.' Lily grabbed Mort's arm in alarm . . . then dropped it, hoping he'd been too distracted by the scene before them to notice the impromptu groping. 'Don't do it, Veronica. Stay strong.'

Veronica had the stricken look of an armadillo pinioned in the high beams of a lifted truck. Lily half expected her to roll up into a ball and go bouncing off to safety.

Nate dropped to one knee, then bestowed a blazingly white grin upon the crowd. Whoops and cheers rose up from the surfers as Nate whipped a box out from his pocket. Alas, not a dad wallet.

'Babe, I know we've had our . . . ups and downs. Like the micropayments situation on Roblox. And the other night at Misty's, with the waitress. And with the whole Amber situation.'

Veronica frowned. 'What Amber situation?'

'The Amber situation indeed,' whispered Lily, unfolding her arms just so that she could refold them emphatically.

'Not relevant now.' Nate waved Veronica off. 'But, like, I want you, babe. I think we're good together. You're amazing at keeping on top of the bills. And no one cooks breakfast like you. And the way you massage my calves after leg day – a guy would kill for a girl like that. What I'm asking is . . . what do you say?'

He thrust the ring box at her. As Veronica reached tentatively towards it, he chomped it on her hand.

'Ow!' Veronica yanked her hand away, sucking on her finger. 'What the *hell*, Nate?'

'That was meant to be like . . . the *Pretty Woman* scene.' Nate shrugged. 'But we're good, right? We're doing this? Because the lease still has six months on it . . .'

Veronica shook her head in disbelief.

Something brushed against Lily's leg: Mort's cat, Esmeralda. Thank goodness, because Lily needed something to do with her hands other than clench them into fists of second-hand rage.

Lily stooped to pick up the fluffy feline, stroking her black-and-white mottled fur – she was the cutest Rorschach kitty Lily had ever seen. As she stroked, Esmeralda's fur crackled. 'Ooh, you've got some static in your fur . . .'

Overhead, clouds gathered in the formerly flawlessly blue sky. Lily's wrist ached where she'd broken it during her short-lived roller derby career as a teen. The pin in it acted as a handy, if painful, barometer.

'We're about to get a storm,' she whispered.

'I can see that,' said Mort, who was riveted by the way this whole proposal was going. 'This proposal has more drama than a Greek tragedy.'

Lily grimaced. 'I was always more of a romcom girl.'

Nate turned to flash a thumbs up at the crowd before returning his attention to Veronica, who was looking *very* squirmy. He grabbed her hands. 'So, what do you say, babe? Are we going to put those missteps behind us, and you know . . . you and me?'

Esmeralda was vibrating with purrs. They were getting louder and louder, to the point that Lily thought she might get dinged for doing construction without a permit.

'Babe. The crowd's getting antsy.'

Veronica swallowed. She looked at the ring – very large, very flashy. Then she looked at Nate's shit-eating grin – also very large and very flashy.

Then, and rightly so if you asked Lily, Veronica's eyes became very large and very flashy.

'You're dead to me,' she snarled, slapping the ring box out of Nate's hand.

Esmeralda's purring hit a crescendo, vibrating not just through Lily, but through the very air around them. The crystal on her collar flashed and spun, casting a rainbow that almost felt like a spell. Its spinning glow tinted the clouds, which turned quickly and ominously from fluffy white to Seattle grey to midnight black. Lightning crackled at their edges, and thunder rolled like timpani, giving the accordion player a tempestuous backbeat to play along with. The gentle breeze kicked up a gear into a hat-snatching, hair-buffeting affair. (One of the perpetually stationed chess players swore as it knocked over his king, forcing a forfeit.)

The gathered crowd let out a marvelling *ooh!*, and a weather alert siren went off on someone's phone, making everyone around them jump.

'My Achilles!' moaned one of the jumpers, clutching at his lower leg. 'I have a game tomorrow!'

'It's the rapture!' screamed a woman in an all-white outfit. She held up a small gold cross to the flashing clouds. (She had apparently failed the storm safety class at school.) 'I've changed my mind! Don't take me! I've barely had a chance to sin!'

A handful of people went racing for shelter – but others stood by, more interested in sharing their videos of the failed proposal with the world than in running from the imminent storm. Veronica stared up at the sky, apparently trying to figure out whether Nate had done some cloud seeding as part of his proposal.

Boom! A particularly loud thunderclap sent Lily cowering, with a shriek, into Mort's side. Down the way, poor Jenkins let out a mournful howl.

'Comfortable?' Mort asked, as Lily wrapped her arms around him as though she were a giant squid seeking the solace of a ship's prow during a particularly gnarly tempest.

'Sorry,' she whispered, unhitching her arms. 'Should we get back in—'

But before she could finish her sentence—

Blam! Another zap of lightning, so bright it was like 4th of July fireworks in a city with an epic fireworks budget and very little interest in public safety.

The sky at the edges of the moody clouds glowed a million magnificent colours, like a kaleidoscope being twirled by a child hopped up on sugar. Both Mort and Lily were mesmerised: they couldn't tear their eyes away from the tumultuous display.

Then, as prefaced by the dramatic thunder and lightning, the skies opened. Rain pelted down on the remaining gawping onlookers who were valiantly livestreaming as Veronica ran off in the direction of 40 Licks, presumably both for shelter and for the largest, most sprinkle-topped sundae she could find.

'I'm hideous! Don't look at me!' cried a middle-aged guy as his beard dye seeped out from his facial hair and down his neck.

A woman with a beehive she'd clearly been re-lacquering since the Sixties snatched up a tiny dog and shoved it down her shirt. 'Make haste! Make haste! I just had Pookie perfumed, and she must not be tainted with wet dog smell! Here, give me those.'

She snatched a handful of cocktail umbrellas from some drenched picnic-goer, holding them over her head as she shoved past a nervous teenager sobbing on the phone with his mom, apologising for not telling her he loved her frequently enough. The poor teen's sobs deepened as an amateur tornado chaser shoved him out of the way to get a good shot of the furiously spinning clouds overhead.

Meanwhile, Nate was on his knees scouring around in the muddy garden beds for the missing ring, the stilts-wearer joining him with an alacrity that suggested she might be the Amber whom Nate had mentioned in his proposal. Although, had it actually been a proposal when he hadn't technically asked Veronica to marry him?

'Damn, dude,' said one of the surfer bros, pulling his T-shirt over his head to protect himself from the sheeting rain. 'You shouldn't have reused the ring.'

'I mean, I couldn't *return* it, bro,' said the saturated Nate, chucking away a beer can ring-pull that had tempted with its shininess. 'You know how bad the deal is on returned engagement rings? It's criminal.'

Thunder boomed again, rattling the wind chimes strung from a nearby tree – and Lily's nerves as well. She half expected a witch to go zooming through the air, spilling purple exhaust from her broomstick. Was this normal? This couldn't be how things went here. Unless Mirage-by-the-Sea had struck some sort of Faustian bargain where it enjoyed a perpetually idyllic existence so long as a freak storm could shake things up once a year or so? (Something which surely should have been mentioned in the fine print of the lease she'd signed.)

'Here.' Draping his suit jacket over Lily, Mort drew her back under their shops' shared awning, the gentle touch of his hand on her arm sending a vibration through her. Lily couldn't help but notice how the rain drenched his shirt, sculpting it to his skin and revealing the shape of the muscles that Lily had spent quite a bit of time hypothesising about since yesterday. Or how the rain plastered his hair messily to his face, giving him a drenched Mr Darcy look that made Lily wish for a daily deluge.

'My weather app didn't say a thing about this.' Lily blinked as the rain poured off the awning in front of them, encasing them in their own private bubble. She was a frequent checker of the thirty-day forecast: volatile weather was not a friend of outdoor weddings, and outdoor weddings were so far basically her whole thing. Also fancy tents, but they were also not a friend of the rain.

Mort shook his head, sending water flying from the messy waves of his hair. 'I've never seen anything like this.'

'Well, it was worth getting drenched for the show, though,' said Lily, with a rueful grin.

All right, so that was a lie. The Veronica–Nate situation had a sort of reality-TV appeal to it, but the real show was happening right here under the pink-and-white half of the awning that belonged to Lily's shop. She was extremely aware of Mort's damp, unfairly good-looking presence. Of the way his damp shirt clung to him, which was surely illegal in some parts of the country. Of the way his bare forearm grazed against hers as he squinted to watch Nate's latest shenanigans. Of the way the spiced scent of his cologne – well, she hoped it was cologne, and not something funeral-related – emanated from the jacket she continued to hold around her shoulders, even though the rain couldn't get to her here.

Mort's dark eyes bored into hers. 'Truly, although . . .'

He frowned, reaching out a hand to . . . to touch her face? Lily swallowed, knowing that she had to stop it – they worked next door to each other! And yet, she was simultaneously extremely okay with this. Ugh, of all the times to contain multitudes!

Lily closed her eyes, waiting. But when the anticipated skin-to-skin contact didn't happen, she opened them again.

Mort was prodding at an inky raindrop in the palm of his hand.

'Well, that's not good,' he said.

Death Becomes Her

Mort

Mort hurried inside the funeral parlour. Rain rattled through an apparent hole in the roof at a rate akin to a fire hose. Mort jumped as another clap of thunder shook the building. Oh joy. Something else to occupy the dwindling resources of his bank account. As if the bill from the fumigation wasn't already haunting his dreams like the Ghosts of Termites Past.

As it turned out, the storm itself was the least of Mort's problems. Something very strange was going on. The pelting water was dribbling down the walls and pooling on the fleur-de-lis carpets . . . but it wasn't just making them wet. It was *bleaching* them somehow. The patterned wallpaper was turning from velvety black to grey to pale pink florals, taking the opposite journey of a kid's paint palette.

With every flash of lightning and sodden squeak of Mort's shoes, the parquetry transformed into white marble, and the rugs bloomed from a restrained Turkish pattern into rainbow shag monstrosities. As the thunder boomed overhead, the black ceiling roses and cornices lightened, becoming yellow with rose highlights, and the gloomy Victorian chandeliers transformed into something plucked straight from a glass flamingo. And most horrifically of all, the coffin display wall was somehow melding into a set of bunk beds.

No, no it wasn't. Because that was not logical at all.

Mort clapped his hands over his eyes, then counted to ten. He opened them again, right as the room flashed white with lightning. He blinked, waiting for his vision to clear.

Nope. Everything was still fucked.

Boom!

Jesus Christ, was this a storm or the coming of the Four Horsemen? Four Horsemen who apparently had a thing for redecorating.

Come on, Mort, there has to be a rational explanation for this. A stroke! He was having a stroke! Thirty year-olds could have strokes, after all – he'd called Dr Rubenstein's emergency after-hours that time he'd smelt burnt toast, and she'd grudgingly admitted that a stroke *could* be a possibility, albeit an unlikely one. (It had turned out that Gramps had just burnt some toast.)

But no, Mort couldn't smell toast, and his limbs were all working as they should. Not a stroke then.

Flash! It was like an apocalyptic nightclub in here. Mort closed his eyes again, trying to figure out why the walls (and everything else) were melting.

What else, what else? Could it be ergot hallucinations from his overnight oats? He'd purchased them from the farmers' market, and there *was* a stand there that did raw milk. Could the same anti-science principles have tainted his breakfast? But no, his muscles weren't spasming, and there was no sign of gangrene.

Mort was running low on explanations. But at least the worst of the storm seemed to have passed: the thunder had softened, and the lightning could no longer be described as 'strobing'.

'Mort?' came Lily's voice from the other side of the ornate

grille on the shared wall between their businesses – a grille that was now taking on hints of the pink paint she'd painstakingly lacquered her side with. 'Did you lace my business cards with LSD or something?'

If only, thought Mort, poking a bouquet that had transformed from funereal white lilies into a tropical explosion of purple passionflowers. Even the scent of the space had shifted – from the eau de parfum of electric air fresheners carefully designed to cover the aroma of embalming fluid into something softer, more summery. (All right, so this was an improvement.)

Mort held up one of the passionflowers, hoping that it would start dancing in his hand or share with him the secrets of the universe. Alas, the passionflower seemed static and normal, and his fingers looked as they should, not rendered by AI. So he wasn't tripping.

'Mort? Something's wrong over here. Everything's drenched . . . but also *backwards*.'

Lily's voice had an edge to it. Even with his business warping around him like a weird fever dream, all Mort wanted to do was whatever it took to file away that edge.

'I'll be right there.'

He hurried out, almost tripping over Esmeralda as he leapt off the front step and into a massive puddle. Fuck – not his best black Oxfords. The ones Gramps had tenderly handed down to him along with the keys to the business.

'Mrow?'

Esmeralda's mismatched eyes regarded him in amusement as he grabbed at one of the black greyhound statues flanking the door for balance. No, not a black greyhound statue. A white *poodle* statue.

What was going on? Whatever it was, it was unconscionable. And there was far too much fluffiness and pizzazz involved.

'Esmeralda!' Appearing from her doorway beneath the safety of a rainbow umbrella with little bonus rainbow ears on top (rain had breached her awning), Lily clapped a hand over her mouth. 'Your *fur*!'

Mort frowned. What about Esmeralda's fur? Was something wrong with her? Was she sick? Had she got into Gramps's Doomsday Prepper Spam cupboard in the funeral home's backup pantry again?

'Don't you see it?' Lily's eyebrows were high in alarm. Her mascara had run – hopefully from the rain, and not from tears, because Mort couldn't abide tears. 'Her patterning. It's reversed!'

Mort regarded the fluffy cat. Lily was right. Esmeralda's swishing tail had previously been black, and the patch on her throat had been white. And her eyes – hadn't it been the *left* eye that was brown?

'You think that someone replaced Esmeralda while we weren't watching?' Mort glanced around for a damp cat thief, but the promenade was empty other than a guy in a raincoat painting a soggy plein air. 'But how?'

'Mort,' said Lily, trying to keep her lips from moving, 'I ink-thay at-thay we're in a eality-ray v-tay ow-shay.'

Maybe Lily was the one having a stroke.

'Do you smell smoke?' he asked gently.

'Of course you don't know pig Latin,' she huffed. She turned slowly, pointing at all the things between the two businesses that had shifted since the worst of the thunderstorm, like she was being graded on a Spot the Differences picture by a particularly stern teacher. 'I think we're in a reality TV show. Look at the signs! The doors! The poodles! The *welcome mats!* It's all topsy-turvy! I think the whole proposal thing was to distract us while someone switched out our businesses.'

Mort pondered this. It *could* be a prank, and with a

sufficiently large group of people and the right resources, you could potentially swap two businesses within a half-hour period. HGTV hosts managed to ruin entire homes in a day, after all. Not to mention the backyards. (As someone well versed in the practice of digging holes, Mort took a special interest in landscaping.)

'Perhaps they planted the seeds for it when the funeral home was being fumigated!' Lily said triumphantly. And a little hysterically, although he couldn't blame her.

'But why?' asked a bewildered Mort, although not without a surreptitious glance around for a hidden camera. 'I thought that candid camera shows fell out of favour a decade ago.'

Lily considered (but thankfully didn't ask how Mort knew this). 'You're right. Ashton Kutcher does venture capital stuff these days, not gotcha shows.'

'But if it's not a stroke, or ergot, or hallucinogenics, or *Punk'd*, then what?'

Lily's eyes widened. She jabbed at the drizzly sky with her umbrella. 'The proposal. The storm. The second Veronica spoke those words – *you're dead to me* – everything changed. It's a curse. A switcheroo. Just like in *Vice Versa*. Only instead of *people* switching, our businesses have switched.'

'Well, that's just . . . ludicrous,' said Mort. Although a switcheroo *did* sound slightly better than a stroke.

'Reality can be ludicrous!' argued Lily. 'I have a friend who only dates men called Kevin so that she doesn't have to keep getting tattoos of new names.'

Fair point. Although not necessarily relevant to this specific situation.

Mort drew in a deep breath. 'All right, so assuming a switcheroo, as you call it, makes any sense at all, how? And why? And why *us*? Is there some deep moral the two of us need to understand in order to reverse the switch and go on with our lives? Because I'll do whatever it takes to turn the poodles back. Unless it's correlated with a high risk of death.'

Lily sighed. 'Maybe we should do this . . . inside.'

Mort swallowed, realising just how many times he'd fantasised about her saying those words since he'd met her. But not like this. Not in a strange weather-related crisis that had distinct *Opposite Day* overtones.

He followed her into Eternal Elegance (Wedding Edition), wiping his feet on the welcome mat, whose message now read *Love Dies*. Oh dear.

Inside was as he'd expected: weirdly, forebodingly funereal. The morbid notes of Eternal Elegance (Funeral Edition) had seeped into Lily's business, infusing its chipper paint job and floral walls with a grimness better suited to Mort's line of work. Unless Lily was open to the idea of getting kickbacks from a divorce lawyer. And she didn't seem the type.

Lily shoved a flower-patterned bucket beneath one of the worst leaks.

'This is real, right?' she said, her chin wobbling as she waved at her newly motley shop, which looked as though Dr Frankenstein had had a go at a business merger. 'You're seeing it, too?'

Mort wanted to hug her. Instead, he watched the murky water slosh into the bucket. 'Maybe it's a mutual delusion.'

'Well, that can't be,' said Lily, wiping her eyes with her free hand. 'I gave up on delusions after my brief flirtation with trying out life as a brunette in seventh grade.'

Mort couldn't imagine Lily as anyone other than who she was. 'But why? You're perfectly cute as a blonde.'

Dammit, why had he said that? Had the switcheroo upended his sense of propriety?

Lily blushed beneath her umbrella. Well, blushing was better than almost crying.

'Well, obviously I figured that out eventually.' She touched shaking fingers to a half-melted wall with distinct Salvador Dalí vibes. 'Ugh, this paint was meant to be colour-fast. I might have a legal case against Pace Hardware.'

Mort picked over the table of bonbonniere, which had transformed from a pile of chirpy kitschy tchotchkes into a sombre selection of mini tombstones, mourning rings and dried flowers. (This was actually an improvement. Well, except for the bracelet made from human hair.)

'I mean, you can try. They have a bulldog lawyer on retainer after Tom Evans walked under every ladder they had and tried to claim that he suffered a lifetime of bad luck as a result of their shop display.'

'Maybe not, then. Is your funeral parlour like this?' Lily gingerly prodded a stack of black candles with the smiley face handle of her umbrella.

'Uh-huh. It's more like a fun parlour,' replied Mort despondently. 'It's not meant to be the kind of place you kick up your heels and dance a jig. It's *death*! Death is serious business.'

'So is matrimony,' said Lily seriously, although it was hard to take her that way under her rainbow umbrella. 'It's not something you do for shits and giggles.'

Mort regarded a black-and-white marbled stationery set. 'Not with these price tags.'

'Those are more expensive now. Limited edition.' Lily sighed. 'They were originally cream. And the supplier has moved to Romania, so I can't return them.'

Mort plunked himself down on an acrylic ghost chair – hadn't this been pink and plush just a few hours ago?

'The rain's starting to slow at least,' he said. 'A good thing, because when I texted Gramps about the last time the roof had been replaced, he sent me this.'

He showed Lily a text message chain with a ' . . .' bubble.

'Sounds like your landlord should be saving for a new roof,' said Lily, twisting her hair into a damp messy bun shot through with a rainbow pin.

'Oh, Gramps owns it.' Mort tried not to stare as Lily, done with her hair, deftly tied a knot in her shirt to keep it from getting in the way as she set to work cleaning up the mess the storm had caused. Ah, so she dealt with trauma by rolling up her sleeves and getting to work.

'So you don't have the same rental terms as me, huh? Cheap rent for a year and then see ya later?'

'None of that,' said Mort, although personally Mort thought that maybe the discounted rent programme had overstayed its welcome. Why *not* let a business properly establish itself? Especially if that business belonged to Lily. 'We're here for life. Well, death. Gramps bought this place decades ago.'

Lily exhaled as she shook out a selection of crystal plates – now streaked black and gold. 'I didn't even get a chance to take out an insurance policy.'

'I don't think that Acts of Switcheroo are covered.' Mort blew on a party blower, which fanned out into a printed obituary. He jumped – all right, so this was going to take some getting used to. 'If it makes you feel any better, my place looks worse. Very . . . matrimonial. No offence.'

'That makes me feel worse, actually.' Lily squeezed out the mop she'd been dragging across the floor. 'Maybe we could swap? I mean, we do share a business name.'

Mort considered this, but only for a second. 'You want to plan weddings with a bunch of coffins as a backdrop? Well, half coffins, half bunk beds – don't ask. Isn't that a bit limiting in terms of clientele?'

'The goth market's huge,' said Lily. 'They're really committed to the whole aesthetic. But you're right. It wouldn't be fair to your Gramps either. I mean, he dedicated how many years to running the funeral home?'

'Way too many.' Mort picked up a pen that was quite fetchingly engraved with an intricate skull-and-bat design. 'Anyway, who's to say it won't just all swap back? Maybe this is just a strange . . . mirage or something. A temporary glitch in the matrix. A quirk of the full moon.'

'Quarter moon,' corrected Lily, leaning on her mop.

'And by the time we wake up tomorrow everything will be back to normal.'

'And if not?' asked Lily, pausing to pick up a set of playing cards shaped like caskets. 'Those were shaped like hearts a few minutes ago, you know.'

Mort swallowed. 'And if not, well, we'll have to figure something out.' He held up the pen. 'Can I keep this?'

Lily made a face. 'You can also have that weird lava lamp one filled with what looks worryingly like blood. Hey, it's sunny outside again. Maybe a reversal is in the works.'

Setting down the mop, she hurried outside, Mort in tow, to where the skies were their familiar deep blue once more. The puddles steamed as they evaporated under the warming touch of the sun. The abrupt rainstorm already forgotten, people thronged down the promenade, eating vinegar-drenched chips on the benches of the rotunda, sharing gelato from 40 Licks, and browsing the shelves of The Naked Bookshop. Apparently none of the other businesses in the village had been affected, thought Mort, peering around for signs that the switcheroo might have cast a wider net.

Taking it all in – the bright flowers, the quaint businesses, the colourful bicycles and roller skates – Mort couldn't help but see Mirage-by-the-Sea through Lily's eyes. The *romance* of it. This wasn't just a place where the elderly carked it and needed abrupt funeral arrangements. Or the spot where season seven of *The Love Question* had filmed, citing the sunny weather and the tax breaks. (They hadn't renewed after learning just how hostile the promenade area was to any vehicle larger than a moped.)

It was a place that people came to for birthdays, for holidays, for respite from the business of everyday life. A place that celebrated joy over seriousness, whimsy over the sedate. And, of course, poodles over greyhounds.

As Mort had known she would, Lily made a beeline for what had been until a few minutes ago two very elegant twin black greyhound sculptures perfectly aligned with the funeral home's dark, elegiac branding.

'Okay, so it's not all bad.' Lily giggled, patting the poodles' snouts. Pulling a paper crown from a back pocket, and then a floral lei, she proceeded to dress up the poodles, snapping a quick photo of her handiwork when she was done. 'If we're stuck with this whole switcheroo thing, this *would* make a great spot for couples shoots.'

'Oh yes,' said Mort. 'Right in front of a funeral home. Perfect start to married life.'

As though summoned by Mort's statement (and why not, for stranger things had happened in the past hour), two goths sidled up, the woman of the pair in shoes so tall she towered over Mort – rarely did anyone tower over Mort. Her partner was decked out in a magnificent pirate's cloak. On his shoulder perched a green and gold budgerigar, whistling happily to the tune of what Mort picked out as a Sisters of Mercy song.

'Greetings, meat puppets,' said the woman, closing her

parasol. She spoke in an impressive monotone, like a chatbot trained on Coleridge poems and episodes of *Daria*. 'The word on the wind is that you do goth weddings? Or is that next door?'

Lily raised an eyebrow at Mort. 'See, the poodles are already working.'

The goth woman squinted carefully so as not to mess up her red-and-black eyeshadow. (Mort understood – he knew only too well just what went into creating the perfect corpselike visage.) 'I was told there were black dogs of death guarding the premises, and yet . . .'

She regarded the poodles with the look of someone who has just been Rickrolled. Although, in a way, she had been.

'They're on loan . . . to a mortuary museum,' said Mort.

'Acceptable. So, you're the master of nuptial ceremonies?'

Lily waved gaily from under her rainbow umbrella, which was slightly superfluous at this point. 'That'd be me.'

'A rainbow goth,' mused the woman.

'More like a hi-Visigoth,' added the man, with a chuckle.

The woman considered, then assented. 'Well, the goth umbrella casts a wide shadow.'

'Sure does,' said Lily, giving her umbrella a twirl. 'Also, I love your budgie.'

She reached out a finger for the budgerigar to nuzzle. The budgie gave a little chirrup, then did a little dance. 'What's your name, cutie?'

'He goes by Sunny. It's not our preferred moniker, of course,' noted the woman, retreating urgently from a patch of sun. 'It came pre-bestowed.'

'He's a good little dude,' added the guy. 'Picked him up at the shelter about five years ago. This is Desdemona. I'm Ambrose.'

'Lily.' Lily held out a hand, which Ambrose took, with a bow, and Desdemona with an incredibly stern curtsey. 'And this is Mort. He does funerals.'

'Excellent. We'll stop by anon – funerals do inspire me so.'

Mort nodded politely. 'Please do. But no rush, of course. Unless you're at risk of imminent death.'

'We're all at risk of imminent death,' intoned Desdemona.

Fair. Mort watched Lily lead her new clients off to her dramatically redecorated shop, wondering how she was managing to stay so chipper when everything had turned upside down and inside out.

Mort went back inside the upsettingly refurbished funeral parlour, preparing to practise his scales on the pipe organ – something that always helped soothe his anxiety when it came bubbling up and over, which it was certainly doing right now. But the organ was no longer an organ – it had somehow melted into a marimba.

Wonderful. Mort grabbed the soft pink mallets sitting on the marimba's wooden keys and banged out a mournful scale.

Now what?

You Goth This

Lily

'Excuse the mess,' said Lily. Although oddly, there wasn't all that much to excuse. The pools and puddles had evaporated, leaving just the blotches of dark ink and funereal twists on Lily's decor in their wake. Something occultish had occurred, and assuming everything didn't go back to rights overnight as Mort had suggested, she'd get to the bottom of it.

But for now, she had some walk-in clients (her first!) relying on her to deliver the exceptional customer service her Yelp reviews promised. All right, the one Yelp review that actually related to her services. (The rest were for the *other* Eternal Elegance, who apparently had some problems with the attitude of the current funeral director. And also the direction of the wind when it came to the spreading of ashes, although Lily personally thought that was a user error issue.)

'Deliciously odd vibes.' Desdemona nodded at a wilting dahlia in a bud jar as she took a seat on one of the clear acrylic chairs. The dahlia had been delivered just this morning, alas. (Although Lily wasn't about to complain about the ghost chairs – she'd always wanted a set, but they'd been out of her budget.) 'I do love to see it. So, my dark love and I are embarking upon a till-death-do-us-part journey.'

'A wedding,' added Ambrose. 'In case that was ambiguous.'

'Well, I do get the odd cult leader in here,' joked Lily, even though after the whole switcheroo business she wasn't feeling particularly mirthful. Who was to say that the business wouldn't continue down its funereal path in the coming hours? What if her oven turned into a crematorium or the local bat community decided that her chandelier was an appropriate napping place?

Hand shaking, she passed Desdemona a handle-less coffee cup that looked terribly like a miniature cremation urn. At least the coffee brewer had been working – although the milk in the fridge had curdled. ('Fortunately I like my coffee black, like my soul,' Desdemona had purred.)

'Cult leaders? Do tell me more,' said Desdemona, her long nails rattling against her coffee cup and sparking in Lily the opposite of an ASMR response.

Sunny, apparently also triggered by the nails, wolf-whistled, then squawked *I do, I do!*, giving Lily a reprieve from having to make up a cult leader story on the spot.

Ambrose gave Sunny a proud pat. 'We've been working on that. He's going to do the rings.'

'The vision is . . .' Desdemona's coffin-shaped nails flashed, which was still better than rattling '. . . something morbid. Something aligned with our way of life. Funereal, yet celebratory. Something that finds beauty in the darkness.'

'But not spiders.' Ambrose took a cautious seat on one of the clear chairs.

'Uh-huh.' Lily was uneasily taking notes with what had been until an hour or so ago her favourite pen. The yellow bobble on the top had turned grey. 'And how many people are we thinking?'

'As few as possible,' said Desdemona.

'Our extended family,' said Ambrose, simultaneously. 'It's

only three people,' he clarified. 'And the dogs. Two dogs. Both pugs. A fawn and a brindle, if that helps.'

'It does, it does.' Dogs. Dogs were normal. *Focus on the dogs and not on the switcheroo, Lily.* Lily drew an elaborate picture of a pug, then wrote *x2* next to it. 'And will the dogs be . . . involved?'

Desdemona clutched the anatomical heart-shaped locket at her neck. 'It wouldn't be a wedding without honouring the canid souls who brought us together.' She opened the locket, revealing the pictures of two well-dressed wrinkly doggies.

'Maybe they could wear a little hat. Lazarus, anyway,' mused Ambrose. 'Edgar isn't really the hat type. A tie. He could have a tie.'

'A bow tie,' added Desdemona thoughtfully. 'Pinstriped.'

'Pinstriped,' repeated Lily, jotting that down. 'And what time of day are we thinking?'

'Midnight,' they said simultaneously.

'That's a great time for a wedding. Just so long as we're not feeding gremlins.'

'We would never,' said Desdemona haughtily.

'Location?'

'Cemetery,' said Ambrose.

'*Graveyard*,' corrected Desdemona. 'It's not the same thing. I want unconsecrated ground.'

Ambrose jumped in to add, 'But not in a problematic way.'

'I'll see what I can do.' Surely Mort had some suggestions – what Angela was to above-ground real estate, he was to burial plots. 'And what kind of celebrant are we considering?'

'Elvira,' said Desdemona. 'But I'll accept an impersonator if she's busy.'

'She's *very* busy,' noted Ambrose. 'I've emailed her agent seven times. I did get a signed photograph, though – we could use that at a pinch.'

'For a summoning circle, perhaps,' mused Desdemona.

'Elvira . . .' repeated Lily, adding a few question marks for good measure. 'And do we have a date in mind?'

'Friday the 13th.'

'That's when we met,' added Ambrose. 'It has a special meaning to us.'

Lily glanced at her planner, which had quite a few more skulls embossed into it than it had this morning. But it was nothing some decorative contact paper couldn't fix. She hoped. 'We actually have a Friday the 13th coming up in a couple of weeks. After that, we'd be looking at . . eight months.'

Ambrose and Desdemona conferred, mentioning something about GothCon and a band they wanted to see in Munich, where Desdemona's cousin Helmut lived. (From the way they spoke about him, Helmut was an extremely cool cousin, and had even had a cameo on a few of Desdemona's movies. Lily jotted down a note to check out Desdemona's IMDb over a glass of wine tonight. Perhaps joined by a gloomy funeral director. *No, Lily.* That was a recipe for business disaster. Although . . . wasn't this *already* a business disaster?)

'The closer one,' Ambrose and Desdemona finally agreed.

Lily swallowed as she eyeballed the distance between now and the next Friday the 13th. The biggest pieces of the puzzle were always the venue and the catering, but those could be overcome. Mirage-by-the-Sea was storybook, but it was *old*, and there was farmland all around. They could definitely find something unconsecrated, which to Lily's knowledge was everywhere that wasn't in a cemetery attached to a church. And if they couldn't find an actual graveyard, surely Mort or the cinema could help out with props.

Then there was the food. Lily hurried over to her library of inspiration photos – she had whole albums with material she'd sourced for different types of weddings. Sure, Pinterest might be the done thing these days, but there was something she loved about poring over a magazine and cutting out an image that she loved.

'So if we're going non-traditional . . .'

She slid over one called *The Black Album (Please Don't Sue Me, Metallica)*. Lily didn't actually recall putting together such an album, having typically stayed on the opposite end of the colour palette, but maybe this whole magic switcheroo thing was working in her favour.

'Ghastly,' said Desdemona approvingly. 'For someone so . . . perky, you do have an exceptional understanding of the macabre ethos we seek to embody.'

'That's high praise,' whispered Ambrose.

'Complimentary! Complimentary!' whistled Sunny.

Lily hid a grin behind her own coffee, which she was sipping from a cobweb-patterned mug. She was doing this whole wedding planning thing, and in uniquely challenging circumstances at that! Sure, she might be destined never to be chosen as the bride, but look at all these happy couples actively choosing her as their wedding planner.

Lily gave herself an imaginary pat on the back. *Self-worth, I love you!*

Desdemona and Ambrose flipped through the book, Desdemona jabbing her coffin nails at charcoal-tinged burger buns, squid ink macarons, figs and dark heirloom tomatoes . . . and, finally, a quadruple chocolate cake decorated with black roses.

Lily was impressed. Contrary to popular belief – or at least, *her* belief, the black food possibilities were endless. Well, not endless. But doable. It would be like feeding the opposite of a toddler on a white food diet, something she had experience with now that JoJo, who had trigged the whole marriage dominoes situation amongst Lily's friends, was now a mother of three and therefore a dino nuggets aficionado. Lily could probably source most of the food from the local restaurants and The Hot Pot. She'd just have to make sure there was enough food dye to go around.

'Excellent thinking,' said Desdemona, when Lily posited this. 'I do have a source, if you need it. A former squid biologist.'

A bell tolled at a distant church, saving Lily from having to respond to that. (How *did* one respond to that?)

'Thrice,' murmured Desdemona, eyes wide. She closed Lily's black food look-book. 'I'm afraid we must bid you adieu. The hounds must feast.'

'We need to feed the pugs,' translated Ambrose.

Well, it was a fair enough reason to take your leave. Lily escorted them out across the newly black-and-white terrazzo floors and back outside, where half a dozen tourists were posing with Mort's new poodles.

'At least we have blue skies again.' Lily averted her eyes from the sight of an old guy sunbathing naked on a sun lounger in one of the flower beds, with only a strategically placed local newspaper saving him from an indecent exposure charge.

Shuddering at the prospect of fair weather, Desdemona opened her parasol with the vigour of a vampire hunter gouging at the undead with a wooden stake. Only in this case the sun was the vampire. Or maybe Desdemona was. Lily had confused herself with her own metaphor.

As Desdemona angled her parasol to avoid as much pesky sun as possible, an older woman wobbled past, dressed in a dramatic frock that she'd topped with a veil and a bouquet of roses. She reminded Lily of someone, but she couldn't quite place who.

'I *adore* your outfit,' said Desdemona. 'It's so delightfully melancholy.'

'Thanks, love.' The woman managed a spin on her glittery pumps. She leaned on the bougainvillea-smothered railing outside the shop for balance. 'It's our fiftieth anniversary, and we just renewed our vows. I'm Fran. This is my beau, Derrick.'

Lily blinked. Derrick? Fran? She'd heard those names before.

An older man in a flat cap who'd been tying his shoelaces stood and waved at Lily, who suddenly wished smelling salts were something people still kept around. Maybe she could duck back inside and find something suitable amongst the wedding favours. Or perhaps Desdemona had some at hand? Someone who wore corsets for fun was surely acquainted with the rousing properties of dilute ammonia.

'Everything all right, Lily?' asked Ambrose.

'All right? All right?' chirruped Sunny, happily nibbling on Ambrose's shoulder.

'Spectacular. Business calls but, um, make sure you grab a macaron at The Hot Pot and let me know what you think. I'll start scouting locations and will be in touch . . . tomorrow?'

'Be sure to scout at night,' noted Desdemona. 'I expect verisimilitude.'

'Verisimilitude,' sighed Ambrose, quite romantically. (He definitely had a touch of a piratey Baudelaire to him.) 'I love that word. If we have a daughter, that's my second choice for a name.'

'Fabulous,' said Lily absently. She had, after all, just figured out where she'd seen the passing couple before.

She'd seen them in passing. Literal passing.

Let's Grow Cold Together

Mort

Hearing Lily's voice, Mort glanced down from where he'd been valiantly attempting to repaint the cornices of the foyer in the wake of the switcheroo. (He still hoped that things would somehow return to rights after a good night's sleep, but even a day of being surrounded by hot pink froufrou decor was too much.) The black seemed to be sticking, at least. He'd never been so glad for Gramps's hoarding tendencies: the storeroom off to one side of the embalming area in the cellar was brimming with paint tins and excess wallpaper and coffin hardware.

Mort squinted, peering through the front windows, which were letting in a highly improper amount of sunlight more befitting of an art studio than a funeral home.

Weird – that woman passing by outside looked like Fran Hemsley of keeling-over-at-the-cinema-fame, which was odd because Fran Hemsley was currently in the morgue alongside her beau Derrick Hemsley waiting to be embalmed prior to their combined funeral on Tuesday.

And why was there a trail of rose petals in the hallway?

Setting his paintbrush down on the lid of his paint tin, Mort followed the rose petals, which as he'd feared led to the cellar, which not only housed the morgue and the cremation urns, but also had the dubious honour of having been his bunk room when he'd visited as a kid. His childhood stuffed owl Hooty, modelled on a taxidermied model crafted by Aunt Dot in her pre-cinema days, still sat on the vintage cabinet to one side of the embalming room.

Alas, Hooty was presently the only inhabitant of the morgue. The rose petals led to what Mort had feared he'd see: the two lockers that had housed the Hemsleys were wide open, with not a single body inside. But that wasn't the weirdest bit. Each of the lockers glimmered with tiny tea candles – a fire hazard that Mort promptly doused. And were those long-stemmed roses? A sticking hazard if Mort had ever seen one – Mort preferred his flowers of the non-thorny variety.

Mort's heart thumped in his chest. The Hemsleys had been *dead*. Thoroughly, absolutely, undeniably dead. The coroner had signed off! They'd been on ice!

And yet, he'd just now seen them flouncing down the promenade, hands clasped and looking the very picture of matrimonial bliss. Something very strange was going on, and it ran deeper than mere appearances.

Mort picked up the mortuary phone – Gramps still insisted on a landline – and pressed the speed dial.

'Coroner Bill speaking. You maul 'em, we call 'em.'

(Bill's mantra was that you couldn't take death too seriously. Except the murders. And even then, you could often find humour in the event. There were silly murders, after all. Mushroom pies that had wiped out a whole potluck, slapstick-style door clobberings, vengeful flocks of sparrows and so on.)

'It's Mort. From Eternal Elegance.'

'Hey, buddy. How's death treating ya?'

'Weirdly.' Mort paused to blow out a candle he'd missed. 'You signed off on the Hemsleys, correct?'

There was a moment of silence as Bill mulled over the many corpses that had apparently paraded through his office in recent days. 'Hemsleys, Hemsleys . . .'

'The older couple with the double cinema death.'

Bill made a rude noise over the phone. 'Oh, I hate that. Nothing worse than having to cut a showing short. Were you doing accompaniment?'

'Mm-hmm. To *Vice Versa*, this old *Freaky Friday* sort of film. Remade in subsequent years a few more times than it deserved.'

There was some shuffling and tapping as Bill pulled up his report.

'It says here that at 3.12 p.m. they were pronounced . . .' Bill cleared his throat. 'Um. Pronounced husband and wife.'

Mort almost dropped the receiver.

'Dead. It's meant to say they were pronounced *dead*.'

'Some April Fools, huh!'

'It's March,' pointed out Mort.

Bill huffed and puffed for a moment. 'I dunno what to tell ya. Maybe the intern got into my files . . . or my brother. It is funny, though, you gotta admit.'

Maybe Bill would benefit from a new line of work. This one was doing a number on his mental health.

'So they're not . . . dead?' asked Mort, his voice querulous. 'They were just visiting?'

'You didn't ask them when they came in?' asked Bill.

Mort counted back from ten, the way Gramps had had him do as a kid when Eliza Doone at school had called him Pugsley with regard to all-black attire. Of course, Eliza was now Sister Eliza and would go about in a black habit until the end of her days, so Mort had had the last laugh.

'They weren't really in any sort of state for that,' snapped Mort.

'Seems like they are now, though,' said Bill.

Mort couldn't handle any more of this. He hung up, feeling numb, like the time he'd suspected he had Bell's palsy. (*You do not!* Dr Rubenstein had snapped.) Zombies! Now there were zombies! Or if not zombies, then a terrible case of medical malpractice that was making Mort reconsider every one of his doctor's assessments regarding his own health.

Although, he thought, dead people who weren't actually dead weren't unheard of. In the nineteenth century, after a few too many people had been buried alive, grave bells had become quite the trend. And there were all sorts of horrible stories about people who'd tried to claw their way out of their caskets. Not to mention that Derrick and Fran *had* been kept on the finest ice the funeral home had to offer, so it wasn't entirely out of the question that Mort hadn't heard anything from them while they'd been napping in the morgue.

Mort was musing on whether resuscitation or resurrection was the likelier option when the doorbell rang. Instead of the snippet from Mozart's Requiem it usually played, the chorus from 'It's Raining Men' blasted through the foyer.

Griping, Mort opened the door to an extremely tall guy with a basketballer's physique (albeit clad in something closer to a candy striper uniform). 'Singing telegram for Eternal Elegance!'

'Which one?' asked Mort suspiciously.

'There's more than one?' bellowed the singer, who had admirable voice projection.

Lily's door opened, and Lily emerged from her shop, a pink-tipped paintbrush in hand. She was wearing an oversized shirt covered in daubs of pink and splashes of glitter, and looked . . . astonishingly, gloriously beautiful.

'I'm the owner of the other Eternal Elegance,' she told the

singer. Then, covering her mouth with her hand, she glanced at Mort and whispered, 'Mort, did you see—'

'I saw,' said Mort, who had been doing his best not to think about the whole Fran and Derrick situation. Although at least the bodega would keep its doors open, which was critical to the happiness of the village's bodega cats and those in urgent need of overloaded deli sandwiches and a vibrant selection of seeded mustards. 'Just a case of clinical misdiagnosis. Nothing to worry about.'

'If you say so,' said Lily, who did not sound convinced.

Propping his foot up on one of Mort's poodles, the singer cleared his throat, then in a stunning contralto, belted out 'Ding-Dong! The Witch Is Dead'. Pigeons and hummingbirds took flight on the vibration of his voice. Elderly neighbours raced to the phones to make noise complaints. A passing middle-aged guy rubbed at his chest, complaining about his pacemaker.

'Wow, you really put your heart and soul into that,' said Lily, scraping her suddenly windswept hair back into place.

'And my poodle,' said Mort, regarding the party-hatted poodle that in his opinion was a poor replacement for his beloved greyhounds. The singer had left a footprint – and was that a crack? Mort wasn't *entirely* opposed to this. Who knew – perhaps shattering the poodle would reverse the switcheroo.

'But what's this . . . serenade . . . about, specifically?' added Lily. 'Or who?'

The singer held up a finger, then pulled two elegant, swan-shaped cards from his pocket. He handed one each to Lily and Mort.

'It's a Save the Date,' said Lily, tracing the precise embossing on the card. (This was definitely Tink's work.) 'But . . .'

'But it's for a funeral,' finished Mort, turning his own card over. 'In October.'

Lily held her card up to the sun, as though this might entice it to reveal its secrets. 'How does that even work? Is this . . . an assisted dying situation?'

Mort was baffled. 'I have no idea. Funerals are usually held on fairly short notice. They're also not typically a singing telegram type affair.'

'Don't shoot me – I'm just the messenger,' said the singer. At least he'd taken his foot off the poodle. 'And it's not my name on that card.'

'Well, whose name *is* on it?' muttered Mort. He fiddled with the card, which had a complicated opening mechanism (swans *are* notoriously beastly).

'Candice Shelby,' read Lily over his shoulder. 'Is she the one with the bathtub kombucha brand in all the gift shops? That's really good stuff.'

'Excess kombucha consumption may cause hepatic necrosis.' Mort pointed in the direction of her kidneys.

Lily brandished her paintbrush, fending him off. 'I like to take a walk on the wild side. Aka the tasty side.'

'I love kombucha,' bellowed the singer. 'It's good for the vocal cords. Can I get it at the bodega?'

Sure, if you didn't mind being served by a guy who had been dead half an hour ago.

'And the second-from-the-left stand at the farmer's market,' said Lily. 'Although there might be supply issues after October.'

'Great, great!' The singer mopped his forehead – voice projection was hard work. He nudged the small, open suitcase by his foot. 'Is it all right if I move on? I have the rest of the town to cover.'

'Sure.' Lily popped a lollipop and some change in his suitcase. 'Good luck breaking the news. Especially with Candice's pickleball team. They're really close-knit.'

Mort folded his arms. 'How do you know Candice? You've been in town barely twenty-four hours.'

'I talk to people. It's called being affable.' She winked. 'You should try it sometimes.'

Mort had absolutely no intention of trying it. That was how you ended up with visitors. Or on the board of the library. Or buying half a dozen blocks of chocolate you'd never eat for a school fundraiser.

'Did I hear someone say Candice?' asked a cheerful middle-aged woman in striped athleisure and with a pickleball racquet under her arm. A streak of white in her otherwise dark hair poked out from beneath her sun visor, and she swiped at it with a sweatband-covered wrist. She seemed the very picture of health – and happiness.

'Candice Shelby?' confirmed Mort, although he knew her vaguely from the *Rocky Horror Picture Show* showings at the cinema. She always had a few too many G&Ts and tried to get up on the piano.

'I'm she!' bubbled Candice, with the confident, wealthy cadence of someone who had a foundation set up in her name.

'Um.' Lily glanced down at the swan card in her hand. 'We think there's been some sort of . . . mix-up.'

She handed Candice the Save the Date.

Candice donned a pair of reading glasses and held the card very far from, and then very close to her nose as she tried to make sense of it.

Meanwhile, the resonant strains of 'Ding-Dong! The Witch Is Dead' rang out from a charming set of townhouses across the promenade. The telegram guy really was singing for his supper. And a hot breakfast.

'But that's me!' shrieked Candice, clutching the card tightly enough to fold the swan's neck in half. 'That's *me* on the Save the Date.'

'It does seem that way,' agreed Mort, whose ears were ringing from the double assault of first the singing telegram guy and now Candice. What did one do in this particular situation? Offer a hug? A meeting with an estate planner? A cease and desist targeting the telegram guy?

Mort resorted to an approach that required neither empathy nor self-reflection: sales.

'Do you need some help selecting a coffin?' he asked. 'We have some beauties at the moment. You'd look lovely in cherry. It suits your complexion.'

'No, no, I wouldn't! Not one bit! Because I'm not dead! I'm not even close to it!' shrilled Candice. 'I'm right here! I'm fine! The doctor says my vitals were excellent! I take a shot of wheatgrass juice every morning! *And* I just finished a morning of pickleball doubles. A very productive morning. You should've seen us! Not an awkward grunt or twisted ankle among us.'

Mort nodded calmly. This all seemed like a reasonable argument against an imminent death.

'I'm sure it's just a prank,' Lily reassured Candice. 'A very detailed, very committed prank. Or a typo!'

'That's probably it,' said Mort, although Tink didn't make typos – she was extremely exacting in her work. 'Predicting a death down to the specific day is quite a feat. Unless . . .'

Mort swallowed. A few additional options had struck him.

'Unless what?' Candice cocked her head warily.

'You're not considering . . . you know?'

Candice spluttered. 'Absolutely not!'

'And there's no one else who might . . .'

Candice whacked him with the invitation. The swan's beak gave him a papercut. 'I'm happily single! If I end up murdered, it'll be a freak accident. Or a road rage incident. Or maybe my habit of picking up hitchhikers backfiring on me.'

Hmm, given the fatality statistics associated with all of those, the Save the Date might not actually be far off.

'You might want to switch to a safer habit,' agreed Mort. 'Like riding a motorcycle. Or hard drugs. At least until October.'

Candice perused the Save the Date again. 'Do we know how this happened? Or why? And who I should sue?'

'Hey, Candice!' A pickleball player (Mort presumed, based on the flared skirt and the dayglo shoes) hurried up, a bag of oranges slung over her shoulder. 'I just wanted to let you know I've cleared my calendar for October. Looking forward to catching up!'

Poor Candice stood there stricken.

Lily put a hand on Candice's arm. 'I have wine inside. Lots of it. Shall we?'

Love is the Genuine Article

Lily

Candice was three glasses of wine deep and contemplating whether an ex-boyfriend or an ex-pickleball partner might have put out a hit on her when the phone on Lily's desk rang. She scrabbled around for it, grimacing as she saw that the cute yellow rotary phone had been switcherooed into a plastic push-button affair that looked like the love child of an ash tray and a nautilus. She tentatively picked up, hoping she wouldn't be electrocuted by the ghost of the 1980s.

A Kardashian-esque voice drawled down the phone. 'Hey, babe. It's Coriana, from *The Gown* magazine. Is this afternoon still a good time?'

Oh shit. The magazine feature she'd ambitiously booked the day she'd set up her LLC. It had slipped her mind entirely after the magical rainstorm debacle. And the resurrection of Derrick and Fran. And the looming demise of Candice, who'd pulled up her medical records on her phone and had been walking Lily through them in great detail.

My queendom for a slow news day, thought Lily, whose pulse had been doing double time since the disastrous marriage proposal. She was more than a little concerned that the stress of moving to a new town and opening a business had caused her to break from reality, and that right now she was actually in a highly medicated state in a padded room.

Lily swallowed, glancing around at the absolute state of things that was her shop. What had been hours before a charming, sunlit haven brimming with bud vases and cute apothecary cabinets filled with greeting cards and wedding favours was now a gloomy, moody affair. Even the sun was trying to avoid playing on the shimmery disco ball she'd hung in front of the leadlight door. She'd done her best to put the shop to rights after the rainstorm, but nothing was sticking. The mottled black stubbornly stippled the brightly painted walls and darkened the floorboards. The flowers in their vases slumped like teenagers, and the sample cake pop that Lily had nibbled on when she'd needed a quick pick-me-up, well, the less said about that, the better. (Death. It had tasted like death.) And her Polaroid camera kept spitting out images that looked creepily corpse-like. Not to mention the presence of Candice, who was definitely putting a damper on things with how she was using Lily's newly Gothic stationery table to list out all the people who might want her dead. (It was a disturbingly long list that made Lily a touch anxious about having offered the poor woman a safe haven.)

But business longevity was all about visibility. And she was determined to make this business work, just like Mom had made her consultancy work for all these years. Lily might be the eternal bridesmaid, but Eternal Elegance would not endure the same fate.

'Um, hi?' Coriana drawled. 'Anyone home?'

'This afternoon is perfect!' she chirped, hoping Coriana couldn't hear her grinding her teeth over the line.

'Amazing!' said Coriana, with the tone of someone checking their fingernails. 'I'll bring my camera – we'll get your name up in lights. This could be your big break.'

'Can't wait!'

Hanging up the phone, Lily surveyed the shop around her. Could she make this work? Surely she could make this work. She was a pro at putting a positive spin on any situation. Like the time she'd stood up for a college friend who'd been mocked about her retro hairstyles by insisting that scrunchies were the hot new fashion, and committing to the bit until they damn well were. Or how she'd mostly convinced Candice that knowing the date of your impending death was good, actually, because it encouraged you to tick a few things off your bucket list.

There was clearly more to this whole situation than a simple rainstorm – anyone could see that. (Although hopefully they were wrapped up enough in their own day-to-day business that they wouldn't.) But she couldn't just sit around and wait for these magical shenanigans to pass – she had weddings to plan, and not all of them aligned with the aesthetics of the switcheroo. There was the Christmas in July wedding she'd spent hours on the phone with local fir tree farmers for, and the bootscootin' rodeo nuptials that promised to be very cowboy-forward and very straw-filled. And the hippie wedding that Venus was supposed to be coming in on Friday to discuss.

She had to figure this out – and fix it. And, just like the broken zipper on her friend Emmaline's wedding gown last year, she would. But first, she had to make the place look presentable by 3 p.m. She could do this. She could make this happen.

Well, once she got rid of Candice.

Lily grabbed a feather duster and made a show of dusting the wall clock (a vintage starburst design that since the switcheroo had become less star and more burst). Candice, even with her heightened blood alcohol level, got the hint.

'Oh, is that the time?' Candice dabbed her eyes with a napkin and straightened her pickleball skirt. 'I have an appointment with my personal trainer.' Her mascara-smudged eyes widened. 'You don't think *he's* behind the Save the Date cards, do you?'

'I doubt anyone you're paying money to wants you dead,' Lily assured her.

Grabbing her mini bottle of prosecco (Lily wasn't going to object), Candice skedaddled, leaving Lily to embark upon some hasty tidying before Coriana's imminent arrival.

Cranking a vinyl record on the record player – wait, was Elvis meant to sound quite that . . . spooky? – she went over to the armoire that housed the different paint samples and decals she collected for the inspo packages she put together for her couples (or throuples). She hesitantly cracked a few of the paint lids, sighing with relief when she saw they were untainted by the magical rain.

Adjusting her paint-flecked shirt and tying a shawl around her hair, Lily raced about covering up the most egregious marks on the walls. As she'd found before with her pink paint travails, painting *over* the black blobs didn't work, but painting *around* them did.

Lily tapped the handle of the paintbrush to her mouth, thinking. The dots almost looked like sunflower florets, or perhaps the spots on a cheetah. That one over here could be a heart. She could make a mural out of them – something bright and cheerful.

She'd managed a few sunflowers and a bird when the door opened. Mort stood there, looking quite cocky for someone whose business had had a magical change of heart only hours ago. He was dressed in his usual black formalwear – the man could rock a suit – and Lily felt astonishingly underdressed.

'Transitioning into an art gallery already, I see,' he said.

'Could you help?' begged Lily. 'I have a reporter coming to do a feature on the place at three, so time is of the essence.'

'You didn't . . . postpone? You do realise this is the perfect opportunity to get out of talking to someone.'

Lily raised an eyebrow. For someone who apparently disliked people so much, Mort didn't seem shy about dropping into the shop to chitchat. Was this whole grumpy persona a façade? Or did he perhaps enjoy Lily's company?

'How do I know it won't still be like this tomorrow or next week?' She added some petals to the flower she was working on. 'We could be switcherooed for *years*.'

'At least you'd have a good excuse to ask for a lease extension – the property delivered wasn't the property promised.'

'I bet the Chamber of Commerce would love that rationale.'

'I'd find it quite compelling,' said Mort.

'Here.' Lily went over to her paint stash, browsing for the most garish colours she could find, which was most of them. 'How do you feel about *Fucking Fuchsia?*'

'But I barely know her,' Mort said. Ah, there was that wit. Lily supposed you needed it when you were in a line of work like his.

Lily chuckled. 'What about . . . *YELL-ow?*'

Shaking his head, Mort popped on a pair of tortoiseshell reading glasses to read the tiny print. The glasses were quite becoming – not that Lily was looking.

'There must be something less shouty,' said Mort. 'I'll go with *Rhymes with Orange.*'

He took the paintbrush Lily offered him and gingerly dipped it into the tin. The look on his face when he saw the tangelo hue on the brush amused Lily to no end; she'd never seen anyone so distraught over a paint colour.

Crossing the fingers of his right hand, Mort daubed orange over a dark blot on the wall with his left.

'A lefty, huh?' noted Lily.

'Demon child,' agreed Mort. 'It's why I was dumped on a doorstep.'

Lily messed up the stem she was working on. 'Wait, really?'

'I doubt it. How would anyone have known my preferred hand at the age of eight weeks?'

'The bigger question is how did they carry you to the doorsteps if they were only eight weeks old?'

'Very good question. I think they were winged babies. Putti, like in all those Renaissance paintings.'

'Let me know if you have their details,' Lily added a pink flower around one of the dark blots. 'Winged babies are highly sought after for themed weddings. People will pay extra if the grannies can pinch their cheeks.'

Mort was quiet for a moment as he painted something that sort of resembled a fruit. 'I know it's weird. Being a doorstep baby. But Gramps has always been great. Was it a slightly off-kilter upbringing? Sure. But whose isn't?'

Lily thought about that as she added petals to her flower. Her upbringing had been . . . well, she'd always considered it normal because there'd always been plenty of hugs and food on the table and new clothes to wear, but was it, really? Was it normal to move every year because your mom's consulting work was always a short-term thing? Was it normal to flee every romantic relationship because if Mom wouldn't settle for what she always belatedly called 'just some guy', then why should you? Was it normal that the shop and apartment that Lily was repainting right now represented the first time that she'd felt stable in her life?

Mort understood her silence. '*You* had a normal childhood, I see.'

Lily's flower was wonky. 'I suppose so. But we all come out the other end with our own quirks and foibles.'

'Quirks and Foibles. Sounds like a good name for an esoteric shop.'

'Noted, just in case this whole wedding planning thing doesn't work out. At least we've figured out a way to disguise the blobs. Do you want me to help you do the same at the funeral parlour?'

Mort shook his head. 'Not if these are the colours you have on offer. Anyway, the wallpaper texture makes it look . . . almost deliberate. Although I'm really going to need you to stop dressing up the poodles.'

'If they return to greyhounds overnight, we have a deal. If not, well, you'll have bigger things to worry about than some well-dressed poodle statues.'

Lily was trying to make light of the situation, but in reality her stomach was churning. The goths might be fine with a sprinkling of gloom when it came to their nuptials, but she had a feeling that Venus might not be entirely up for a 'Surprise! Morbid!' twist on her wedding. And a wedding like Venus's was a make-or-break thing.

'Hey, you said that you arrived on the funeral home doorstep as a baby,' mused Lily.

'Correct.'

'So Gramps ran the place for, what, thirty years, at least.'

Mort nodded. 'Fifty or so.'

'Well, has this whole swapsies thing happened before?'

'Not that I've heard of, but it's worth asking. He never picks up his phone – he has bad hearing – but I'm visiting him tomorrow.' Setting down his paintbrush, Mort regarded her with dark eyes. Then, after a beat, he added. 'Would you like to join me?'

Lily's heart thumped at the suggestion. If you were fairly proficient in Morse code, you might even be able to say that it thumped out something like, *yes, yes, I thought you'd never ask, you hot, scruffy fool.*

'Sure,' she said coolly, pretending that she hadn't daubed her own nose with paint in her excitement. 'I was planning to head that way to do some location scouting for the goth wedding anyway. Um, speaking of dark attire – should there be dozens of people in mourning outfits gathering around the shop?'

Mort glanced at his watch. 'Shit. Mrs Fagan's wake. Good luck with that journalist. Remember, if they ask about the decor, just say you're storing it for me while I figure out my flood insurance.'

'Babe, this is *gorg*.' Coriana sashayed back and forth in front of the shop, her camera clicking as she snapped away at what people in the business loved to call 'the details'. She'd brought with her . . . well, Lily supposed it was a dog, but on the rat-dog spectrum it was definitely closer to the non-canine side. Lily wished she'd put it in a carrier basket before it got scooped up by a seagull.

'Although, *wow*, setting up next to a funeral parlour? *Ba-rave*. Do you guys have a kickback thing going on? If it's not working out and they don't want to go through a highly visible divorce, you can . . .'

Coriana clicked her tongue and made a throat-slashing gesture.

'Or poison, if you must,' added Lily, deciding to assume that Coriana was joking.

'Poison's a bit . . . expected, don't you think?'

'Sure. Although I specialise mostly in weddings—' Lily tried to find common ground '—I do love a good true crime podcast.'

(This was a lie. Pop Culture Happy Hour was about as dark as Lily's listening got.)

'Between us girls . . .' Coriana paused to take a shot of Mort's poodle statues, which Lily had dressed up in plastic floral leis a mere ten minutes earlier. 'I had my heart set on the crime beat.

But y'know, gotta go where the work is. Even if that's writing about weddings when your boyfriend of eighteen months just said he wasn't the marrying type.'

'Oh,' said Lily. 'I'm really sorry to hear that. Come in. I have CBD-infused soda.'

She led Coriana inside, hoping that the drink would take the edge off. Although Coriana seemed to be all edges. She was like a human dodecagon.

'Lying ass,' scowled Coriana as she popped open the can with a long, frosted nail. 'He was the marrying type. Just not to me. He's got two kids now. And a back tyre that keeps getting slashed.'

'They don't make tyres like they used to.'

'Right? You really have to stick the knife in, give it a twist. Anyway. Are we ready? I know we're going to get some amazing sound bites. I just feel it, babe. That you're going to be fab. Do you have any reverse osmosis water for Hercules? He has a sensitive belly. Needs those extra 2s in his H_2O.'

Lily had dropped chemistry after her junior year, but as far as she knew, this wasn't how water worked. But she wasn't about to correct someone who wrote for such an esteemed publication. It even had a print edition!

As Coriana strolled the shop, Lily surreptitiously poured some tap water into a teacup and set it down on the floor, hoping that the little dog wasn't actually a water connoisseur with a palate as pronounced as his underbite.

'Interesting decor. Very don't-give-a-fuck.' Coriana squinted at the freshly painted mural. Spooked (understandably) by his own reflection in a mirror propped against the wall, Hercules backed up against the mural, managing to smear himself with *Fucking Fuchsia* paint.

Good, good. This was going well.

'And that mirror with the snakes? I love a good Medusa commentary.'

Lily nodded, hoping that Coriana wouldn't realise that the mirror had been hastily slapped over a poster that post-switcheroo had reconfigured itself to read *Better Dead than Wed*.

'These moody colours – it's so evocative. Very chic, very in. Not like those boho barn weddings from the 2010s, my *God*, they were so passé.'

'You're right!' Lily was hyperaware of her armpits. Were they damp? Did they smell like fear? She tried to reel herself in. 'I'm working with a goth couple on a quick-turn wedding. It's going to be macabre in all the best ways.'

'Macabre! You know your way to a journalist's heart.'

'It's an exciting ask, because if you look around—' Lily gestured in a way that encompassed Mirage-by-the-Sea '— where we are is the spiritual opposite of macabre.'

'True. It's like something out of a particularly charming Wes Anderson movie. Not the one about the asteroid, though. I thought he overshot there.' Coriana snapped a few shots of Lily's recently appeared ghost chairs. 'So how did this couple find you? What made you stand apart? There are, after all, *thousands* of wedding planners in Southern California. And at least a hundred specialising purely in goth weddings.'

Well, you see, Coriana, a magic rainstorm pulled a swapsies on my business and the one next door, so this place is actually far more Gothic than it appears. Especially when I basically covered the walls with colourful pancake makeup – with the help of a funeral director – to hide the evidence.

'Right time, right place,' said Lily. 'Don't let my rainbow attire fool you – I'm a chameleon.'

'I see.' Coriana made a note. Was she using red? Red didn't seem good. Red reminded Lily of her calculus assignments.

And then came the kicker.

'No ring, I see.'

Lily glanced down at her left hand, although why exactly, she didn't know. It wasn't like she'd expected a ring to have sprouted there without warning. (All right, maybe a little, given the events of the morning.) 'No ring.'

'Interesting.' Coriana leaned forwards, her icy eyes boring into Lily. 'So, if you've never been married, why all this? Why do you want to help people celebrate something that's passed you by?'

Lily chugged the rest of her own CBD soda, then popped open another. She hadn't known she was going to be interviewed by Christiane Amanpour. 'Well, I wouldn't say passed me by. Maybe I haven't found the right person yet.'

Coriana's pen scratched accusatorily. 'In that case, are you the right person for this kind of work? How can you prepare someone for their special day if you haven't experienced it yourself?'

'I mean . . . you don't have to have lived something to appreciate it. Mort next door is a funeral planner, and he's never been dead.'

'The place with the photogenic poodles?' Coriana seemed to revel in the concept. 'Now there's a man who understands theatre. Maybe you should rope him in, get him involved in some of your upcoming events.'

Lily could only imagine what a Mort-branded wedding would look like. Probably a lot like what she'd returned to a few hours earlier, honestly. Would he wear a tux, though? Or just stick with his usual black suit with the shirtsleeves rolled up as he carried his bride over the threshold . . .

Lily sipped drink #2, trying to rinse away the very not-safe-for-work image of Mort that had just passed through her mind. It was the phrase 'roping him in' that had done it.

'So, what else is on the horizon for you?'

Lily swallowed, grateful for the opportunity to turn her thoughts away from Mort. Mort, who had nothing at all to do with weddings. In fact, he was the opposite.

'Um, I have a hippie wedding coming up, for Venus Cargill. A cowboy wedding. And a Christmas in July wedding.'

'Curiouser and curiouser.'

'No *Alice in Wonderland* weddings yet,' said Lily, hoping that despite her lowly spinster status she was steering the interview back on track. 'But I'd love to do one. We could make a photo booth out of the Cheshire cat's grin. And a shisha out of the pipe-smoking caterpillar. And of course there'd be croquet.'

Coriana nodded. 'I do like the prospect of hitting things with a mallet. I make a mean schnitzel.'

Hercules, apparently not a fan of mallets, trotted over to Lily, sitting on her foot and whining. She picked him up and gave him a snuggle – after all, even the less aesthetic members of the canine persuasion deserved snuggles. As she did, her ears picked up the faint strains of the 'Wedding March' being played. Perhaps *that's* what Hercules was responding to.

But *she* hadn't put on the 'Wedding March'. Her record player was still crooning Elvis at half-speed. And she'd disconnected her doorbell after it had started blasting Metallica's 'Fade to Black' on repeat. So where was it coming from?

Then she realised. There. From the grate above her desk, the one that connected to the funeral home.

Was *Mort* playing the 'Wedding March'? And on a . . . was that a xylophone?

'Everything all right, babe?' said Coriana.

'I just . . . need to grab something from next door. Thank you for the interview. Did you get everything you need?'

'And then some.' Coriana picked up Hercules, who was

rainbowed with damp paint splodges. 'Is there a doggie day spa around?'

'Keep heading down the promenade, and you'll see it next to The Hot Pot. It's called the Barkingham.'

Coriana hustled out the door with the tiny dog, then paused. 'Babe, one more question: is it normal for a dead person to be carried out of a funeral home on a chair by a crowd of clapping revellers?'

Oh shit, thought Lily. Her old nemesis musical chairs had struck again.

Danse Macabre

Mort

Mort was at a loss. The funeral guests were *not* comporting themselves in a way appropriate for people in mourning. First, there'd been a hubbub because the deceased's sister-in-law had shown up wearing the same outfit as the deceased, which apparently made her a narcissist. Then, someone had taken over the funeral marimba with an upbeat rendition of 'Here Comes the Bride'.

And now, instead of heading out towards the back of the funeral home where the hearse awaited, poor Moira Fagan was being hoisted down to the cemetery on a chair.

'Can we please bring Mrs Fagan back in?' he called politely. Even though what he wanted to say was *what the fuck! What is wrong with you!*

'Who wants to swap fish for chicken?' brayed a woman who definitely had someone of the equine variety somewhere in her family tree. 'Fish for chicken?'

At some point, the funeral had become a catered event well beyond the club sandwiches and devilled eggs that Mort was used to vacuuming out from the carpet or peeling off the ceiling. (Chucking sandwiches at ceiling rosettes was a universal kid-at-a-funeral thing.) A series of round tables had been rolled in and decked with lacy tablecloths. There was even a seating chart and tiny seating cards printed, perhaps not entirely sensitively, with a cheerful header that read 'Moira Fagan, survived by . . .' followed by the name of the guest in a rolling cursive typeface.

Not only that, but there were funeral favours. *Funeral favours!* Bags of sugared almonds shaped like skulls. Lily's wedding doodads had truly infected his business.

And what was that clicking noise? Mort pulled back a velvet curtain to reveal . . . a photo booth. Where had that come from? Who had shouldered this giant contraption in here without him noticing?

Mort grabbed the photos that poured out from the side of the machine, feeling slightly worried that there might well be a corpse in them. Wait, *was* that a corpse? He squinted at the overexposed photos, which showed an impressively wrinkled individual draped in a feather boa and flamingo sunglasses.

Mort's stomach wrenched. This whole thing was flying extremely close to the sun of losing his funeral director licence, which he'd studied hard for. Was this interference with a corpse? Was there even a law for what was going on in here? For there to be a law meant that something like this had happened before, which . . . surely not.

Momentarily, the short curtain on the photo booth slunk aside, revealing a tiny old woman who'd been bent in half by the combination of age and gravity. Thankfully she seemed very much alive.

'You look like you've seen a ghost,' she creaked, in a timbre that suggested the family might have done well to pay for a two-for-one deal.

'You look just like . . .' And she did. She looked exactly like the woman that Mort himself had embalmed, dressed, and made up for her final day above ground.

'I'm Moira's twin sister,' said the tiny woman, unlooping the feather boa and tossing it to a middle-aged guy at the front of the photo booth line that had gathered. 'Mirella. And thank you. For putting the fun back in funerals.'

'But I didn't. I would never,' Mort stammered, extricating himself from the frivolities and hurrying back towards the foyer. Fun? Funerals? All right, so there was some convenient wordplay there, but that was where the overlap ended.

Besides, this was not at all the brand mission that Gramps had fleshed out with that flashy advertising exec after winning a branding grant from the city a few years back. But was it so wrong? That people were celebrating a life instead of weeping on each other's shoulders and rending their clothing graveside?

Yes, thought Mort, watching out the front window as someone in head-to-toe black, including a veil, took a selfie with the poodle statues, an injury that was made all the worse by the rabbit ears they were propping up behind one of the poodles. Yes it was.

And worst of all, here came Lily, cheery, bright, rainbow-clad Lily, traipsing up the walkway, skirts swishing and bangles clanging. She even paused to take a photo for the veil-clad mourner, who had for some reason grabbed a bucket from Jorge the gardener and was now standing awkwardly astride one of the poodles. The shame. The indignity. (All right, all right, the hilarity, thought Mort gruffly.)

'Welcome to the festivities,' said Mort drily as Lily let herself in.

A group of mourners who'd gone to town on the open bar that had been set up on Moira's coffin (it had been a closed coffin affair, at least) wrapped her in a tipsy hug. Lily, of course, did not seem to mind. She hugged right back, never mind that these were all strangers, and drunk ones at that.

'I'm just here to get your stamp,' she said to Mort after she'd extricated herself from the clutches of a woman opining loudly about Moira's one-of-a-kind fried chicken batter, the recipe for which she'd apparently taken to the grave, bless her heart. 'And enjoy the party.'

Mort harrumphed. 'I don't partake in town treasure maps. Or parties.'

'All right, all right, to get a better look at the switcheroo and the number it's done on your place,' said Lily. She jabbed at her treasure map. 'And also, you're listed right here.'

'No, that's Eternal Elegance, Wedding Edition,' lied Mort. He did not give out his stamp to women he barely knew. Even if they were unfairly becoming.

'Sure, sure.' Lily rolled her eyes. 'Wait. Is that a photo booth? At a *funeral*?'

'Sure is.'

'You sly dog.'

'It's a switcheroo thing,' said Mort. At least he hoped it was, because that was a better option than a mourner deciding, of their own volition, to immortalise Grandma Moira on Polaroid.

'Have you indulged?' asked Lily curiously.

'Absolutely not. I have a reputation to uphold. This is a memorial service, after all. Whatever it might look like.'

Mouth open in mock horror, Lily smacked him lightly across the chest. 'I'm sorry, but what kind of business owner doesn't sample their own goods?'

Before Mort could protest – and he *did* have quite a protest ready – Lily had dragged him into the booth. The space was cosy and plush, with the sort of satin upholstery you might find in a coffin . . . and a series of discarded props that you might find on the person in said coffin. Mort was, well, mortified. They had to find a way to reverse this switcheroo immediately.

'Here, this is for you,' said Lily, draping an elastic bow tie around Mort's neck. She wrapped a lace cuff around her own, then grabbed a black veil for good measure.

Oh, but she looked good.

All right, so the switcheroo didn't have to be reversed *immediately*, immediately. But soon.

The photo booth whirred as it prepared to snap their likenesses. Mort was painfully aware of Lily next to him: the warmth of her leg against his, the lightly floral scent of her shampoo as her hair grazed his neck. And now, the gentlest touch of her breath as she turned to him, her smile broad.

Mort wondered, not for the first time, what it might be like to kiss her.

But neither timing nor confidence was on his side.

'Say . . . Rest in Peace!' Lily called, throwing her arm around Mort as the camera clicked and whirred, clicked and whirred.

And fairly so because, in this moment, Mort had quite possibly died and gone to . . . well, whatever came after all of this.

It was not as easy as you'd think to find an organ repair guy, although Mort was a little under the weather in the wake of yesterday's wake. Thankfully the party had moved elsewhere eventually, and Mort had managed to chase down the missing deceased in time to get her to her plot before the graveside workers clocked off for the day. Lily had excused herself after someone called Venus had texted her fifteen times in a row about tie-dyed tents, a recusal that Mort – although trying to keep his focus on the funeral he was managing – had somewhat mixed feelings about.

Anyway. Feeling moody about the fact that the switcheroo hadn't magically resolved itself overnight, Mort sipped a decaf as he reviewed his latest set of organ-related search results, which had pulled up records for a handful of transplant surgeons who had holiday abodes in Mirage-by-the-Sea, followed by a farmers' market booth specialising in oregano, a clarifying question from Siri about whether he had meant to type in the state of Oregon instead, and then a series of bullet points from an AI about organic chemistry.

Mort huffed in frustration; it wasn't just that the organ-turned-marimba situation meant that he was going to have to resort to playing Enya on repeat on the temperamental Bluetooth speaker Gramps had hooked up in the viewing room. It was that the organ was his outlet – it was the closest thing he had to a piano in the funeral parlour, and therefore the closest outlet he had for his anxiety or for when he needed to get his thoughts in order.

'Still switcherooed over there, huh?' called Lily through the grille in the wall. Had she been listening in on his grumbly googling the whole time? Hopefully she hadn't heard him get a tad testy with the guy who'd shown up on the front page of Google as an *organ donor near me*. It wasn't Mort's fault that Siri had assumed the guy replaced musical instruments for free.

'Clearly,' said Mort. 'And you?'

'Oh no, it's all sunshine and rainbows over here. There's so much white that I feel like I'm in an ad for Philadelphia cream cheese.'

Mort straightened in his chair. 'Are you being serious?'

'Never. Unfortunately we're stuck with our weird magical mishmash. But I think I can help you with the organ situation.'

'You know how to reverse the switcheroo on an organ?' Mort called. Even his smartphone assistant hadn't been able to help with that.

'Well, no.' There was some scuffling as Lily climbed up on her desk chair so that she could talk more freely through the grille. 'But there's a player piano up for grabs not far from the cinema, if you want to take a walk with me.'

'All right.' Mort regarded his side of the grille. He'd done his best to repaint it, but the switcheroo pink kept oozing back through the endless coats of black he'd applied. In the end he'd moved a particularly tall floral display in front of it, feeling endlessly grateful for the local florist's obsession with height. (She took the same approach with her hair, whose bouffant every day exceeded the previous day's.)

In Mort's humble, morbid opinion, pink and funerals did not go together. He needed the pallid, the wan, the ashen. It was right there on the two-toned colour wheel Gramps had put together years ago and had subsequently kept in his desk: ivory and black. Variations on the theme were accepted, but nothing that veered into the colour spectrum. If a dog couldn't see it, Mort didn't want it in the funeral home. Grief was a thing with feathers, yes, but crow feathers, not parrot ones.

The grille rattled as Lily clapped her hands against it. 'I'll be right over. Wear sensible shoes.'

Mort looked down at his polished Oxfords. He had never been accused of not being sensible.

Moments later, 'Oh Happy Day' rang out on the musical doorbell, startling Mort. Well, it was better than yesterday's 'It's Raining Men'.

Lily shoved open the door, sweeping into the funeral home in an explosion of pink and yellow taffeta.

'You look like the human embodiment of Pop Rocks,' observed Mort. (Mort would never admit it, but he loved Pop Rocks.)

'Why thank you!' Lily showed off a pair of orange-heavy leopard-print sneakers that presumably counted as sensible in her world. Oh dear, did they light up when she moved? Yes, yes they did.

'You're welcome,' replied Mort, amused.

'Are we ready?' Leading Mort outside, Lily rubbed the noses of the poodle statues out of the front of the funeral home (today they were in sunhats and beach towels), then dragged Mort up the winding pedestrian pathway that meandered through the heart of the village, connecting a hundred shop-lined laneways and ivy-smothered kiosks and seating areas fit for a fairy picnic.

'Mostly I just wanted an excuse to walk the promenade,' Lily admitted, pausing to wave to Jorge, the gardener whose magical botanical gift kept the flower baskets and huge planters lush and bright.

'Morning, Lily!' Jorge danced over with a vibrant zinnia for her. (Jorge never walked – he shimmied everywhere. He was quite the star on the dance floor and had proudly stood in as a seniors' Zumba instructor at the YMCA a few times.) 'A bright flower for my bright lady.'

Beaming, Lily tucked the flower into her curls. 'Thank you, Jorge. Make sure you come by for some wedding cake. I just got some lemon poppyseed and some chocolate caramel in. We'll do a taste test and you can let me know what you think.'

'I don't say no to cake.' Jorge's grin was so broad it took up all of the available real estate on his leathery face. Snipping his secateurs up and down like extremely sharp castanets, he pranced off towards a garden bed rainbowed with the reaching blooms of gerberas. The vibrant flowers' feet were warmed by a colourful carpet of verbena and lantana.

'Cake testing, huh?' Mort held out a hand for Jenkins, the extremely personable Jack Russell who guarded the premises of The Hot Pot with threats of doggie kisses and an endless game of fetch. Jenkins usually stayed on site, but around lunch he'd trot up the promenade for extra treats and belly rubs, which locals and tourists alike were happy to give. The stumpy-legged pup slobbered a welcome all over Mort.

'None for you until you wash your hands.' Lily stooped to give Jenkins some belly scratches and a treat she produced from a hidden pocket. 'I didn't take you for a dog person.'

Mort raised an eyebrow. 'Should I be offended?'

'Well, maybe it's just the Esmeralda thing. The two of you seem to get along, and most people are one or the other.'

'But Jenkins isn't just a dog. Look at him. He looks like Wishbone.'

Lily gasped. 'You watched *Wishbone*?'

'Sure. Just because I look like I grew up in *The Munsters* doesn't mean we didn't get TV reception. Besides, Gramps liked Wishbone's outfits.'

'Ah, now it's starting to make sense. Although I don't remember Wishbone's goth phase.'

'Wishbone could be anyone he wanted to be,' said Mort haughtily.

'You're thinking of Gumby.'

Sending Jenkins back down towards The Hot Pot with a butt pat, Lily directed Mort up Oleander Avenue and around the pedestrian roundabout that let on to Juniper Way. Mort swallowed – Whispering Waters, which Angela had suggested as an option for Gramps, was just around the corner. Mort knew that Gramps needed something more low-maintenance than the current rambling family home, but a retirement home didn't feel right.

Lily yawned, self-consciously covering her mouth. 'Sorry. After I got done with Venus I spent half the night trying out spells to undo the switcheroo.'

Mort shot her a sidelong glance. 'No luck, I see, unless your shop looks better than mine. But I appreciate the effort.'

'I was going to fast-track a witchcraft kit from Amazon, but I didn't want poor Roddy running around at 3 a.m. I made do with some river pebbles from the planters outside, some old spices from the cupboard, and a poem about change from a Hallmark card I found at the back of the wardrobe.'

'Ah. I think I see the problem.'

'Trader Joe's 21 Seasoning Salute apparently doesn't reverse dark magic. Smells good, though.'

'Should've tried the Everything But the Bagel seasoning.' Mort sighed. 'Still, you did better than me. After the boys put poor Moira in the ground I went to the library and went through old newspaper articles looking for reports of something similar happening.'

'Anything?'

Mort shook his head. 'Although the press hasn't covered our situation, so who knows.'

'Other than Coriana.' Lily made a face. 'I can't wait to see her article. *Unwed Spinster Lives Matrimonial Dreams Vicariously through Wedding Planning Business*.'

Mort wasn't sure what to say to this. *Did* Lily dream of a wedding for the ages? Was that why she'd started the business? Or was she being self-deprecating? Mort glanced over at Lily in her adorably ridiculous outfit, wondering what kind of wedding she might plan for herself. She *had* looked cute in that black funeral veil last night.

'A Vegas elopement,' Lily said suddenly. 'That's what I'd do. With or without Elvis. Hey look, it's Derrick and Fran. They look well. And they have an entourage!'

A small group had surrounded the resurrected couple, heads bowed in reverence (and phone cameras out).

'Please bless my market tomatoes, Derrick,' pleaded one.

'Will you minister to my turtle, Fran?' begged another.

'Did you see a white light?' a third was asking.

Derrick looked quite pleased by the attention, and was handing out discount vouchers for the bodega as he anointed his new fans. Fran, on the other hand, was fiddling with a cross around her neck and seemed to be having a bit of a crisis of faith.

'It was just a spot of bradycardia!' she snapped. 'We overdid it on the beta blockers at Toastmasters before the movie!'

'Maybe I won't say hi,' whispered Lily. 'They look . . . busy. Besides, we're just about here.'

Jogging up the last of the hill, Lily pointed to a purple fairy-tale house with green trim and an extravagant assortment of glass frog garden ornaments.

Out the front sat an ancient pianola with a FREE sign stuck to the front. One of the local peacocks (a family of them had escaped from a nearby zoo and had since bred) regarded him from its perch upon the closed keyboard cover.

'How on earth did you hear about this?' Mort regarded the battered old pianola, which someone had had a go at decorating with a paintbrush and sponge, and which sported crooked candelabra holders covered in wax.

'I was talking to Desdemona and Ambrose about their wedding, and they were very insistent that their nuptials involve a piano-like instrument in some shape or form.'

'Well, you've got the "piano-like" and "some shape or form" down.' Mort tentatively depressed the rickety middle C key, which was missing its plastic veneer.

'And then on my way out from the funeral yesterday I found this guy bashing out "The Lion Sleeps Tonight" on that— glockenspiel?'

'Marimba.'

'Right. I mentioned something about the organ, and he said

that his cousin had this beauty sitting around looking for a new home. Kismet!'

Kismet was certainly one way of putting it. Getting a warning call from the Board of Funeral Directors about the seven noise complaints that had apparently been lodged in relation to the funeral was another. They had to find a way to reverse this thing. Even if it took all the Trader Joe's herbs in the world. Mort was prepared to stand in front of a midnight mirror and recite *back to reality* three times, if that's what it took.

But then he caught sight of Lily's sunny smile as she turned from the top step of the house, where she was happily knocking away with the brass carp doorknocker ('Like the ones in Malta – my bestie Annika is always sending me pictures of those!'), and he wondered if maybe, just maybe, this switcheroo wasn't *entirely* terrible.

After all, if their businesses hadn't performed their own *Freaky Friday/Vice Versa* dance, he wouldn't be here with Lily collecting a deformed piano from one of the all-singing, all-dancing mourners at yesterday's disastrous funeral.

All right, so maybe it wasn't a *great* defence of the switcheroo. But it was *a* defence.

'How are we going to get this thing back to the funeral parlour?' Mort regarded the rickety pianola with the critical eye of his high school musical composition teacher. It looked held together by a whisper and a prayer. A pianissimo prayer.

'It has wheels.' Her shoes flashing, Lily crouched to demonstrate. 'We can push it back down the hill.'

'And risk a runaway player piano? Absolutely not.'

'Oh go on,' said Lily. 'Live a little. Haven't you always dreamed of hauling a piano around in public? I feel like one of the helper birds in *Cinderella*.'

The door to the purple house opened. One of the mourners

from yesterday stood there, looking askew in every way. He wore sunglasses so dark they were possibly black holes and sipped a bright-orange drink Mort recognised from the handful of times he'd played piano through the night and had lived to regret it.

'That you, Lily? Oh, and Mort, buddy. Chief party man, eh! Excuse the state of me – last night was a bit of a rager.'

Mort blanched. *A rager?* They'd been seeing off poor Moira Fagan to the great beyond. Granny Fagan had been a character, but her death shouldn't have incited an all-night street party. The rather robust send-off at the funeral home had surely been enough – and then some.

'Thanks for the piano,' said Lily. 'We're going to put it to good use, promise.'

'All I can play is "Chopsticks", and my nephew chewed up all the sheet music, so I know it's going to a better home. Oh fuck, my head. Can you take it from here?'

Lily give him a thumbs up and a grin so bright that he rubbed his temples.

'Drive safe,' said the guy, closing the door gingerly.

'We're going to regret this, aren't we.' Mort eyed the pianola, then the gentle slope of the promenade. All sorts of horrible deaths were parading through his mind. In the past century, some thirty-six people in the US had died from piano accidents – from being crushed, from falling through a less-than-sturdy floor, and most commonly, from attempting to move the damn things.

But Lily wasn't one for regrets.

'Oh go on.' She gave him one of those affectionate whacks on the arm that Mort was learning to associate with Lily – and like a happy Pavlovian dog rather wished she'd repeat. 'Don't look a gift pianola in the mouth. All I ask is that you let me borrow it for the goth wedding. I'm going to dress it up with flowers and cobwebs and candles – the whole lot.'

She got behind the pianola and started pushing. 'Maybe I can borrow Esmeralda, too. What do you think? Would she sit quietly if I tempted her with enough tuna? Maybe I could get a laser pointer for her to keep her on her mark.'

Hoping that death wasn't ready for him just yet, Mort tried to steady the pianola to keep it from tipping from side to side or gathering too much speed down the hill. Fortunately the promenade was bumpy with its cobblestones and Spanish tile, so a runaway pianola turned out to be an unrealised fear.

'Now there's a fun partner exercise,' hollered Dierdre from The Hot Pot, who was hurrying up the street with a delivery of fresh tea leaves.

'Play us a song, Mort!' shouted Tink, who was sharing a sandwich with Angela at one of the small patio tables in one of the promenade's wisteria-hung pocket parks.

'If you get sick of funerals, I've got a job for you,' called Roddy, passing them by with a stack of packages in hand.

Even the koi in the stream that crisscrossed beneath the promenade here and there popped up to lend their silent support. Candice the pickleball player, who was hunched beneath a blanket tossing coins into the water and muttering wishes to herself . . . did not.

'I hope she doesn't blame us,' whispered Lily.

'Well, if she doesn't die, at least she'll have a new perspective on life. And if she does . . .' Mort grunted as he tried to keep the pianola from rolling into an azalea bush. 'Well, she'll have bigger problems to worry about.'

Mort was sweating unbearably by the time they wheeled the pianola through the front door of Eternal Elegance (Funeral Edition). Not that he'd ever admit it in front of Lily, but a suit was not ideal piano-moving attire. Although surely she wouldn't hold it over him if he loosened his tie. And undid a button or two.

Apparently not — because she averted those bright blue eyes as he did so, using the moment as an opportunity to pull out a marker from the same invisible pocket from which she'd produced the dog treats. She wrote something on the exposed wood of the bare middle C key, then gave Mort's arm a squeeze.

'Enjoy,' she said. 'Come get me when you're ready to visit Gramps.'

Mort took a seat at the rickety pianola, taking a moment to read what Lily had written.

Mort's piano, from Lily. With a heart. Of course with a heart.

As Mort put his fingers to the keyboard, he could've sworn the key gave him a zap. Just like Lily's blue-eyed gaze had.

Pushing up Wildflowers

Lily

When Mort knocked at Lily's door later that night, Lily was in quite the tizzy.

Yes, they'd made plans to check out Mort's favourite graveyard (of course Mort had a favourite graveyard) on the way to visit Gramps. It was a two-birds-one-stone situation: lock in a location for Desdemona and Ambrose and also hopefully get the 411 from Gramps on just what, precisely, was going on, and how it could be reversed. Well, three birds, really: Lily was looking forward to spending time with Mort, who, in his odd, dark, grumpy way, fascinated her. Certainly, he was the opposite of anyone Lily had ever dated, except perhaps Aubrey (an assumed name) in her junior year of high school, who had sported a fantastic single sabre of black hair trained down over his face and rows and rows of spiky bracelets that functioned a bit like a razor wire fence. (Curious and tipsy on canned sangria one night, Lily had googled dear Aubrey, learning that these days he was a 2-IC shop assistant at a family hardware store chain, with a charming young family and a much more mainstream haircut – the Superclips Dad special.)

But all that personal life planning can only go so far when you're a wedding planner and you have clients texting you all day about emergencies such as a bridesmaid who is not au fait with the mandatory sleeve length the wedding party simply must adhere to, or the mechanical bull called Rosa who is being shipped across the country and needs to be tracked in person, or a best man who has stated his intention to get a facial tattoo at the Portland Tattoo Expo a week prior to the wedding. Not to mention the seating chart issues. There were *always* seating chart issues.

In between texts from Mom about Mom's life love (which was going disastrously, as always), Lily had been dealing with seating chart issues for the past two hours, and as such was not in a state for public consumption. Her cheek had a huge red blotch where she'd had it propped on her palm, and her comfortable trousers were covered in cookie crumbs. And cupcake crumbs. And also full-sized cake crumbs.

'Down in a sec!' she shouted, brushing herself off.

Donning an orange floral dress whose wrinkles she hid beneath her favourite pink jacket, she gave her hair a quick comb with her fingers, then swiped some lipstick over her lips. Oops, she'd gone a bit over the vermilion there, but the overlined look was in. She hoped. Wait, deodorant, just in case Gramps still had a sense of smell.

Shoes in hand and feeling acceptably presentable given the low-lighting situation of their graveyard destination, Lily clattered down the stairs, wondering when the stair runner had turned black, and the banister adorned with bat decorations – she'd have to do something about that tomorrow. She opened the door to Mort, who looked like he was, well, on his way to a funeral. The only concession to colour was the band on his watch, which was dark brown. And also Esmeralda, who padded into the shop behind Mort, then proceeded to sharpen her claws on the fluffy mohair cushion on Lily's desk chair.

'The safety orange look suits you,' said Mort. 'It brings out your . . .'

'Fake tan?' guessed Lily, laughing. Oh, but he was bad at compliments. But she loved that he was trying. 'Meanwhile, you're begging to be run over by a boomer with poor night vision.'

'They'd never,' said Mort. 'Not if they want a discount on their funeral plot. Ready?'

'I'm ready, I'm ready.' Giving Esmeralda a stroke on the head, Lily squeezed into her heels and followed after him.

Mort held up a hand, stopping her before she could step over the threshold. 'Those shoes.'

'They're amazing. I know.'

'But are they . . . apt for a cemetery stroll?'

'Graveyard. And oh yeah. Watch.' Lily bent and snapped off one of her heels, converting her shoes into flats.

Mort blinked. 'Wow.'

'They roll up, too. Girls have to be ready for anything.'

'Anything, hmm.'

His dark eyes regarded her thoughtfully. Lily's heart was doing something odd in her chest. Was Mort . . . flirting? Was Mort capable of flirting? Or did he mean death? Because everything always seemed to come back to death with him.

'I can use the heel as a blade, too,' she added hastily, trying to fill the very noticeable gap in their conversation. 'In case you're thinking of trying something.'

'Do I look like the kind of guy who would try something?'

Lily gave him an assessing look.

Mort leaned against the doorframe. 'Are you . . . funeral director profiling me?'

'Always. It's the wedding planner in me. So are we done judging my footwear?'

'If we're done judging my overall aesthetic.'

But it was so fun! 'Never.'

Mort chuckled. 'Fair.'

He led her down the vine-smothered laneway that ran to the left of Eternal Elegance (Wedding Edition), all quaint archways and mossy flagstones. Lily loved browsing its teeny-tiny shops in her off hours: the cramped gallery behind a curved wooden door and a deeply rusted hanging hurricane lantern; the jewellery shop with its breathtaking custom rings (and equally breath-taking prices); the fancy wine shop that she was too terrified to enter lest she bump into a bottle and have to mortgage her future firstborn.

Above them, on curved wooden arbours, wisteria and string lights bobbed in the gentlest breeze.

'This place is magical,' Lily breathed. 'I feel like every time I say something I'm casting a spell.'

Mort smiled. 'It has its charms. Even if . . .'

'Please don't say something about death.'

Mort groaned. 'But there's *so much* death. It must be the ocean air. And all the rollerblading. The car's over there.'

The alleyway opened out into the cosy parking lot where the residents of the downtown area stashed their cars – the promenade was strictly for pedestrians and well-mannered bicyclists. Lily's Miata sat there primly, covered in bumper stickers and filled with pink stuffies, its pop-up lights (complete with eyelashes) staring happily at her.

She gave the little car a pat on the hood. 'Hi, Lucille! Don't be jealous, but we're taking . . . what's the name of your hearse?'

'The hearse,' said Mort.

'How about Hearston Gloomenthal,' suggested Lily. 'Like the chef.'

'Absolutely not,' said Mort.

'Herbie the Death Bug? The Black Widow?'

'Please stop.'

Mort unlocked the hearse and opened the passenger-side door for Lily, who climbed in, her gaze flickering over the vehicle's curved hood, which was topped with a silvery skull ornamentation. Matching skulls shimmered from the silvery centre of each wheel. Apparently the hearse hadn't been switcherooed – perhaps there was some sort of geographical limit on the impact of the spell. (Maybe Lily could look at working remotely. From the beach, perhaps.)

Inside, the hearse was plush and roomy, with . . . oh, look, more skulls. But it was pristine, and smelled gently of pine and sage and not of, well, what Lily had worried it would smell of. There was not a single whiff of a corpse.

'I feel like Wednesday Addams,' she said, as she buckled up and Mort cautiously pulled out from his spot, checking around him multiple times for possible pedestrians.

They cruised slowly – excruciating slowly – down Jupiter Street, the thoroughfare that connected the various residential streets of the village, with their storybook houses and their tiny pocket parks. Every street sign was hand-painted and decorated with tiny hanging sculptures and baubles: disco balls, gleaming birds, glimmering windchimes that sang softly in the omnipresent breeze.

'You know you don't have to drive this slowly when you're not part of a funeral procession, right?' prodded Lily, although she didn't mind so much – not really. The town was so pretty, with its pink cottages and rose gardens and roundabouts decorated with sculptures and string lights. She wound down the window, drinking in the feel of it all: the gently salted ocean breeze and the fragrant wildflowers exploding from the garden beds, all topped with a dash of cinnamon wafting up from The

Cakery, which was the residential part of the town's answer to The Hot Pot. (Lily received cake samples from both on a daily basis, and had quite the cake stash going. Not to mention that her treasure map was looking pretty well filled out. She'd also had the joy of reciprocating with her own stamp, a pink heart with wings.)

'I'd rather be late than dead,' said Mort firmly. His knuckles gripped the steering wheel with the strength of a thousand panic attacks. Lily said nothing, but she added it to the dossier of facts about Mort that she'd been collecting.

'Would you prefer me to drive?' she asked gently.

'Absolutely not.'

They drove in silence for a few minutes, Lily pointing out her favourite houses along the curving road, and then the gorgeous eighteenth-century Spanish basilica that loomed in all its tiled glory over the top of Mission Hill.

'If only they were looking for consecrated ground,' said Lily wistfully. 'What a beautiful spot.'

Mort put on his indicator. 'Let's take a look anyway.'

'But there's no point,' said Lily. 'They specifically said . . .'

Mort shrugged. 'Maybe you can get some inspiration for another event. Or who knows, maybe . . .'

He trailed off, leaving Lily's imagination to run off in all directions, a bit like the fluffy alpacas flocking around on the other side of the fence that divided the mission from a nearby farm.

Mort pulled the hearse with sloth-like form off the road and beneath a huge fir tree that had carpeted the ground with needles and tiny pinecones. Lily grinned as she stepped out of the car, her heels sinking into the spongy combination of moss and tile.

'It's perfect,' she breathed, turning on the spot as she took in the peaceful courtyard and the tranquil mix of greenery –

cycads, olive trees, even a herb garden with a central fountain decorated with patterned tiles.

Lily made a beeline to the fountain, on the way crumbling a lavender flower between her fingers, then rubbing the fuzzy leaves of a lamb's ear plant.

'Do you have a coin?' she said suddenly.

Mort pulled out the thickest wallet Lily had ever seen. She hoped Mort had a permit for carrying a deadly weapon, because you could absolutely kill someone with it.

'You're going to get scoliosis walking around with that thing in your back pocket,' she warned.

'The things I suffer through to have a readily available collection of coins.' Mort passed her a quarter. 'Well, just the one coin. It's my quarter for the bodega basket.'

'You really are making sacrifices for me, huh? Such a gentleman.'

Mort folded his arms and harumphed. 'Make your wish. And make it a good one because I'm going to have to use my bare hands next time I shop for food.'

'How did you know making a wish was what I was going to do? There might be a pinball machine around the corner.'

'Ah, yes. Pinball. Very on brand for a Spanish mission.'

'One of those and a claw machine, and they'll have new converts lining up.'

Mort snorted.

Closing her eyes, Lily tossed her coin in the fountain. Well, she tried. It clinked off the edge of the fountain and bounced off into the bushes. 'Noo,' she moaned. 'And I had such a good wish, too!'

'Do tell.'

'A woman never tells.'

'It was about the switcheroo, wasn't it.'

Lily zipped her lips.

Mort stooped, then straightened. He opened his hand, revealing the slightly muddied quarter. 'Want to try again?'

Lily winced. 'I don't trust my aim. Here, let's do this.' She pressed her palm against the back of his hand, trying to ignore the warmth of it, the way he seemed to angle his arm just slightly towards her, so that his bare forearm brushed hers . . . But was she trying, really? Was she not thinking about pressing up against him and letting him wrap those arms around her, about kissing the damned grief out of him, showing him that maybe, maybe, there was more to life than death?

Shut up, brain.

Because if she let the impulsive side of her win out, things would be weird. Well, more weird. And there was already plenty of weird to go around.

'We'll split the wish,' she said valiantly, her voice definitely not cracking under the weight of all the unspoken thoughts her brain had been sending its way, only to yank them back at the very last second. 'On the count of three . . .'

She counted down, and together they hoisted the coin into the fountain. A few flips, and it plopped into the water with minimal fanfare. A tiny frog blinked up at them, disappointed at their pathetic theatrics.

'Well, I guess we'll see if it worked when we get back,' said Mort.

'If there's a freezer full of gelato in my kitchen, you'll know it did.'

'Excellent priorities there,' said Mort. 'Do you want to explore the grounds, just quickly?'

Lily clapped her hands. 'Do I ever!'

'I used to wander around here as a kid,' said Mort.

'Ah, so you've always been weird.'

'I used to get ammo from my slingshot off that tree.' He pointed to a massive, stooping olive tree shaped like a ballet dancer mid arabesque. 'And there was a nest of wrens that would rebuild every year. They had the prettiest eggs. And Father Bronson would sit on that bench drinking sacramental wine as he watched the sunsets.'

Lily chuckled. 'Part of his duties, I'm sure.'

'So much blood of Christ. It was like a transfusion centre.' He guided her to the huge double doors that led to the chapel, then pulled one open a crack, peering in. 'Take a peek.'

Lily gasped at the sight of it: all rough-hewn wood and soaring buttresses that came together like the hull of a ship. Crystal chandeliers winked at her. It wasn't the grandest space she'd seen, but it was majestic in its own way.

'Impressive, no? But the real tour de force is over here.' Gently closing the massive wooden door, Mort led Lily down a tiled garden path from which wildflowers sprouted from every crack and divot. It was so beautiful, and in her colourful outfit, Lily felt just right.

Before them, sun was starting to drift down in the sky, setting the evening clouds alight with stripes of pink and purple. All the world had become the most glorious ice-cream sundae.

'This place really is perfect,' said Lily.

Mort's dark eyes twinkled as he led Lily to a wire fence framed with ancient wooden posts. Behind the fence lay a sprawling field overhung with massive trees and afire with wildflowers: patches of purple and yellow dotted the grass, and California poppies waved their pretty heads in the delicate breeze. 'And now, for the best bit.'

Lily cocked her head. Was it wise to be heading off into the woods with a man she barely knew? Or worse, climbing a fence wearing an excellent thrifted dress she'd never be able to find again?

'Do your shoe conversion thing,' said Mort. 'I know you have it in you.'

Well, Lily had made her wish. She might as well see it through.

There's Mortal Life than Love

Mort

Mort hid a smile as Lily effortlessly scaled the wire fence in her stripped-back shoes. He had to hand it to her: the girl had gumption. Especially since there was a gate a few feet further down the fence. Mort let himself through this, chuckling as Lily stomped her foot at him.

'What?' he said. 'I'm thinking about buying myself a pair of those shoes and want to know that they're up for the task.'

If Lily had been anyone else, say Angela or Tink or Dot, she would've thrown one of those shoes at him. But being Lily, she grinned good-naturedly and pulled out her phone.

'*Five stars,*' she recited as she typed. '*Great for fence-climbing and . . .*'

'. . . Running towards alpacas,' Mort finished, as one of the fluffy creatures trotted up to him. He wrapped his arms around its neck, giving it a kiss on its fawn-coloured head.

Lily raised her eyebrows. 'Did you just . . . demonstrate affection? Should I check you for a fever?'

Mort scratched the alpaca's forehead. 'This is Lulu. The patchy-coloured one is Whiffle. They're part of Aunt Dot's herd.'

'As in Movies Dot? She has an alpaca herd?'

'Herd is kind of overstating it. There are only five of them at the moment. But it seems like there are more when they're at peak fluffiness. Once a year they get shorn down, and their wool gets spun into the skeins you see at The Crotchety Crocheter. Begonia Alleyway, two down from ours,' he added for good measure.

'I'll have to visit,' promised Lily. 'Although the one time I tried crocheting I almost smashed my phone because the woman on the YouTube tutorial kept saying "and just pull it through the loop, easy as that!" and it was not, in fact, easy as that.'

'I didn't know you were so full of rage,' said Mort. 'I like the complexity.'

'Inside me are two wolves,' said Lily. 'The sunny one, and the one who rages against poorly described YouTube crochet videos.'

Mort bit back a laugh. Lily wasn't just funny, she was *smart*. Part of him was looking forward to her meeting Gramps, although he knew, just *knew* that Gramps was going to ask a whole lot of questions about matching funeral plots and his and hers caskets. Which was precisely why Mort was always so cautious about dipping his toe into the dating waters: even if things worked out perfectly, the prospect of death coloured everything. Every minute you spent with someone was a countdown until they weren't there anymore.

And yet. Here he was with Lily, who was here for a year tops – because that was the duration of the Chamber of Commerce grant. Unless she applied to extend her lease (at market rate), but was she going to, really? When she'd opened up shop next to a funeral home with the same name, had become embroiled in a magical switcheroo, and was constantly being double-texted by Candice, who was convinced there was a fatwa on her head?

'Lead the way,' said Lily, breaking into his thoughts with that luminous grin.

'Over here,' said Mort, turning on his phone torch and leading

Lily over to a fenced-off section of the field where a handful of crumbling stones poked up from amongst the colourful wildflowers.

'Oh wow,' said Lily, as she stooped to read the age-faded names and dates on the stones. 'I thought those were rocks or something. They're gravestones? The goths will love this. It's perfect.'

Something odd was happening inside Mort's chest as Lily snapped photos of the gravestones and the stunning wildflowers – phlox, bluebonnets, black tulips – that grew in a rainbow river all throughout the field. His heart attack risk was definitely increasing.

'Thank you,' she said, reaching up on her tiptoes to graze a kiss across his cheek. 'I can't wait to take this back to them.'

Swallowing, Mort nodded. Lily was so free with her emotions. Wasn't she terrified of getting hurt? Of getting it wrong?

The two alpacas trotted up, nosing at Lily's hair and making her giggle. 'They have the funniest little faces! They're so expressive and yet . . . so vacant.'

'They're the best.' Mort gave Lulu a scratch on the head and exhaled. 'Are you ready to go meet Gramps?'

Lily snapped a photo of the wildflowers against the sunset. 'Am I ever.'

'Wow, it's *exactly* what I imagined,' said Lily, as they pulled up to Mort's childhood home, which *did* have a touch of the ghoulish to it, especially now that Gramps was finding it ever harder to get through the chores and maintenance that the huge Victorian house required. The home was all peaks and gables and towers, with spiky embellishments and garden beds that prickled with dark mondo grass, irises and foxgloves. The cast-iron outdoor furniture was pillowed with black velvet cushions that had seen their fair share of the area's salty breezes, and the hedges that formed mazes and labyrinths were shaggy and overgrown. Bunnies peeped out from them, shyly regarding Mort and Lily as the duo climbed out of the hearse and picked their way up the wonky flagstones, Mort lugging Gramps's groceries like a packhorse.

'Everything I know about you is starting to make so much sense,' whispered Lily. She bent to pluck a dandelion clock from a thick patch of weeds, then puffed on it, sending dandelion seeds flying. 'What?' she asked, seeing the aghast look on Mort's face.

'That's how you get *more* weeds,' he pointed out.

Lily cocked her head. 'I thought the robust dandelion field was on purpose. A statement about rebirth or something.'

'If everyone would stop dying, I'd have more spare time to help out with Gramps's lawn. Come on.'

The porch steps sagged from decades of comings and goings, and Mort held out a bag-laden arm for Lily just in case she became a slip-and-fall statistic. Lily took him up on the offer with a grin, and Mort, who could feel his face flushing, was grateful that the porch light had blown. (He made a note to replace it once his flush had faded.)

Gramps opened the door before Mort even had a chance to knock. Thankfully – because Mort didn't have much in the way of a free hand.

'He's so tiny,' whispered Lily in delight. 'Like a shrunk-down Uncle Fester.'

Fair, thought Mort: Gramps had always been diminutive, and his hair hadn't been seen for years. His eyebrows, on the other hand, were another matter.

'Oh, but it's good to see you, Mort!' Gramps wrapped Mort in one of his usual effusive hugs, which landed roughly at hip height given the height difference. Grocery bags swung all over. 'And who's this? Your girl? Did you get a girl, Mort?'

Mort spluttered, although he should have anticipated this, honestly. Gramps had always shown untold interest in Mort's private life – well, everyone's private lives, really. You had to, when at any moment you might have to start helping a bereaved bang out an obituary to send to the *Mirage Daily Mirror*. But though Mort had finally stepped up to the funeral home plate, there was still the question of *beyond* that. Would the business stay in the family if there was no more family? The question had kept Mort up since he'd taken over running things. It wasn't just people that could die – businesses, landmarks, legacies could, too.

Lily, sensing that Mort was off in his own world, stepped forward, giving Gramps a taste of his own medicine with a giant hug of her own. 'I'm Lily. Mort has told me *all* about you.'

'*All* about me, huh?' chuckled Gramps, looping his arm through Lily's. 'Did he tell you about the giant perch I caught when I went fishing with a shoelace by the lake as a joke? Ooh, and the sandcastle I made on the beach one day that was so good the locals thought it was made by Banksy?'

'That never happened.' Mort dropped the bags of groceries on the kitchen counters, which were made from black Formica rimmed with striped chrome. He eyed the single bowl and single spoon drying by the sink and felt a pang. When was the last time Gramps had had company that wasn't Mort? 'Lily has moved into the shop next door.'

'A business called Eternal Elegance,' said Lily. 'Wedding Edition.'

'Great name.' The ancient floorboards creaked as Gramps led Mort and Lily into the living room, where his current jigsaw-puzzle-in-progress took up most of the massive coffee table in the middle of the room. (Gramps had been a jigsaw puzzle fiend for as long as Mort had known him.) 'I love a business that dabbles in finality. Watch that missing floorboard there.'

Lily side-stepped it, then took a seat on one of the sprawling black chesterfield couches in the living room, laughing as she sank so far into it that Mort had to help her back out again. Once he'd rescued her, Mort perched on the opposite end of the couch. With the black-and-white photos of the funeral home through the ages surrounding him, he felt like he was back in high school, introducing Gramps to a date who'd inevitably ask to see the back of the hearse, beg to tour the downstairs preparation room at the funeral home, and then report back to their friends about what a freak Mort was.

Only now, things felt . . . sad. It was no longer Gramps watching Mort grow into his life. Now it was Mort watching Gramps wind down from his. He swallowed. He needed to call Angela about Whispering Waters. Or about a place that wasn't a giant ramshackle home.

'What are you working on here?' Lily was trying to figure out the theme of the jigsaw puzzle.

'The Spanish Steps in Rome. Glorious place, if you haven't been. Near the Villa Medici and the Spanish Embassy.' Gramps popped a piece into a section of the puzzle marked by pink and yellow planters, then headed over to a black rattan bar cart. He hefted a bottle of whiskey in Mort's direction, a bottle of port in Lily's, then as both nodded, poured a shot of each into twin cloudy tumblers. 'The widow Nesbitt – Hyacinth, remember, Mort? She always brought you liquorice? – gave me my first jigsaw puzzle years back as thanks for the work I did on her husband's funeral, and I got into the habit of puzzling. It got to the point that everyone would give me a puzzle when all was said and done.'

'Wow,' said Lily. 'That's really sweet. I get a lot of cake.'

'Cake's not a bad perk.' Gramps recapped the whiskey bottle. 'I put my heart and soul into that business, you know. Proudest day of my life when Mort agreed to take it over. I just *knew* he'd do a brilliant job. Keep our five-star rating on that, what's it called? Yowl? Yawp?'

Gramps passed Mort the whiskey, which Mort promptly downed. Yep, everything was going just fine. It was perfectly normal to have bouquets of hot pink zinnias delivered for a wake, or for mourners to call up asking about whether Mort had a DJ on his roster, or better yet, a live band. And the growing stack of Polaroid selfies taken with the deceased was nothing to worry about at all.

'He's doing a great job at it,' agreed Lily.

'Although I did hear you had an energetic one the other day.'

Mort felt like a deer in the headlights. As pressing as the issue was, he couldn't bring himself to ask about the switcheroo. He couldn't disappoint Gramps, not now. Gramps finally, *finally* had a chance to relax after all these years. He didn't need to know about the strange spell that had bizarrely merged the two businesses. Not unless things got worse, anyway. And maybe they wouldn't. Maybe it would all resolve itself. (Even so, Mort had been stocking up on mixed spices in an effort to try to help things along.)

'Um, that was just . . . some overflow from . . .' he began, shooting Lily a *please save me* look.

'One of my clients,' said Lily quickly. 'They get a bit frisky on the prosecco samples, and before you know it, they're dancing down the street.'

Mort breathed a sigh of relief.

Gramps chuckled. 'Ah, weddings. There's a reason I stuck with funerals. No surprises. Isn't that right, Mort?'

'Absolutely.' Mort set down his glass on a coaster. 'So, how about you two set to work on that jigsaw puzzle, and I'll get your groceries put away. And I'll deal with that porch light.'

'Deal,' said Lily. 'Although I should warn you, Gramps, I *never* do the edge pieces first.'

'An agent of chaos, I see.' Gramps grinned. 'But you get to do the sky.'

Lily flicked her hair and pretended to crack her knuckles. 'Ready to watch the master at work?'

Mort paused in the doorway to watch just that, but all he saw was the most beautiful woman he'd ever seen glowing in the soft light of the half-dark Venetian chandelier overhead.

Live, Love, Party Plan

Lily

Floating on cloud nine, the only type of cloud that could regularly be spotted in the blue skies above Mirage-by-the-Sea, Lily pushed open the door to The Hot Pot, the town's favourite purveyor of hot beverages and ridiculously decadent pastries. Lily was making it a personal ambition to visit at least one shop in town a day, a mission that was turning out to be highly delightful, and a good distraction from the switcheroo, which was not responding to any of her spells, wishes or pleas to the universe.

In the past week, she'd stopped in at The Naked Bookshop, the outdoor (but not nudist, as a little sign warned) bookshop; Brolligarchs, purveyors of fine umbrellas; Nods and Ends, a hat shop; and Catastrophic Feltdown, a very niche boutique specialising in felted feline artwork that surprisingly did a roaring trade. And the bodega, mostly because she was curious about how things were going with Derrick (cult-like, apparently – the man was selling votive candles with his own likeness on them). Oh, and also the library for the small business owners' meeting (where she'd met the Jaws, the resident fish), and the town hall (worth visiting for the bathrooms alone). Her treasure map was fat with stamps, seals and stickers – her inner Pokémon trainer had been waiting for this moment.

As Lily stepped over the coffee shop threshold, a tiny caramel-latte-coloured terrier with one floppy ear and a tail that whipped from side to side like trees in a category-five storm bounded up to Lily, planting happy kisses all over her pink flats. Jenkins!

She stooped to give Jenkins some belly rubs and some head scratches. Then some more. Jenkins was a bottomless pit when it came to attention.

'Lily! What'll it be this morning?' Dierdre, whose outfit today had a punk-rock Rosie the Riveter vibe, waved as she swung by with a tub filled with anarchically mismatching cups and teapots. A spotted bandana tied her purple hair back, and her apron was thick with political patches that would scandalise Lily's stern great-grandma. (To be fair, everything scandalised GG Edna.)

'I'll take a pot of the Garden Variety Insolence – Angela was raving about it.'

'I love a good rave. I accept rants as well. Pastry? All the ravers are saying that the lavender croissant is the way to go.'

Dierdre slapped the display counter, which was filled with an incredible assortment of pastries crowned with beautifully piped chocolate, cream and ornamental flowers.

'Done. I'll take some extras back to the shop for my clients.'

'Ah, they're going to a good home. All I ask is that you promise to share all the best gossip with me. I live for romantic friction.' Dierdre nodded to the bookshelf at the back of the room, which was crammed with well-loved romance books. 'So does my book club. Next meeting is this Thursday, if you want to talk tropes and yearning.'

Lily's whole life was yearning. 'Sold. I'll bring some

personalised bookmarks – I've been talking to a prospective client about a bookworm wedding.'

'What do I need to do to get on that guest list, huh?' Dierdre grabbed a croissant with a pair of red and white decorative tongs. 'Pick a room, and I'll bring this out to you in a few. They're all perfect, but you know my favourite is the sunroom out back. Views so criminally good I should be in maximum security.'

Lily strolled through the shop, which was a creaky, sun-filled house not unlike the one that Gramps lived in – but in terms of decor, its spiritual opposite. Every window beamed with striking stained-glass motifs, and each doorway had been painted a different colour. The hardwoods beneath Lily's feet looked original, and showed the passage of thousands of people over many years.

'They're from a local mill,' came a drawly voice from behind Lily as she tested the floorboards beneath the toe of her pink Keds. Aunt Dot! 'Their son and I went steady back in the day. I didn't get a ring, but I did get a custom kitchen.'

'Not a bad investment.' Lily stepped out of the way of the kaftan-clad cinema owner. 'Sorry for holding you up.'

'Not at all. It's nice to see a gal taking some time to appreciate the beautiful things in life, and these *are* beautiful. And it's a tea house. There's nothing urgent going on here. This place is all about letting life steep. Just like the movies.'

Angela's bob waggled as she popped her head around the doorframe. 'I dunno, Dot, things get pretty urgent when you're trying to share one of Dierdre's éclairs. They have a habit of disappearing when you turn your head.'

'Always take the first bite. It establishes dominance,' said Tink, grinning. She was dressed in a swishy polka-dot jumpsuit today – apparently spots and dots were her thing. 'We're heading to the sunroom. It has the best views, and the best board games. Want to join us?'

'I do love a spot of Boggle,' said Lily. 'If you don't mind me sending a few texts. Wedding stuff.'

'Wow, you and Mort already?' Angela waggled her perfect eyebrows.

Aunt Dot feigned extreme astonishment – she took her cues from the silent movie actors she loved so much. 'You found your way into the heart of my piano man?'

Lily flushed the red of the velvet cape lining she'd been frantically trying to source for the upcoming goth wedding. 'It's just a client thing.'

'Ignore these two.' Angela gave Tink a jab. 'They're horrible human beings. Besides, we all know that Mort doesn't do human contact. He's like a bubble boy, but the bubble keeps him safe from emotional wounds.'

'I get that,' said Lily. 'What with his line of work and all . . .'

Dierdre appeared with a rattling tray of mismatched teapots and pastries. 'Are we talking about Mort?'

'How did you know?'

'Psychic. And we went to school together.'

Angela moved her enormous handbag out of the way (what on earth was in it? Scale models of her property listings?) so that Dierdre could set down the jumble of colourful plates and teapots. Lily's was shaped like a haunted house, and the giant pot that Angela and Tink were sharing was a rainbow, with a shooting star functioning as the spout. Aunt Dot's was an art deco delight redolent of her gorgeous cinema.

'Yes, Rainbowpot! Our trusty steed.' Tink happily walked the teapot over to her teacup.

'So, speaking of Mort, he and I on a missing person case,' said Lily. 'Well, mostly me, because he doesn't know about it yet. But still.'

'Do *tell*,' mumbled Angela through a giant bite of flaky pastry.

'I love a good murder mystery podcast. The gorier the better. Especially when the quiet, keeps-to-himself neighbour did it.'

'The neighbour, in the basement, with the kitchen utensil.' Tink's eyes widened excitedly over her spotty teacup. 'Clue should do a serial killer special edition.'

'Do you remember the girl from the movie night when Frank and Derrick temporarily died?' began Lily.

How was she even going to broach this subject? *So, absent of all logic and evidence, Mort and I suspect that same girl accidentally caused a magical rainstorm that switcherooed our businesses, and that she alone can reverse the spell. And yes, I did stand under the Grand Gazebo screaming, 'You're not dead to me!' until my throat hurt, but no dice.*

'Sorry again about the temporary death thing,' called Aunt Dot from the next table, where she was playing Scrabble with herself (quite competitively, too). 'I still think it was a photosensitivity thing. Bastien is still figuring out the projector.'

Oh yes, thought Lily, *definitely* a photosensitivity thing. Definitely not a black magic swapsies issue at all.

'At least the whole second-coming-of-Derrick thing has been good for the bodega,' added Angela. 'He's talking about expanding into the building next door.'

Tink frowned. 'The old church?'

Angela sipped her tea. 'There are no zoning laws against what a group of consenting adults do in their spare time. Besides, cults are always good for their lease terms. They tithe.'

Lily was beginning to wonder if perhaps the switcheroo wasn't the weirdest thing that Mirage-by-the-Sea had endured.

'But anyway, back to what Lily was saying about the girl from the other night,' said Angela. 'The one with the smarmy boyfriend, right?'

Tink made a face. 'Ugh, I heard about the proposal.'

Angela made an even worse face. '*Everyone* heard about the proposal.'

'Not everyone can do it in El Ateneo in Argentina, babe,' said Tink, smugly. 'That's where we got engaged,' she added, in a stage whisper.

'It was a good time,' said Angela. 'Except for the bit where I had an allergic reaction to something in an alfajor and was rampaging around the pharmacies begging for antihistamines and then the antihistamines made me a raging bitch and we got in a fight at the restaurant where that waiter was being a total dick because tourists are the lowest life form, and I almost shoved his pepper shaker up—'

Tink put a hand on Angela's gold-bangle-adorned wrist, patting it soothingly. 'And despite all that, love prevailed.'

'Wow.' Lily giggled around the mouthful of lavender cream that her croissant had dissolved into. 'This sort of thing is why I do what I do. So, back to the disastrous proposal that did not end in loving matrimony, but has had bizarre repercussions that I can't talk about just yet.'

'Oooh?' Angela tucked her bob behind her ears to show just how well she was listening. 'I *love* repercussions. You can tell us.'

No, nope. As far as the town needed to know, nothing out of the ordinary had happened, save for the fact that Mort had discovered a sudden soft spot for poodle statues. Lily was not going to broadcast the switcheroo any more than she needed to.

Lily shook her head. 'I have a very strict NDA. Anyway, I need to find that girl, and since the two of you know everyone . . .'

'We really do,' said Tink. 'Social butterflies, we are. Dot, can you help?

Aunt Dot shook her turbaned head. 'Mr Smarmy paid for their drinks, so he's the only one I carded. And he paid in cash, so no credit card trail.'

'Cash, hmm,' said Angela. 'The currency of a person trying to get away with something. Also old people. Who, if my Pops is anything to go by, are also usually trying to get way with something.'

'Her Pops has his whole change scam going,' explained Tink. 'He's banned from the bodega. And the local fountains. So we're trying to find this girl, huh? Do you have a smart doorbell?'

'I do!' said Lily. She'd spent hours online with Tech Support last night begging for them to stop said doorbell playing 'My Heart Will Go On' every time Roddy came up by with a delivery. The best they'd been able to manage was a universal mute function.

(Mom, who'd been on the phone during the whole conversation, had been dismayed to hear that anyone could consider muting Celine. And had also enquired about Roddy's relationship status for the next time she came back on the market, which would most likely be soon.)

Tink drummed on the wonky table, which almost tipped over. 'All right. Just pull up the recordings from the day of the proposal, then screenshot it. We're going to Nextdoor this baby.'

'We have a Nextdoor community like you wouldn't believe,' said Angela. 'If anyone so much as sneezes weirdly, there's a day's worth of debate about it. It's also great for buying furniture. I outfitted my whole house for, like, thirty bucks and some gossip about the provenance of Ophelia Heinz's art collection.'

'Aha!' After some tapping and updating and two-factor authentication and a backup email code, Lily pulled up the feed from the doorbell. Hmm, was that Mort loitering around outside? Just what was he doing? And why was he holding such a massive pink bouquet? Hang on, was he sweeping up rose petals from outside the front of her business?

It took every bit of self-control to ignore the current goings-on outside the shop and scroll back in time to the disastrous proposal.

Angela and Tink looked on with interest as Lily found the right day, then placed her phone on the table. She thumbed backwards through her and Mort huddled beneath her awning, looking *very* close, then the thunderstorm, Veronica's heated response to the proposal, slimy Nate getting down on one knee . . .

'There. Pause it there.' Angela jabbed at the screen. 'Screenshot that and forward it to Tink.'

'And . . . got it,' declared Tink, holding up her phone as though it were the holy grail. 'Posting it now. Ha, looks like Sammy's chihuahua escaped again. If you see a tiny barking menace in a pink collar, her name is Cassandra the Seer, and she lives in the pink house just off Celestial Lane, the one that opens out to that bit of the promenade with the big koi pond. Where Angela once caught a fish *by hand*.'

'I put it back,' said Angela. 'After I gave it a kiss for good luck.'

'Ooh, and the reports are already rolling in. She's Edna Flaherty's grand-niece. Her name's Veronica Teuer, and she's from Encinitas.'

Lily opened up her various social apps, looking up the name. 'Oof, all of her social accounts are locked down. Even her website's offline.'

'Not the website!' said Tink. 'According to Edna she was an *Elementary Whiz Kids* champ and leveraged that success into the fame and fortune of a civil engineering career, with a focus on bridges.'

'Ooh, bridges,' said Lily.

'She apparently did a daily engineering equation thing on her website,' added Tink. 'Although now we'll never know.'

'Pfft, an online presence. Who needs that when you've got the

MLS?' Angela was thumbing through property listings (at least half of which appeared to be related to the current conversation, and the other half to the other conversations happening in the room – realtors never stopped working). 'Bought a cute apartment with bay views. Nice work, girl. Love the windows. That'll appreciate at a solid ten per cent annually. And here . . . is her phone number.'

Angela triumphantly spun her phone around to Lily, who typed it into her phone.

Tink checked her watch. 'A minute twenty-eight.'

The two women high-fived each other.

'You do this a lot, don't you,' said Lily.

'All the time. A realtor and a stationer?' Angela bit into an éclair with relish. (As in verve, not the tomato-based sauce.) 'We're like the ultimate PI team. Plus we're young, hot women, so no one ever suspects us.'

'Oops, too much tea, gotta pee.' Leaning in to grab a bite of the éclair as a parting remark, Tink hurried off to the bathroom. Angela looked around conspiratorially, then leaned in. 'Okay, coast is clear. I know your thing is weddings, but Tink's birthday is coming up, and I want to do something *big*. Costumes, music, someone jumping out of a cake, the whole shebang. May I engage your services?'

'You may. My rate is another one of those croissants.' Lily pointed to the crumbs that remained on her decorative plate.

'They're *good*, aren't they? I would sacrifice someone's firstborn child for one of those. Not mine. I'm child-free.'

Lily scooped up the croissant dregs and popped them in her mouth – they were too good to waste. 'Come by the shop when you have a few, and we'll sort it out.'

'Sort what out?' Tink swanned back in, a doughnut and local paper in hand.

'That was quick,' noted Lily.

'The jumpsuit has a little flap – no need for a full-nudity situation. One button, and you're in and out like that.' Tink snapped her fingers. 'By the way, I got you a *Mirage Daily Mirror*. It's full of gossip. It's basically if you printed off Nextdoor and added photos.'

'Sold,' said Lily, turning first to Pets in Show (the cutest section), and then to Births, Deaths and Marriages (the most important section).

Oh. Oh no.

The switcheroo was at it again.

Burying the Lede

Mort

Mort was not having a good morning. He'd spent an hour on the phone sorting out a funeral plot double booking, Candice had asked if she could nap in each of his coffins to test them out ahead of her imminent demise, someone had yarn-bombed the greyhounds, and now Molly Lambshead was demanding a refund on her mother's obituary. Mort was delicately trying to explain that the obituary was part of the package, and he'd submitted precisely what the family had signed off upon, but Molly was not having it.

'*Mort*,' she seethed – Molly was exceptional at seething, having presided over the town's most expensive homeowners' association with the pugnacious attitude of a bulldog. (She'd cut her teeth managing the town Facebook page, and before that, the local MMA page.) Her earrings swatted the air, almost whacking Mort as though he were an annoyingly large mosquito. 'Read it aloud, and tell me that this obituary bears any resemblance to anything a sane person would have submitted.'

Mort cleared his throat. 'Oh frabjous day, callooh callay . . .' he began. 'Nice "Jabberwocky" reference.'

'Is it, though?' seethed Molly, extra seethingly.

All right, so nice was relative where obituaries were concerned.

'We are delighted to announce the passing of our mother, Calla Lambshead,' he went on.

'*Delighted!* It says *delighted!*'

Mort cleared his throat. 'Well, families can be complicated.'

'It gets worse!' shrieked Molly (whose anger had broken the bounds of seethingness, and was now on another level entirely). 'It ends with Monty Python lyrics!'

All right, so that was a hard one to explain. Especially since the lyrics were in question were from 'The Lumberjack Song' and not from, say, 'Always Look on the Bright Side of Life'. The switcheroo had struck, and in appalling fashion. But perhaps he could salvage this situation.

'A bit of levity can help with the grieving process,' Mort offered awkwardly.

'Levity! More like indignity! This is grounds for a lawsuit! It's . . . defamation! It's . . . not how we want our mother to be remembered!'

Mort swallowed. 'Black cat?' he asked, offering Molly a candy from the bowl he kept on his desk. 'Or black tissue?'

Molly recoiled, but then took one of each. Mort had learned from years of watching Gramps at work that comforting people via food and thin sheets of paper went a long way.

'We'll publish a correction,' he said, stroking Esmeralda, who'd leapt into his lap and was unapologetically shedding white fur all over his black suit.

And then after that, figure out how to reverse this whole switcheroo situation so that he could get back to being yelled at for regular funeral things. Like why a funeral couldn't be delayed to accommodate someone's multi-stop flight itinerary or the quality of soil being shovelled over a casket or why even the most careful mortuary makeup application in the world couldn't make Grandma Kelly look like she had on her wedding day.

'It'd better be a full-page apology,' snarked Molly, chewing as she blew her nose. (The multi-tasking energy was admirable.) 'And there'd better not be a single iota of joy *or* cheer at the funeral. Doom! I want doom! Doom and gloom! *Sturm und drang*!'

'The eighteenth-century German literary and musical movement?' asked Mort, intrigued.

Molly slapped Mort's desk hard enough to leave a handprint. 'No! In the turmoil sense!'

The doorbell rang, crooning out The Three Degrees' 'When Will I See You Again'. Molly's aghast expression suggested that she had mentally added a few items to her potential lawsuit.

'Sorry,' said Mort. 'I've got the doorbell guy coming to look at that. It's meant to play "Gloomy Tuesday".'

Roddy wobbled in under the weight of a huge stack of boxes. His Lycra-clad legs strained, but then Lycra-clad legs always did, for the whole point of Lycra was to flex your muscles and show off your gams. Even if you were eighty. 'Where would you like me to put the confetti cannons?'

Molly gulped like a restaurant aquarium fish with a disturbingly full view of the sushi counter. '*Confetti cannons?*'

'Oh, they're not for me,' said Mort placatingly. 'They're for next door. Eternal Elegance, Wedding Edition.'

Roddy shook his head. He prodded at the delivery label. 'No, says here they're for you.'

Two switcheroo symptoms in one day. This was not a good sign.

Pretending to have a revelation, Mort took the box, squiggling a signature on the device that Roddy held out. 'Right! They're um . . . for personal use. Not funeral-related.'

Molly folded her arms. 'I think that's worse. Now, correct this obituary nonsense *anon*, or I'll take my business elsewhere.'

Mort sighed. 'I can accommodate that, if you must. Assuming you have a chilled van.'

Molly harrumphed. Literally. She literally harrumphed, like something out of a British children's cartoon. But apparently she did not have a refrigerated van, for she waltzed out, leaving her mother on ice in the morgue. Mort was relieved that she'd left so easily, because the definition of 'on ice' had changed substantially since the business swapsies, and it wasn't out of the question that poor dead Mama was sticking out of a champagne ice bucket.

'Ding-a-ling!' called Lily from the doorway. At least she hadn't set the doorbell off – who knew what was next on its playlist. 'I'm Walking on Sunshine'? 'Don't Stop Believin'? 'I Believe in a Thing Called Love'? 'It's Lily, the local newspaper delivery girl.'

Mort sighed. He assumed that Lily wasn't here to share a particularly good coupon for Brolligarchs (they did make brilliant umbrellas) or a delightfully optimistic horoscope that spoke of bakery riches and good surf (Kit von Diesel, the local psychic, knew what the locals wanted to hear). 'Tell me this isn't about the obituary. I have heard all one man is capable of hearing about obituaries. Ask Molly Lambshead what topic she could do an impromptu TED talk on, and apparently it's what's appropriate to put in an obituary.'

Lily grimaced. 'Well, unfortunately I've just spent the past half hour engaged in similar speechifying from one Bronson Roibles.'

Mort's desk shook from the violence with which she slapped down a copy of the *Mirage Daily Mirror*, which had a wedding announcement that began: *We regret to inform you that Bronson Roibles and Tiffany Ferguson are tying the knot.* The announcement ended with *The lucky couple are survived by their families and their dog Delilah.*

'Bronson Roibles,' said Mort, taking a seat at his comfy leather desk chair, which had been studded with spikes until recently, but was now adorned with feathers. At least they were grey, which was close enough to black. 'Quite the name. Evokes an affable aristocratic golden retriever who travels through time solving mysteries.'

'Unfortunately for all of us, Bronson Roibles is a human, and not a particularly affable one at that.' Lily prodded judgementally at the jar of black jelly cats on Mort's desk. Hang on, were there some jelly beans among them? Mort scowled – the switcheroo was a constantly moving target.

Picking out a selection of jelly beans, Lily flopped down on the chaise longue to one side of Mort's desk. (This was for the fainters. There were also some more standard chairs for the sitters, and a moody, ornate doorframe for the leaners.)

'It's so *fuzzy*.' Lily stroked the chaise in a way that made Mort rather wish he were a piece of furniture. 'Anyway, Bronson is one half of a couple with a space-flight-themed wedding I'm working on getting on the books two years from now.'

'Two *years*?' Mort was so surprised that he spun his chair in a full circle. 'Must be nice to be able to schedule your work. Every time I think about a holiday, someone kicks the bucket. Even Pickleball Candice's proposed funeral is only six months out.'

Lily regarded her jelly beans, which were disappearing at a worrisome rate. 'It's a very elaborate wedding, with a scale Mars Rover as a ring bearer and engraved meteorites as bonbonniere. Oh, and a performance of "Major Tom" from that astronaut who went viral. They're hoping that space tourism will be a little further along by then, and that everyone can join them on a jaunt to the stars. A jaunt paid for by the guests, of course. Well, and some funding from NASA. The ultimate destination wedding.'

'They are *not*.' Mort was appalled, but also fascinated. 'What possesses a person to throw away so much effort and money on a single day?'

She threw a jelly bean at him. 'Love, you fool! And a little bit of social pressure. And you're one to talk. Funerals can be just as expensive, and the people who are the subject of yours are *dead*.'

Mort couldn't argue with that.

'You're right,' he said. 'I'm sorry. I shouldn't make fun. I know you're brilliant at what you do, or the Chamber of Commerce wouldn't have picked your application over all of the others. And the runner-up does mirror-ball sculptures, so it was close. It just seems like an enormous undertaking for one day.'

'But it's not for one day,' said Lily, picking out the yellow jelly beans and arranging them into a sugary flower on the chaise. 'That's the whole point. The one day is just the *start*. Speaking of starts, or rather starts that never were: Veronica of disastrous-proposal-rejection-that-spoke-the-switcheroo-into-being fame – I found her. Veronica Teuer.'

Mort was impressed – what could he say? Lily impressed him. Especially her switcheroo origin story hypothesis, which was much more appealing than Mort's, which was that he was actually dead, and all of this was a final, hallucinatory gasp from his poor, dying brain.

Yep, the curse option sounded much better than brain death.

'You'd make an excellent stalker,' he said. 'Very unassuming. And very creative.'

'Why thank you, kindly.' Lily leaned to one side, striking a femme fatale pose. Alas, the funeral home's blinds were now chiffon and didn't offer the dramatic striped shadows a set of

Venetians might have. (The jelly beans also detracted a tad from the scene.)

'I had some help from Angela and Tink,' she admitted.

'Ah. Learning from the best.' Tink had famously tracked down an elusive post-rock composer based on the birdsong found in the background of their compositions. Mort leaned back in his chair, wriggling a bit to avoid a peacock feather. Had that been there before? 'So, assuming you're right, and she's behind this whole . . .'

'Switcheroo? Topsy-turvy? Reverse Uno card?'

'Terrible. You should be ashamed.'

'I'm not the one whose doorbell plays "It's Raining Men".'

Mort could feel what little colour lived in his cheeks draining away. 'Nor does mine. It tolls, like all good doorbells should.'

Lily's blue eyes twinkled in that terrible way that made Mort want to climb over the desk and seize her in a fit of passion. *Why* was she lounging on the chaise longue like that? Was she, despite her outward cutesiness, a proponent of cruel and unusual punishment?

'Sure, whatever keeps you going,' said Lily. 'Anyway, yes, the goal is to get her back here to reverse the spell. But Veronica has gone dark.'

That's right. They'd been having a conversation. Mort had lost the thread a bit there, what with this delectably clad woman lying seductively before him, sexily eating jelly beans. Well, eating jelly beans as sexily as was possible. (Which, honestly, wasn't very. And yet, Mort was still intrigued.)

'Gone dark,' Mort repeated.

'Offline. Incognito. Away from the public eye.'

'Yes, I assumed you weren't just saying she'd dyed her hair.' Mort slumped in his chair, fiddling with the crossbone studs that stamped the leather to the wood beneath (at least those hadn't been switcherooed, or he would've been spending the day digging up the receipt to demand a refund). 'So chances are we're stuck like this for a while, huh. Opposite Day land. Well, fuck.'

Images of increasingly unhinged obituaries and dancing on freshly filled graves swirled through Mort's head. And just what did the switcheroo have planned for those confetti cannons?

'Well fuck indeed,' said Lily. 'Because while the goths might take this whole thing in stride, Venus sure as hell won't.'

'She's not as laid-back as her PR team would have us believe, huh?' asked Mort. 'Imagine that.'

'And then there's my mom! I've been sending her strategic close-ups of my decor, but there's going to be a point where she demands a video call, and what then?'

'You could take it outside. By the bougainvillea.'

'What if Zoom applies a switcheroo filter? We don't know how deep this thing goes!'

'I take it your mom isn't big on doom and gloom?'

Lily shook her head, then affected the deep, gravelly voice of the film preview voiceover guy. '*In a world . . . of toxic positivity,*' she intoned.

'Ah. Understood.'

Lily scooped up her jelly bean flower and ate it. 'So, while I'm here. How much for a couple of coffins? The goths registered for a his and hers number.'

Mort raised an eyebrow. 'Thinking ahead, I see. Definitely a better investment than an ice-cream maker.'

'Don't besmirch the humble ice-cream maker. Truly. It's a solid twenty-dollar gift for someone you don't really know or like. And if ice-cream isn't your thing, you can always throw it at someone. They're quite heavy. And come with a vicious blade.'

'You sound like you have first-hand experience with this.'

Mort led Lily to the coffin display. Well, coffin/bunkbed display, which was proving very difficult to explain to his clients.

'Wow,' said Lily. 'Is this a switcheroo thing, or are you exploring space-saving burial options for our overcrowded future? Because the goths also want plots for their dogs.'

Mort considered. 'How big are we talking?'

'Pugs.'

'Oh, thank God, I thought you were going to say a Great Dane. I'll throw in a pug plot gratis.'

'Two pug plots.'

'You drive a hard bargain, but I can't say no to a wrinkly face.'

Lily set her hands akimbo. 'You'd better be talking about me, because I will not have you slandering our puggy friends.'

Mort couldn't help but laugh. 'Of course, of course. Lucky for you, there's a botulism voucher in that Chamber of Commerce treasure map of yours. Just be careful, because it *is* a neurotoxin.'

'At least if you have to embalm me, I'll be a perfectly blank canvas. You can pancake me up in a single swipe. Now help me up this ladder so I can check out these coffins.'

Not a Mourning Person

Lily

Friday the 13th rolled around with all the usual social media fanfare and quippy menu items and sales. And why not? The date was a solid excuse for a miniature Halloween, and who didn't love an excuse to give their costume a trial run?

At least Lily had all day to finalise the plans. Which were extensive. Channelling her inner goth took a good deal of work. Honestly, *finding* her inner goth had been a large part of it; Lily had been one of the few kids in her class who had skipped the phase, opting for an ethereal theatre kid vibe instead. Hand pressed to her forehead, she'd swanned around in full-length pastel gowns, climbing every balcony in sight and sighing theatrically. She'd promptly discarded the affectation when the hem of one of her gowns had caught on the non-slip tread on a step, leaving her half-naked above a major road during peak-hour traffic. The police had arrived, worried for her safety. And her pride.

Still scarred from the experience, which (along with her bare butt) had made the local news, Lily had opted for a three-quarter LBD with bell sleeves that doubled as pockets. (Said sleeves had a handy drawstring in case she needed to reel them in to avoid a repeat of the stair-catching situation.)

She felt incredibly underdressed next to Desdemona, who wore a majestic velvet and tulle mermaid gown and stacked boots so tall that she could conceivably dunk a basketball without having to leave the ground. (Alexander McQueen would have been proud, and perhaps a little scared.) The bride's eyes were sharp with expertly executed liner, and her lips were a matte black so deep that they swallowed stars. Briony, the event photographer, spun around Desdemona with a massive camera on a gimbal. Briony was a thin, austere-looking individual who looked as though she'd come off the set for a film steeped in German Expressionism. (This was because she actually had – it turned out that Desdemona was an esteemed independent film director, and Briony was her director of photography. Tonight's wedding was in part supported by a film grant, and would air at Rerunning Up That Hill in a few weeks' time, with piano improvisation provided by Mort.)

'Lovely touch with the black carpet.' Desdemona nudged the carpet roll with a toe. Lily was astonished she could even lift her feet in those boots. The woman must be a powerhouse in the gym. 'I might repurpose it for the film premiere.'

'Thanks,' said Lily. 'There was a leftover bolt from the seamstress who leased the shop before me.'

The familiar rumble of Mort's hearse shook the light-studded streets.

'Your chariot,' said Lily, with a grin.

Desdemona nodded approvingly. 'Now *this* is how one travels on to the next stage in life.'

Pulling the hearse around in front of them, Mort climbed out, looking oddly . . . shevelled. His black tux was impeccable – and set off with a black and red paisley bow tie – and his usually tousled hair was neatly combed. Was that product?

'You did your hair,' noted Lily, impressed.

And damn, he smelled so good. Unless that was cedar from a coffin she was smelling, in which case . . . okay, he still smelled so good.

Mort scoffed. 'It's Friday the 13th. Not dressing up would be most improper.'

He paused, taking in Lily's uncharacteristically monochrome outfit. 'You look . . . lovely.'

These were effusive words coming from Mort. Lily tried to swallow back the enormous grin that threatened to take over her whole face. This was Desdemona's night, not hers. 'Thanks, but it's just the moonlit beauty of our bride reflecting on to me.'

Said moonlit bride was presently posing in front of a decorative lamppost like something out of a French horror film. But she *did* look great.

Mort popped the back of the hearse, which creaked open deliciously to reveal a profusion of black satin cushions arranged in the shape of a coffin. Behind the cushions was a wall of black roses sourced from Whoops-a-Daisy (whose treasure map stamp was a dried daisy nested in acrylic), arranging them so that they filled the back of the hearse in a solid black wall of petals.

Quoth the raven: Evermore, was spelled out in spidery writing atop the roses. (This had been Ambrose's suggestion.)

Lily squeezed Mort's arm; the display was the epitome of the macabre. It was perfect.

Clopping forward on her astonishing boots, Desdemona clapped her hands over her mouth – although carefully, so as not to ruin her purple-lined lipstick – overcome with emotion at Ambrose's thoughtful addition to the celebration.

'It's deliciously sombre,' she whispered. 'The soul aches at the very sight.'

'Let me know when you're ready,' called Mort from the driver's seat, as Lily adjusted Desdemona's hem so that Briony could snap a series of shots of the bride in repose. Desdemona snatched up one of the roses and held it to her throat, inhaling deeply.

'Ah, the sweet scent of the night, of the little deaths it offers,' she murmured.

'Sorry I'm late,' whispered Mort as Lily buckled up next to him. 'I had an issue with a body. It was a whole thing.'

Desdemona was high on the scent of the roses she'd been huffing (maybe Lily shouldn't have spritzed them with all that hairspray as a preserving agent). 'Mort, tell me,' she murmured. 'How many corpses have made the journey back here?'

'Hundreds,' said Mort, crawling down Jupiter Street at a speed so slow it was surely an arrestable offence. 'Some of them couples.'

'How romantic,' breathed Desdemona dreamily. 'Heading back to the earth together, becoming one with the mushrooms . . .'

Lily cranked the stereo, which was preloaded with a goth rock playlist she'd spent hours putting together as she worked on the 'sky' chunk of the jigsaw puzzle Gramps had assigned her. She had a fairly solid area of blue on her upstairs table, and a newfound appreciation for fuzzy guitar and nihilistic lyrics.

'I never pegged you as a Ministry fan.' Mort braked for a tourist who was a solid three metres away from the road and could therefore conceivably do a running jump onto the hood.

'What?' Lily danced along in her seat to the amazingly Eighties drumbeat. 'What part of me doesn't suggest I live my life like every day is Halloween?'

'You really embody each wedding you work on. It's . . . impressive.'

'Thanks. And you do a lot for the dead denizens of Mirage-by-the-Sea.'

As the hearse inched along, Lily leaned out the window, marvelling at the giant moon that hung like a very brave trapeze artist in the mist-shrouded sky.

'Perfect for Friday the 13th,' she mused.

'Here.' Mort pressed a button. The sunroof opened, giving Lily whatever the opposite of the bird's-eye-view to the moon was. She reclined her seat, staring up at it.

'What an idyllic night to come together as one,' whispered Desdemona from behind her.

Lily shot a glance at Mort, then hastily averted her eyes as she realised that he was doing the same thing.

'Watch the road,' she murmured in a sing-song voice.

As the hearse climbed the top of the hill, the Spanish Mission rose up before them, its quaint arches and massive trees reaching up at the sky in celebration.

'Almost there,' said Lily, producing a makeup compact from her purse. 'Are we ready?'

'Deadly ready,' said Desdemona.

Lily climbed through to the back of the vehicle, gently pushing the roses aside. She cracked open the compact, then grimaced. The thick, cake-like makeup was not what Desdemona had handed her earlier that evening. *Casket Case* was tooled in silver on the front of the compact. Shit. It was Mort's mortuary makeup. The switcheroo was at work.

Desdemona gasped, then clasped her hands to her throat. 'Where did you get that? It's all the rage after Kat Kadaver showcased it on TikTok. It's been sold out for months.'

'And it's . . . all yours!' said Lily brightly. 'A wedding gift from me. Oh look! There's even a lipstick.'

She passed Desdemona a matte pink lipstick (*Frigid Fluid*) that didn't quite seem the bride's style until Desdemona gave another gasp – 'The lipstick hue from *The Corpse Bride*! You've thought of everything!'

'It's my special brand of magic.' Lily carefully adjusted Desdemona's gown in preparation for the bride's arrival at the wildflower field. 'Now let's get your cape on.'

'I've got the step stool.' Mort came around with a child's mourning chair, which was *not* the chair that Lily had sourced. At least the switcheroo was working for this particular wedding, she thought, as Desdemona waxed excitedly about olden-day mourning rituals. It was the others that were going to be more of an issue.

But, she thought wistfully, as a shooting star launched itself overhead, maybe they'd have this whole spell reversed by then.

When Desdemona appeared against the giant studio-style lights that Lily had borrowed from Rerunning Up That Hill, a murmur arose among the small knot of guests like the flapping of a cave full of bats – which to be fair, was probably the vibe they were going for. The bride's black beaded corset skimmed her hips, making the explosion of her tulle mermaid skirt all the more eye-catching. A beaded floor-length cape in matching tulle clung to her shoulders like the most extravagant raven wings.

Ambrose stood at the far end of the field by the gravestones, which Lily had carefully lit with additional cinema lights. ('We're going for a spooky Ed Wood vibe,' she'd told Dot, who had needed little coaxing.) He wore a majestic black velvet tuxedo over a purple silk shirt studded with skull buttons, and a canted brimmed hat that straddled the line between pirate and steampunk. (In a good way.)

Sunny the budgie perched happily on his shoulder, nibbling sweetly at Ambrose's chain-link earring, which swung from his left lobe like a miniature obstacle course. Meanwhile, beside him, two pugs – one in a top hat and the other in a pinstriped vest – panted happily from black satin cushions, their curly tails waggling.

Breaking character from her usual funeral vibe, Desdemona beamed as she drank in the stunning scene: the vibrant wildflowers bobbing in the gentle evening breeze, the small knots of black-clad guests on the ancient pews the mission had generously lent them for the night, the table of dyed-black burgers sourced from Burgermeister and the equally dark desserts from The Hot Pot, the haunting light of the moon that hovered high above them.

'It's perfect,' she whispered to Lily. 'I could die happy. Not that I would, because that's not my particular aesthetic. But you know what I mean.'

'I do indeed,' whispered Lily, giving her hand a squeeze. Ouch, those nails! 'Are we ready to hit the music?'

Desdemona nodded. 'Let's do it.'

Mort rolled a score into the rickety pianola that was now enjoying a pleasant semi-retirement inside the funeral home. Lily had set black candles into the candelabras at its front, and had shrouded it in a length of black lace that Janessa Hodges had left at the back of the upstairs wardrobe. (Having all of this excess fabric around was proving a boon.)

Mort set the pianola to play, then stomped his foot on the pedal. He gave Lily a thumbs up as the discordant notes of 'Hurt' by Nine Inch Nails rang out crookedly into the moody night. A self-playing piano in a cemetery field under a full moon: it was deliciously haunted, if Lily could say so herself.

'How on earth did you get a score for that?' whispered Briony, her camera snapping as Desdemona slowly made her way down the ornate Turkish-style carpet runners Lily had dragged into a line to form an aisle. Black candles glimmered in hurricane lanterns along the edge of the runners, casting a soft light on Desdemona's ankle-twisting platform shoes.

'Internet,' said Lily proudly. 'I printed it out and cut the little holes myself.'

'Wow. Dedication.'

In astonishing testament to her capacity to her childhood

ballet lessons – that ankle strength! – Desdemona made it to Ambrose without injury.

'My bride.' Ambrose's dark eyes sparkled as he pulled Desdemona to him. Desdemona sank into his arms, her black-painted lips curving into a smile as the gentle light of the moon played over them.

Lily's heart swelled – this was why she did this. She loved seeing people in love celebrating that love, however that looked. And as a wedding planner, it looked all ways.

The celebrant – an older woman clad in flowing black robes and with a pair of goggles pushed up on her head – stepped forward. (Elvira had been double-booked.)

'Where are my glasses . . .' she muttered, before pulling down the goggles.

'Unexpected,' said Mort.

'Very steampunk,' whispered Lily.

'We are gathered here tonight under the watchful eye of the full moon, upon this unconsecrated ground, to bring together two dark souls in eternal darkness together.'

Someone whooped.

'Our couple have chosen to recite their own vows in the form of T.S. Eliot's *The Waste Land*. Our bride will begin.'

Nails flashing, Desdemona spread her arms, intoning the poem's famous first line.

'I hope you brought snacks,' whispered Mort, 'because this is going to take half an hour.'

At the next stanza, Ambrose took up the mantle, his words embellished by Sunny's twittering.

On they went, taking a line each and sending it off into the night. The moon coasted overhead as the couple recited the poem with surprising accuracy (Lily was scrolling it on her Poem a Day app on her phone) until, finally....

'*Shantih*!' repeated the crowd along with the bride and groom. Everyone stood for a moment, lost in the puzzling disillusionment of Eliot's words. Even the pugs panted mournfully.

The celebrant pulled up her steampunk goggles to wipe a tear from her eye. 'A masterwork befitting of this union. And now, do we have the rings?'

Lily grinned. It was her inner theatre kid's moment to shine. Well, someone else's theatre kid, anyway.

A ring box between two of his fingers, Thing from the Addams family leapt up onto a nearby tombstone, evoking claps from the crowd.

Desdemona, rather uncharacteristically, chuckled. 'How did you . . .'

Thing leapt from tombstone to tombstone, then trotted over to the happy couple, climbing up Ambrose's leg to hand him the ring box, which was shaped like a black skull and opened up to reveal pink innards in which two ornate rings had been planted.

'Thank you, Thing.' Thing hurried off into the night, just as Lily had planned: she'd booked a local high school kid for the gig. Fifty bucks, a meal, transportation and a job reference for anyone who wouldn't mind getting dressed up entirely in theatre blacks (Thing hand excepted) to provide a fun little cameo at a goth wedding. Every single thespian at the local high school – which, of course, was an arts high school – had auditioned. It had been a tough decision.

As a smattering of applause broke out (goths were a tough crowd), Ambrose took the ring box, then held it up to Sunny, who pulled out Desdemona's ring – a black floral band with elegant little rubies – passing it to Ambrose to slide onto Desdemona's finger.

Desdemona and Sunny then did the same with Ambrose's ring (a giant silver skull that could double as a knuckle duster).

'And now . . . kiss the night – and each other!' shouted the celebrant, rather ominously, thought Lily, who was a bit worried that frogs might rain down from the sky. If she'd known, she would've at least brought her rainbow umbrella.

Ambrose gently dipped Desdemona, the two kissing so passionately that Lily's cheeks flushed. Her hand, apparently taking inspiration from Thing, reached for Mort's, and her fingers were twined around his before she realised what she was doing.

But Mort didn't recoil – at least not immediately. He was staring down at their clasped hands in surprise, as though he couldn't believe what he was seeing. Gently, he placed his free hand over hers, gave it a squeeze, then pulled away.

Lily's heart tugged. Had she overstepped?

'I think you're needed,' he said, nodding at Briony, who was waving frantically at Lily.

Fingers tingling from where Mort had clutched them moments before, Lily swished through the wildflowers over to the ornate buffet table, hoping there were no snakes. Wildflowers always seemed like such a good idea from afar, but the reality was that all sorts of creepy things lurked there. And divots! Secret divots preparing to grab a hapless walker and break their ankle.

'It's the cake.' Briony pointed to the tiered cake with its skull and gargoyle piping work. 'There are . . . maggots.'

'Maggots?' Lily's stomach wrenched. Switcheroo, no! Even for the goths, this was going too far. 'But it's fresh! It was made specially for tonight.'

'Maggots!' boomed Desdemona from over Lily's shoulder. She'd followed Lily, somehow avoiding all ankle breakage. Avant-garde film directors were built from stern stuff. 'Show me immediately!'

Briony pointed to a cream skull with a maggot wiggling out

of its eye socket. Lily, unable to decide whether she needed to scream or retch, clapped a hand over her mouth. How did one even go about salvaging a situation like this?

'I'm so—' she began, ready to launch into the most impassioned apology of her life, followed by a madcap dash to The Cakery for a backup cake. She'd take Mort's hearse into fifth gear if she had to.

Desdemona reached for a fork, scooping off the offending buttercream skull and marvelling at it. 'Nothing better encapsulates the eternity we're embarking upon like maggots. They represent life. Death. Rebirth. *Emptiness*. It's perfection. All of it, perfection.'

Well, Desdemona was the one paying the bills.

'I'm so . . . glad you like it.' Lily's prior urge to retch had shifted abruptly to an urge to whoop. She'd done it! Her very first official wedding was a success! She couldn't wait to tell Mom and Annika all about it. (Well, not *all* about it.) 'A wedding is all in the details. Well, there's the love part, too. But mostly details.'

Desdemona's expression almost crossed into smile territory. 'The hearse, the coffins, the Thing cameo, and now this? I'm as ecstatic as a goth bride has the right to be. Now, if you'll excuse me, we're about to do the cake smash.'

Oh no, thought Lily. Oh no. No to that.

Briony took a step back and popped the lens cap back on her camera. 'I think I have what I need.'

Lily nodded. 'Let's go wait by the hearse. I'll do the *just married* shaving foam.'

'Deal.'

Say it with Funereal Flowers

Mort

Ah yes, the endless weepy hugs that came with being a funeral director. Mort was presently enveloped in a bosomy embrace that seemed to have gone on a solid minute too long. (Alas, not even a switcheroo thing, but a came-with-the-territory thing.) Over the sturdy shoulder of Aunt Agnes, he could see a line of similarly distraught women waiting for their turn at the hug dispenser.

There was entirely too much physical contact involved in this job. And none of it the good kind, like how Lily had gently reached for his hand last night . . .

No, no, Mort. Stop right there. Feelings were bad. They inevitably ended in pain. And there was a high possibility that said pain involved death.

Exhibit A: the funeral he was overseeing this very moment. This was what happened when you loved someone. They carked it and left you with endless decisions to make about caskets and flowers and liturgies. Not to mention the estate. Oh, the angsting over estates that Mort had endured throughout his youth, and now, especially now, as the de facto psychiatrist in the room. Estates were terrible things because they meant divvying up assets, or worse, debts. Given that he'd seen family members fighting over lasagne apportionment, the prospect of dividing up a home was a thing to be feared.

There. Mort felt much more grounded after that. All thoughts of Lily were gone. It was just Mort and the corpse and the hugging women. And now a man.

'I miss her,' sobbed the man, unloading a set of false teeth on Mort's lapel. Mort gingerly handed them back using his pocket square as a buffer. 'She was my queen. My *queen*!'

'Uncle Irv,' said a woman with a magnificent purple rinse through her hair. Ah, Cousin Domenica. 'Beverley wasn't your queen. She was Poppy Clive's queen. Remember?'

'No! Not Clive's!' Uncle Irv's eyes were red-rimmed. (The potential cause of this seemed manifold.)

Mort suspected there might be some skeletons in the Alberi family closet, and not all of them in the casket at the front of the room.

'How about we take our seats,' Mort said gently. 'We'll begin the service shortly.'

'Me first! Bags the shotgun seat,' shouted Uncle Irv, muscling several aunties and a few kids out of the way.

Not trusting Uncle Irv to behave for the duration of the service, Mort ran to fetch a Rubik's cube to keep him busy. Hopefully Irv wasn't a pro at algorithmic problem solving. (He'd run into this issue before.)

Finally, the rowdy crowd settled down, and the pastor stepped forward to begin the eulogy. But the siblings weren't having it. The purple-rinse woman pulled a knife from her purse and started banging it against a funeral urn from Mort's display.

'Toast time!' bellowed a guy in a Seventies velvet suit with astonishingly expansive flares.

'*Roast* time,' corrected Cousin Domenica.

Ah. So *here* came the switcheroo action. Mort desperately

wished he'd stocked up on distractions and diversions. There was a slinky somewhere in one of the back rooms, and from memory a game of Hungry, Hungry Hippos in one of the cabinets of the morgue. But they weren't enough to distract from the fact that Purple Rinse was carefully working through sixty years of the deceased's sexual exploits in strict chronological order.

'And then there's the horrible kids,' howled Cousin Domenica. 'I see you here, counting your inheritance on your little phones. That should've been mine. Poppy Clive, you've got some explaining to do!'

'Don't blame me,' shouted Poppy Clive. 'The kids are Uncle Irv's doing.'

'I told you she was my queen!' Uncle Irv leapt up in his chair and flung his solved Rubik's cube at Poppy Clive's shiny head. He missed by a fraction. The cube bounced off the coffin, leaving a smudgy red dent. 'How else do you think they all got into MIT? It certainly wasn't *your* brains, Mr Unranked Two-Year Technical College.'

(Well, that explained the speed cubing and the terrible arm. Apparently a lot of temperamental MIT alumni retired to Mirage-by-the-Sea.)

Mort tried to position himself between Poppy Clive and Uncle Irv, who it seemed had some unfinished business that spanned generations. Specifically, the generation that came directly after theirs. 'Um, let's move on to the next part of this . . . celebration of life.'

'Righto. Who's ready for the bouquet toss?' Sister Margaret (sister as in genealogically, not as in the devoted to Christ type) had grabbed the bouquet of lilies from the casket and had leapt atop a chair. Her back to the crowd, she held the bouquet between her knees, ready to show Uncle Irv a thing or two about hurling things across a room.

A bouquet toss was not what Mort had in mind.

'We don't really . . .' Mort swallowed. 'That's more the remit of next door.'

But the mourners – revellers really – were not having it. A gaggle of wrinkled women had shoved aside the chairs that Mort had carefully set out that morning and were primed for a crucial moment of athleticism.

'Let 'er rip, Marge!' shouted Aunt Agnes, whom Mort did not doubt for a second was ready to perform a tackle if needed. She'd absolutely played rugby during her college years. Her quads strained as she settled into a catching pose.

'Agnes, you were first to get married. You're not wining this race, too,' grumbled Cousin Domenica, who had no shortage of grievances today. She'd been fourth in the family to be married, although she'd managed it four times, so perhaps she'd prevailed in the end. Well, her wedding planners had, anyway, although Mort wasn't sure that wedding planners had been a thing half a century ago. He'd ask Lily next time he saw her.

'Please let it be me,' wheezed Great-Great-Auntie Petunia, who was hooked up to enough oxygen to keep a submarine crew underwater for a solid six months. For some reason she carried a bucket filled with kitchen utensils. (Advanced age brought out odd proclivities in people.) 'I don't ask for much . . . only death.'

It was a fair ask, Mort had to admit.

There was jostling and grumbling as the mourning women hoicked up their skirts and kicked off their shoes in preparation for the athletic feat about to follow.

'And a-one! And a-two! And a . . .' Sister Margaret hurled the lilies over her head and into the circling crowd of funereal sharks. It was a solid throw: Sister Margaret had a better arm than Uncle

Irv, and the lilies flew through the air on an impressive arcing trajectory, racing through the too-slow grabbing hands of Aunt Agnes and tumbling to the floor.

It was a bloodbath. Great-aunts and sisters and cousins-twice-removed and a bearded gentleman with The Dude vibes who'd introduced himself as the pool guy descended in a frenzy of high kicks and elbow jabs and hair pulling. Mort had never seen anybody at a wedding so desperate to catch the bouquet. And he'd certainly never seen anyone at a funeral fight to be next in line to die.

Through all the chaos, Great-Great-Aunt Petunia was sneaking in on her chair, brandishing a pair of tongs she'd pulled from the quiver on her back like some sort of elderly kitchen-hand assassin.

A snapping of tongs – not quite, *almost* . . . yes! The tongs grabbed at the bouquet, clasping at the ribbon that held it together. Great-Great Aunt Petunia yanked it towards her like a fisherman triumphantly landing a fish, then cradled it like said fisherman in his dating app photo.

'I got it!' whispered Great-Great Aunt Petunia, a tear trickling down her wrinkled cheek. 'Oh, happy day.'

Mort swallowed. This was not precisely how he would've categorised the outcome, but she seemed happy, and who was he to argue with that?

Bouquet in her lap, Great-Great-Aunt Petunia rolled up to Mort. She reached for a black Glomesh purse, pulling from it a hefty pen and a not-so-hefty chequebook.

'Mr Mort, will you do me the honour of being my funeral planner?'

Mort spluttered. This was almost as romantic a proposal as the one that had caused this whole situation.

And then, because the switcheroo couldn't get enough of

making fun of poor, sad old Mort and his dreadful career choice, Beyoncé's 'Crazy in Love' started blasting over the speakers.

Once he'd taken Great-Great-Aunt Petunia's deposit, Mort went off shakily to the kitchen to pour himself a champagne.

Swan Song

Lily

Venus Cargill was the embodiment of the verb 'to swan'. All long neck and long beak, she glided into Eternal Elegance (Wedding Edition) with the ease of a water bird coasting around on a golf course water feature. And given the din of the private helicopter that had landed in the amphitheatre, she was going to glide out just as easily.

She took so long to shimmy through the front door that Lily had time to make a quick prayer to the switcheroo gods *and* bang out a quick text to Annika about the arrival of the heiress.

!! texted back Annika.

Right?? responded Lily.

Their correspondence would be fit for the Smithsonian one day.

(Mom, meanwhile, had just sent Lily seventeen screengrabbed boomer cartoons from Facebook. She'd figure out a way to respond to those later.)

'Lily, darling!' Venus came in for a three-kiss greeting that involved lots of *mwah!* sound effects. 'I cannot tell you *how* excited I am for you to bring my vision for my nuptials to life. Thank you for taking over from the previous wedding planner at such short notice. She just didn't get my vibe, you know?

Oh, I brought you some toothpaste. Our new Pearly Whites range, made with natural pearls. It's the decadence your teeth deserve.'

Typically, the most decadence that Lily's teeth enjoyed was a bag of M&Ms scoffed while binge-watching *Suits*. But she wasn't one to say no to a treat.

Venus passed Lily a tiny gift bag filled with toothpaste tubes and mouthwash and floss. Lily felt like she'd just visited a celebrity dentist, but in a majestic turn of events, the dentist was paying her, which was a welcome change from how these things usually went. (Expensively. Painfully.)

'So, how are we faring with the tent?' Venus took a seat on one of the ghost chairs, which Lily had draped with a rainbow kantha quilt in preparation for this visit. (She'd shoved the more morbid results of the switcheroo into a nearby cupboard, and had run over to Mort's to grab a few of the bouquets of dried wildflowers that been mysteriously delivered to his shop for reasons that the florist simply could not explain. She'd even managed to get the Mamas & the Papas playing through her sound system after a few false starts that had involved 'Tears in Heaven', 'I Am Sailing', and then *The Exorcist* theme song.

'The tent is . . . *enormous*,' Lily assured Venus, who was inspecting a bonsai tree wedding favour. 'I had a structural engineer come in to make sure it could sustain its own weight, especially once we have the Moroccan lanterns and mirrors added.'

'Oh, it's going to be so chill, so relaxed, so *zen*. Our very own Burning Man, but somewhere with more acceptable weather. And proper beds. And honouring me. And of course my love . . .' Venus frowned, then twisted a lock of hair that had clearly come straight from a blow-out appointment. 'Um, Desmond. Oops, blanked for a moment there, silly me.'

As one did when it came to a small detail like your fiancé's name.

Venus pulled out a gilded planner. A literally gilded planner. Were those actual pieces of jewellery welded together?

'Oh this old thing? It's a family heirloom. When my grandmother passed she gave me all of her old rings, and I decided to give them new life. Now I carry them with me forever, just like she wanted. I mean, her will did say *wear*, but they were so dated. And besides, I didn't want her to feel bad competing with this.'

Venus waved an iceberg in Lily's face. Oh wait. That *Titanic*-sinking chunk of white was actually a diamond.

'It's blood-free,' promised Venus. 'Canadian. Now, let's talk vendors. So, we were in talks with a renowned tie-dye artist from Seattle, someone huge in the textile mural scene, but they refuse to work with the colour blue. Something about it being unlucky in their life after an open-water boating incident. So we'll need someone new. Someone unafraid of blue.'

Tie-dye artist, wrote Lily.

'And I had a photographer lined up, but they did this frankly *mid Vogue* cover. You saw the one for March? The outdoor shoot with the breeze blocks and the Marilyn vibes? Too structured. Too inorganic by far. I need someone free-flowing, unfettered, someone capable of capturing the love of the moment.'

Photographer, wrote Lily.

'But well connected,' Venus went on. 'Media placement is everything. This is more than a simple wedding, of course. Although we do want it to be simple – pastoral, even. It's two empires coming together to form a dental hygiene superpower. But a flower power superpower.'

??? wrote Lily.

'And then there's the food.' Venus spun her planner around to reveal an extensive list of ingredients. 'These are all the things my guests are avoiding, whether for allergies, ethical reasons, or just the vibe of it all. I had a raw vegan chef lined up, but he's taking some personal time away after an unfortunate mango overdose.'

'You can have too much of a good thing.' Lily was now suddenly concerned about her own strawberry intake, which was substantial. (Who could resist the giant strawberries from Farmer Vikram's stall, which was set up a few lanes over, and which happened to be part of Lily's just-stretching-my-legs stroll that her smartwatch demanded she take multiple times a day. Between the strawberries, the honey and the dates, Lily had been feasting like an ancient queen.)

'You truly can. Hence my ketamine detox.'

Right.

'How about the vows?' Lily decided that now was a good time to brew some tea. (Dierdre from The Hot Pot had come by earlier with a calming blend somewhat oddly called GABA-Gool, and it had been calling Lily's name all morning.) 'Are you feeling good about those?'

Venus's phone buzzed. 'Oh, it's what's-his-name. Desmond. Here, I'll put him on speaker.'

Ah yes, what's-his-name, perfect pet name for the person you were about to commit yourself to for life. Or at least for a while. She wondered Venus had a prenup, or whether Desmond did, or whether you needed a prenup when you were each as rich as each other.

'Hello?' Desmond's voice crackled over the phone, stirring Lily out of her imaginary prenup showdown.

'Babe, we're doing wedding planning stuff.' Venus scrubbed her hands with a lotion that Lily only recognised because Honour Nivola had sparked a giant media commotion by saying that her beauty routine was simple, really – she flew to Paris for a tub of this very affordable over-the-counter skin cream made by a local company. Ten euros! Bargain.

'How are we feeling about vows?' went on Venus, slathering herself in the scent of gay Paris. Lily could just about hear the dollar signs ringing out.

'Vowels? I like "e".'

'No, vows. *Vows*. "I do" and all that.' Venus was on to a fancy lip balm now, which from its tropical pattern was likely from Brazil. *So* affordable – just a quick jaunt to Rio away!

'Right. Right. Um, whatever you think. I'm heading into a board meeting about that whole dental floss thing—'

'Someone lost the top of their finger because they wound the dental floss too hard,' explained Venus to Lily, smacking her lips. She held out the pot of – was it gold? Yes, probably – to Lily, who used all of her willpower to politely decline. Sure, she'd never know the gentle touch of Brazilian royalty, but she also wouldn't have to worry about cold sores for now. (She'd learned this lesson the hard way, having shared a straw with a friend back in elementary school.)

'That's not the company line, babe.'

'We're amongst friends, *babe*,' replied Venus, in a majestically bitchy sing-song tone.

'You said the same thing about the whole microplastics debacle. My family put that law firm's entire collective of kids through college.'

'They *did* have a lot of kids, didn't they? You'd think lawyers would be too busy.'

Desmond – or what's-his-name, which, who knew, maybe he preferred to go by – pressed on. 'Anyway, I wanted to ask about the mouthwash burns situation. The reputation firm is on it, but that hashtag is moving really fast.'

'Winston can be the fall guy,' said Venus airily. 'He owes us after we covered up the whole . . . oh. Um.' Remembering that Lily was in the room with her – or perhaps simply because she'd met her daily conversational quota with poor Desmond – she rang off. 'Anyway. Back to more important things. Dinnerware!'

Setting a mental reminder to donate Venus's generous gift of class-action-lawsuit-pending dental hygiene goods to Estelle, her frenemy from college who kept popping up on her social media feeds being *suspiciously* successful, and whose blinding smile was what Lily had always assumed was how Estelle hypnotised people into doing her bidding, Lily showed Venus over to the art deco cabinet that housed her curated assortment of crockery and silverware.

'If there's nothing here that works,' she said, 'we can always browse one of the vintage shops in the village.'

'Hmm, there are some quaint pieces here,' said Venus. 'Is this one hand-thrown? I have this wonderful artist out of Puglia I work with sometimes. So sweet, so bucolic. She does all of my scarves, too. You might know her chocolate box collab with Zodiac? You should absolutely bring her on as a vendor. Imagine the bonbonnieres!'

Which reminded Lily: they hadn't discussed wedding favours. She'd been thinking something like vintage Loteria matchboxes or personalised fragrances. But perhaps honey imported from the ends of the earth or hand-gathered meteor fragments would be more suited to Venus's sensibility, which was somewhat hilariously disconnected from reality. Or a puppy for everyone. Or a tortoise, a really long-lived one that could see the happy couple through multiple generations of delighted matrimony.

She bit back a grin, imagining how Mort would respond to any of these suggestions. She could just see the furrow between his brows as he tried to make sense of why someone would need a hundred monogrammed baby pots of honey to take home with them after a bland meal and three hours of dancing to an equally bland cover band. (Mort's prior words, not hers – Lily did not do bland.)

There was something that delighted her in the way simple things baffled him so. He was crotchety and grumpy, yes, but it came from a place of deep compassion. You could see it in the way he was with Esmeralda. Or in how he was doing his utmost to help Gramps with the huge rickety house that clearly had poor Gramps bested. But that was life, wasn't it. That was relationships. You were never done figuring it all out. You could only hope that you got a little bit better at it all, day by day.

(Not Mom, though. There was no hope there. But maybe Lily could one day break that particular family curse.)

'Hmm, I'm liking the tortoise idea more and more,' mused Venus, chugging a shot of ultra-water she'd pulled from her purse as a pre-tea palate cleanser. 'Could we write a little note on their shells?'

Lily gulped. This wasn't the way she'd expected things to go. She was learning the hard way that wedding planning was like the security area at the airport: not the place for jokes.

'They do have a habit of escaping,' offered Lily. This was, of course, a valid concern when you were choosing wedding favours, and why salt and pepper shakers or the classic sugared almonds tended to be the preferred option.

'Oh, but I love that.' Venus stooped to stroke Esmeralda, who'd wandered in looking for a second helping of tuna. She inspected the cat's crystal collar ornament. 'Don't you think it's the perfect metaphor for love? How it's something we chase, slowly, inexorably, for our whole lives?'

Even Esmeralda seemed to cock her head at this analysis. Venus had clearly gone to the Hollywood School of Philosophy, the one where luminaries like Grimes and Jim Carrey lectured.

'Sure, sure,' agreed Lily, sipping her tea as calmly as possible. The customer was always right in matters of taste and bizarre pseudo-philosophical rantings. 'We can talk about the tortoises. Um, are your guests experienced in working with small reptiles?'

Venus sipped her tea and made a face. 'Are you sure this is organic? Hmm. I do know someone who's big in the zoo space. Maybe we could throw in some care and feeding classes. And a terrarium. And a dedicated veterinarian.'

A rumbling overhead shook the building. Lily hurried to her cabinet of stemware, enveloping it in a giant hug lest the whole thing should come crashing down. Was this another switcheroo? Had Veronica finally checked her emails and returned to put the world back to rights? (Lily really hoped she was on the right track with this Veronica business because muttering a nightly incantation over some leftover birthday candles certainly hadn't worked.)

'Oh, that's my helicopter,' said Venus. 'I asked Jim to pop up to that farm that does the fresh wasabi; I guess he's done. So circling back to the dinnerware, I'm liking the mismatched vibe. Like this teacup. But not just, oh, some of these are different; more like *oh, every single plate is unique*. But themed. But with no repeats. But holistic. Do you get my gist?'

Lily mentally added another *???* to her list. And a *?!?!* as well.

'You're a star, Lils. I'm amazed that Honour even shared your details instead of keeping you all to herself for her future wedding – she's not even seeing anyone seriously at the moment, but you have to keep a good thing to yourself just in case. It's the same with realtors. And lawyers. And plastic surgeons. Look, really, I'm super laissez-faire about the whole thing, assuming you run every decision past me for approval. Just not on Wednesdays, because that's when I do medicinal micro-dosing, and my decision-making energy shifts in ways that I have to undo later. Just ask my PR rep.' Venus finished her tea and set the cup back on the pink doily coaster, another fabulous farmers' market find. 'I bet you've never had a bride so laid-back, right?'

'You're amazing,' said Lily kindly. (This was not a lie – Lily was *quite* amazed right now.)

Venus's fox eyes narrowed. 'Just as long as there are no surprises. I cannot abide a surprise. Especially on a day as big as this. Well, toodles!'

'Toodles!' said Lily brightly, even as her heart sank. She *had* to undo the switcheroo situation before Venus's wedding, or she faced a potential reputational disaster that could end up covered in *People* magazine, or worse at every family dinner until Lily's eventual demise.

Trader Joe's seasoning summoning circle, here she came. Well, once she got back from plate shopping.

Death by Embarrassment

Mort

Mort always enjoyed a quiet browse of a vintage shop. They were such peaceful, still places, ones where every creaking footstep counted and items were picked up and replaced with care. He especially liked Then Again, which was run by the magnificently churlish Theo Giordano, who'd plonked himself and his ever-present vintage *New Yorker* issue behind the counter some forty years ago and had never left. Theo never asked you whether you were looking for something in particular, or whether you needed help, or if he could interest you in a twenty per cent off sale or a fundraiser for some obscure charity whose name was so depressing that you simply had to buy an armload's worth of flavoured popcorn or consign your soul to hell.

Theo simply unlocked the front door in the morning, spent all day reading luminary short fiction of years past, then locked the door at night. It was a charmed existence, and just quietly, Mort wouldn't have minded being dropped on Theo's doorstep as a baby, if this was how his life might have turned out. Although maybe it was for the best. The man was of so few words that if he'd raised Mort, Mort might never have learned to talk. But he'd be very knowledgeable about the short stories of thirty years ago.

Anyway, Mort was here on business today. Well, mostly

business. And a bit of . . . not pleasure, exactly, but *curiosity*. For the pink-and-black grille between the Eternal Elegances had informed him that Lily was heading this way in search of plates, which had reminded Mort that he had a client's record collection that needed dealing with. And if Lily happened to arrive while Mort was still browsing the shelves, so be it.

'Mort?' A familiar pair of large blue eyes regarded Mort through a gap in the wall of vintage records. An equally familiar pair of pink lips quirked into a grin. 'Fancy seeing you here. Shopping for some new tunes?'

'I'm helping a family with an estate sale,' said Mort.

'Always good to diversify your income streams. Have you considered becoming an influencer? I think you'd be fab. Morbid Mort would kill it as a live-streamer.'

Mort shook his head in disbelief. 'I've never been more disappointed in you.'

'I should hope you've never been disappointed in me at all.' Lily hefted a hideously ugly brass sculpture of a hand making a thumbs up.

If only she knew the half of it.

'I'm actually fairly impressed with how you're handling this whole switcheroo thing. You were very sanguine regarding the maggots.'

'Ah, the maggots. My only other option was to go screaming into the night, which would have been terrible for my Yelp reviews.' Lily upended the sculpture to make an ostentatious thumbs down. The sculpture clanged against the shelf, but unfortunately didn't break. 'Besides, switcheroo or not, the show must go on. And believe me, when it comes to weddings, they *must* go on. Bridezillas are no joke.'

'I bet. At least the dead don't complain. Just their families. Hence this trip. There's been a whole . . . kerfuffle—'

'Kerfuffle! Such an emotive word.' Lily returned the sculpture to its thumbs-up position. 'Must be serious.'

'*Kerfuffle*,' repeated Mort. 'Regarding someone's uncle's music collection. Some guy with a statement moustache came in offering to take it off their hands for the princely sum of a hundred bucks.'

'And you think it's worth more than a hundred bucks.'

'I think we're definitely looking at a few extra zeros.'

Lily set down the thumb. 'Righteous indignation looks good on you. And maybe a moustache, too. You could beat that guy at his own facial hair game.'

'Absolutely not.' Mort picked up a terrible still life of some pomegranates – or possibly juggler's balls (or possibly *a* juggler's balls) – positioning its oversized frame as a way to hide the fact that the colour was rising in his cheeks, like the first flush of embalming fluid through a corpse. No, not like that. Goodness, this job was doing a number on him. Or was it Lily? Lily with her bright eyes and brighter personality and, brightest of all, those outfits that appeared to have come straight out of a My Little Pony cartoon?

'Death can be expensive. And it can bring out the grifters. I want to make sure that they're not getting ripped off. Theo's going to look into it for me when he's done with his current short story.'

'Almost there,' came Theo's creaky voice over his magazine. 'Just at the good bit. Well, I think so – you never can tell with literary fiction. Just another ten pages to go.'

'So how's the plate shopping going?' asked Mort.

Lily cocked her head. 'How did you know about the plate shopping?'

Mort spluttered. He couldn't exactly say *eavesdropping* and *borderline stalking*, could he?

175

'Your basket,' he said eventually, pointing at the mismatched plates Lily was pushing along the floor in a wheeled floral basket – her own? Was it normal to have a floral rolly cart? How did one procure such a thing? 'I like the practicality,' he added.

'Thank you.' She beamed, scooting the basket back and forth. 'Well, I need 250 plates – all different – and so far I have ten. And also a jigsaw puzzle in a jar for Gramps. Anyway, daisies, starbursts, Puebla, lapis, floral, rooster . . . That one's for me.'

Of course it was. Nothing said Lily more than a hand-painted rooster plate. Except maybe a floral rolly cart that Mort was just now seeing was embellished with a flying rainbow bread-cat sticker. Mort had no idea what this was meant to symbolise, and was afraid to ask.

'Dierdre at The Hot Pot might be able to help,' offered Mort. 'When it comes to crockery she puts the Smithsonian to shame.'

Lily smacked herself on the forehead, the vintage rings she'd picked out from the shop's jewellery overflow bowl glinting. 'Of course! Why didn't I think of that?' She paused. 'How is she with ridiculous menus for the trend-forward and ingredient-averse? We're talking more substitutions than teachers in a school plagued with norovirus.'

Mort shook his head. Dierdre did her best, but there was a limit to the bullshit a small business could reasonably handle without having to close their doors.

'Actually,' he mused, 'I *do* have someone who could help you.'

'Whispering Waters,' read Lily, who upon Mort's recommendation had made the smart decision to come back for her cartful of plates. They'd hiked to the top of the promenade to arrive at an ivy-clad steamship-style building that loomed, all curved walls and metal-framed windows and sad-eyed sculptures surrounded by tulips.

'I'm getting distinct end-of-life-care vibes here, Mort,' she added, running a hand along the railing that travelled the entire length of the pathway from the street to the front door. The paramedic sitting on the front step sipping a cup of coffee probably didn't help much with that impression, either.

'No, it's not like that,' he said, perhaps a touch defensively. 'It's just . . . a retirement community. Angela and I have been talking about a place here.'

Lily balked. 'A place here? For whom? Not for Gramps, surely.'

Mort swallowed. 'He can't manage that huge house all by himself. Even *I* can barely manage it. And it's at the point where everything needs to be redone or it'll just crumble into the ground.'

'House to house, dust to dust.' Lily nudged a toe at one of the plaques in the ground. Of course it happened to commemorate someone dead. No matter what he did, Mort wasn't going to come out of this discussion looking like the good guy.

'It's not a done deal. It's just an option. Something needs to change about Gramps's living situation, is all.'

Lily nodded in that thoughtful way that Mort suspected meant she was internally screaming at him in outrage.

'Well, are we going in? Because I suspect that this place knows all about bland, inedible food with limited ingredients.'

'I hope you're not speaking disparagingly of Jell-O,' said Mort.

'Oh no,' said Lily, 'we stan a Jell-O.'

The plastic alarm duck by the front entrance quacked as Mort pushed open the front door, gesturing for Lily to go ahead.

Inside, the home was as cosy as Angela's brochures had claimed: all streamlined wood panelling, sturdily upholstered furniture and ornate fixtures brimming with the softest of light. Golden oldies crooned on an antique gramophone, and everything smelt ambitiously of lavender, as though the residents had been making potpourri for arts and crafts for a solid six months. A few residents sat about, reading the paper or musing over chessboards.

An old guy with a knitted blankie over his legs and a skein of yarn in his lap carefully stood, giving Mort a wave. 'Mort! It's Mort!'

Mort smiled, although his heart wrenched slightly – the last time he'd seen Edward was at Edward's sister's funeral about six months ago. A few years ago, though, Edward had been one of Rerunning Up That Hill's most devoted patrons, showing up just about every day for the matinee session, and occasionally even banging out a few crowd favourites on the piano. But time, and death, marched on. Now there was just Edward.

'Good to see you, Edward,' said Mort. 'How's life treating you?'

Edward chuckled. 'Well, it's a treat to still be here. Who's your girl?'

Mort coughed. 'She's not . . . I don't . . .'

'I'm Lily.' Lily waved sunnily, bestowing one of her trademark giant grins upon Edward, who drank it up like a desert plant a longed for rainfall. 'Did you make that blanket, Edward? Think you could do me a frog when you get a chance?'

'Could I do you a frog? Of course I could do you a frog!' Edward beamed. 'She's a keeper, Mort. You'd better hang on to her. Or I'll give you what for.'

He made a fist.

'He means it, too,' said another old-timer Mort recognised as Lorraine, a hand tentatively on a chessboard rook. (Lorraine's husband of fifty years, whom everyone had nicknamed Rick the Prick, had died three years ago. Bill the coroner had had some suspicions, but figured that Lorraine deserved a few years of peace.) 'You know Edward was a boxer back in the day. He had his share of knockouts.'

'Knocked out a few of my teeth, too.' Edward loosened his dentures in demonstration.

'Edward, when did you last clean those?' snapped Lorraine, horrified. She pulled out her own falsies, showing off their bright, white enamel. 'That's what they should look like. I've had dogs with cleaner teeth than that.'

Edward waved his yellowed dentures about. Both Mort and Lily ducked for cover. 'They didn't have the off-brand solution at the bodega. So I've been using coffee. It's hot – kills the germs.'

Standing out of the line of spittle fire, Lily reached into her handbag and dashed forward, dropping a handful of dental hygiene supplies in Edward's lap. Then she retreated. 'Something in there should do the trick.'

'That's right – this wedding of yours is for a toothpaste magnate, isn't it.' Mort checked his shirt for wayward saliva.

Lily cocked her head, giving Mort the look of someone who'd caught a co-worker leaving the bathrooms without washing their hands. 'Hang on. Have you been listening through the grille? Is that how you knew about the plates? Because it's how I knew about the photo booth. And how I know that you have an ungodly amount of hummus delivered each week.'

Mort found himself wishing that Mirage-by-the-Sea were in a liquefaction zone, because he could really do with the earth swallowing him up right now.

'Who doesn't like hummus?' he protested weakly.

'Anyway, the whole toothpaste thing seems to be less of a wedding, more of a merger,' said Lily. 'They're talking about combining their surnames and adding "Corp" as a middle name.'

Lorraine moved her rook. 'Well, if the bride needs to make it look like an accident, tell her to call me. I know what's up.'

Lily grabbed Mort's hand. 'Could we . . . um . . .'

'That's right. Our meeting,' said Mort pointedly.

Before the two of them overheard something that couldn't be unheard, Mort ushered Lily out of the main room and over to the reception area, where a cheerful dark-haired nurse with half a dozen novelty pins on her shirt waved at them. Lily, apparently having found a kindred soul, showed off the patch on her pink knitted bag.

'I love your Eat-the-Rich Hungry Caterpillar!' she said.

'And *I* love your Fuck-Off-I'm-Sparkling unicorn!' said Crystal. (She was wearing a sparkly nametag.)

'I do weddings. I'd give you my card, but I'm having some new ones made. There was a bit of a printing error with the last ones.'

(Said printing error being that the switcheroo had turned them from the kissing couple display into a bouquet of roses that wilted when you folded the card. Mort personally thought that the switcherooed version was quite fetching, but Lily did not agree and was using the box as a doorjamb instead.)

'If my boyfriend *ever* proposes, I'm calling you,' said Crystal. 'Although it's been eight years, so I'm not getting my hopes up. We've had the talk three times, and you know, I might be ready to move on to more committed pastures.'

'I'm here either way,' said Lily. 'Even if you just want to eat your feelings – I get so many cakes in for tasting. It's great.'

'Deal.' Crystal turned to Mort. 'How've you been doing, Mort? I've missed the last few shows at the cinema because of life stuff – although I *did* hear about Derrick and Fran. I heard it was monkshood poisoning from a bespoke perfume. Almost enough to be deadly, but not quite. Divine intervention for the win. Are you going to Derrick's sermon this weekend?'

'Maybe,' said Mort generously. This cult thing was progressing as quickly as the switcheroo.

'Don't wear shoes if you do. How's Gramps?'

'About eight thousand pieces into a new jigsaw puzzle,' said Mort.

'We're helping,' explained Lily. 'He picked a doozy of a puzzle – I'm officially putting myself in charge of the next one.' She pulled out the puzzle-in-a-jar she'd bought from Then Again. 'I don't even know what this is meant to be, but there's no way it's worse than the one he's currently working on. Look – patches of contrasting colour! Outlines!'

'Well, there's plenty of space in Beverley Alberi's old unit for a jigsaw puzzle collection. Number 51. Still interested?'

Mort felt the floor wobble beneath him. With Beverley's funeral looming large in his memory, it was impossible not to make the connection between this place and what came after.

'We'll pop our heads in,' said Lily gently, filling the space that Mort, in the moment, simply couldn't. 'But we're actually looking for . . . what was their name again, Mort?'

'Jefferson,' stammered Mort. 'Is he around?'

'Airplane or Starship?' joked Crystal. She gestured behind her, waggling her sparkly nails. 'He's in the kitchen, whipping up some chocolate pudding. Go right on through. See you Saturday!'

Mort and Lily's footsteps echoed as they walked together down a wood-panelled hallway filled with fake trees and residents' artwork. Their fingers brushed not entirely accidentally as they navigated around clay sculptures of small dogs or paper chains decorated with loved ones' names.

Mort tried not to notice the numbers on the rooms they

passed, but according to the decorative numbers hot-glued to plump ovals of fabric on each door, they were presently in the 40s, which meant that Gramps's possible future apartment was just steps away.

47. Now 48, 49 . . . 50.

As they reached 51, Mort stopped short. Lily paused beside him, putting a gentle hand on his wrist.

'Do you want to go in?' she asked. 'At least see what it's like and whether it's a good fit for Gramps?'

Mort ran a finger over the polished wood of the doorframe. How many hands had done the same thing over the years, rallying themselves for a visit with someone ailing, or someone who might look at them with confused eyes? Lily was right. Either the space would feel *right*, and Mort would feel comforted knowing that Gramps was in good hands, or he'd know he had to figure out something else. A motorised chair lift for the rickety stairs, perhaps (after Mort had the stairs repaired, of course), or maybe a Roomba he could program to help with all the puzzle pieces under the couches. Oh, and perhaps some extra buttressing for the gargoyles that kept falling off in the middle of the night.

'You could always move back in with him,' suggested Lily. 'Or I could. Imagine all the jigsaw puzzles we could do together. Just so long as he let me open the curtains. And maybe paint the walls.'

'Ah, you want to perform a switcheroo on poor Gramps, huh?' teased Mort, trying to find levity in the moment. 'It wasn't enough that you took over the funeral parlour?'

Lily grinned. 'To paraphrase a classic, I see a black door and I want to paint it pink. Like this one.'

'It's cherry,' Mort pointed out.

'Yes, but is it *cheery*?'

More to shut Lily up than anything, Mort pushed open the door – just a crack at first, then all the way.

The apartment was sunny and soft. Light streamed in through the lace curtains on the far wall, playing off the cushioned furniture and gleaming against a gold mirror in the shape of a sun. *Home sweet home*, read the throw pillow on the armchair in the corner. A family of padded fabric ducks migrated up the pastel wallpaper, apparently trying to escape the lavender chenille bedspread (and the heart-shaped packets of lavender potpourri in a dish on the side table).

Lily chuckled. 'Wow, Gramps would hate this.'

'He really would,' admitted Mort.

'Especially the ducks,' they both said simultaneously.

Mort sat down on the bed, feeling its aged springs sag under his weight – it was designed for tiny elderly people, not thirty-year-old funeral directors with the weight of the world on their shoulders. Setting her handbag on the floor with a fearsome *whump* – had she brought the plates with her? – Lily sat beside him, a puddle of colourful fabric next to Mort's all-black outfit. Her arm grazed his, infusing him with a warmth that scared him. One day, it would be Lily in a bed like this. And then what?

'Whatever you're thinking, stop it.' Lily took Mort's hand in hers, giving it a squeeze.

There must have been an ungrounded electrical wire in the room, because Mort felt a zap. He stared down at their twined fingers, at how slim and tiny Lily's, with their rainbow nails, were next to his. He wasn't sure how did she did it, but her presence made everything feel brighter and more delightful somehow. Not that he was asking that of her – it wasn't someone else's job to put you in a good mood – but there was something about those joyful blue eyes and the way she cocked her head and the sheer effort she put into connecting with everything around her that made Mort want to be, well, less grumpy and more . . . grateful. Grateful was the word he was after.

Putting his free hand over hers, he squeezed back.

'I'm thinking that Gramps should stay in his house,' said Mort, trying to avoid the gaze of a kitschy ceramic cat wearing huge glasses. 'Somehow, even if it means getting him a butler.'

'Or a nice European au pair,' added Lily.

'But since the reason we came up here is for your spearmint-peppermint toothpaste merger or whatever it is, let's go talk to Jefferson about catering your event. Trust me, he'll be perfect. The pickiest eater I've ever met, and firmly opposed to all texture.'

'How does he feel about different ingredients touching?' asked Lily.

'The same way he feels about the word "mouthfeel": strongly.'

'I love him already.'

Like a Mechanical Bull in a China Shop

Lily

Phone on speaker waiting for Venus to come off hold (the toothpaste heiress had been called into an urgent investor meeting about some sort of water laser dental floss), Lily sat at her desk, containers of allergen-friendly, low-mastication retirement home food in front of her. Jefferson was a genius. There was simply the matter of branding to deal with, and that was where Lily came in.

After her nightly Google session to see if Veronica Teuer had surfaced, Lily had spent the rest of the night on Canva whipping up an edgy brand identity aligned with all the most on-trend content – Venus was going to love it (if she ever came off hold). Even better, she'd be slightly baffled, but that bafflement would be what clinched the deal. The fashionable *always* leapt on what they didn't understand because they'd rather be clueless than late to the party. Better to spend the money and then have your assistant do a deep dive than miss out on an opportunity to be the *it* girl.

As Lily bopped along to the folksy hold music, Mort's low, calm voice wandered through the grille above Lily's desk. Lily wished she were on the other side of the wall, watching Mort try to pick the jelly beans out of his beloved black cat candy jar. Or helping him show a newly widowed professor of medieval studies the newly arrived handcrafted replica of the Anglo-Saxon Loveden Hill Cremation Urn, a striking piece of ancient craftsmanship that looked to Lily very much like a garden planter that had been sitting out in the rain for too long.

And yet, here she was talking about . . . what was she talking about again?

There was a rattle as the hold music ended and the clatter of helicopter blades came over the line. Lily had been on hold so long that Venus had managed to take flight.

'Premetheus,' said Lily triumphantly. That was it!

There was a pause over the line – or maybe just lag. 'Like with the fire?' crackled Venus's voice.

'*Predating* the fire,' said Lily. 'This is a restaurant so essential, so back to basics, that it doesn't even cook its food. Everything is raw, vegan, easily chewable.'

She frowned – there was a commotion outside. Had Veronica returned to the scene of the failed proposal to undo the switcheroo?

'Amazing,' breathed Venus over the line (and the chopper blades). 'Chewing feels so primordial, don't you think? And this also ties into our new dental sensitivity line. How are the plates coming along?'

'You'll have more range than Mariah Carey,' promised Lily, leaning in her chair to get a better glimpse of what was going on outside.

'Lily?' boomed Mort's voice. (He'd apparently moved on from murmuring soothingly to the newly bereaved.)

'The line's cutting out,' lied Lily. 'I'll call you back when you land.'

Hanging up, she hurried outside to see exactly what the

switcheroo's latest shenanigans entailed. Mort was already there, standing arms folded in front of his decorative poodles (which Lily had dressed up with glow-stick necklaces and thermochromic T-shirts that changed colours when the sun hit a certain way or someone patted them).

'Please tell me this is a misdelivery,' said Mort, extremely judgementally. 'Because I know that I didn't order this, and I'm fairly confident that you wouldn't either. Would you?'

Alas, Lily was about to thoroughly disappoint Mort. She clasped her hands in a please-forgive-me motion in front of the mechanical bull that poor Roddy had somehow carted in from the parking lot behind the shops using an elaborate combination of wheeled carts and leather pulls. (Lily was beginning to see how the pyramids were built.)

'It's for my cowboy wedding. Although it wasn't meant to come here – it was meant to go to the venue.'

Mort prodded the mechanical bull distastefully. 'Which is where?'

'A barn with million-dollar views of the beach.' Lily had been jealous of pets before – lapdogs led a charmed life – but this venue was the first time she'd ever been jealous of a horse. 'Oh, to be a rich person's thoroughbred. Or even their mechanical bull. Are you going to hop on?'

Mort took a step back. 'You're pulling my leg. There's not a chance that two people declared, oh, let's tie ourselves together romantically and legally, and invite all of our friends and family to hoe down with us at a pretend ranch. With . . . *this* as the centrepiece to it all.'

'*One* of the centrepieces.' Lily shooed away a pigeon that had decided to give the bucking bronco a go. 'It's just the unifying element. You should see the cowboy boot vases – oh, and the branding station.'

Mort looked deeply insulted by the prospect of all of this, which Lily found quite gratifying.

'Live a little, Mort,' she said, giving him a light jab in the ribs.

'Die a little, more like, given the fatality rate of those things,' he retorted. 'What are you going to do with it, anyway? You can't just leave it there.'

'Why not? You've got the dogs; I can have a bull. Maybe it'll bring in some extra business.'

'I'm not sure the kinds of people who ride a mechanical bull on the street for the sheer joy of it are the marrying type.'

Lily couldn't help herself – she burst out laughing. 'Exactly who *do* you think is the marrying type? Elizabeth Bennet? Anne of Green Gables? The Madonna? You have a very, very strange concept of what this institution means to people, Mort.'

Mort was visibly preparing a comeback when two very buff, very Palm Springs–looking gents in boat shoes, denim cut-offs and astonishing tans stepped out from behind the laneway next to Eternal Elegance. Lily brightened: Amos and Bernard, the couple behind the rodeo wedding! Until now she'd only seen them over Zoom (well, and their many, many social media selfies), but they were as movie star-ish as she'd imagined.

'Oh. My. God. Is that the bull?' Bernard, who had combed-across hair and Paul Newman eyes, clapped his hands with the glee of a collector looking at an Eames chair priced at five dollars at an estate sale.

Amos, all stylish salt-and-pepper locks and a smile so white it was a portal to the land of cosmetic dentistry, clapped the bull on the butt. 'That's our Rosie girl!'

Lily rushed forward to give them each a hug. 'You made it!'

'We certainly did! The things we have seen. We followed Rosie all the way from Nashville,' said Bernard. 'It is *quite* the drive.'

'Santa Fe has its charms, though,' added Amos. 'I got a great hat that I plan to wear on the big day.'

'But not Amboy. Big murder vibes.' Bernard shuddered. 'Well, except for Roy's. That's a cutie-patootie of a place. I'm a sucker for a Googie sign.'

'This is Bernard and Amos,' said Lily, introducing them to Mort, who was shooing a small child with an ice-cream away from the mechanical bull (for their own safety, and sense of pride). 'They're getting married next weekend.'

'But we're staying in town until then,' said Bernard. 'It's going to be a *blast*. We've rented out this charming farmhouse out by the Spanish mission . . .'

'It's not all black and falling apart is it?' said Lily warily. 'With the house numbers displayed on a tombstone? And owned by a small man with a half-halo of hair and a commitment to dapper dressing and 25,000-piece jigsaw puzzles?'

'That is extremely specific, but no,' said Amos. 'It's yellow and charming, with a red door, and a small population of alpacas. Although I suppose there could be jigsaw puzzles.'

'Ah, Aunt Dot's cottage,' said Mort, sounding relieved.

'Were you worried Gramps was going to crash at your apartment?' teased Lily. 'Lucky you have the coffin bunk beds, if you need them.'

'The what now?' asked Amos, from astride the mechanical bull (which thankfully wasn't plugged in, for Lily's liability insurance only went so far).

'Mort's the town funeral director,' explained Lily.

Mort nodded. 'We have a two-for-one deal on plots at the moment, if you're interested.'

'Ooh, making a liar of *till death do us part*, I see,' said Amos, running a hand over the fake bull's spotted hide. 'It is kind of a romantic gift, though, isn't it. What kind of caskets do you have? Or do you think cremation is the way to go? What about cryogenics?'

'That's entirely up to your preferences,' said Mort, adding drily: 'Although I'd have to direct you to a start-up in the Bay Area for the cryogenics option. I believe there's an app subscription involved.'

Lily bit her lip, amused – Mort's sharp sense of humour always seemed to come out of nowhere, but it got her every time.

'Hmm, worm food or judgemental remains sitting outside the Conservative Ladies' Township Society.' Amos rested his elbows on the bull as he pretended to think it over. 'Oh, they'd be *so* pissed off. Let's do the one that pisses off Republicans. Help me down?'

'A good call, as always.' Lily offered Amos a hand as he scrambled off the bull, cackling. She knew the giddy feeling, although she hadn't ridden one of these since orientation at college. Sadly, she couldn't remember much of that night. 'When I say this wedding is going to be amazing . . .'

'Expect the cops to be called,' said Bernard. 'Multiple times. It's not a party if there's no public disturbance complaint!'

Mort nodded politely, but Lily could see the alarm in his expression. Noise complaints and police escorts were not Mort's preferred way of partying. He was more the paperback book and a glass of wine kind of guy, which Lily was slowly starting to come around to, especially in the wake of her phone calls with Venus.

'Do you want me to run you out to your accommodations?' Lily asked. Although she'd have to borrow Mort's hearse to make it happen – her Miata was only a two-seater, and she wasn't sure that either of the two men would fit inside.

Bernard shook his head. 'We've got our trusty Stormy Daniels with us.'

'The . . . adult star?' clarified poor Mort, who rather looked like he'd happily step into an open grave.

'Now *that* would be a hoot. No, no, our car. It's stormy blue. Let us know if you need help getting poor Rosa down to the venue.' Bernard gave the mechanical bull a hearty pat, and with some cheek kisses and waggling of fingers, they set off back down the laneway, ready to check into their accommodations.

But because comings and goings always coincide in some sort of Newtonian twist of narrative, Gramps appeared from down the laneway, eating a croissant and pushing a rolly tweed suitcase along the cobblestones. It was not a subtle entrance; Lily had heard armoured vehicle parades that were quieter.

'Mort, my boy! Your visitor, checking in! Nice bull, Lily. A good way to draw in happy couples to your business. And if someone dies, Mort can do the funeral.'

'I pride myself on my holistic approach,' said Lily.

Mort, in the meantime, had turned the colour of one of the ghosts that presumably haunted the funeral home. 'Visitor? But I thought Amos and Bernard had rented Aunt Dot's?'

Gramps shook croissant crumbs off his ruffled black shirt. 'I don't know who that is, but good for them. No, the pipes in the bathroom backed up like something out of a horror movie. You should've seen it: ooze and sludge all over the place. Stribley's out dealing with it, but he said it'll be a few days. It'll be like old times – you and me and a jigsaw puzzle!' He pulled out the jam jar Lily had found at Then Again, giving it a hearty shake. 'No picture, so we'll just have to wing it. I love what you've done with the greyhounds. Poodles – a nice touch.'

'Me too,' said Lily, pulling Mort and Gramps in for a selfie. 'Say switcheroo!'

The Little Sleep

Mort

'It's good to be back in the old digs.' Gramps set aside his rolly suitcase and cast a squinty eye around the funeral home. 'Even if it does look ... different. Although my vision isn't what it used to be. What happened to the organ?'

'The termites,' improvised Mort. 'Lily found me the pianola as a temporary replacement. Elsie does the job, but she lacks a certain gravitas.'

'Elsie, hmm?' Gramps thumbed the middle C key that Lily had written her note on.

'One of Lily's names. The girl names everything. Her car, large appliances, that plant that Jorge had dropped off as a thanks for all the cake, novelty kitchen sponges ... She'll name her pot of tea if she thinks it's going to take a while to drink.'

Mort had spent his whole life trying not to get attached to things, and here was Lily giving the local pigeons a cohesive backstory told in three parts, complete with character charts and star signs.

Gramps lazily thumbed out 'Twinkle, Twinkle Little Star' on the pianola. 'Sounds like you're in love with her.'

Mort spluttered. 'Why would ... What gave you that idea?' Mort folded his arms indignantly. 'Absolutely not!'

'Definitely love,' diagnosed Gramps, letting the last note of 'Twinkle, Twinkle' linger. Then he tapped the long rectangle of photo booth pictures that Mort and Lily had taken a few weeks back, which Mort had stuck under the lid of the pianola. All right, so Mort had kept the picture, but so what? He needed proof of the switcheroo in the event of a legal claim. And besides, he looked quite fetching in the third photo, and it never hurt to have an updated head shot available.

Gramps ruffled Mort's hair, something Mort had always felt should fall under cruel and unusual punishment. 'I've seen enough partners sobbing over their dead lover's corpse in my time to know love when I see it.'

Mort scraped his hair back into its usual messy state. 'Really selling it there for me, Gramps.'

'Oh, pshaw.' Gramps settled on the chaise longue, propping his moccasins up on the coffee table. A gift from a casket company a few years back, the slippers had little coffins etched into the soles – even in retirement Gramps was still living that funeral planner life. 'What's life, without love?'

'It's plenty,' countered Mort. 'It's the bills paid and a roof over my head and movies when I want to watch them and ice-cream when I want to eat it.'

And none of the risk. None of the fear of losing someone.

Gramps grabbed the guest book and started flipping through, frowning as the book started its transformation from morbid to mawkish, with glittery stickers and googly eyes, and a surfeit of the sparkly ink that had for some reason started spurting from the once-solemn pens that Mort kept by the book, like a weeping statue of Mary, if Mary were suddenly into disco.

'Yes, but those things aren't all they're cracked up to be when they're done alone.' Gramps flapped the guest book at Mort as evidence.

'I'm not alone. I have . . . friends,' snapped Mort. Well, sort of. 'And I have you. And besides, there's nothing wrong with being alone.'

'Of course not,' said Gramps. 'If that what makes you happy. When you're alone because you're afraid of getting close to anyone, now that's a problem. Now, where am I sleeping tonight?'

Mort could hardly ask Gramps to sleep in the casket bunk beds or on the chaise longue – Gramps's back was held together by pins and painkillers. Besides, the upstairs had been least affected by the switcheroo, and was therefore the safest bet, although Gramps might have a few questions about the linens-filled glory box that had suddenly appeared at the end of the bed (which itself suddenly sported a canopy that Mort had had nothing to do with).

Mort sighed. 'You can take my bed. I'll . . . figure something out.'

This was not going to work.

Gramps was snoring at a volume that was surely registering on the local earthquake tracker apps. A 5.0-level snore, maybe more. Something that would trigger a tsunami warning and send the oarfish racing up to the shores, warning of the end times.

Mort lay pretzelled up on the bench seat in the kitchen area upstairs (he'd wanted to remain close enough to Gramps to intervene in case the switcheroo reared its pink sparkly head), cursing Gramps's clearly haunted plumbing, cursing Airbnb for renting out the only other nearby cottage to Lily's clients instead of leaving it free for Gramps, and cursing his own excellent hearing. He should have at least *some* hearing damage by now. Damn his passion for unamplified classical music and his short-sighted commitment to earplugs.

Clad in his pyjamas (torn black tracksuit trousers and an even more torn black T-shirt), Mort slunk out to his balcony, wondering if the double glazing on the doors would provide some respite from Gramps's nasal chain sawing.

'Can't sleep?' came Lily's voice from next door.

Mort started. Why was she out here? Why, when he was so vulnerable in his stupid shredded clothes and with bed hair that had him looking like the most pitiful rooster in the pecking order? He smoothed his hair, hoping he looked vaguely human. Then he cast a glance over at Lily, who . . .

He burst out laughing. For Lily was dressed in a Cinderella nightie that barely skimmed her thighs. But never fear, she was not to be caught in a state of undress: beneath the nightgown she wore a striped pair of thermal long johns. And fluffy slippers shaped like raccoons.

'What?' said Lily. 'If you can't handle me at my comfiest, you don't deserve me at my sparkliest.'

'Fair,' said Mort.

'I'm sleeping, not presenting a case in the Supreme Court. And even then, attire shouldn't matter. The substance of the argument should.'

'Spoken just like Elle Woods. That was a compliment,' added Mort.

Lily toasted with a cup of peppermint tea. 'I would never take it as anything else.'

'You look . . . adorable,' Mort admitted. Then flinched as a particularly loud snore rattled the door.

'Is he always like this?' whispered Lily.

Mort shook his head ruefully. 'It depends on the night, and whether he's remembered his CPAP machine. But this is . . . quite the display.'

'Even the poodles out front are cowering,' said Lily, grinning.

Then, after a moment's consideration, she said: 'Do you want to come over?'

Mort, as usual, found himself looking for something to say. Or rather, let's face it: an excuse. A way out. He knew, he just knew, that if he went over to Lily's right now, he'd embarrass himself so fundamentally that he'd have to sell the business and move to a small town in the deep south that didn't have internet access and therefore couldn't watch the viral video that would inevitably result.

'I should keep an eye on Gramps to make sure he doesn't die.' Mort's tone sounded as half-hearted as it felt.

'Oh, come on. We'll know he's dead if the window panes stop rattling.' Lily tossed a cookie crumb his way. 'And if the worst happens, he'll be in a good spot for it.'

'You are a ghoul,' said Mort, trying not to laugh.

'The sweetest ghoul around,' said Lily, placing her hands beneath her chin in an angelic gesture.

'All right, all right. Unlock the front door.'

Whisper Sweet Hereafters in My Ear

Lily

Never before had Lily so regretted her choice of bedtime attire. All right, so her usual sleepwear combination definitely erred on the side of comfortable, but this particular ensemble screamed Slumber Party, circa 1996. All she needed was a hair crimper and a three-pack of Lip Smackers, and she'd have reverted to her twelve-year-old self. Not even that – her *mom's* twelve-year-old self.

(Speaking of Mom, Lily owed her some pics of Rosa the mechanical bull, and some upvotes on a contest Mom had entered to win a Winnebago.)

But maybe this was good, Lily told herself. There was absolutely nothing in her choice of outfit that could suggest to Mort that she had designs on his surprisingly fit body. Or those arresting dark eyes. He'd know she was being polite and neighbourly, and had no intention of muddying the waters between the two businesses whose waters were, let's face it, muddied up as though they'd been infested with carp. The Eternal Elegance x Eternal Elegance mashup was already primed for epic drama – Lily had just fielded a call asking about a graveside wedding – and the businesses' owners getting similarly mixed up hardly boded well. And Lily wasn't renowned for her relationships' longevity. What if she started something and it petered out? Or worse, flamed out? Then what? They'd have to grit their teeth and smile at each other every day until Lily's lease was up. Which was . . . months.

Mere months, she thought sadly. Then what?

The doorbell rang, intoning the Star Wars 'Imperial March'. Was it too late to renege? Could she pretend she'd fallen asleep? Or that she had a sudden migraine?

More important, was it too late to change her outfit? But if she did that, then Mort would know that she was worried about his opinion of her. Which she absolutely wasn't, of course. But he couldn't argue against throwing on an elegant dressing gown – that was simply protecting herself against the elements.

Lily prevaricated, struggling with the endless 'what ifs' of this scenario. Why had she spoken to him in the first place? She could've just hung out on the balcony in silence like a creeper, but an imperceptible creeper. But *no*, she had to let her impetuous streak prevail. (To be fair, her impetuous streak had always treated her well.)

'I can see you in there,' came Mort's wry voice over her smart doorbell. 'And I know that if I'm waving my hand it's activating the motion sensor.'

Was he doing the hokey-pokey? She'd never taken Mort for the hokey-pokey type, but people could be complex. For example, Lily had once written a strongly worded review after her favourite chocolate shop back in La Jolla had run out of peppermint frogs during a particularly brutal bout of PMS. She hadn't known she'd had it in her, and apparently neither had the business because they'd sent her a $25 gift card. (She'd retracted the review.)

Lily opened the front door, gesturing self-consciously at her outfit.

'Welcome to the catwalk,' she said doing a shimmy.

'Fierce,' said Mort. He pirouetted awkwardly on the spot.

'Very Derelicte,' said Lily.

Mort chuckled.

'I'm surprised you got that reference,' she said, raising an eyebrow.

'I spent a lot of time as a kid watching movies.' Mort tapped a finger against the latest wedding favours Lily had ordered: a set of slap bands. 'It was how I dealt with the whole being surrounded by death thing. Although I *did* gravitate towards horror movies. Not really sure what that says about me.'

'Probably that you were surrounded by horror and grief and needed a safe way to process it.'

The slap band Mort had been toying with curled around his wrist like a sparkly shackle. 'That's quite the analysis,' he said slowly.

Lily shoved her sleep mask higher up on her tangle of hair. 'I'm not just a pretty face.'

'You're certainly not,' agreed Mort, unrolling the slap band. Sexily, somehow. Lily had never considered that a slap band had the potential to allure, but stranger things had happened. (Mostly within the last couple of weeks, to be fair.)

Lily hesitated. What now? If some other equally good-looking guy with whom she had a complicated relationship had shown up on her doorstep late at night looking so gloriously dishevelled, Lily would've dragged him upstairs and stripped him on the spot. But this was Mort, who was anything but some other guy. Shoving him down on the bed – or couch, or hell, the dramatically decorated table right in front of them – seemed wrong, somehow. And not because Mort would somehow come out with an anecdote about someone who'd died being pounced upon by a lover. It was more that . . . Lily had feelings for Mort. She'd never really sat with the whole idea of feelings before, and she wasn't quite sure how to handle them. Or act upon them.

In the past, perhaps scarred by the many disastrous relationships of her mom's she'd had to endure, she'd simply had her fun and been on her way. Which was probably why she was so trepidatious; part of her worried that if she took the same approach here, the part of her that always cut and bailed would rise up like an overly yeasty loaf of bread. *No, no, not yeast, Lily. Don't liken yourself to yeast.*

Lily didn't want to bail on Mort, or Gramps, or Angela and Tink, or Mirage-by-the-Sea – at least not before her lease forced her to. For the first time in her life, she was starting to feel *settled*, and the thought of pulling up the roots she was just starting to dig into the earth of this quaint town created a pang in her heart. But would that happen? If she started something with Mort, would the familiar lizard brain flight sense kick in? Or would this time be different?

Lily swallowed. She was worried about what it might mean to find out.

'Mrow?' asked Esmeralda, appearing from some secret shadowy pocket. She wound figure eights around both of their legs, pulling them together.

Lily grabbed at Mort's threadbare shirt to keep from stumbling. His hands caught gently at her shoulders, his fingers curling lightly. They were warm through her pyjama top, and not for the first time she wished she'd worn something more normal to bed. Or maybe *less* normal. And more scant.

'Esmeralda, you sly thing.' Avoiding eye contact with Mort, Lily grinned down at the fluffy cat, who was staring innocently up at them.

'She looks like she's hungry for sardines.'

'I can't help there, but I do have tuna. C'mon, Esme. And Mort, if you must.'

She reached for Esmeralda, who lolled in Lily's arms as though someone had performed a disappearing spell on her bones. Her purr rattled through Lily, a low and happy rumble.

'She has a soft spot for you, I see.'

'Ah, she has a soft spot for everyone. The first day I met her I thought she was dying of starvation. Turns out she's been visiting every business in town – and half the homes – for a snack every day. No wonder she's a bit of a chungus.'

'She's not. She's just . . . Rubenesque.'

'She certainly knows how to get what she wants.' Lily hesitated, a foot on the steps that led up to her apartment. Architecturally it wasn't a threshold, but emotionally it was. Okay. They were doing this. Whatever this was. Nothing. Probably nothing.

'The place looks . . . cute,' said Mort, as Lily ran to grab a tin of fish for Esmeralda. From his tone, Lily suspected he'd never used the word before in his life. Not even for a puppy! The sacrifices he'd made for her.

Lily emptied out the tin onto a decorative lobster plate, scooting it towards Esmeralda, who daintily tucked in.

'Nice dish.'

'I found it when I was scouting for the vintage dishes. I couldn't resist. It was from a Swedish Kräftskiva, according to Theo.'

'A lobster party?' asked Mort, the very picture of credulousness. He stood awkwardly in the centre of her rug, as though it were some sort of protective circle.

'Do you want me to put some salt down?' she asked, eyebrow raised. 'To keep the switcheroo spirits out? Anyway, how on earth do you know what a Kräftskiva is?'

'The things you learn in the funeral directing business. Truly – I overhear the most magnificent gossip.'

'Ah, so our professions do have something in common. Cake?'

Lily pulled out a massive platter of cake from her pink vintage fridge – if there was one thing she was never short on, it was wedding cake. And prosecco. And sugared almonds, but that was mostly because no one ate those. They just kept multiplying in the cupboards like coat hangers, or the lids of takeaway containers.

Oh God, she'd just realised that the strip of photos from the photo booth had pride of place on the fridge – it was right there next to her scribbled grocery list and the Polaroids of Annika and Mom that she'd pinned up the day she'd arrived, and which had mercifully survived the switcheroo. Had he seen it?

But no, Mort was perched on her love seat, clutching a plate of cake and perusing the crumbled, tea-stained papers on Lily's coffee table instead. Lily strategically shifted a novelty San Diego Trolley magnet around just in case, then climbed up beside him, pulling her feet beneath her.

'What're you working on here?' Mort dug a fork into a multi-tiered slice of coffee-flavoured cake. 'This looks like the work of a crazed serial killer. Not the cake, though. The cake is excellent.'

Lily took a forkful of cake and nodded in agreement. 'It is delicious. I have a night owl wedding coming up and they're insisting on coffee-infused everything. I'd share the tiramisu, but I ate the entire batch. Fell down the stairs after, too – whoever made it went heavy on the Marsala wine. How good are you at solving puzzles?'

Mort blocked her fork as she went in for a bite of his cake. 'Sounds like you've been talking to Gramps, huh.'

'All the time. We have a whole text thread going. When he's not on the jigsaw puzzles he's all about his Wordle streak.'

Mort raised an eyebrow. 'You, Lily, astound me.'

Lily hid a smile behind her fork. Was that . . . two compliments in one night? Had *Mort* been switcherooed?

'I *do* aim to astound,' she said lightly. 'But I have this seating arrangement thing I need to sort out, and it's a doozy.'

'Oh no. Not a doozy.'

'It's for this Christmas in July wedding I'm working on.' Lily unrolled the rest of the seating arrangement – what Mort had seen was merely the tip of the musical chairs iceberg.

'Wow, it just keeps going,' he said, pulling out his reading glasses. 'It's like one of the scrolls for the pianola.'

'It's definitely the most complicated seating sudoku I've ever tried.'

Lily reached under the coffee table for one of the vintage board games she'd inherited with the shop. She upended the shabby box, spilling hundreds of colourful wooden pawns all over the scroll. These she arranged into sets of twelve, with each one representing a wedding guest.

'I think you missed your calling as a military general,' said Mort, impressed.

'The military couldn't handle me.' At least, the military men she'd met over the years hadn't been able to. She tapped her fork on Table 1, then waggled a green pawn. 'This is Aunt Jemimah. She can't sit near Grandma Beatrice on Table 2 because she had an affair with Grandpa Joe. And Table 4 is out of the question because she gave Auntie Edith brutally honest feedback about the pelmets in her living room.'

Mort nodded thoughtfully. 'Problematic but tasteful. I see how she could be an issue. Go on.'

'I'd choose to scoot her over to Table 8, but I already have Cousin Miriam there, and she can't be moved to any of the other tables after what she did at ChickenFest back in 1988.'

Mort's fork screeched over the cake plate. 'What did she do at ChickenFest?'

'No one will tell me. But the nine other people at the table are the only ones who'll abide it.'

'Ah, we've found the chicken fuckers.'

Lily snorted, giving his bicep a squeeze. Oops, getting handsy – she probably shouldn't have taste tested that prosecco this evening. 'Mort! I didn't know you had it in you.'

For good measure, she pulled out the prosecco and waggled it at Mort.

'Sometimes I get tired of gallows humour and veer into the world of crass humour instead. Fill me up – I think we're going to need the help.'

'Crass suits you. It's unexpected.'

She poured Mort a drink, then passed it to him with a cheersing motion.

Sipping away, Mort tapped the table plan. 'Mm, that's good. Much better than what we get stuck with – people in mourning say that everything tastes like ashes, so they just go with whatever's on sale. So, what about if we move this chunk of Table 7 over to Table 12.'

Lily put a protective hand over a jumble of multicoloured pawns. 'Those are the Mopsy triplets and partners. They come as a set. And they're vegan, so they can't be seated near Cousin Isaac, who runs a brisket truck.'

'I see why Isaac would want to be spared a tarring and feathering. With vegan feathers, of course.'

Between sips of prosecco and mouthfuls of cake, Lily and Mort worked on the chart for a solid half hour, making very little progress on the wedding's seating arrangements – but making quite a bit of progress in terms of their own.

'I'm afraid,' said Mort seriously, 'the only way this seating situation gets resolved is if someone dies.'

'I *do* hope you're talking about the wedding,' said Lily, whose leg was now pressed up against Mort's. Mort's arm had at some point made its way around Lily's shoulder, and Lily leaned into him, conscious of the confident thrum of his heart against her arm, painfully aware of the warmth of his breath in her hair. Would it be so wrong to kiss him? She spent her days bringing happy couples together, after all – why shouldn't *she* get to be on the other side of that arrangement? She had a whole basket of out-of-season mistletoe sitting right there, for fuck's sake. Not to mention the rude party favours she'd ordered as part of a hen's night side business she was working on. (Although she should probably wait to bring those out.)

Mort brushed her hair gently from her face, and Lily turned, her pulse quickening.

His dark gaze met hers, full of the usual warmth and humour . . . and something more heated.

Lily was first to break away.

There was a moment as they both collected themselves, still living in a world of what might be. Lily's hand was on Mort's knee, and Mort's rubbed her shoulder ever so gently. One of them had to say something – or one of them had to *do* something before this whole situation imploded into messiness. Or worse, into nothing.

Oh, fuck it. Turning, Lily reached for Mort, her fingers curling around the back of his neck, running over the soft, short hair that gave way to bare skin. Their eyes met again, but this time neither looked away.

Lily pressed her lips against Mort's, tentatively, then hungrily. She'd been longing to taste him since they'd first met, and the feeling didn't disappoint: heat sparked between them like a feral magic, and Lily drew him in closer, shifting on the couch so that she could straddle him. Mort's hands found her sides, his fingers wrapping around her waist with an urgency that surprised her.

'I've wanted to know what you felt like for so long,' he murmured, his voice husky against her lips, her chin, now her throat.

The feeling was mutual. So damn mutual. Desperate to close the space between them, to find the smallest distance between her skin and Mort's, Lily grabbed at her ridiculous Disney nightie, dragging it over her head – grateful that she hadn't gone to bed wearing her loosest, most threadbare sports bra, the one with the red wine stain on the front and the hole in the side.

So too was Mort, because his hands roved from her sides up to her breasts, cupping them reverently, his thumbs finding her nipples as his lips found the edge of her collarbone. Lily groaned, leaning into him as he gently explored her skin with his fingers, his mouth. Every inch of her felt primed, electrified, ready to ignite.

But then Lily's phone vibrated on the table, startling them both. They jerked apart, suddenly shy, the spell broken.

The phone buzzed again, then again, slowly making its way across the seating chart like it was possessed by a very small but very determined demon.

'Fucking hell,' said Mort, his gaze averted once more. Lily shyly hid her breasts under one arm, although, she supposed, that ship had sailed.

'I thought that was one of Gramps's snores,' Lily admitted sheepishly, as the phone buzzed away.

Mort nodded, but the energy between them was . . . *off*. Lily wondered if he regretted coming over, if she'd taken things too far. She grabbed her nightie, holding it against herself, wondering what on earth Mort's eyes were seeing right now. A lunatic in thermal leggings covered in cake and marker? A sex fiend who lured shy men with prosecco and cake and then had her way with them?

Or the business owner next door he had to endure until her lease was up?

'I . . . should go,' Mort said. Lily could see he was running through excuses in his head.

'Ah, you've left something on the stove,' she said wryly. She pulled on her nightie – dammit, Cinderella was on backwards. 'A body?'

Mort ran his hands through his gorgeously mussed hair, the hair that seconds ago Lily had been twining her fingers through. 'No, it's not that. It's just . . . I don't know how to do this. I don't know what I'm doing. I'll . . . see you tomorrow. Sorry.'

He hurried downstairs, then out the front door, which as it swung let in a moment of late-night song: an owl, a drunken conversation between tourists, the hum of bass from somewhere up the hill. All intermingled with the heavy sigh that Lily let out.

'Mrow,' said Esmeralda, in a tone that was both sympathetic and judgemental.

'Well, that wasn't how that was supposed to go,' Lily told the cat. But Esmeralda had already moved on and was busy inspecting Mort's fork for leftover Chantilly cream.

Lily's phone buzzed again, and with an aggrieved huff, she turned it over, scanning the text messages, which were not, as they usually were, from Annika or Mom. (Well, not all of them – Annika *had* sent a few screenshots of an initiative in Italy where you could buy a home for one euro so long as you promised to renovate it. And Mom was asking Lily's thoughts on the zodiac compatibility of her current partner, and whether it was time to call things off.)

Now it was Lily's turn to run downstairs.

'Mort! Are you up?' she hissed through the grille. 'We've found Veronica!'

A Corpse is a Corpse,
of Corpse of Corpse

Mort

Like any film buff, even as one steeped mostly in the scarier side of what the movies had to offer, Mort had seen *My Big Fat Greek Wedding*. He'd chuckled along and had even come around to the value of Windex as the ultimate panacea. But he hadn't anticipated that he'd end up hosting one. Because weddings weren't really his remit. Or at least, hadn't been until recently.

Mort knew the deceased, of course; he knew just about everyone who ended up wheeled through the funeral home's doors in some capacity.

Christos Georgiou had been a semi-famous local architect known for his ability to seamlessly add modern extensions to the storybook houses of Mirage-by-the-Sea without violating any of the heritage laws. You'd never know from the street, but if you snuck into many of the village's back gardens, you'd find multi-storey additions with vast floor-to-ceiling windows, ivy-wrapped greenhouses, and elaborate tiered gardens with squared-off fish ponds all overhung by glass-framed patios that made it feel like you were hovering over a magical forest.

Christos had consulted on the funeral home's pre-switcheroo

casket displays and had helped Gramps expand the consultation room. The expansive windows had been his addition, although the cupcake-patterned chiffon curtains that now adorned them had not. That said, they were starting to grow on Mort, and the families seemed to like them. Even if they'd increased the client consumption of complimentary cake by a degree, that was not good for Mort's bottom line. Or his waistline. Which in turn was not good for his EKG line. At least Mort had cultivated a strict fitness routine over the years – he was not about to invite Death in by slacking on his daily push-up regimen.

'Sorry for your loss.' Mort greeted the black-clad mourners one after another, turning his head to ignore the grille that connected the two Eternal Elegances – and the flashes from last night that simply would not stop bubbling up at this incredibly inappropriate time. He was meant to be overseeing a funeral, not thoughts of Lily's body. He should be mourning a dead guy, not the chance with the girl next door that he'd horribly, irrevocably blown.

'Christos's buildings live on,' said a burly man Mort recognised as a local general contractor. Mick something, or so the personalised licence plates on his enormous work truck parked out back proclaimed.

'He designed my favourite rooflines,' sobbed Timbo Jones, the roofer who'd come in to assist with the post-switcheroo leaks. ('Can't explain it. Roof's sound. Just a freak leak. That'll be five hundred bucks.') He'd since become one of Lily's best friends, and regularly stopped by to taste-test the club sandwiches she was trying out for upcoming weddings. According to the commentary Mort had overheard through the grille that joined the two businesses, Timbo was a fan of sandwich pickles, but had thoughts about smoked salmon.

'Mort!'

Angela and Tink swanned through the door in head-to-

toe black lace (polka-dot lace in Tink's case), looking like an extremely cool punk rocker duo. Tink definitely played drums, while Angela definitely sang while attacking a bass guitar.

'You knew Christos?' Mort leaned in for an awkward hug.

'My uncle,' said Angela. 'Or thereabouts. The man got around, let me tell you. I'm not sure where I saw him more often: at family dinners, or in my real estate listings. Speaking of, we need to talk about Whispering Waters.'

Mort nodded. They did in fact need to talk about that, because there was no way that Mort was shipping off Gramps to that place. (Unless Gramps kept up the snoring.)

'I'll never forget that grill out on the beach,' said Tink dreamily. 'Just us and the ocean and half the contents of the ocean on a firepit. And wine. So much home-made wine.'

'Retsina, my first great love.' Angela dramatically clutched her hands to her heart. 'Oh, there's my Yia-yia. I gotta go say hi – make sure I keep my rightful place in her will. Joking, joking.' She dropped her voice to a stage whisper. 'Half joking.'

'Quarter joking.' Tink waggled her fingers in a *toodles* and strode off to sign the guest book. 'Oh look, someone's drawn a dick. Three dicks. Mort, what's your policy on dicks?'

Mort groaned internally. The funeral home had various policies on dicks, depending on what part of the funeral one was talking about. But in general they had a no-dick policy when it came to the guest book. This hadn't typically been a problem in the past, but since the switcheroo, there'd been an alarming uptick in drunken dick drawings. And off-colour jokes during the eulogy.

'I'll get the white-out.'

Mort stalked over to his office to grab the pencil case he kept inside his desk drawer for stationery emergencies. But as he made his way back to the foyer, a scene at the viewing room caught his attention.

Mort stopped in his tracks. A group of suit-clad men were gathered around the coffin. Well, not around the coffin, precisely. They'd hauled Mr Georgiou out of said coffin and had propped him up against its side. This was, of course, against every single rule or regulation in the funeral director's handbook, and several laws as well.

'What's going on in here?' asked Mort, brandishing his pencil case.

The group of mourners – if mourners was the word given the upbeat mood in the room – stepped back. One held a squirt can of shaving cream, while another held a fancy, multi-bladed razor with a lovely ergonomic grip. All held guilty expressions on their faces.

'We're shaving the corpse,' explained a guy Mort recognised from the local hardware store. Alex, from memory. He'd helped Mort pick out a safety ladder a few years back.

'But ... why?' Mort had personally ensured that Mr Georgiou had been stubble-free during the embalming and makeup session. Speaking of makeup, the men had scraped half of it off with the razor. Poor Mr Georgiou looked like he'd been attacked by a bear. Several bears.

'It symbolises his separation from his family,' said another of the men. 'And since I'm currently going through a divorce, I'm top choice for the blade.'

The man went in for another scrape with the razor – he clearly had some unfinished business with his divorce lawyer.

Mort had heard enough about Angela's family's escapades that he knew the tradition. And while he wasn't an authority on Greek funerals, he was fairly certain that this was not a funeral tradition. The switcheroo was at it again.

'Give me that,' he said, snatching away the razor from the deceased's ageing friends.

The divorced guy tried to grab the razor back. 'Hey! That's a good one! It's got the fancy head and the built-in soap. Its native habitat is in a locked case at CVS.'

Mort was thankful – as he often was – for his great height. He'd been a childhood keep-away champion, and his prodigiousness in this area of life continued to bless him. If he'd been more of a joiner (and didn't take issue with sand being in his bits) he might have been a volleyball champion.

'Look, we can honour the deceased,' he said. 'And we should. But scraping at his skin with a rusty metal blade is not how it's done.'

'Boo,' said one of the would-be shavers, swigging from a slender bottle of Ouzo. 'Boo!'

Mort ushered them out of the viewing area and back to the eulogy room, where a group of mourners was clustered around the deceased's widow, who had overdone it on the sugared almonds and was snoring like a champ. Were they . . . writing on her shoes?

'It's so we can see who'll be next,' whispered a pretty young woman he recognised as a regular from The Hot Pot. She crossed her fingers as she used a sparkly pink pen to write her name on the bottom of the widow's best black pumps.

The switcheroo was really pushing its luck at this funeral, thought Mort. Maybe it was the scale of the thing – there were *hundreds* of mourners milling around, hurling rice and bopping along to Zorba's dance. And those who weren't inside the funeral home were cruising past the back of the building in their cars, honking cheery tunes on their car horns. The town's Nextdoor group had plenty to keep them occupied.

But amidst the chaos, which Mort was doing his best to quell with his patented Placating Hands™ and Gentle Hushing Voice®, came a noise that caused horror to rise in his heart. A high-pitched *smashing* sound. The sound of porcelain hitting the floor. Lots of porcelain. About a hundred and fifty pieces of it, in fact.

Mort's eyes widened. He followed the source of the smashing to the kitchen, where he'd been storing Lily's carefully curated stack of kitschy mismatching porcelain ahead of the toothpaste heiress's wedding.

A half dozen aunties danced around, grabbing plates from the stack and hurling them to the floor. They cheered and twirled with each smash, clapping their hands with the kind of joy that made Mort wonder whether Christos's death had in fact been due to suspicious circumstances. The women were giddily happy.

'Not that one,' he snapped, grabbing the rooster plate that Lily had wanted to claim for herself, and positioning it high up in the cabinets. 'Everyone out! We'll be heading to the cemetery soon enough, and I expect you to be on your most funereal behaviour until then.'

The women sauntered out, one of them giving him the evil eye. Mort gave her one right back – with all the ills that the switcheroo was raining upon him, he wasn't scared of an extra curse or two. All right, perhaps a little.

'You can ride up front,' he called placatingly to her back.

He sighed, stooping to gather the shards of the hundreds of plates that carpeted the floor like a dusting of extremely sharp snow. Alas, he thought, sucking at a cut on his thumb and hoping it wouldn't turn septic – 350,000 Americans died of sepsis every year – this was a job for the big broom and the big bucket.

'There you are.' Angela poked her head around the doorframe. 'Wow, did we have an earthquake?'

'Just some very intense mourning.' Mort scraped a pile of plate shards into the bucket.

Angela picked her way across the floor towards the dessert table, which groaned aromatically with pistachio-topped pastries. 'You're going to need a bigger bucket.'

'I think you're right.' Mort couldn't see the carpet through all the shards. 'The worst part about it is that these aren't even my plates. They're Lily's.'

Angela paused, mid bite of baklava. 'Lily has an extensive collection of plates she keeps at your place? Why not start small? Like a toothbrush.'

Mort spluttered. 'No, no, it's not like that.'

Although it was like that, after last night. Or could be. Mort could still feel Lily's lips on his neck, could still see the delicious shape of her body right there in front of him, inviting him to explore it . . .

Mort! You're at a *funeral!* Funerals and sexy thoughts were mutually incompatible, even with the switcheroo looming over everything.

'The plates are for a wedding,' he explained, mopping his forehead with his skull-patterned kerchief. When had it got so hot in here?

'Well, at least they smashed the plates and not the baklava.' Angela closed her eyes dreamily as she chewed on a mouthful of honeyed pastry. 'I can't resist it. It's just so good. Pistachios. Filo pastry. It's heaven on a plate. I sort of feel like Christos would want me to eat it. So, I hear you stopped by Whispering Waters. With Christos gone, you've got an extra residence to choose from. This one has ocean glimpses, and an original pink bathroom.'

'I need to think about it,' said Mort.

'You're bleeding, by the way.' Angela pulled a Band-Aid from her giant handbag. (Realtors always came prepared.)

Mort wrapped the Band-Aid around his finger, then with a sigh went to fetch the broom and bucket he kept in the janitorial closet. How was he going to explain this to Lily? She'd worked so hard on the weird hippie wedding, and now the fabulous plating styling she'd organised was a pile of shards that even the most diligent archaeologist would struggle to put back together.

He could imagine her lips turning down at the corners, and her chin doing that slightly walnutty, wobbly thing, like when she'd knocked on the door worried that Esmeralda had disappeared (but was just at a neighbour's eating a second dinner. Third dinner, probably.)

He'd fix this. He'd come up with a way to fix this. Even if it meant individually gluing together every single plate in the stack until Lily had something to serve her uncooked retirement home food on.

Wait, there! A plate had survived the drop to the ground, courtesy of a well-placed napkin. Mort was reminded of the egg drops his class had done from the school roof in fifth grade. Mort picked up the plate and held it aloft. It was a sign that not everything was ruined. That something could be salvaged.

'Opa!' came the cry from behind Mort. '*Opa!!!!*'

Mort, who never responded well to people bellowing in his ear, dropped the plate, which shattered on the tiles.

Smashing, he thought.

Once Smitten, Twice Shy

Lily

It was perhaps for the best that Lily's week had been so busy that she'd scarcely had time to think about the fact that she'd thrown herself at Mort, only to have him run off screaming into the night. No, instead of reflecting extensively on how they'd spent hours pressed up against each other just to wind up with that damned pink-and-black grille dividing their lives again, Lily had been corralling the various vendors for Venus's wedding into a shared space ready for the rehearsal dinner ahead of the big day next weekend. And rather than fretting that Mort had reacted to her bare boobs with a flight response, she'd been calling around attempting to source a whiskey from every state for Amos and Bernard's 'bourbonniere' (bonbonniere, but make it boozy). And rather than reliving the backwards Cinderella nightie situation again and again, she'd been bribing the middle school's art students to make giant papier-mâché nutcrackers for her Christmas in July wedding.

All right, so she *had* had time to ruminate extensively on the whole disastrous debacle and about how her feelings for the funeral planner next door were rooted in something far deeper and more complicated than trauma bonding over the switcheroo. Plenty of time. But she hadn't had time to blow up

Mort's phone, which was good. Okay, so that was a lie as well, but she'd accidentally sent that stream of mortifying texts to Annika instead, so in practice she hadn't made things worse.

Wow, Lily, this is messy even for you, Annika had texted back. *I love it.*

Annika had followed up with a few emojis and then some photos of a ramshackle stone house in the Italian countryside.

One euro! I bought two. I just have to fix them up in between gorging myself on pasta and finding love in Tuscany. I'm going to livestream the whole thing.

Annika had finally done it: she'd made good on all that cheap house scrolling.

Homeownership seemed so . . . *adult*. So long term. Even more long term than marriage. And definitely more long term than Lily's year-long lease at the shop. Which she was now several months into, which meant that the prospect of giving up her shop to the next Instagram-scrolling entrepreneur was increasingly on her mind. Maybe she could take Mort's advice and explain the switcheroo situation to the Chamber of Commerce, then beg for an extension given that the first few months of her lease hadn't, as Mort had noted, strictly delivered the commercial premises she'd been promised.

'Love, are we doing this?' This was Reba, the effusively dressed tie-dye artist behind the decor of Venus's manifold glamping tents. Reba had shown up in a rattly Kombi van last night, emerging from it in a profusion of colour, swearing, weed smoke and The Grateful Dead jangling away at full blast. She wore cat's-eye glasses and a million rings and an expression of constant amusement, and fiddled with a tiny vessel around her neck.

'My husband Frank, with a dash of my dog,' she'd said by way of explanation (not a thoroughly comforting explanation, but

Lily had decided not to ask further questions). 'Damn, Mirage-by-the-Sea. I haven't been out here since Fire in the Grass back in, what, '89? Good times, good drugs. Not like your poor generation gets.'

She gave Lily a sympathetic pat on the shoulder.

Reba, proprietor of a company called Dyer on the Mountain, was basically the Dale Chihuly of tie-dye (although she asked not to be described that way because apparently there'd been a whole fuss after she'd tried to repurpose one of Mr Chihuly's sculptures into a bong at Tie-Dye Palooza a few years back). Honour Nivola's sister, Gracie Nivola – Venus's wedding photographer and a childhood friend of the bride's, who should be here any moment – had recommended Reba wholeheartedly. Apparently the two had collaborated extensively in a hole-in-the-wall art gallery in Brooklyn. Something called Riffraff, which sounded very Brooklyn-y and legit.

Anyway, both were available, both were here (well, Gracie was almost here – GPS issues) and Reba was doing a good job of talking Venus off the emotional ledge she'd been hanging out on all morning, worrying in turn about her toothpaste empire and quarterly earnings and the worrying reading that her psychic had given her. And also distracting Lily from the whole Mort fiasco, which was sorely needed right now.

'We are indeed doing this,' Lily told Reba. Steeling herself, she flashed one of her sunny grins, then twirled in a circle, showing off the food truck that Jefferson from the nursing home had put together for Venus and what's-his-name's wedding rehearsal. Lily had never invented an entire business for a wedding before, but she did have a literal blank cheque to work with, and expectations were high.

'Presenting . . . Premetheus,' she exclaimed, with a clap of her hands.

'Oh, I love a good food truck,' said Reba. 'Especially one with a punny name that only works on paper. I got my start selling grilled cheeses on tour with the Dead, you know. Well, not just grilled cheeses. But I'm all about diversification. And running from the cops.'

Venus smiled faintly as Lily showed off the truck, although that was possibly because she'd just had her makeup trial and couldn't risk the slightest bit of facial expression. The gold tones in her eyeshadow really brought out the gold in her bank account, which she was checking right now. How could so many zeros fit on a phone screen? Ah, her banking app had landscape mode.

'We'll be dishing out dinner out right here from the truck,' said Jefferson, who scrubbed up in very hipstery fashion when he put his mind to it. Well, when Lily and her entourage put their mind to it. He'd even acquiesced to wearing a fake man bun, which apparently you could buy as clip-ons, and which Lily vowed to use as an alternative to pin-the-tail-on-the-donkey at Tink's forthcoming birthday party, which she'd been working on behind the scenes with Angela.

Lily passed Venus a tiny froyo tub with a paper straw poking out from it. 'Here, give it a try. Just sip gently so that you don't mess up your lipstick.'

'Oh, it's seventy-two-hour colour stay. It's a thing NASA is working on. I wish they'd got to the eye makeup faster, but, you know, their chemists have competing priorities.'

Of course, that exploring extra-terrestrial space and advancing human knowledge and all. And also the demands of the space-themed wedding Lily was working on, which had definitely diverted some research funds.

'Mm, that's really . . . apple sauce forward.' Venus rolled the meal around her mouth, nodding thoughtfully. 'Is this how we're serving it, though? Weren't we doing plates? Don't get me wrong, I like the recyclability of the paper cups. Very earthy, very organic, which you know is *so* important to me. But I was expecting something with more . . . pizzazz. If the emissions are an issue, I can buy some carbon credits. Just say the word.'

Lily held up a finger. 'And this is what I call the tour de force. Reba?'

Reba pulled away the sheet of tie-dyed fabric that had been strategically draped over a vintage bathtub filled with shattered plate pieces.

Venus tapped her lower lip. 'I'm seeing the vision . . . we use the shards to scoop? Like corn chips, but porcelain.'

Lily laid a selection of shards out on the table, arranging them into a vague circle.

'We're going to make our own,' she said. 'Each plate will be individually crafted by a guest, then glued together by Reba using a ceramic glue coloured to your choosing.'

'Bet you've never seen tie-dyed glue before, babes,' said Reba, peering down through her cat's-eye glasses.

'I have not,' said Venus, who was poking thoughtfully through the tub of shattered plates to put together her own plate.

'Well, it'll be closer to marbled, but you get the gist.' Reba downed her Irish coffee and motioned for Cleo, the assistant barista from The Hot Pot, to bring her another. 'Nice brew here. Who do you use for your beans? Because I've got a supplier back home who grows a solid harvest. It's a whole cemetery greenhouse setup – don't think about it too much. I reckon your funeral home friend next door might like it. Suits his vibe.'

'I'll let him know.' Mort would indeed love the idea of cemetery coffee. But now everything was weird; she hadn't even yelled any of the Veronica updates through the grille, even though Veronica would shortly be arriving in town to hopefully undo the switcheroo.

Had she scared Mort off for good? She'd seen how tentatively he approached the world – driving the hearse in first gear at all times; keeping everyone but Gramps at arm's length for fear that someone might die – and instead of honouring that, she'd just pounced on him like a particularly grabby raccoon might approach a burger wrapper.

Presumably all of these thoughts surfaced on Lily's forehead, because Reba tapped her arm.

'You look like you could do with one of these as well.' Reba poured half of her spiked coffee into a cup for Lily.

'Thanks,' said Lily, as they clinked cups.

'Romantic troubles, huh?' Reba's cat's-eye glasses sparkled as she regarded Lily.

'I thought you were the tie-dye lady, not the psychic.'

'There's a lot of overlap, believe me. Tie-dye is where people come when they want to be free of something, but they don't know how to express it. I mean, look at this one here.' Reba nodded surreptitiously at Venus, who was digging around in the tub of shards, looking more and more perturbed. She was making a fine old racket as well, thought Lily; like the heart-pounding noise of her friend Jojo's kids upending a giant box of Legos.

'There's no right or wrong way to do it,' said Lily gently, stepping forward. 'Just put the pieces together, however they seem to fit.'

'That's the problem,' snapped Venus, her airy, soft-spoken bohemian mask slipping. And one of her false eyelashes as well. 'They *don't fit*.'

'That's what the glue's for, hon.' Reba waggled a squeezy bottle of glitter glue. 'Enough of this stuff and you can make anything geometric. Trust me, I've hallucinated every possible shape in my time, and then some. You haven't lived until you've seen a sixty-four-sided triangle.'

Lily wasn't about to argue with that.

'And then once we're done,' added Lily, watching as Reba applied glue to Venus's trial plate, 'I thought the guests could write a note on the plates. Sort of like a functional guest book. I know someone who can do a custom frame. After our dishwashers have cleaned and sterilised the plates, of course.'

'A custom frame for two hundred plates, huh?' Reba whistled. 'What are you going to transport it in? A tour bus? If you need one, I can hook you up. I've got half the jam bands in the country on speed dial. They're huge on tic-dye. And they have the best weed. It's a mutually beneficial arrangement.'

Lily chuckled. Where *had* Venus found this remarkable woman? A new-age shop in the Haight? A drug odyssey in some self-proclaimed shaman's house in Santa Fe? An internet chatroom dedicated to rainbows? A truck stop?

'Ooh, there's Gracie! You're going to love Gracie!'

Reba waved over the tallest, blondest, most beautiful woman Lily had seen in her life. She seemed to have thoroughbred somewhere in her genetic tree, or she'd had limb-lengthening surgery.

'Wow,' said Lily, wondering what it might be like to see over the shelves at Target. 'How do you get jeans to fit?'

Gracie broke into an easy smile. 'One of the great challenges of my life. Gracie Nivola.'

She held out a long, slim hand with a sensible, tidy manicure.

'Lily,' said Lily. 'I'm so happy to finally meet you! Venus knows you through your sister, right? Honour. I really love her on *Time After Time*. She's the perfect villain.'

'She's a sweetheart in real life, though.' Gracie's huge grey eyes crinkled at their corners – she clearly loved her sister. 'And handles the fame like a pro. But me, well, I prefer to be on this side of the camera.'

'I've seen your portfolio,' said Lily. 'You're a miracle worker. The photos you did outside that coffee shop with that hot tattooed guy and that cute girl with the curls? *Wow*, Marie Curie wishes she had that chemistry. And Reba's wedding? Reba, you were a *vision*.'

Beaming, Reba patted the vessel she wore around her neck. 'Best bloody day of my life.'

Gracie squeezed Reba's hand, and the two were silent for a moment. Lily wondered if she was missing something – but maybe they were just reflecting of the joy of the day. There was something so sweet about Reba marrying late in life, although from what Lily had gleaned, it had been more a renewal of vows.

Venus threw down the shard of plate she'd been considering. 'I need a moment,' she said. 'All this . . . makeup . . . is getting to me.'

Venus hurried off to the massive tie-dyed bridal tent which, according to the invoices Lily had received, Reba had spent the better part of the past month (and the better part of an Olympic swimming pool) dyeing.

'Uh-oh,' said Reba. She reached into her tie-dyed handbag and chucked Lily a pair of rainbow socks decorated with equally colourful bobbles. 'Might want to bring these because I reckon she's getting cold feet.'

'Everything's *fine*,' insisted Venus, who was sitting cross-legged on one of the daybeds that Lily and her crew had spent the past few days putting together. She was sucking on a CBD vape as though it held the meaning of life. 'And the vape is a work thing. Not an addiction. We're trying to get the dental association's approval on this. But the damn dentists keep holding out. Every new product, it's double-blind trial this, peer-reviewed that. You have no idea how stressful my life is.'

Lily took a seat on a tie-dyed pouffe, blinking: the sunlight playing off the tent gave the psychedelic decor an even trippier effect. She'd have to add some seasickness pills to the debauchery baskets that were going in each of the guest tents.

'You're right. I don't,' she said. 'But I do know that you're surrounded by amazing people who want your happy day to be perfection. And you have me.'

Venus sucked so hard on the vape that it made a warning beep. 'Can we . . . go see a movie or something? Get my mind off rehearsals and all the questions from the M&A lawyers.'

It seemed like Reba might be right about those socks. 'You don't want to practise your vows?' she asked gently.

Venus fiddled with her enormous engagement ring, turning it so that it faced her palm. 'We can have my understudy do them. I'll channel my energy as strongly as I can in their direction.'

Lily bit her lip. 'But we already have a stand-in for Desmond. Isn't it . . .'

Venus brightened. 'That's great. They can practise the wedding dance together, too – let me know how the choreography goes. Now, what's playing?'

Lily dutifully pulled up the playlist for Rerunning Up That Hill on her phone. 'If you're lucky, we might catch a *Barbarella* showing, with Mort on the piano. But are you sure your family won't mind?'

Venus, who'd recovered her composure, waved a hand airily.

'They won't even notice. You should invite Gracie and Reba as well. I like them.'

'Whatever you say,' said Lily, with false cheer. 'You're the bride, after all.'

Hopefully Venus knew what she was doing when it came to true love, because Lily certainly didn't.

Oh, Good Grief

Mort

If there's a song you don't particularly want to hear blasted over the speaker in the downstairs prep room while you're readying a body for an upcoming showing, it's Journey's 'Don't Stop Believin''. Mort – who'd been halfway through preparing Mrs Prescott (renowned boules player and cupcake baker, taken too soon after an unfortunate incident involving a fall from a stepladder while reaching for a mixing bowl on the top shelf) for an upcoming viewing – swore.

The embalming machine ticked as it slowly filled Mrs Prescott with a fluid that would keep her looking spiffy for years to come.

Mort lifted his gloved hands. Was it urgent? Was there a dead person on the front doorstep? Had those solar sales guys not taken the hint after he'd stuck the NO SOLICITING, THIS MEANS YOU, SOLAR SALES sign to the front door? Was Pickleball Candice back for the fourth time, beside herself that the fateful day marked on her funeral Save the Date was growing ever closer?

Or . . . was it Lily?

Lily, whom he'd given signals more mixed than anything that Dierdre's KitchenAid could achieve. Lily, who'd made herself so vulnerable in showing that she cared, and whom he'd repaid by effectively shunning.

She'd probably come from the Chamber of Commerce, fresh from cancelling her lease, effective immediately.

No, not that. Anything but that.

Determined to get ahead of his intrusive thoughts, Mort paused the machine and stripped off his gloves. Hurrying upstairs, he frowned at a flash of pink peeping out from his office. Was that a fuchsia mohair rug? Where had it come from?

Mort opened the door, slumping (hopefully imperceptibly) as he saw that his visitor was not in fact Lily. And not even a student flogging novelty sunglasses as part of a fundraiser. Well, at least that meant that Lily hadn't fled back to La Jolla just yet.

'What are you doing here?' he asked the grizzled group of men that had gathered at the door. One was patting the poodles, which Lily had dressed up in 1980s leotards, including sweatbands and slouch socks. Where did she get the time? Or the fashions? Perhaps she'd arrived with a trunk full of dress-ups for her weird themed weddings.

Well, this was still better than the Jehovahs.

'Is there something wrong with the plumbing?' asked Mort, recognising the combed-over pate and overall-covered form of Andy Stribley, the local plumber. Had Gramps gone on a flushing spree while he'd been visiting? (Thanks to Stribley, Mort had lost only the one night's sleep, having sorted out Gramps's plumbing woes before Gramps could reprise his wall-rattling snoring endeavours . . . or before Lily had a reason to invite Mort over again. Mort was still kicking himself over how all of that had played out, and had a bruise on his own shin to prove it.)

'Grief support group?' repeated Mort. This was the first Mort was hearing about any group. He wasn't the social club type, and had no intention of changing that.

One of the men, a rotund fellow Mort recognised from the chair-dancing funeral, scratched the shock of curly grey hair beneath his peaked cap. Orson, a name Mort remembered because Orson always followed up any introduction with: *like Welles, only not very*.

'The girl next door said you did a weekly meeting for men who've lost their loved ones,' said Orson. 'Well, and women, but apparently they don't need it as much.'

'They've got hobbies,' said another of the men, a scarecrow-like gent with a thin, scraggly beard to match his thin, scraggly aspect. Ah, Mort knew him from the cemetery – Duggo. He had a whole family plot, and a recent addition to it as well. His wife Ernestina. It had been a quiet funeral: just Duggo and his 'doggo', Sausage, a fluffy dachshund with very long ears and very short legs, such that the latter ended up standing on the former. Sausage was presently sniffing the butts of the poodles outside.

Mort shook his head. 'You must have the wrong address.'

'Nah, quite sure we're in the right place,' said Duggo, reeling in Sausage and picking him up. Gosh, that was a long dog, thought Mort. How did its spine work?

What would it take to get rid of them? Even the solar sales reps took the hint after you underscored for the third time that the sun didn't shine on your particular property because of all the death and ghosts. 'Look, it's not a great time. I'm part-way through an embalming.'

'Is it Mrs Prescott?' Stribley craned his neck as though hoping to catch a glimpse of the poor old dear laid out on the coffee table in the foyer. 'Very sad about the fall. I was always telling her not to go up high in those slippers of hers – it's an OSHA risk – but she always was a risk-taker.'

'And a fiery one. She made me chilli pepper cupcakes once after I gave her some constructive feedback on the height of her wall-mounted television,' said Orson of the chair-dancing funeral. (That's right – he worked for an AV company, as evidenced by the branding on the pen he was presently, rather annoyingly, clicking.) 'Went through a whole roll of TP recovering from it.'

'Do you cater?' asked Duggo. 'Because I was told there'd be doughnuts. All good grief support groups have doughnuts. I saw it on TV.'

'Grief makes you hungry,' agreed Orson, twirling his pen.

Sausage, who'd caught a glimpse of Esmeralda perched on the banister to Mort's apartment, gave an excited *ruff* and tried to squeeze past Mort.

'Looks like we're coming in,' said Duggo. 'Don't blame me, blame the doggo.'

Mort sighed and pulled open the door fully. 'Come through to the office. I'll fetch some snacks.'

By the time Mort returned with a platter of baklava and tiered fruitcake left over from his recent funerals, the men had rearranged the furniture in Mort's office, turning it into a cosy living room setup. Although for some reason the chaise longue was now turned sideways, dividing the room like an upholstered ping-pong table.

'All we need is a widescreen there, and the game on.' Orson made a rectangle with his hands. 'I can hang it for you, if you'd like. I've got some spare brackets in my van.'

'I like what you've done with this rug,' added Duggo, as Sausage flumped down on the pink mohair, long ears lost in the shaggy carpeting. 'Really ties the room together.'

Stribley sprawled over the armchair in the corner, flopping his legs over the side. He kicked off his shoes, revealing tartan socks with holes in them. And the likely reason that his poor wife had departed the earth, thought Mort, nose wrinkling.

Sausage, bless him, set to work on one of the stinky shoes, happily munching away on its toe until Stribley snatched it away and shoved it back on his foot. The air quality in the room noticeably improved, thankfully, as Mort had already lit a candelabrum's worth of candles and feared he'd burn the place down.

'I'll be back with the coffee in a moment,' he said. 'Talk amongst yourselves.'

Alas, when he returned with the coffee, the men were not, in fact, talking amongst themselves. They were sitting there, all three of them (and dog) in silence, quietly eating their stale pastries and cake.

The silence prevailed as Mort poured each of the men a cup of coffee. Stribley emptied seven sachets of sugar into his.

'My Maureen never let me do that,' he said sadly. He added enough cream to overflow the cup – Mort had to spring forward with his pocket square to prevent the liquid from marking the table. The coaster was right there! 'Or the creamer.'

'Ernestina and I had different ideas about how hot a cup of coffee should be,' said Duggo, dipping a finger into his coffee and nodding happily. 'Lukewarm brings out the flavours, if you ask me.'

'I'm not much for coffee,' said Orson, looking distastefully at his cup. 'Got any beer?'

Mort tried to recall what was left in the fridge following the most recent funeral fiasco. 'I have champagne.'

Orson pursed his lips. 'Weird for a funeral home. But it'll do.'

'Talk amongst yourselves,' said Mort, heading off again. This was why he didn't entertain unless it was for work. Although, he supposed, it was kind of for work.

He returned with a bottle of half-flat champagne and a few decorative flutes etched with the words *Congratulations: he's dead!*

'Wow, hope they don't put that on my tombstone,' said Orson, turning the flute in his callused hand. His wedding ring flashed; Mort realised that all three men were wearing their rings.

Orson had apparently caught Mort staring at his ring finger, because he raised an eyebrow. 'Any plans for your girl next door?'

For want of something to do with his hands, Mort poured himself a flute of champagne, wincing when it bubbled over. He quickly sucked the foam off the top of the drink.

'She's not my girl. We're . . . just neighbours. Colleagues. Friends. Confidants.'

Who'd shared a passionate few moments that he couldn't get out of his head. And who, despite their divergent dress codes, were perfectly suited.

Duggo snorted. 'That's a lot of words to say that someone's not your girl. My Ernestina was all those things, too. Literally started off as the girl next door. Freckles, head of red curls, denim cut-offs – oh, I was a goner the day she moved in.'

Mort sipped his champagne, thinking back on how he'd felt when he'd first crossed paths with Lily. That giant smile, those sparkling eyes, those ridiculous business cards with the kissing couples that had been his very first introduction to her. And how she just *rolled with everything*, no matter what happened. She'd been unflappable when Derrick and Fran had abruptly carked it at the cinema (and then when they'd come back to life). She'd handled the switcheroo with surprising aplomb (much better than Mort had, in fact). And no matter the difficulties her clients hurled her way, she took it all in stride.

'He's off with the fairies,' chuckled Stribley, giving Mort a clap on the back. Mort inhaled his champagne, and burst into a spluttering coughing fit. 'Look at him, one of us.'

Mort set down his glass and took in the motley group of men lounging around his office. Between the coffee and the desserts and their shared interest in Mort's love life, they'd relaxed a little. He could see a sense of relief in all three of them. Maybe all they needed was a place to come together.

'So,' said Mort. Where to from here? How did you start a conversation with a group of strangers? He was used to delivering the usual polite condolences, but beyond that he had little. He'd always tried not to empathise too much, because otherwise this career would drown him with its pain.

Orson shifted on his seat, spilling his champagne, which to be fair, Mort had overfilled. (Bubbles were hard to anticipate, especially when you were dealing with half-flat champagne.)

'Sorry,' said Orson, on the verge of tears as he looked down at the spill.

'Not to worry,' said Mort stiffly. He pulled out his desk drawer, which contained his overflow store of handkerchiefs – but then spotted the pink corner of an ice-breaker card game that Lily had given him after listening to one of his more awkward client intake meetings through the grille. Hang on. Perhaps this could be of use.

Handing Orson a black handkerchief (he'd hidden the ones that had turned rainbow in the switcheroo at the bottom of the drawer), he reached for the box of cards, then set it on the table.

He grimaced as he took in the name of the game – *Dirty Laundry* – but pressed on, proffering the box to the men in front of him.

'A dear ... friend gave this to me. It's to help us get comfortable talking about our feelings and getting to know each other.'

'But we already know each other,' said Stribley warily. 'We're sitting here, aren't we.'

'We've eaten lunch near each other in the same room before,' added Duggo. 'We're old friends.'

'Good start,' said Mort slowly. 'But I think we can go a bit deeper. Let's start by taking a card. A few cards. I'll go first.'

Have you ever had sex outside? read the card.

Maybe not.

'What's the longest you've gone without bathing?' he said, improvising.

Stribley whistled. 'A week? No, no, a month when I lived on a boat in Thailand.'

That tracked, thought Mort, who still hadn't shaken the pong of Stribley's feet. But maybe you had to have an absence of olfactory sensitivity to work as a plumber.

Orson was aghast. 'You didn't even jump in the ocean?'

'Too many jellyfish.'

Orson shifted his chair away.

'I've always wanted to touch a jellyfish,' admitted Duggo. 'But I'm scared of being electrocuted.' He gave Sausage a solid pat instead.

'I don't recommend electrocution,' agreed Orson. 'I worked on telegraph poles for a while before I switched to installing TVs.' He pointed out a burn on his inner wrist. 'Got a right zap during a storm. My whole life lit up in front of me. Well, I thought it was my life – it was my hair. That's when I went grey. And the smell! Like bacon frying.'

This was a good start, thought Mort. Gory, and not particularly on topic, but the men were talking. They'd got past the grunting stage. That seemed positive.

'I'll go, I'll go,' said Orson, brandishing his card. 'I've got a good one. *Have you ever streaked?*'

'Streaked, like past tense of . . . strike?' Orson was still stuck on the lightning topic.

'Like running naked through a sports game,' said Duggo, helpfully.

'Oh, I have!' Stribley's eyes lit up. 'It was chess, though – does that count?'

'I think that counts extra,' said Mort, chuckling. Perhaps the switcheroo had hit the chess scene at some point as well.

'Ooh, me next,' said Stribley 'Ready? *If you had a gang, what would you call it?*'

'That is good one,' agreed Duggo. 'I've always wanted to be in a gang. But a nice one.'

'This could be a gang,' said Orson thoughtfully. 'The Grief Guys.'

'I quite like that,' said Stribley. 'Has a ring. What do we do, though?'

'We channel our grief productively,' said Duggo. 'Through public works and stuff.'

Mort leaned back in his chair. This was all going . . . surprisingly well. Lily was a genius. Well, her card game was a genius. He'd have to email the inventor and let them know that they'd single-handedly helped form a gang. (A nice one.)

Mort's phone buzzed in his pocket, quite insistently. And then again. Oh shit. It was Aunt Dot from Rerunning Up That Hill. He'd forgotten all about *Barbarella*!

'I hate to cut this short,' said Mort, slapping his thighs in the universal sign of *well, it's getting late*, 'but I need to get to the cinema. The piano calls.'

Stribley scooped the remnants of a diamond of baklava from

his cup with a spoon and devoured the squelchy mess. 'Can we . . . come too?'

Mort glanced around at the wrinkled, hopeful faces of the men he'd spent the past few hours chatting with. Why not? They'd bonded so well over their grief and stories and bottomless appetite for coffee and cookies and flat champagne. And besides, the walk to the cinema was good exercise.

'Get your cardigans, Grief Guys,' he said. 'We're heading up the hill.'

Barn to be Wild

Lily

Lily tapped her pink cowboy boots together and took a deep breath. The cowboys' wedding was going to be perfect. Nothing weird was going to happen. There would be no corpses, no maggot-infested cakes, no rending of clothing. Amos and Bernard were funny and delightful and deserved a wedding that reflected that. It wasn't their fault that Veronica still hadn't pinned down a date to stop by and hopefully reverse the switcheroo. (Veronica apparently had odd priorities.)

'Switcheroo, if you mess up this wedding, I'm taking it as a hate crime,' Lily whispered to her black-and-white ceiling, which she'd managed to partially cover with colourful cloth draping, hoping that her visitors were so enamoured of the bonbonniere table that they simply wouldn't look up. Ugh, was that black splodge on the far wall further encroaching upon her side of the building? Pulling up her stepladder, she grabbed a pot of yellow paint and a paintbrush, and swiped over it with a quick approximation of a daisy.

All right, now she was ready. Well, once she donned her pink cowboy hat. Perfect: Dolly would be proud.

She texted a picture of said hat to Mom, who responded with a blurry thumbs-up selfie. *I believe in you, Lils. Make Aunty*

Karen regret her inferior offspring! Also, which candle would go best in the bathroom?

Lily helped Mom with the difficult candle decision (it took twelve texts), then headed out.

'Hey, Lily!' called Jorge, who was out and about watering the endless assortment of planters and flower beds that gave the village loop its unending rainbow of colour. He'd even gifted Lily a pothos that she hadn't managed to kill.

'Got some bluebonnets for the gents today,' said Jorge. 'Send them my best wishes.'

Lily took the vibrant flowers, which Jorge had wrapped in a square of brown paper and tied with string. 'Thank you, Jorge! You're too kind. Will I see you at the cake tasting on Tuesday? I'll have a new lemon one for you to try.'

Jorge lifted his trowel. 'Wouldn't miss it. I'll come hungry.'

'I wouldn't expect anything else.'

Waggling her fingers goodbye, Lily waltzed down the laneway to the parking area. She dug through her handbag to unlock Lucille, but the jangling of her keyring-laden keys was absent. Oh crap, she thought, peeking in the window, where a familiar disco ball keyring flashed and gleamed in the ignition.

'You got locked out. Of this.' Mort folded his arms, regarding the tiny car, which probably looked like a diecast Matchbox model from his great height.

'I get locked out of all sorts of things,' admitted Lily. 'I'm like the anti-Houdini. I called the locksmith, but he's run off his feet. Something about a swingers party and a bowl of keys that went missing. He has to rekey a whole subdivision.'

Mort grimaced. 'I'm not sure I needed to know that. Although it *does* explain the awkwardness at some of my recent funerals.

238

It's beyond frustrating having to call security every time I see more than two grieving spouses in the front pew.'

'You said you were off today,' said Lily pleadingly. 'Can you drive me down to the barn?'

Mort shot her a wry look. 'Will you reimburse me for the mileage?'

Lily huffed in exasperation. 'I won't even touch the radio. There'll be plenty of old people there – you can hand out your business cards.'

'Wow, callous. I didn't know you had it in you.' Mort shook his head. 'All right, let's do this.'

Lily jumped up and down in her gleaming boots. 'Really?'

Before she realised what she was doing, she'd leapt in to give him a kiss on the cheek. Except Mort, famously not a fan of being tackled (tackling had a high mortality risk), turned his head just in time . . . so that their lips met. Lily's cowboy hat tumbled to the moss-smothered cobblestones.

'Oh, shit. I mean, not shit. I just . . .' Lily gulped as all the tension from that fateful night a few days ago came roaring back.

Mort was silent, his dark eyes hooked into her own.

Once could be shrugged off as a mistake. Twice was . . . a pattern. A pattern that Lily desperately wanted to continue, but that Mort apparently did not.

'You've got a little . . .' She reached up to rub the hot pink lipstick from the side of his lip.

As she did, he caught her wrist, gently, holding it momentarily as though he deeply wanted to say something. As though he wanted to kiss all the way down the length of her arm.

But he didn't. Instead he stooped to fetch her fallen cowboy hat, then unlocked the hearse.

'I like the hat,' he said. 'Suits you.'

A unprompted compliment! Was Mort coming around to her wiles?

'Good, because there are plenty extras at the barn,' she teased. 'And I just happen to have a spare one of these.'

She brandished a bolo tie.

'Oh goodie.' Mort looked as though she'd suggested brain surgery without anaesthesia.

'You slip it over your neck and adjust it like this.'

She demonstrated, trying to ignore the thrum of Mort's heart against her hand as she adjusted the tie.

'How do I look?' asked Mort drily.

'Like you're ready for some very depressed boot scooting.'

'There will be no boot scooting of any sort.' Mort motioned for her to buckle her seatbelt. Off they trundled, Mort driving at his usual funereally appropriate pace.

'We're going to miss the wedding at this rate,' said Lily. 'And their first anniversary.'

'Better late than dead,' said Mort seriously, turning his head left, then right, then left, then right, then left, then right as he went to pull out into an intersection. It was like watching someone watching the tennis watching someone watching the tennis.

Fortunately the barn was a relatively short drive, even at what was close to a walking pace. The wedding space came into view, and through the huge open doors Lily admired her handiwork: the embedded tractor tyre aisle, the seats fashioned out of hay bales (for the groom's side) and out of whiskey barrels (for the other groom's side), the enormous horseshoe beneath which they were going to deliver their vows. (This was a prop from a movie about giant horses she'd found on Facebook Marketplace.) She'd really outdone herself with this one.

'Park here,' said Lily, pointing to a gravelly area a few hundred feet from the barn, and well away from the guests' cars. 'We can't show up in this thing. It's not good for morale.'

'Why not?' said Mort, although he pulled over as told. 'Elderly family members have heart attacks all the time at weddings. We're just covering our bases.'

'Speaking of covering,' said Lily, as Mort opened her door for her. She craned her neck towards a commotion outside the barn. 'Or rather, the opposite of covering . . .'

For up ahead, eight enormously buff guys dressed in what Lily could only describe as Chippendale chic seemed to be rehearsing carrying an emperor on their shoulders. Lily hadn't heard anything about this. Was it a protest? Or a cheerleading routine?

Mort in tow and clipboard and walkie-talkie out, Lily hurried over, her cowboy boots clacking on the tractor tyre path that extended out from the barn. Oh, but it was quite comfortable – it was like running on a track.

'I'm sorry, but . . . are you on the guest list?' Lily flagged down the guys, who turned in a flawlessly coordinated demonstration of muscle and sinew. Lily hadn't known that abdominal muscles came by the dozen. 'I don't mean to be rude, but it's a private party. A wedding. And the grooms are going to be making an appearance any second now.'

'We're the Paul-bearers,' explained the buffest of the guys, like this somehow made sense. 'Well, except for him. He's the Peter-bearer.'

'Sorry,' said Peter, who somehow *did* look like a Peter and not a Paul. 'Paul #8 wasn't feeling well, and we figured another P name would do. I was in Thunder from Down Under, if that counts.'

'It definitely counts,' said Lily, taking a sneaky photo to send to Annika, who'd spent much of their last Vegas trip appreciating the muscular troupe of Aussie performances. (Carrot Top had been sold out, she'd said, not meeting Lily's eyes.) 'But . . . why are you here?'

'We're here to carry the lucky couple down the aisle.' A guy with an elaborate frangipani tattoo on his very large upper arm (a sizeable canvas for a sizeable tattoo) mimed holding someone propped against his shoulder.

Lily frowned, flipping through her notes. She didn't remember ordering a set of Pauls. Was this some sort of bachelor party thing? Then she realised, watching the guys simultaneously mime their whole carrying thing . . .

'*Pallbearers*,' she and Mort whispered simultaneously.

'It's the switcheroo,' muttered Lily to Mort. 'But sexy. I'll allow it.'

'At least we're not graveside,' said Mort.

'This time,' said Lily, with a grin. Her phone beeped. 'Okay, we're almost up. I'll go find Bernard and Amos, and we'll get this rodeo started.'

Lily rapped using the stirrup door knockers on the silvery his and his custom horse trailers the boys had chosen as their dressing rooms. Each was plushly upholstered with gleaming leather and draped with saddle cloths. (All right, Pendleton blankets, but close enough.) Flowers bloomed from cowboy boots.

'How are we going in here, boys? The Paul-bearers are waiting.'

'Oh yes, we *saw*,' said Bernard, extremely happily. Spinning on the silver heel of his cowboy boots, he showed off his magnificent custom suit, which sparkled with elaborately embroidered western scenes. 'What a gift from the heavens.'

'I am not complaining,' agreed Lily.

'Is that your boy Mort out there?' whispered Amos, who was in a fabulous corduroy vest that Lily desperately wanted to touch. 'Good for you for bringing a plus-one.'

'Oh he's not . . .' started Lily, then gave up. Today's wedding was going to take all of her focus – and she didn't want to expend valuable energy explaining the complicated Mort situation. 'C'mon, boys, it's showtime.'

The Pauls gathered around the grooms as they emerged from their trailers.

The Paul with the frangipani tattoo knelt with his hands knotted into a human stirrup. 'Who needs a leg up?'

Amos and Bernard shared a delighted grin.

'Boost me,' said Amos. He guffawed as he was hoisted skyward and onto the carefully staggered shoulders of half the Pauls, to some resounding applause from Bernard and Lily (and a quieter golf clap from Mort, who was watching with a quirked eyebrow). The remaining Pauls (and Peter) knelt, ready to give Bernard a lift.

Lily blew them a kiss. 'Off you go, boys.'

She jogged inside, giving the thumbs up to the bluegrass band standing ready by the giant horseshoe altar.

The gentle strains of 'I Will Always Love You', with vocals from a stunning drag Dolly, rang out through the barn, bringing tears to Lily's eyes. Amos and Bernard were such a gorgeous couple, and they deserved all the happiness in the world. To be even a little part of that happiness was an honour that she could hardly believe had been bestowed on her.

The guests, decked out in their best western finery (including one guy in a Best Western uniform – awkward), turned as the grooms made their highly unusual entrance.

'Oh my God,' muttered Bernard, as he was carried down the aisle on the shoulders of the Pauls (and the one Peter), one hand outreached to clasp Amos's, 'I've died and gone to heaven.'

Moon(shine)struck

Mort

Mort was in hell. He'd never seen such a . . . festive . . . wedding reception. The barn had been dressed to, as a cowboy might say, hog heaven. The guests sat on whiskey barrel chairs around huge round tables dressed with horse blankets and centrepieces that ranged from candle-topped saddles to fake saguaro cacti hung with string lights. Some of the drunker members of the wedding party were doubling down by doing shots at the saloon, which had a full vintage storefront and swinging doors and staged shoot-outs held at half-hour intervals (upon learning about Mort's new social club, Lily had enlisted the Grief Guys to do the honours). The Pauls had retreated to some of the cowhide armchairs that Lily had arranged into miniature living room setups.

Fringed leather vests, cowboy boots, and ten-gallon hats bobbed and weaved around the room as the guests snacked on fried pickles and brisket that had been smoked on-site overnight.

Mort had never felt so out of place. He said as much to Lily, who'd just now boot-scooted up to him in a flurry of sparkly pink.

'Never felt so out of place *yet*,' she said, waggling her hips. 'Wait till you see the Christmas in July wedding setup – I've got Tink on stationery, and she's outdone herself. Besides, you'd make a good Santa. Just let that five o'clock shadow grow out a bit.'

Mort rubbed his cheek, trying to come up with a good comeback for that. But Lily had been swept away by a tall blond cowboy in a tasselled leather vest sporting a hobby horse in one hand. Kicking up a booted foot, she waggled her fingers at Mort.

Mort nibbled on his corn on the cob, which was a challenge given that his jaw was so firmly clenched from all the banjo music.

'Damn, this moonshine is *strong*,' croaked a guy in chaps and a dramatically printed flannel shirt. He perched on a nearby barrel, his eyes watering. 'Who needs a nostril hair trimmer when you've got this?'

He waved his glass demonstratively under Mort's nose.

Mort's eyes widened – and watered. Oh no. That was no moonshine. And not because Mort had any idea what moonshine smelled like. But he *did* know what embalming fluid smelled like. And the guy in chaps was about to be immortalised at the age of thirty-five for life.

Mort slapped the drink to the floor.

'Oops, sorry. Nervous tic,' he said.

'You're okay,' said the guy, flagging down one of the cowboy waiters hurrying around in flannel aprons. 'Plenty more of that sloshing around.'

Which was precisely the problem. Where was Lily? Mort glanced about, trying to spot her blonde curls and pink cowboy hat amidst the line dancing hordes and the costumed 'horses' trotting around the room. But Lily was, as usual, by far the smallest person in the room – and even with her pink outfit it was impossible to pick her out from amongst the leather vests and blinding belt buckles.

'Lily!'

He pushed through a crowd of whooping cowboys testing their lasso skills on one of the Pauls, who stood on a stool making bodybuilding poses. (Fortunately for the Paul, they had no such skills.) Then shoved through a Jell-O pistol shoot-out. (Messy, and squelchy, although the Grief Guys were fully in character.) Then fought his way through the Dolly Parton shrine, which featured an enormous Dolly crafted from flowers. (Beautiful, just like Dolly.)

He found Lily reorganising the hobby horses on the back wall.

'There you are!' he exclaimed, relieved.

'Miss me, partner?' she drawled, in a regrettable, but still adorable, southern accent. She pressed the hobby horse's ear, making the horse neigh dramatically.

'Very much.' Mort leaned close. 'We have to swap out the drinks, immediately.'

Lily frowned, trying to see where he was going with this. 'What's going on? Are they making the martinis with vodka? Are the champagne snobs refusing the prosecco?' Her eyes widened. 'Did someone get into the secret stash of absinthe? The boys promised me that was for their inner circle only.'

Poor Lily had erroneously assumed that if the switcheroo had struck once, she'd be safe for the rest of the night. Wrong. As the Greek funeral had shown him, the switcheroo knew no limits.

'Embalming fluid,' he said. 'The spirits have been switched out for embalming fluid.'

Lily's clutch on the hobby horse grew so tight that it unleashed a series of whinnies. 'So, how bad are we talking here? What kind of side effects? Will it help them age gracefully?'

Ah, the sweet summer child.

'They might not get the chance to age if they keep it up. We're talking blindness, if we're lucky. Death, if we're not.'

Over at the Queen Dolly shrine, one of the Dolly worshippers broke into an anguished, caterwauling rendition of 'Jolene', with the lyrics rewritten to be about the 2019 version of Andrew Lloyd Webber's *Cats*.

'Although death doesn't sound *so* bad right now,' Mort admitted.

'It could be worse. You could be gamely trying to stick a Rosa landing.'

Lily pointed to where Rosa the bull was bucking and spinning, her hydraulics in fine form. No fewer than three would-be cowboys were sitting groaning beside her, clutching various parts of their anatomy. A sexy male nurse was tending to them with novelty Band-Aids and platters of ribs and fries.

To be fair, fries did fix a lot of things. Except perhaps an artery blockage. And the effects of the formaldehyde shots that a group of cowboys were toasting with over the saloon bar.

Mort raced forward, swiping the shots off the bar. The shot glasses shattered, exploding around the bartender's cowboy boots.

The Grief Guys, who were just about to run in to reprise their shoot-out, backed off. Duggo (who had a dressed-up Sausage on a leash) shot Mort a confused look.

'I'll explain later,' Mort told him. 'Come back in ten.'

'Dude, what the fuck!' exclaimed a guy with hair so sun-bleached it was translucent. He wore a shark tooth on a leather strap around his tanned neck, and cowhide patches on his jeans. Ah, a surfer cowboy.

'Sorry. I'm ten months sober . . .' extemporised Mort. 'And it hurts to see you hurting yourselves like this.'

'Aw, man. Thank you for thinking of us.' The surfer guy

wrapped Mort up in a brutal hug. 'I love this sobriety journey for you. If you want to come on my podcast and talk about it, let me know. Here's my card. I'm one half of The Dudes Hang Low.'

Wheezing for air, Mort took the card.

But then, disaster.

Bernard stood, whacking a cowbell with a butter knife to get everyone's attention.

'It's speeches time, cowbabes! And then after the worst of you have roasted us like the brisket very kindly provided by the Flaming Galah, we're going to boot scoot up a frenzy. Does everyone have a drink?'

A murmur went up as everyone raised their glasses.

'*No!*' shouted Lily and Mort together.

'Barkeep, get those two in the back a drink,' said Amos, raising his glass of moonshine. 'We can't have empty hands at an event like this.'

'Not him – he's sober,' shouted the surfer guy, pointing at Mort.

Mort waved awkwardly as everyone congratulated him on his sobriety.

Lily took the helm, drawing the attention away from him with an even worse pronouncement. 'I mean . . . no, we can't toast with the basic moonshine! That's not how cowboys do it. This stuff hasn't even been stirred with a raccoon's penis bone.'

'A what now?' whispered Mort.

'It's a whole thing. Google it sometime,' murmured Lily.

'Don't,' said the surfer guy, holding out his hands placatingly. 'It's better someone in your position doesn't know.'

Lily turned her attention back to the guests. 'If you've got moonshine in your hand, get yourself to the spittoon because the good stuff's coming around.'

A puzzled murmur went up around the crowd.

'Sit tight: the Grief Guys are coming around with the bubbly. It's three times stronger, and not made in a Red State.'

The confusion shifted to approval.

Lily jumped on her walkie-talkie, sending out an urgent announcement to Mort's gang of gents.

'*Champagne in every glass, stat.*'

The Grief Guys hurried about, pouring bubbly and handing out champagne flutes as the speeches began. (*Bloody hell,* but they were rude. Was it normal for speeches to be this rude? Or was this a switcheroo thing?)

'Not a switcheroo thing,' Lily said, smiling mischievously as one of the guests made a joke so off-colour that even Pantone didn't have a number for it. She reached out to clink glasses with Mort, then looped her arm through his as they sipped. Mort indulged her, because it was extremely hard not to indulge Lily.

Oh, but he wanted to kiss her again. But after how badly he'd messed up last time, it was probably best to keep a respectful distance. Even if Lily was a vision in glittery pink right next to him, so close that their shoulders, their arms, their hips, kept brushing in a way that felt too close – and nowhere near close enough. It was a cruel and unusual punishment. Just like the fact that in a few months, she'd be gone from his life entirely.

'Just make sure the gents dispose of the embalming fluid thoughtfully,' said Mort, as they leaned against the back wall, slowly drinking their champagne. 'It's highly . . .'

A fireball erupted in the night sky, eliciting whoops and cheers from the tipsy crowd.

And also from Lily, who was clapping riotously.

'Yes, that,' said Mort, rubbing his temples. There were far too many unexpected events at weddings. It was impossible to keep track of all the moving pieces.

'Wow,' Lily exclaimed. 'Free fireworks!'

'No one died,' reported a guest with an astonishing handlebar moustache so long and styled that it seemed to have been taken from an actual bicycle. 'No one died!'

'To not dying!' cheersed someone in a sexy cow outfit. (Mort wasn't sure whether they'd misinterpreted the dress code, or accurately interpreted it.)

'Cheers to that!' said a guest, raising a wayward glass of embalming fluid.

'Oop, not that one.' Lily jumped up on a chair to switch out the drink for a Salty Dog. 'This one's stronger.'

'I like you,' said the guest, knocking back the cocktail, then wrapping Lily in a drunken hug. 'Anyone who brings me drinks is a friend of Jack's.'

'I wouldn't want it any other way.' Lily gave Jack a good-natured pat on the head, then climbed back down to the floor.

'*Amazing*,' purred Amos, who was sidling past with Bernard. 'First the Paul-bearers, and now surprise fireworks? I love you as much as I love Bernard. Almost.'

'I'll let it slide just this once,' said Bernard, whose grin took up most of his face. 'Because the feeling's mutual.'

Lily winked and gave them both a kiss on the cheek.

The band kicked up, breaking out into a fascinating bluegrass rendition of 'I Will Survive'.

Amos clapped his hands in delight. 'Sorry, babe, but we can't *not* dance to this.'

The newlyweds raced off towards the dance floor, which was densely populated with everyone who hadn't (yet) been injured by Rosa the mechanical bull.

'Well then,' said Lily to Mort, teasingly, 'I suppose we might as well hit the dance floor.'

Mort swallowed.

Lily regarded him thoughtfully. 'Ah, but you don't dance.'

Mort raised an eyebrow. 'I dance. Just not to . . . this.'

Lily managed a wobbly, champagne-influenced turn in her cowboy boots. 'Oh, I just think you're scared. I hear that dancing is correlated with an increase in torn Achilles tendons. You might even get stabbed with a stiletto and die.'

'I don't know who you've been dancing with, but that's not typically how these things go. Besides, the floor is more likely to collapse than anything.'

'Well, then, prove me wrong.' Lily murmured something into her walkie-talkie, and as if on cue, the lights dimmed. The gentle intro to 'Can't Help Falling in Love' shimmered across the room.

'I've heard you playing this on the pianola,' whispered Lily.

'All right, I can't say no to that. May I?' Tipping back her cowboy hat so he could see her face, Mort gently put one hand against Lily's back, his fingertips lightly grazing her bare skin. With his other he reached for her hand, gently enclosing her fingers in his.

'Look at you, Mr Slow Dance.'

'You don't run a funeral home without learning some tips from the old ladies,' said Mort, pulling her in. She was so small in his arms, yet strong. There was a fiery strength to her that he loved: the strength of a huge personality squished into a tiny package. She seemed to overflow with it, with a brightness and energy that Mort suspected you'd be able to see even with the lights dimmed.

As the rest of the crowd pressed onto the floor, rocking and swaying together, Mort and Lily danced quietly on the sidelines. Lily followed his lead so beautifully – she'd definitely partner-danced before. Even slightly addled from the champagne, she was strong and balanced on her feet, adding little footwork embellishments that provided the perfect flourish to the music. Mort was impressed, and enthralled. He could have danced with her for hours, moving smoothly across the dance floor, in time with the music, in time with each other.

But any funeral director knows that all good things come to an end.

The lights dimmed. The guy on the banjo picked up a fiddle and bowed a handful of notes that sent fear trickling down Mort's spine.

The microphone squealed as he howled: 'Who's ready for "Cotton Eye Joe"? Get in line, folks!'

You Can't Hurry Love Spells

Lily

Lily stretched out in her desk chair, trying to loosen the kinks and knots from hours of administrative emails combined with hours of line dancing. By the time she'd sent Amos and Bernard off to their new lives together, the sun had been peeping over the horizon, and Lily had been practically pickled on Pol Roger. But at least she hadn't thrown herself at Mort again, not *technically*, unless dancing cheek to cheek counted. (Well, cheek to shoulder given the height difference.)

Lily never slept well after a big boozy night, and she'd come downstairs at seven scrabbling around for some emergency ibuprofen and Berocca to help counteract the drumbeat in her head. Esmeralda had joined her, and by then Lily had decided that she might as well start work for the day because she sure as hell wasn't going to manage her morning run down to the beach. If someone saw her shambling up the promenade in her current state they'd probably get on Nextdoor sounding the alarm about a pod people invasion.

Besides, she had emails to catch up on, texts about Annika's new Italian pied-à-terre to respond to, and the imminent arrival of Veronica – who was going to do her best to reverse the switcheroo spell – to prepare for. Not to mention some eavesdropping through the grille in case Mort was sharing with Gramps or his Grief Guys his innermost thoughts about their dance.

Alas, judging from the murmured conversation coming from the other side of the wall, Mort was taking some heat for the inscription on a newly placed bench over a late judge's grave. Apparently it read 'all rise' instead of the requested 'please approach the bench', which was not entirely off brand, but might open the judge's estate to liability should a zombie apocalypse occur.

Lily's phone buzzed, startling her away from her eavesdropping. Mom!

'I finally caught you, Lils! Take that, phone tennis.' Mom craned her neck all around, trying to get a look over Lily's shoulder. 'Is that your shop? It looked different in the photos you sent me. Are you in a basement? A dungeon? I suppose grey is making a comeback this season.'

'It's just . . . the light,' said Lily awkwardly.

'You should work on that. Good lighting is everything on someone's big day. Speaking of, I sent the photos from that cowboy wedding to Aunty Karen. Her jaw? On the floor. That's how you know you're doing a good job.'

'Thanks, Mom. It's going really well.'

'Never a dull moment, I'm sure – I know it all too well – but I knew you'd be brilliant. You've got your mom's genes. And that space! Is that a cat? Do you have a cat?'

'Sort of. Her name is Esmeralda.' Lily angled the phone to capture Esmeralda in the shot. The fluffy cat frowned, then slunk off to scratch up Lily's desk chair.

'And you're making friends? You should join a sports team. Or bingo. I love bingo – mine has such a good buffet! Or how about a jogging club? Are there joggers there? There must be, being so close to the beach.'

'That's a great idea,' said Lily, who was exhausted at the thought. She'd been so busy with work that clubs were out of the question – she'd missed every single one of Dierdre's book club meet-ups so far, even though she'd had good intentions.

'How's . . .' Lily had given up keeping track of Mom's boyfriends.

'It's Rick. He's . . . fine. Not the one, though. Although are any of them?'

Maybe *some* of them, thought Lily. Well, one of them.

'The only condiment he can abide is yellow mustard. Yellow mustard! That stuff's radioactive, I know it. Life's too short.'

It really was, wasn't it? Lily's stomach clenched as she caught sight of the calendar on her wall. How much longer would she get to call Mirage-by-the-Sea home?

'By the way, did you check Facebook?' Mom asked knowingly.

Lily had not; she wasn't even sure she still had an account. There were just so many boomer memes from her older relatives to sort through, and why bother when said relatives would just take a screenshot of the memes and text them to you anyway?

'Sure did,' she said brightly.

'Isn't it great?'

'Sure is,' she said. She'd learned over the years that when it came to memes, the best thing to do was just smile and nod.

'Oh God, Rick's just come in with a box of Costco-size mustard. I need to deal with it. Can I call you later? Oh! I just saw your ceiling. Do you have a leak? If it's a leak, you should get that sorted out right away. It could be mould. Is it mould? Oh God, the mustard. I have to find space for it.'

Mom rang off, leaving Lily feeling grateful that for all its faults, at least the switcheroo hadn't brought mustard into her home.

She checked the time. A few minutes remained before

Veronica was due to arrive, so Lily busied herself emailing the local dovecote about the homing pigeons that were to be released for Venus's wedding this afternoon, and following up with the Christmas in July Santa about how his beard growth was coming along. (Santa, an early riser who was presumably on North Pole time, sent pics of said beard, which was looking very festive.)

She was texting with Reba their planned carpooling itinerary when the doorbell started blasting 'Highway to Hell'. Dammit, the switcheroo's ever-shifting playlist startled her every time.

Lily leapt up to wrap the nervous, dark-eyed Veronica in an effusive hug. The woman looked fabulous, as though she'd spent several months at a day spa for the strong and single. She wore a floral maxi dress that Lily wished she had the height to pull off, and huge hibiscus earrings dangled from her earlobes.

'Hi,' said Veronica shyly. 'Sorry it took so long for me to get back here. I was a bit scarred after the whole proposal.'

'I don't blame you,' said Lily. 'It was a weird evening. For a lot of us. But sometimes good things come out of weird occurrences. Tea?'

She gestured to the pot she'd just brewed: the Sit a Spell blend from The Hot Pot, which she hoped might help with the magical shenanigans they had planned for this morning.

'Tea sounds perfect.' Veronica plopped down on the yellow love seat that had had so many visitors over the past few months – happy couples with bizarre wedding themes; chatty townsfolk who stopped in for a break between the top and bottom of the promenade; the grieving widowers whom she'd fed and watered and gradually sent Mort's way. Mort himself, when a conversation through the grille that separated their offices simply wouldn't do. And, of course, the fluffy and delightful

Esmeralda, who found the couch's vintage fabric perfect for all of her claw-sharpening needs. (Lily now understood why her grandparents coated everything in plastic, but didn't have the heart to do so herself.)

Lily poured them each a cup of tea, then gathered a plate of Christmas-themed cupcakes and laser-engraved sugared almonds to snack on.

'That's a lot of sugared almonds,' said Veronica, as Lily scooted aside a jumble of stationery, setting down the teetering platter on the coffee table.

'Turns out even the switcheroo can't break through those candy shells,' said Lily. 'Watch your teeth, though.'

'I'm sorry I caused all of this,' said Veronica, peering around at the black-and-white-splodged decor. She ran her fingers over a two-way sequinned cushion, flipping it from a golden crown that read *VIP* to a black tombstone that read *RIP*. She grimaced. 'I can see why you were so desperate to track me down. I swear, I didn't mean to cast a spell or whatever happened. I just . . . I couldn't say yes.'

'If it makes you feel better, everyone who saw it is on your side.'

Veronica grabbed the pillow, hiding her face in it. 'Apparently the whole internet is, too. I'm *dead to me* girl. They're selling T-shirts with my face on them. People are using gifs of me to quit their shitty jobs.'

'So the whole thing was a net positive,' said Lily cheerfully. 'Well, except the switcheroo.'

'I still don't quite understand what happened there.' Veronica scooped up a piece of cake with a fork that had tarnished to black sometime in the past five minutes. 'Your businesses . . . merged? But weren't you both called Eternal Elegance in the first place?'

'It's complicated,' said Lily. 'Really complicated. But it's not all bad.'

'True,' said Veronica. 'It's given me the impetus to focus more on me these days. I started learning German on Duolingo so that I can visit the Cinderella castle in Bavaria. I have a trip booked and everything.'

'*Sehr gut*,' said Lily, testing the limits of her German (which extended to various types of sausages and select words ending in *-bahn*.) 'Once Desdemona gets here, we'll be good to go. She's a goth film director whose wedding I did a few weeks ago,' she added by way of explanation. 'She'll be helping you with your lines and everything.'

'Wow, this town is all about the theatrics, huh.' Veronica sipped her cup of tea, then nodded at the pink neon sign on the wall that read *we're getting hitched!* 'So, when's your turn?'

Ah, there it was. But there was something in the way that Veronica said it that wasn't patronising or judgemental – not like the way everyone else asked it.

'I'm not sure,' said Lily, wishing not for the first time that the sign would short-circuit. 'Maybe never. I've never even been in a long-term relationship.'

Veronica crunched on a sugared almond. Wincing, she probed her back molar with a tongue. 'It's okay, I still have a tooth. But you know, me neither, really. I keep dating these guys who treat me like crap, and then when I go to leave, they try to tie me down. That was my third proposal.'

'*Third*?' Lily couldn't keep the horror out of her voice. 'But you're like . . . twenty.'

'Twenty-two,' said Veronica. 'I'm definitely not ready for any of that. I'd side-eye a promise ring, honestly.'

'Good for you,' said Lily. 'Although I have some good mood rings in that box of wedding favour samples, if you want to try one.'

'I do love a good mood ring.' Veronica popped one on her finger, watching as it turned hot pink and then purple. 'Ah. "In the mood for love," according to the key.'

'Sorry. They're kind of rigged. But they're cute.'

A tall figure in black swept towards the front door, a black parasol spinning hypnotically as it moved.

'Oh God, it's the spectre of Death,' whispered Veronica. 'I'm too young! I have dreams! I want to travel the world!'

'Ah, to be mistaken for Death. Vindication is mine,' said Desdemona, putting down her parasol and tromping through the door on her enormous high heels. She was well over six feet tall today – more if you included the voluminous black bonnet she wore. An eyeless broken doll peered out from the tulle wrapped around the brim, waving with a blood-red hand. She stared ominously around the room, taking in the floral mural and the rainbow displays of wedding favours and stationery that Lily had so painstakingly arranged to cover up the worst of the switcheroo.

Desdemona's drawn-on eyebrows dove. 'Oh, but it's bright in here. Such a surfeit of pink, even for a rainbow goth.'

'Sorry,' said Lily. 'It's a lighting thing.'

Desdemona uncapped a calligraphy pen and used it to sketch a tiny crow in Lily's test guest book. 'Delightful pen. I could write some ghastly marginalia with this.'

'How's married life treating you?' asked Lily, as Desdemona scribbled some – was it poetry? – in the guest book.

'It's morbidly wonderful. We're going to pick out our coffin lining while we're here. Your Mort has an incredible selection of black silks.'

Of course Mort did. Only Desdemona came anywhere close in her worship of black fabrics. To be fair, it did make eating pasta with tomato-based sauce less of a risky endeavour. Or drinking red wine. Or blood. Not that she suspected that Desdemona drank blood.

'This is Veronica,' said Lily. Veronica murmured a hello around a chunk of sugared almond. 'She's the one you'll be coaching.'

Desdemona gave Veronica an assessing look, as though she were grading a piece of roadkill for possible taxidermy. 'I can work with that. Have you ever acted before? Been on camera before? Been in front of stage lights before?'

Veronica shook her head. 'Only factory lights. I'm an engineer.'

Ah, that was right: bridges.

'Which reminds me,' said Lily, 'while you're here, I might get your thoughts on my ceiling upstairs. Is it normal for it to bend in the middle?'

'My expert opinion is . . . probably not,' said Veronica.

'I like a good structural bend,' said Desdemona. 'It speaks to existential angst in both the architect and the materials. Creates a liminal space where the demons can float in and out. And a nice perch for gargoyles.'

'I do like gargoyles,' mused Veronica.

'An agreeable pronouncement.' Desdemona tapped her razor-like nails to her heavily made-up cheek. 'I can work with her. To the great outdoors we go.'

She raised a sinewy hand adorned with a sparkling cobweb of chains and directed Veronica outside to the pagoda where the disastrous proposal had taken place just weeks earlier.

'I can't even look.' Veronica shielded her face from the beautiful structure, which was wrapped with blooming wisteria and bougainvillea. Jorge had been by to hang fresh flower baskets, and the local elementary school had added painted rocks as part of their Art on the Go unit. (A few of these cuties sat outside Lily's door on an upended painted flowerpot – her favourite was one that was possibly a smiling sun or a smiling crab. Whatever it was, it made her heart sing every time she glimpsed it.)

'So, according to my brief we're reversing a curse,' noted Desdemona, generously slathering on sunscreen so thick it was almost solid. Lily hadn't even known you could get 200+ SPF – you might as well coat yourself with exterior house paint. 'A shame, as I do like a good curse.'

Just quietly, Lily agreed. Yes, the switcheroo had caused all sorts of mayhem and devastation. But it was also . . . fun in its own way. And it had given her so many opportunities to spend time with Mort, whose darkly humorous presence she happened to adore.

Speaking of. The disco strains of 'Stayin' Alive' coloured the air, which meant that Mort had emerged from Eternal Elegance (Funeral Edition) and was making his way past the poodles and over to the pagoda.

Like Lily, he looked a tad worse for wear, although the scruffy look suited Mort. There was something about a loosened tie and those rolled-up shirtsleeves that set off her inner swoony Victorian.

'Good to see you, Veronica, Desdemona.' Mort shook their hands, then folded his arms, which Lily had learned was his protective stance when he was feeling uncertain.

'Oh, the piano guy!' Veronica played some air piano. 'You were great at the *Vice Versa* showing. Until the whole death thing.'

'He's not bad on the marimba, either,' added Lily.

'And he has a fabulously macabre vehicle,' added Desdemona, tilting her sunhat. 'If I weren't married . . .'

Flushing, Mort scooted closer to Lily.

'. . . I would carjack it and hide the body,' Desdemona finished. 'But I couldn't do that to poor Ambrose. Our credit scores are linked now. And a felony is not ideal for a first-time homebuyer.'

Well, that had taken a turn.

'Veronica, this is your mark.' She pointed to an X that she'd marked out with gaffer tape.

Veronica obediently went to it, standing awkwardly as Desdemona walked around her in a slow, anticlockwise circle, sweeping the tiled floor of the pagoda with an ornamental broom whose handle was wrapped with trailing silky ribbons.

'Are we quite sure that this is going to work?' whispered Mort, with a tone that sounded almost like he didn't want it to.

Lily, who felt similarly ambivalent, shrugged. 'I went through a wiccan phase in seventh grade, but that's about where my knowledge of magic ends. I *did* get Nick Rosenburg to fall in love with me, though.'

'Good for you. Did it last?'

Lily grinned. 'A solid three days, which is pretty good by seventh grade standards. Turned out he didn't like tacos, and I just couldn't get past it.'

(Like mother, like daughter, apparently. Although a disdain for tacos was far worse than an affinity for mustard.)

'Tacos? That is a dealbreaker.'

'Any folded food, actually. Gave him the squicks.'

'So no gyros, no falafels, no onigiri, no crepes? What about an omelette?'

'A folded omelette could be hiding anything, Mort. Anyway, he's married with three kids now, according to my mom, who keeps a close eye on the Facebook pages of everyone I've ever met.'

'A whole family living in a taco-less world. Astonishing. There really is someone for everyone.'

The way he caught her eye when he said it made Lily flush the deep, deep pink of the coneflower bouquet she'd wrapped with matching ribbon. She feigned a cough, hiding behind the florals. Had there been something behind that comment? But Mort was against marriage, or anything lasting, by the sound of it. Because in his eyes, nothing lasted, not really. Even the most promising unions ended up with at least one person being worm food. Or wedding confetti.

Desdemona stepped forward, wafting the black velvet of her skirt around her. She waved magnificent cobweb-painted nails as she introduced a tall, bespectacled man who had arrived while Lily and Mort had been dissecting Lily's tweenaged love life.

'This is my cousin Helmut,' pronounced Desdemona. 'He's an aspiring actor – he had a supporting role in my short that made the Nicholl semi-finals. And received several other laurels as well, if you care to view my website. He'll be playing Desmond today.'

Helmut bobbed his head in a shy greeting. With his side-combed hair and cautious attire, he had a shy Clark Kent vibe.

'Hello,' said Helmut, with a grin that sparked a similar grin in Veronica. He had a gentle German accent that explained those cheekbones, although not his tardiness.

'Hi,' whispered Veronica, twirling a lock of hair around a finger.

'I'm sorry I'm late,' said Helmut. He held up a reusable bag. 'I was told it's mandatory for any visitors to buy pastries at The Hot Pot. So I took a detour.'

'Pretty sure Veronica just went weak at the knees,' whispered Lily to Mort.

Mort raised an eyebrow. 'I have a great physiotherapist, if she needs it.'

'*Bist . . . du zu . . . Besuch?*' stammered Veronica.

'Very good! Yes, just visiting. For work,' said Helmut. 'I'm an engineer when I'm not acting. We have a factory in Munich.'

Veronica's eyes widened. 'Munich? Near the Sleeping Beauty castle?'

'Ah. Schloss Neuschwanstein. Not too far.'

Veronica's eyes were sparkling. 'And what kind of engineer?'

Desdemona clapped her hands, the cobweb lace of her sleeves wafting. 'Enough! You're meant to loathe each other to the depths of hell and back, and the energy is all wrong. Your auras, they're . . .' Desdemona wrinkled her nose. '*Lustful*. Ground yourselves.'

'I don't even care if this works,' whispered Lily. 'This is amazing.'

'Helmut, you're Nate. You have a complex relationship with fidelity. You don't listen to actual music, only algorithmically generated playlists. And you hate puppies.'

'I'm a monster,' whispered Helmut, green eyes wide.

'And you think surprise public proposals are a good way to corral someone into marriage. Veronica, you're you from earlier.'

'Okay,' said Veronica, although she looked *far* happier than she had the night of the switcheroo.

'You've learned that your partner is a lothario in the worst possible way. And worse, he wants to tie you to his pathetic little world. A world with *surfers*.' Desdemona shuddered. 'Your job is to channel the emotion you felt when you told Nate to go fuck himself. Take this spoon. It will help.'

She turned to Lily and Mort, hiding her mouth as she muttered, 'Psychosomatic. But we do what we must in the name of the art.'

Spoon clutched between her fingers, Veronica stood upon her mark, brow furrowed as she thought of how badly Nate had treated her.

'Do you need me to prompt me with your lines?'

'I've got it,' said Veronica.

Helmut stepped forward, looking bashful. 'Sorry for what I'm about to say.'

'No hard feelings,' said Veronica. 'It wasn't you.'

'Wrong!' proclaimed Desdemona. 'It *was* him. Inhabit your character!'

Veronica closed her eyes and inhaled deeply. The spoon bent between her fingers.

'I'm ready,' she said, her voice icy.

'And, action!' Desdemona's clapperboard clacked.

Affecting a jerkish pose, Helmut got down on one knee, producing a novelty matchbox, which he popped open to reveal a bunch of rainbow-tipped matchheads.

'Yours?' whispered Mort to Lily.

'Extras from Venus's wedding,' said Lily. 'Ten bucks a box.'

'The anti-capitalist spirit is strong, I see.'

'Veronica,' said Helmut in a passable American accent. 'Babe. Let's do this.'

There was a beat as Veronica bit her lip. Lily had the suspicion she was considering whether it might be worth taking Helmut up on his proposal and running off to the Sleeping Beauty castle on a whim.

'Veronica, that's your cue,' whispered Desdemona.

'Oh, sorry.' Veronica cleared her throat. 'Nate, you're dead to me!' she declared to the heavens.

'Well, that's not very nice,' muttered Pickleball Candice, who was shuffling past in head-to-toe safety gear. 'It's not fun to mock someone's mortality.'

'Are you feeling lost, Candice?' asked Derrick, poking his head out from the shelves of the Naked Bookshop. He reached out a robed hand. 'Because I have the answers you seek.'

'Jesus, Derrick,' snapped Fran. 'It was a misdiagnosis, not a miracle.'

(A schism already threatened the Cult of Derrick.)

'That was quite good,' said Helmut, giving Veronica a thumbs up. 'I believed it.'

'Any signs of a reversal?' asked Desdemona.

The sky was a mesmerising blue above them. Lily held out a hand, considering. Perhaps the humidity had increased a percentage point or two? 'No rain.'

Desdemona nodded, clapping her hands sternly. Veronica's performance was not up to her directorial standards. 'Again, with *feeling!* Look into his eyes and imagine you want him to keel over right here.'

Veronica stared up Helmut, then blushed. She cleared her throat.

'You're *dead* to me!' she said, voice breaking.

Helmut pretended to swoon.

Veronica covered her mouth, hiding a smile.

Desdemona raised a carefully painted eyebrow. 'Amateurs,' she muttered. Then, loudly, 'Imagine the worst moment of your life. The darkest betrayal.'

Veronica fanned her hands in front of her face, then hopped from foot to foot as though she were getting ready to run up a flight of stairs with 'Eye of the Tiger' blasting in the background.

'Now imagine that Helmut was behind that betrayal.'

'Sorry,' whispered Helmut.

Veronica scowled. She took a deep breath, then shoved Helmut. '*You're dead to me*,' she snarled.

Helmut regained his balance, then clapped slowly. 'Wow. So good. And yet I live.'

Veronica looked hopefully at Lily, who pointed to the unbroken sky.

'Still blue,' she said sadly.

'Still poodles,' added Mort, pointing to the poodles outside the funeral home. Some clown who was definitely not Lily had strung pom-pom garlands around their necks.

Desdemona folded her arms, drumming her nails against her cobweb sleeves.

'Any other suggestions?'

'We could . . . try it in reverse?' suggested Lily. 'What's *you're dead to me* backwards?'

'Em ot daed er'uoy,' said Helmut instantly.

'Wow,' marvelled Veronica. 'You must kill it at parties.'

'Oh, I don't party. Or kill things.'

'Sounds like a keeper,' whispered Lily to Mort, who – wait – blushed? Lily winked, setting off an extra layer of redness in his angular cheeks. Lily sucked thoughtfully on her bottom lip, imagining a world where the wall between the Eternal Elegances, between their lives, disappeared, and the two of them spent the rest of their days tangled up in bed together.

Would Mort, with his fear of loss, ever allow it?

'Take four,' called Desdemona, with a clack of her clapperboard.

Lily blinked, yanked out of her imaginary world and back into the real one.

Veronica balled her fists and tried valiantly to repeat Helmet's backwards-speak.

'Em ot . . . daed er'uoy . . . ?' she said, then burst into giggles.

'Pretty good,' he said.

'What about . . . *you're alive to me?*' suggested Mort.

Veronica nodded, then waited for Desdemona's clapperboard.

Helmut dropped to one knee, waving the matchbox. 'Babe,' he intoned in, for some reason, a southern accent, 'let's go to Vegas and let Elvis do this marriage thing.'

Lily stifled a giggle. For someone so stoic, he had some decent comedic chops.

'Vegas. A man after your own heart,' whispered Mort.

Lily was impressed. 'You remembered.'

'I remember everything.'

'Shh!' hissed Desdemona, waving her clapperboard.

'You, Helmut, I mean Nate – are alive to me.' Veronica's eyes sparkled as she said it, but apparently not enough to set off a magical rainstorm. After a pause, she shrugged. 'Sorry, guys. I really tried.'

'You did a fabulous job,' said Lily, giving Veronica a hug. It was not, however, lost on her that Veronica was peering over her shoulder at Helmut, who was sifting through the pastries bag in search of one good enough to give to Veronica.

'I think it might be picnic time,' she added. 'Let me run back to the shop.'

Moments later, she was back with a picnic basket stuffed with desserts and canned cocktails.

As she spread out a mushroom-print blanket, pinning it down at its corners with weighted toadstools, she was aware of Mort beside her, helping to set out the plates and cutlery – doing a fine job of it, even though Lily's table setting was, well, maximalist to say the least. She had a feeling that Mort might be the kind of guy who would actually do the dishes instead of leaving them in the sink to soak, or feigning some sort of gendered inability to understand the function of a sponge.

'Don't forget the umbrellas for the drinks,' she added. She wasn't even done speaking before Mort, as though he'd anticipated her words, pulled out a series of tiny rainbow umbrellas (and one black umbrella for Desdemona, whose black lips pursed approvingly).

Lily poured them each a sparkling water, adding a twist of lemon and bitters.

'To amusing failures,' she said, raising her glass.

'The best kind of failure,' said Desdemona.

'To Bavaria,' added Veronica, toasting happily with Helmut.

Mort looked pensive as he clinked his glass to hers – what was going on in that thunderous head of his?

Thinking Outside the Casket

Mort

As seemed to be the case wherever Lily was involved, the sedate picnic had quickly turned raucous. Lily had produced a bottle of Pimm's, and things had become increasingly tipsy and increasingly loud, with half a dozen of the village's locals popping by for cake (non-wormy, thankfully) and sandwiches with more layers than your average sedimentary rock.

Mort, who became a tad introspective when alcohol was involved, and accordingly avoided it for the most part – unless he was reading something that required moody introspection, like the Schopenhauer paperback that a mourner had left on a pew after an ancient philosophy professor had kicked the bucket – had excused himself before he'd blurted out something about how he actually quite liked the way their businesses had become strangely intermingled. How he quite liked the way their *lives* had become intermingled. How he wanted their *bodies* to become intermingled, dammit.

Sure, animated corpses in the morgue weren't ideal. And the fluffy poodle statues out the front of Eternal Elegance (Funeral Edition) set certain expectations about the number of hugs Mort was willing to give strangers. But he enjoyed hearing Lily's voice come through the decorative grille that separated their offices whenever she had a question about napkins or typefaces or just wanted to tell him she'd spotted a hummingbird outside.

If everything went back to normal, if their businesses reverted to their original forms, what reason would she have to keep doing that? Why would Lily want to stay in Mort's life when Mirage-by-the-Sea was brimming with an endless parade of men who'd happily sweep her off her feet? Would she even want to stay on in town after her lease expired, or would she just pack up and head off to less picturesque but less problematic pastures?

Mort sighed and prepared to make his way down to the prep room, where Barrett Hodgkins's body lay, waiting for Roddy to deliver a new vat of embalming fluid after last night's moonshine switcheroo shenanigans. (Mort had given his current vat a sniff, and had nearly burnt his eyebrows off with the low-quality alcohol of it all.)

But because life is one big slew of interruptions all the way through to the final interruption of all, the funeral home door swung open to the upbeat tones of 'Don't Stop Till You Get Enough'.

It was Duggo from the Grief Guys, with Sausage in tow. Sausage shuffled in over the threshold, his ultra-low belly scuffling on the doormat.

'Duggo,' said Mort, confused. 'Do we have a Grief Guys meeting today? I'm out of doughnuts, but I do have some cowboy wedding cake. It's shaped like a wagon wheel.'

Removing his hat, Duggo shook his head sadly. 'We don't. Which is mostly why I'm here. Do you have . . . anything for me to do? That I could help out with?'

Absolutely not, was Mort's first thought. What was he going to have Duggo do? Embalm Barrett Hodgkins? Haggle for a discount on the commemorative brass plaques that had doubled in price this quarter? Censor the rude comments in the switcherooed guestbook? Gas up the hearse?

'It's just so hard without my Ernestina,' Duggo went on, prodding at Mort's jar of black cats and making a face. Mort, feeling bad for him, plated up a slice of leftover wagon wheel wedding cake and handed Duggo a fork.

Duggo dug in, but dispassionately. 'I just rattle around the house all day with nothing to do and only Sausage to talk to. And he's a good boy, but not the best conversationalist.'

Sausage whined sadly.

'Sorry, Sausage, but you know it's true. I've done all the odd jobs around the place – changed to a water-saving showerhead, patched the bad shingles, straightened all the paintings. I've been doing three loads of washing a day just for something to do. And making Sausage six-course meals. Look how low his belly is getting.'

Mort wasn't one to body-shame, but Sausage's belly *was* about as low as the tips of his ears. At least he was doing a good job of dusting the floor.

'So I suppose that's why I'm here. I could use the company,' said Duggo sadly. 'And the purpose. I'm thinking about getting one of those robot roommates. For company. I even looked at Whispering Waters, but it's not conducive to Sausage going out for his night-time wees.'

The more Mort heard about Whispering Waters, the less sold on it he was as an option for Gramps. Especially since Gramps was also known for his late-night wanderings. When he wasn't snoring the roof down, anyway. But the germ of an idea was beginning to sprout in Mort's brain, a bit like the seedling wedding favours that Lily presently had on display (and which hopefully wouldn't turn into Venus flytraps).

'Are you and Sausage up for a drive?' asked Mort.

An hour later, Mort and the three Grief Guys – for they'd stopped to collect Stribley and Orson, both of whom had been slouching around at home watching daytime TV and snacking on Girl Scout cookies (Stribley) and shredded cheese (Orson) – pulled up at Gramps's house. Mort grimaced; the house was in progressively worse shape every time he saw it, and he could no longer accept that the garden looked like that because Gramps was 'rewilding' it.

'Mort!' exclaimed Gramps, wrapping Mort in one of his squeezy hugs. 'And . . . friends!'

'Heya, Gramps,' said Stribley. 'How's the plumbing holding up?'

'Good, good,' said Gramps. 'No clogs or glugs, and the toilet's draining as it should.'

'We're here for an impromptu working bee,' said Mort. 'The boys have some time on their hands, and I figured you might have some work that needed doing. Between them we have a plumber, an AV guy and . . .'

'I can handle the weeding,' said Orson. 'A dandelion-free lawn is the pinnacle of human existence. Oh, and that light. I'll get out the bug gunk and put in a new bulb for you.'

Gramps beamed. 'It sounds like we're going to have a brilliant day. And if you need to stay over, I have plenty of room. Now, how do you feel about jigsaw puzzles?'

Love and Marriage Go Together
Like a Hearse and Carriage

Lily

Well, it was turning out to be an interesting day. Lily had failed to reverse the switcheroo, but she *had* brought Veronica and Helmut together. Knowing that new love needed time alone to properly take root – after all, she was living the experience first-hand – she'd left them to their picnic not long after Mort had raced off, muttering something about a graveside vigil. Of course, Lily had her own obligations: Venus's wedding was this afternoon, and Lily's phone battery was already redlining from the gazillion text messages she'd received about it, as well as a series of cryptic emoji-filled ones from her cousin Tessa, who had presumably given her phone to one of their younger cousins to mess around on. (Never a good idea, Tessa.)

Ah, there came another message – a horribly mistyped one from Reba, who was swinging by to pick Lily up in the Kombi. Lily could only hope that she'd used voice-to-text, because otherwise Reba was in no state to drive.

Quickly changing into a floral midi dress with an embroidered peace sign across the bodice and donning her convertible heels,

Lily hurried down the leafy, fairy-light-studded laneway to the tiny parking lot behind the shops.

The jangling tones of the Grateful Dead blasting (Lily could feel the essence of the Nextdoor group gathering around her in neighbourly indignation), the bright yellow Kombi van screeched to a halt next to Lily's Miata.

A cloud of smoke billowed from it as Reba rolled down the window, her cat's-eye glasses flashing as she poked her head out. The woman looked like she'd rolled around in a set of marbled endpapers. Or acid papers.

Reba pointed at the side door with a heavily beringed finger. 'Lily, babes! Hop on up!'

Lily yanked open the door, climbed up into the rickety van and plonked down on the velvet bench seat, which was smothered in tie-dye throw pillows and grandma rugs. Every inch of the vehicle was decorated with vibrant fabrics and brand posters; even the roof was adorned with a psychedelic blanket that looked like a portal to another plane of experience.

'Hey there,' said Gracie Nivola, from the far end of the bench seat. She wore a simple pale blue sundress and a silver headband, without even a dash of makeup on her face, and would still outshine every single person at the wedding. How did the Nivolas do it? Had they made a bargain with the devil on a crossroads late at night? Lily suspected she knew why Venus had hired Gracie to be behind the camera rather than in the bridal party. 'Love the shoes.'

'Thanks! They're convertible.' Lily demonstrated.

Impressed, Gracie snapped a photo.

'Where's your fella?' shouted Reba over a particularly noodly guitar riff. She jabbed the accelerator, sending the clunky van roaring out onto the backroads.

'Mort? He's not my . . .' Lily paused. 'He has funeral stuff.'

Lily felt a pang as she glanced back at the empty spot where the hearse was usually parked. She'd been hoping for an excuse to invite Mort along to the hippie wedding. It was going to be utterly ridiculous, and she knew that Mort would have plenty of commentary to offer about the on-site florist and the house-sized custom tents. And it was only fair that he got to see what had become of the smashed plates. And perhaps the inside of one of the house-sized custom tents.

Ahem, Lily.

Reba snorted as she hauled on the steering wheel. 'You two, with all your beating-around-the-bush nonsense. You should go for it before one of you dies.'

Lily blinked.

'It's kind of a personal crusade with her,' whispered Gracie. 'Her husband Frank died on their wedding night.'

'Second wedding night,' corrected Reba. 'But the moral still stands.'

As the Kombi puttered around the cresting hills and coasting valleys of the farmland that surrounded Mirage-by-the-Sea, Lily realised they weren't far from Gramps's place. There it was: the gothic Victorian with its rickety chimneys and dark foliage. Although the lawn was looking good today. Hang on – was that Mort's hearse?

'Pull in here,' she told Reba. 'Just for a second.'

As the Kombi rolled up, Sausage raced towards them, barking valiantly in between awkwardly standing on his ears. It looked like the Grief Guys were here.

'Hey, Lily.' Orson stood, rubbing his back. He held a weeding tool, and was surrounded by the corpses of dandelions. 'Looking for Mort? Mort! Hey, Mort!'

'Here.' Reba leaned on the Kombi's horn, startling a family of squirrels.

Mort came over, looking deliciously scruffy with his

shirtsleeves rolled up and his hair mussed as usual. He pulled down the pair of Ray-Bans he was wearing. 'Lily? How did you find a worse vehicle than the Miata?'

'How do you feel about being a plus-one?' shouted Reba.

Lily hid her face behind her hand. 'We could do with the extra help, if the Grief Guys aren't too busy here?'

'We're coming back tomorrow,' said Duggo, who'd appeared on the porch with Stribley. 'This place has years' worth of work to do on it. But I'm up for a wedding, if you are, Stribs?'

'What about Gramps?' asked Lily. 'He's welcome, too.'

'I've got a date with a jigsaw,' shouted Gramps from the front door. 'I just found where your sky bit fits with the edge pieces, Lily! I'm a roll, and I can't stop now!'

'Come on, hop in,' called Reba. 'The dog's welcome, too. If he doesn't mind some cat hair. My Ember sheds like you wouldn't believe.'

The Grief Guys piled in, and off they went, coasting along on the plaintive strains of Jerry Garcia's vocals.

'It's no Woodstock, but it's close. And probably with a bigger budget,' said Reba, as they pulled up to the event site, a vast estate zoned as farmland for the tax breaks. But today at least it was a spot for hippie glamping, and Reba had been busy tie-dyeing every inch of its fifty-acre footprint. Dozens of personal tents swept out like rainbow fractals from a central clearing demarcated by astonishing floral arrangements that emerged naturally (and expensively) from the ground. Beanbags had been carefully lined up in angled rows around the ceremonial arch, and a variety of stations offered all the booze and entertainment you could dream of. Even the Portaloos – which were more like portable, multi-stall bathrooms – were a work of (hand-painted) art.

'I hear that from a helicopter's-eye-view it looks like a very trippy crop circle,' said Lily, waving hello to the lighting guy who was busy stringing Moroccan lanterns from the sculpted trees.

'Ooh,' said Duggo, holding Sausage up to the window so the short-legged dog could get a better view. 'How do we get a peek from all the way up there?'

'Be born rich,' said Orson. 'Unless there are drones. Are there drones?'

'I don't do drones.' Gracie tapped her camera. 'I'm strictly analogue.'

'I could hook you up.' Orson dug around in his overall pockets for a business card. (The one he produced looked lightly electrocuted.) 'I do AV of all sorts.'

'Thanks, but I have a vision.'

Oh, to have that facility for shutting down men when they tried to turn you around to their ways of doing things. Lily had suffered through plenty of girls' nights that were suddenly gate-crashed by guys who couldn't fathom that a night out could be complete without a dose of testosterone. A confident Gracie-style 'fuck off' would've gone a long way.

'And out we get,' exclaimed Reba, putting the Kombi into park with a crunch. She offered around a pungent tin of weed gummies. 'Anyone for a gummy? No? Well, more for Reebs.'

The little gang hauled themselves out of the Kombi, waiting for Lily to go through her clipboard and assign them tasks. (Watching the incense during wind gusts, assisting wayward guests back to the camp, venomous snake spotting and reporting, and poop shovelling in the event that guests' lapdogs failed to adhere to the designated pooping area. Sausage looked quite indignant at this last one.)

'Basically, if you see anyone looking anything other than delighted, offer to help,' she said. 'I promise to keep you all in food, cake, alcohol and goodwill.'

'The good stuff,' said Orson approvingly.

Reba held up a finger. 'And before you go: uniforms.'

She dragged over a giant basket, digging through it for tie-dyed outfits for each of the Grief Guys.

'*And* we get free clothes.' Stribley struck a pose in his new rainbow button-down shirt. 'Living the high life.'

'And you, Mort.' Reba tossed a purplish blazer in Mort's direction.

Absolutely not, thought Lily.

'Absolutely not,' said Mort, just as she'd anticipated.

'At least do a tie. Lily can help you with it.'

'I know how to . . .' began Mort, then trailed off. 'All right,' he said gruffly.

He stooped, his dark gaze thoughtful as he let Lily gently tie a double Windsor for him. She was mindful of her hands on his shoulders, against the warmth of his throat, as they had been during the night he'd come to visit her apartment. A frisson of electricity sparkled through her as she smoothed the paisley-print fabric.

'Suits you,' she said, straightening the knot and trying to ignore the intrusive voice telling her to use the tie to yank Mort towards her.

'I'll take your word for it,' said Mort.

What if she kissed him? What then? What if she just pulled him off into one of the carefully crafted flower beds and pinned him down? What if she finally figured out a label for this unusual situation they were in, so she wouldn't have to keep calling Mort the 'guy next door with whom she happened to share a business name'.

But no, this was Venus's day, not hers.

'These two,' said Reba as Gracie ducked in, snapping a photo of Lily and Mort before Mort could put up a hand in protest.

Blushing from the extreme turn her thoughts had just taken, Lily checked the time on her phone. 'All right, everyone, let's get to it. Reba, can you make sure the Grief Guys have a tent?'

'On it. Who wants to help me pop one up?'

Stribley and Duggo followed after the colourful hippie as she led them off between the rows of colourful tents. Sausage trotted after them, ears dragging and tail wagging. (Gracie snapped a brilliant action shot of the little dog leaping over a leaf.)

'This is going to be quite the event,' said Mort, as Lily took him past a set of plush couches dressed with plump cushions and surrounded by giant vegan leather ottomans.

'Look at you, Mr Compliments. Here's Premetheus, by the way,' said Lily, as they rounded what Reba had dubbed the Reclining Tent and came upon the glossy food truck.

Mort waved at Jefferson, who was pouring an amuse-bouche for an extremely thin, extremely wealthy-looking woman. Although Lily supposed that everything on the menu could be considered an amuse-bouche.

The remaining few hours before the nuptials quickly disappeared into an array of last-minute tasks and frantic questions about where best to land a helicopter. Throughout it all, Lily was extremely mindful that Venus had not yet made an appearance, and worse, wasn't answering her texts. Or even her Instagram messages. Perhaps she was just still in hair and makeup. Or a hyperbaric chamber. Or whatever it was that the rich did to prepare for a major event.

When Venus finally did show up, she was munching on the tin of gummies that Reba had been offering around earlier. She did look fabulous – she wore a macramé gown that bridged the gap between Greek goddess and hippie idol, and her hair spilled in gentle waves so far down her back that it almost touched the ground. (Nature had received some assistance from a hair stylist.

Or at the very least a special prenatal vitamin for the very rich that offered miraculous hair growth properties.)

But she also looked ashen and peaked – more like someone who might be graveside at one of Mort's funerals than a bride about to join her partner in a lifetime of love.

'Low iron,' Venus explained airily, when Lily asked if she was okay. 'It's the low-everything diet I'm on. The wan look is terrible in person, but photographs well. Which is vital, because I did hire a few paparazzi to take pictures on the down-low.'

She must have caught Lily's surprised look, because she added, 'Don't worry – you'll never pick them out from the other guests. They do this sort of thing all the time. Ooh, the revellers are starting to arrive.'

Sleek tour buses in hippie livery were pulling onto the property, interspersed by Bentleys and very low sports cars nervously chugging over the divots in the field that had been designated for parking. The sky was dotted with helicopters waiting for the chance to land, their blades churning the sky.

'That's Desmond,' said Venus, pointing out one of the helicopters with a tone that rather suggested she wanted it to crash. Hoping the gummies went to work sooner rather than later, Lily scooted the bride off to her dressing room tent, which was magnificently decked out with a huge antique dresser, hanging mirrors that shimmered on golden chains, and elaborate clusters of fat candles and Moroccan lanterns. She let the tent flap fall – a nervous bride deserved her privacy.

Meanwhile, the guests had begun trickling onto the grounds, dressed in dramatic, designer bohemian style, as if they'd all been diverted from Coachella with promises of better drugs and cooler weather. Air kisses and air hugs flitted about, as did gossipy murmurings about affairs and second homes and bankruptcies and patents.

Back from putting up their tent, the Grief Guys helped direct the guests to the eclectic ensemble of beanbags, couches and Adirondack chairs. Lily, meanwhile, gathered the folk musicians who'd been lounging around in one of the tents, ushering them to the thatched riser near the altar. Ah, and there was the groom, who was changing from his work attire into a pair of tan trousers (with braces) and a smart grey sports jacket. And a pair of Allbirds, of course. It was an impressive costume change given that he managed the whole thing while dictating a cease-and-desist letter over the phone.

Now there was just the matter of the celebrant. Where was she?

Lily checked her emails, her texts, her social media messages, but to no avail.

'Can I help?' asked Mort, who'd returned from Premetheus with a bamboo container of something liquidy in hand.

'The celebrant is AWOL, and there are only so many Lord Huron knockoff songs you can play before people get restless,' whispered Lily.

'Can you get her on the walkie-talkie?' asked Mort.

'No luck.' With Mort in tow, Lily wandered the fields, looking for signs of the colourfully named – and clad – celebrant. Rainbow Soleil (the moniker of someone who was almost certainly on the lam from decisions made in a past life) was nowhere to be seen. But hang on, there was a whole lot of giggling coming from Reba's Kombi. And smoke as well.

Biting back a grin, Lily knocked on the door, then yanked it open.

The cloud that poured out was enough to set off every smoke alarm within a five-mile radius.

'We were doing a cleansing ceremony,' explained Reba, whose eyes were tellingly red.

Rainbow Soleil, who was dressed precisely as her name suggested, coughed. 'We ran out of sage,' she rasped.

'I think you've got it handled,' said Mort drily.

'The guests are seated,' explained Lily, handing Rainbow an earpiece. 'Are you ready?'

'To join two like-minded souls in matrimony? The goddess that runs through me says yes indeed.'

They hurried over to the ceremony area, Rainbow Soleil taking her place by the altar. Lily hurried in to fetch Venus, who was swigging from a bottle of organic, sugar-free sparkling wine. Spotting Lily, Venus dabbed self-consciously at the front of her dress, where a good deal of said bottle now made its home. At least she wasn't drinking rosé.

'Ready?' said Lily, donning her biggest, brightest smile.

'As I'll ever be,' said Venus, with the excitement of someone preparing to clean cat vomit out of the carpet.

Lily held her smile, hoping the vaguely excited Venus of the early wedding planning meetings would return. Because if not, well, perhaps Mort should take over the formalities.

The folk band (who had some membership crossover from the cowboy wedding) struck up a jaunty tune, and the guests *ooh*ed lightly as Venus, shoulders back and a bouquet of California poppies in hand, walked quietly down an aisle thatched with pink pampas grass fronds and woven grass mats.

Buoyed by the background notes of the band, Venus took her place before the dramatic floral altar, smiling nervously at Desmond, whose phone was ringing in his pocket.

'Just a sec,' he muttered, glancing down at his phone.

This was going well. Distraction. Lily needed a distraction.

They'd start with the doves.

Lily signalled for the dovecote owner (known locally as the Bird Man) to release the doves from their tie-dye-draped enclosure. Giving her a thumbs up, the Bird Man pulled back the latch and urged the cooing birds to their freedom. Only they weren't cooing birds of the sweet and gentle turtledove variety. They were huge and black, and their caws struck up murmurs of confusion among the crowd.

'Portentous,' muttered Mort.

'Rainbow and I have a bet going on this whole thing,' whispered Reba.

Mort was intrigued. 'Isn't that a conflict of interest?'

'You two,' warned Lily.

As the crows flapped and cawed overhead, Gracie stepped forward with her camera, snapping a series of shots of Venus cowering beneath raised hands. Desmond, finger held up in the international symbol for *hang on, with you in a sec*, was on his phone typing an urgent email. Or at least he was until a crow tried to dive-bomb his lifted finger, thinking it was a workaholic worm.

A smattering of confused applause broke out.

'It's . . . good luck,' called Lily. Of *course* the switcheroo had to strike now, when she was finally having some success taking Venus's attention away from her frigidly cold feet. 'Two crows is good luck. They symbolise transformation and . . . fate.'

'But there are six,' said Reba matter-of-factly. 'Six symbolises death.'

Lily shot Reba a look. 'It's a regional interpretation,' she called. 'It doesn't have to mean death.'

Reba flapped a hand smothered in chunky rings. 'Whatever helps you sleep at night.'

'Just go on with the vows,' whispered Lily into her walkie-talkie.

'Roger,' said Rainbow Soleil, a hand over her earpiece. 'Over.' She spun a circle, her kaleidoscopic robes flaring. The sequinned peace symbols on her scarf flashed, and Lily crossed her fingers that they wouldn't attract the crows.

'Oops, too far,' said the celebrant, putting a hand on the massive wildflower arch for balance. 'Dizzy. Let me unwind for a second. All right, got it.'

'This is the best you could get on a multimillion-dollar budget?' whispered Mort.

'The first four cancelled,' whispered back Lily. 'I had to get this one from Celebrant City. She doesn't believe in currency, so I had to pay her in Phish tickets. And Ben & Jerry's Phish Food ice-cream. She also doesn't believe in the restrictions of temporality, so we're lucky she's here on the right day. And mostly the right time.'

Mort chuckled. 'I don't know how you do it.'

'With flair,' said Lily, with a wink.

'No arguments here,' said Mort appreciatively.

Lily beamed. 'Rightly so.'

'Wonderful souls!' shouted Rainbow Soleil.

'Eh?' shouted an old guy dressed like the Monopoly Man. (Given the blood-diamond-studded guest list, it might have in fact been the Monopoly Man.)

'She also doesn't believe in microphones,' added Lily. 'It's a wonder I got her to wear the earpiece.'

'We are here today to bring together these two entities of solidified stardust into one unbreakable union,' bellowed Rainbow Soleil, her voice cracking.

'Bah, unions!' huffed Monopoly Man.

'Now, each of you have in your lap a vessel of fine silt sourced from two asteroids that passed each other in space. When the couple speaks their vows, I want you to combine jars, forging the space dust into one single meteor. Because this is a love that burns bright.'

'Oh shit,' said Lily. 'Rainbow,' she said over the walkie-talkie, 'we scrubbed the asteroids idea. We're doing toothpastes instead. One blue and white bright stripe on a single toothpaste brush.'

Mort snorted.

'Last-minute decision from marketing,' explained Lily.

Rainbow Soleil communicated this to the crowd, who awkwardly dug about for the bespoke toothpaste tubes under their chairs and squeezed as directed.

'Minty fresh,' observed Reba.

Once everyone was awkwardly holding a toothbrush, Lily gave Rainbow Soleil the thumbs up to proceed with the ceremony. 'Now, the couple have written their own vows. Desmond, would you like to share your love for Venus with your favourite people in the world?'

Desmond, who'd been talking into a pair of smart glasses that he'd pulled out from an inner jacket pocket, looked up, startled. 'Rich, can you hold? I'm at an all-hands meeting.' He pressed a button on the glasses frame, then blinked as his vision adjusted. 'Thanks, all, for coming out today. I know we're all busy, so I won't keep you long.'

Lily grimaced. Were these wedding vows, or a speech for a quarterly investor meeting?

'When I met Venus, I knew she represented some epic ROI. Our families have been competitors. Allies. Co-sponsors of some great legislation. And together we're going to keep up that growth. Here's to a dental hygiene empire.' He clasped his hands over his head like he'd just kicked the winning goal in a soccer match. Or like he was the owner of the team who'd kicked said goal.

The crowd clapped politely. Gracie circled with her camera, doing her best to find a modicum of love and romance in this decidedly business-like affair. Lily cast her gaze to the sky and tried to place a wish upon each of the fluffy clouds that resided there. She'd worked so hard to make this event perfect. And it *was*. Everything about it: the rainbow beanbags. The huge field. The floral arch and cleverly decorated trees. The folk band composed entirely of nepo babies. The tie-dyed tents that made for a hippie hobbit experience. The asteroid she'd had ground down by the Smithsonian that now sat uselessly in baggies under the chairs and which hopefully nobody would take it upon themselves to snort.

Everything except the romance between Desmond and Venus.

'If you have any questions or comments, my girl Kiki in marketing will sort you out,' said Desmond, miming shooting a basketball from the three-point line. 'Shout-out to Kiki.'

A young woman in a chiffon romper sitting primly in a beanbag as she typed away on three different iPads held up a hand. 'My "out of office" is on,' she said. 'But not really.'

'Wow,' said Mort, whose eyebrows said it all. 'Was *"for immediate release"* written at the top of that speech?'

'I think he was reading it off his smart glasses,' whispered Lily. 'My guess is that Kiki was writing it as he was reading it.'

'Outsourcing your wedding vows. Very efficient.'

'Shh, Venus is up.' Lily glanced around, meeting Reba and Gracie's eyes, as though by triangulating their gazes they could somehow prevent this whole thing from falling apart into a disaster to be gleefully covered by the tabloids and TikTok reaction videos.

Venus, a vision in her hand-stitched gown, flashed a nervous, slightly tipsy grin at the crowd. The pearls sewn into her hair glowed gently in the light of the golden hour. 'Hi, everyone. Babe, can you turn off your meeting?'

Desmond tapped his smart glasses again. 'Sorry. All yours.'

'There you are.' Venus laughed, slightly giddily, and Lily wondered if she'd sourced some additional chemical help from the medicine cabinet in the dressing room tent. 'Wow. How does a girl follow that. I . . . um, love you. Ever since that first day we met in the lobby, and we got our helicopters mixed up. I knew it was meant to be. And, um . . .'

Venus stood there, the most stunning bride that Lily had ever seen, and yet the most conflicted. Beneath all of it – the wealth, the decor, the glamour – was a gap that not even a bottomless bank account could bridge. Venus took a deep breath, then wiped her mouth with the back of her hand. Her unsmudgeable lipstick smudged away, and she stared down at it, frowning.

Lily's heart squeezed as she considered all the futures that must be running through Venus's mind. All of it with the wrong person. A person who didn't even care. A person who wouldn't wear a silly bolo tie for you or help you paint flower murals on your shop or humour your requests to bang out the solo from Supertramp's 'School' on their personalised pianola.

Lily's walkie-talkie crackled.

'What do I say?' muttered Rainbow Soleil, who was swaying in front of the flower arch like a piece of half-time hippie entertainment.

'Nothing,' said Lily. 'But we'll have the band on standby. Just in case.'

'Roger that.' Rainbow Soleil continued swaying.

'And um . . .' repeated Venus, but with a newly revelatory tone, as though she'd just returned from a quick trip to another planet. 'No. No. I . . . can't do this,' she said, taking half a dozen steps back in her custom-made wooden flip-flops. 'I don't. I can't. I'm sorry. I don't want to be the blue stripe in a blue and white toothpaste tube. I want to be the meteor. I want to be me.'

'Called it,' whispered Reba.

Lily barely managed to keep from shouting out, '*Go Venus!*'

But she had to remain an impartial professionalism. Or at

least seem that way. All right, so it wasn't the best look that Lily's marquee wedding had stalled at the *I do* part of the ceremony, but she'd rather have a runaway bride on her books than a disastrous divorce. Her whole goal was to bring happy couples together in celebration, after all – not force them to go through with a major life decision just because the vendor deposits weren't refundable.

But what now? There were hundreds of guests sitting about, most of them with a vested financial interest in this whole affair. And there were only so many helicopters to go round.

Lily's heart was pounding. She could salvage this. It was all about the guest experience, after all. She just had to act fast.

'Babe, no,' Desmond was saying, not particularly emphatically for someone whose bride had just turned him down at the altar. Probably because he was splitting his attention between this and a Discord chat group.

Drawing herself up to her full height and setting her jaw, Venus hurled her bouquet of California poppies at his head. Desmond ducked. The bouquet hurtled on, arcing exactingly towards one of the bridesmaids. The bridesmaid, ordinarily part of a class that was exceptional at catching wedding bouquets, flinched and stepped aside.

'What? I don't want the jilted juju to rub off on me,' whispered the bridesmaid to her brethren. She whipped out a bottle of hand sanitiser and scrubbed her hands clean. Then she followed this up with a bottle of moon-charged water.

'Venus! Think of the market cap!' shouted Venus's mother (whom Lily recognised from the financial pages of the newspaper), fiddling with her phone. 'Ugh! How am I meant to see the stock ticker when there's no 5G?'

Lily had moments before chaos erupted. First she had to check on Venus, and then she'd sort out the crowd.

She grabbed Mort's arm. Of all the people here, she knew he

wouldn't let her down. 'Mort, can you tell the band to play? I'll be back in a minute.'

Mort nodded, his dark eyes a gentle port of solidarity amidst the madness that Lily knew was about to ensue.

For the second time in as many weeks, Lily hurried after Venus, who'd fled with the dedication of a horror movie final girl sprinting away from a serial killer sporting a chainsaw. Lily found her seated on the drooping bough of an elegantly decorated eucalyptus tree draped with string lights and sprigs of tiny tie-dyed flowers. She looked like a forest fairy who'd emerged from the woods, curious about human traditions. A forest fairy whose eye makeup wasn't as waterproof as its manufacturer liked to claim.

'I'm sorry,' Venus said, dabbing her eyes with the handkerchief Lily gave her. (She'd taken it from Mort's breast pocket.) 'The thought of going through with that was just . . .'

Lily sat down beside her and let Venus lean her head on her shoulder. 'I get it.'

'I know it doesn't have to be forever. I know divorce is a thing. I know that people in unhappy marriages go overboard on yachts all the time.'

'Um,' said Lily.

'But I don't want that to be my life. I don't want to be dragged along by inertia, saying yes to something just because I feel like I should, and then spending who knows how many years trying to find the right time to stop it.' Venus sighed. 'Is he still on a conference call?'

Lily crushed a eucalyptus leaf between her fingers, enjoying its aromatic scent. 'It's hard to tell with the smart glasses, but I think so.'

She pulled out her walkie-talkie. 'Come in, Rainbow Soleil. Is the conference call ongoing? Over.'

'Roger that. Conference call is underway. We've added a projector screen for a Zoom.'

'That was meant to be for the movie under the stars,' moaned Venus, running her hands through her hair and plucking out the pearl pins one by one. In a move that had Lily setting a mental reminder to come back for a recon trip tomorrow, she tossed them to the ground, grunting with rage as each one bounced off the wildflowers and greenery.

'It's not that he doesn't care,' she added. '*I* don't care. If only my parents had let me date that Italian toilet paper magnate ... but *no*, I had to keep my dating prospects within the same vertical.'

Lily chuckled. 'That is one problem we mortals will never share.'

'True. You and that funeral guy – you've got the matrimony to grave pipeline all tied up. Diversification, as my mom would say.'

'She would, wouldn't she,' said Lily, trying not to laugh.

'Yeah, we are not alike.' Venus sighed again, staring down at the makeup-smeared handkerchief. 'I really did have fun planning the wedding, though. It was nice to have something to focus on other than the family business. And I loved what you did with the plates.'

'That was all Mort,' admitted Lily.

'And the food. Spectacular – so unique.'

Lily bit back a grin. 'Also Mort, although that one's a long story.'

'Jefferson should come visit me in Santa Monica. We could collab – he'd be drowning in James Beard Awards.'

'I'll let him know.' Lily ran the toe of her shoe back and forth across the wildflower carpet. 'How do you want to handle the rest of tonight?'

Venus groaned. 'I can't show my face back out there. There'll be talks of a toothpaste boycott. I can just see it. I'll be a viral joke. Like that dead-to-me girl. I have to leave before anyone spots me.'

Lily passed Venus her keys. 'I'm going to stay here overnight, so you can stay at my place, above the wedding shop. It's not fancy, but it's private. Except for the grille downstairs – don't spill any trade secrets if you're near it.'

'Noted.'

'Do you need someone to drive you?' asked Lily.

Venus shook her head and pointed to one of the fixed-gear bikes stacked in a makeshift bike rack (just in case the guests wanted to explore the grounds). 'I'll ride. The fresh air will do me good.'

'Just make sure you wear a helmet, or Mort will be on my case.'

Venus wrapped Lily in a hug. 'Deal. Thank you so much for not judging. For not making me go through with it.'

'Of course,' said Lily, who absolutely meant it. 'I just want people to be happy.'

Venus flexed her left hand, watching the diamond mine on her left finger sparkle. With a sigh, she pulled off the ring and handled it to Lily.

'Here. Can you pawn that for me and send me the proceeds?'

Then, donning a vintage helmet decorated with flower buds, Venus rode wobblingly off into the dusk.

Eat, Drink and Be Unmarried

Mort

The night had risen proudly, shaking the stars and the giant moon out into an inky blanket that twinkled and shone. Although perhaps that was Mort's organic sparkling wine talking. And whatever had been in those cookies he'd accepted from Venus's grandma.

As the night stretched on, the energy of the party roared, then ebbed. The wedding goers broke off into groups – raucous *woo* girls flailing wildly in front of the valiant folk group; older people toasting snacks and making bets on whose marshmallows would catch fire; younger folks in the larger tents playing board games and snapping selfies; a PR team shouting about how best to handle the reputational disaster that was trending on social media. Gracie roved around with her camera, quietly snapping shots of the lamplit decor and the couples snuggled up on the love seats and beanbags – and definitely a few of the shouting marketers.

'I have some stellar photos of your Grief Guys,' Gracie told Mort as she came back around, sinking into one of the ring of beanbags that Mort and Reba had claimed. And Sausage, who was sleepy from treats and belly rubs.

'They did a great job,' said Mort, with a touch of pride.

'What a day,' said Lily, plonking down on a beanbag and wriggling her toes in her convertible shoes (which had been in flats mode since they'd arrived). She'd spent the whole evening running about consoling distraught family members with alcohol and cake and trying to identify hidden paparazzi like she was playing a game of Among Us.

She yawned hugely, as though sleep were chasing her down.

'You know what,' she said, covering her mouth, 'I'm calling it before I fall asleep here and Gracie snaps an artsy shot of me snoring that ends up at MoMa.'

'I would never,' said Gracie, idly. Her grey eyes crinkled at the corners. 'Mostly because I have an exclusivity agreement with LACMA.'

Lily chuckled, then stifled another yawn. 'All right, off I go. Night, Gracie, Reebs.' A pause. Then, meaningfully. 'Night, Mort.'

Mort froze. What had she meant by that? Why the pause? Why the separate address? Had there been invitation in her voice? Or something else? Could she possibly have forgiven him for the other night?

But by the time he'd parsed the sentence, Lily had disappeared into her tent.

'Ah, you win some, you lose some,' said Reba, swigging her Irish coffee, which she'd brought along in a thermos and had been topping off throughout the night. Alas, Premetheus wasn't equipped to do hot drinks, and The Hot Pot cart on site had been instructed only to do decaffeinated nootropic mushroom brews.

Mort wasn't sure how to respond to this.

'Better to do it now than after all the paperwork,' Reba went on.

Oh. She'd been referring to the wedding, not Lily.

'Although I do feel bad for all the time the lawyers spent on the SEC filings. Only a bit, though. Lawyers – fuck 'em! Still, could be worse. At least he didn't die.'

This was true, thought Mort, poking at a gelatinous something that had presumably made its debut as dish of the day at Whispering Waters earlier this week.

'That's what happened at my wedding,' explained Reba, tapping the ornament that hung from her neck. 'The second time around. The second time, to the same guy. The timeline's confusing, but the love wasn't.'

'Sorry for your loss,' said Mort. He mulled it over, wondering how anyone could truly commit to love when death was only ever a knock away. 'Would you do it again?'

Reba stared down at him through her cat's-eye glasses. 'Course not, he's scattered all over the Golden Gate Park. It'd be a logistical nightmare.'

Mort laughed heartily.

Reba did as well – she had no issue laughing at her own jokes. And fair enough, she was funny as hell. 'I'd marry my Frank a million times over, even if he died every single time. He was my person. My crossword finisher, my complaints hearer, my grilled cheese maker. Great taste in music, terrible taste in footwear, but you can't have it all. The worse prospect would've been not giving it a shot. I would've missed out on the love of my life, and all because of what? Fear? Ego? Pettiness about shoes? Bah. Although they were bad. He wore the same pair of Birkenstocks for thirty years. Said Jerry Garcia had blessed them. Although that I believe.'

'Me too,' added Gracie.

'So you know what I think?' Reba angled her head towards Lily's tent. 'I think you should go be with your girl. Repeat after me: fuck it.'

'Fuck it,' said Mort quietly.

'Fuck it!' cried Reba, waving her hands over her head.

'Fuck it,' repeated Mort, more animatedly this time.

'Fuck it all, we're all gonna fucking die anyway!' howled Reba, adding a few coyote howls for emphasis. The wedding guests picked up on her vocalisation, and soon the whole campsite was awash with fiendish howls and calls.

Gracie Nivola, ever the anthropologist, captured it all with her camera.

They *were* all going to fucking die anyway. Maybe it was Reba's motivational words, or maybe it was the open bar talking, but something had shifted inside Mort. He gave Reba a peck on the cheek and quietly went over to Lily's tent.

'Knock, knock,' he said, tapping a finger against the tie-dyed fabric.

A few moments of scrabbling, and then Lily pulled aside the tent flap. Her eyes widened. 'What are you doing here? Shouldn't you be running from coyotes or something? They're out tonight.'

'Can I come in?'

Lily crawled aside, ushering Mort in. He stooped to avoid hitting his head against the tent ceiling, which although generously pitched, still wasn't designed for his height. Only the bridal parties' tents were – although probably unnecessarily, given that half the wedding party was sitting around murmuring about what this meant for the future of two significant toothpaste empires, and the other half was on a conference call with their C-suites.

'What a night,' whispered Lily, who in the soft light of the tent's Moroccan lamp looked as beautiful as Mort had ever seen her – even clad in the pair of novelty tie-dye pyjamas that was part of each tent's care package. 'Is it bad if I'm glad she didn't go through with it?'

Mort shook his head. 'Better now than later. Is she okay?'

Lily sprawled over a tie-dyed multi-piece floor-couch – the same as the one that Mort had helped the Grief Guys install in their own tent earlier that day. 'She's spending the night at my place. Don't worry – she'll take the first helicopter out tomorrow. But it makes you think, doesn't it.'

'How so?' asked Mort, who to be fair, *did* have some thoughts about the travel habits of billionaires.

'Well, they're sort of the opposite of us. On paper, their union was perfect. The same businesses, the same backgrounds, the same goals. All carefully orchestrated for seamless . . . synergy.'

'I see that Harvard MBA of yours is being put to good use.'

'I only went for the sweatshirt. But look at them, and look at us. We're messy, and unplanned, and our opinions on good design couldn't be any more divergent. And yet.'

'And yet,' agreed Mort, who had never known that such a simple phrase could carry every possibility in the world.

'And yet . . .' Lily fixed her bright blue gaze on him '. . . why are you all the way over there?'

Mort's heart was thrumming, and he briefly worried about the likelihood of a heart attack. But then: fuck it, if a heart attack was how he went out, then it would all be worth it.

He rustled over to her, moving awkwardly in the confines of the tent.

Lily giggled. 'You're like a weird Gothic caterpillar.'

'*That's* how you're going to seduce me?'

'I'm not wearing my contacts,' added Lily, squinting intently. 'You're going to need to come closer.'

Mort did: close enough to see that the top button of her tie-dyed pyjamas was unbuttoned. He was pleased to see that although Reba had committed to tie-dyed everything, she was less exacting about button integrity. 'How's that?'

'Closer,' said Lily, crooking a finger. 'My vision is terrible.'

Mort inched forward, mentally counting the buttons on her pyjamas.

'Oh God, not that close,' shrieked Lily. She burst out laughing at his startled expression. 'I'm sorry, I couldn't resist. But I do like having you this close.'

Mort couldn't help himself. He leaned forward and kissed her, seeking out her soft lips with his, melting at the sweet taste of her lipstick, yearning for the taste of the rest of her. As all first kisses – well, second kisses – are, it was a maddening mix of exploration and compromise, pulling back just slightly to avoid bumping teeth even though he wanted nothing more than to wrap his fingers into the hair at the nape of her neck and pull her close – as close as possible.

Lily took the lead for him, dragging a hand hungrily up his cheek and twisting it into his hair. Her eyes were wide as she pulled him down with her to the amply cushioned floor of the tent.

'Wow, this is too many cushions,' said Mort, as he fought not to drown in the stack of throw pillows and novelty cushions. 'It's worse than the couch in your apartment.'

'You'll thank me when you don't get stabbed in the butt with a stick.'

'Kinky,' said Mort, balanced precariously upon a cushioned yoga mat and a Moroccan ottoman.

'You don't know the half of it,' said Lily. Her breath was hot on his neck as she grazed her lips along his throat and jawline, and Mort thought of the card he'd pulled from *Dirty Laundry* – the one he'd been too embarrassed to share during his first meeting with the Grief Guys.

'You look sexy in tie-dye,' Mort whispered, his fingers tracing the loose outline of the pyjamas, which did an exhilaratingly poor job of shielding Lily from his hungry gaze. His thumb slipped beneath the tie-dyed hems and over the soft skin masking her collarbone, the warm and inviting curve of her shoulder. 'Almost as sexy as you do in fluffy slippers.'

'I love that you love my slippers,' said Lily, unbuttoning the remaining holdouts on her pyjama top, giving Mort a teasing glimpse of bare skin shadowed by the too-soft light of the stippled Moroccan lamp. 'Because I have an entire basket of them. We'll put them on rotation, and you can drag a different pair off me each time.'

Mort chuckled, amused, and also honoured that Lily was thinking ahead, was thinking of a future with *him*, with *him* of all people.

'I can think of nothing I want more than being part of your slipper rotation,' he said, sliding a hand lower, where the solidity of her collarbone gave way to the gentle curve of her breasts, the stiff nub of her nipple. As his thumb grazed it, Lily moaned softly, biting at her lower lip.

He let his hand slide over her body, marvelling at the warmth and softness of it – the dips of muscle, the gentle curves, the endless undulations he could explore forever.

'You know I'm not a patient woman, right?' asked Lily, squirming as his fingers wandered over her hips, then down to the warmth between her legs.

'You know what they say about patience.'

'It's hyped up beyond belief?'

Lily's hand found his, and she guided him to the warmth between her legs, her fingertips soft on his knuckles as she enticed his fingers to part her, to explore the slick heat of her, to attend to the hooded part of her that made her moan.

Over in the next tent, a couple giggled, and Lily clapped a hand over her mouth.

'Oh my God,' she whispered. 'Am I that loud?'

'I'm pretty sure someone now has very solid proof that Bigfoot exists, and he has a very distinctive mating call.'

Lily smacked him on the arm. 'Stop being funny during sex. I find it very alluring, and I don't want to give the Bigfoot people more fodder.'

'It's the flat-earthers I'm worried about,' said Mort. 'What if I push you over the edge?'

'Challenge accepted,' said Lily, eyes sparkling. 'Two edges, though.'

Mort bit his lip. Oh, but she was witty. And gorgeous. And wonderful in every way. He desperately wanted her. In fact, he had for *so long*. But he couldn't deny himself anymore. Couldn't deny that every moment he was close to her was a moment he'd replay for the rest of his life.

Mort hesitated. First, the administrative stuff. Then the fun.

'Do you have . . . um.' He pantomimed a condom.

'A balloon animal?' Lily grinned wickedly. Increasingly wickedly as Mort grew increasingly red. 'Mort, you know I never disappoint. I am an incomparable planner.' In an exceptionally mermaid-like move – and an impressive demonstration of abdominal strength – she stretched to the right, returning with a lidded basket that she plunked in her bare lap.

'Debauchery basket,' she explained, opening it to reveal an assortment of goodies more fit for Burning Man than a wedding: airport bottles of alcohol, nitrous balloons, protein bars, questionable-looking organic matter – and of course several packets of condoms. 'May I do the honours?'

The time it took for her to tear open the packet was some of the most brutal anticipation in Mort's entire life. Her blue eyes staring into his, she unrolled the condom, her fingers gently working down his length, one hand cupping him from below. Cruelty. Sheer, exhilarating cruelty.

Mort pressed a hand gently to her shoulder, pushing her back into the maelstrom of pillows. Damn, she was dazzling in this light, surrounded by this ridiculous bright decor that looked somehow like an aura extending from her. Mort ordinarily didn't believe in anything of the sort, but when it came to Lily, he believed in anything. In everything.

Arms flexing beneath his own weight – it turned out there was a benefit to all those push-ups beyond the additional life expectancy – he kissed her hipbones, so soft and inviting, then followed the light lines of the muscles in her belly upwards, to the slope of her ribs, to the soft mounds of her breasts. She quivered beneath him, biting back a giggle.

'That tickles,' she whispered, trying not to alert the Bigfoot hunters next door.

'I'll bear that in mind,' he said, his lips grazing her nipples. She squirmed, knitting her hands around the back of his neck and holding him there as he licked, sucked, his hand cupping the curve of her breast.

'It doesn't tickle anymore,' she breathed, eyes clenched shut as she gave in to him.

Then, momentarily, the tension from her fingers increased; she was drawing him upwards, so that their eyes met and their hips were aligned. Mort reached a hand down, parting her legs, parting her lips, and revelling in her wetness.

Lily swore, cursing his name in invitation.

'May I?' he asked, wanting more than anything to hear that affirmation.

'You'd fucking better,' she whispered, her eyes hooded now, their lids lowered in anticipation.

He entered her gently at first, waiting for her to accept him, which she did, warmly, hungrily, her legs rising up to lock around his hips. He couldn't help himself: he let out a groan that would certainly grab the attention of the Bigfoot fans.

'Fuck, you feel good,' Lily whispered, her fingers twining around his wrists. 'I've been thinking about how you'd feel for so long.'

Mort was too aroused to be surprised. He'd known it, on some level, as much as he'd tried to deny it. 'How long?'

'Since you came to me bearing my business cards, like a dark prince of nerdiness.'

Mort tried not to laugh. 'I'm glad I do it for you.'

'Goddamn do you do it for me.' Lily's heels were tight against his back; her gaze was locked on his. 'There. Like that.'

She reached down to touch herself, her eyes widening as she found her own rhythm – one that she moved to until her tightly wound desire unravelled.

'Holy fuck,' she whispered, over and over, so breathless that she seemed to be hyperventilating. Her fingers dug hard into his arms, then his shoulders, leaving shallow crescents from the pressure. Mort had only the one tattoo – a tiny Milton quote – but if he were to get another, he knew exactly what it would be: the outline of her frenzied nails against his skin.

The gentle waves of her orgasm against him pulled him towards his, and moments later he joined her, tumbling over the edge of pleasure into something bright and perfect and then peaceful. He collapsed against her, positioning himself slightly to her left so that he could bury his face in her neck, stroke the sweaty perfection of her hair.

Mort sighed contentedly, then rolled over slightly so that he could regard her. The soft light of the Moroccan lamp painted her almost as beautifully as his mind's eye did, and he wanted nothing more than to shout to the night sky that she was the

302

most stunning creature to have ever graced the world, and that she was *his* – well, not his, because he'd never presume something like that, but she was here, in this moment, with him, as opposed to with anyone else on earth.

Lily cuddled into the curve of his bicep, squirming so that she had adequate neck support from the cushioned floor. 'You mock the cushions, but I couldn't do this on a regular bed without getting a crick in my neck.'

'Next time we'll have sex in a foam pit,' promised Mort, tucking a wayward curl behind her ear. In fact, all of her curls were wayward right now, but he wasn't about to let her know that. He like dishevelled Lily; it reminded him of the Lily from the day of the switcheroo, when they'd both hid out beneath her awning, drenched from the magical rain that had brought their businesses – and them – together.

'Next time, huh?' Lily considered this. 'Well, I do have a circus wedding coming up. Just so long as you disinfect it first. Those things are vectors for norovirus.'

'Of course. As much as I love having sex with you, even a moderate norovirus risk is unacceptable.'

Lily chuckled. 'Fair.'

'In fact, I'd choose celibacy over a moderate cold.'

She bit his bicep lightly. 'Oh, shut up.'

Mort did.

After a moment, Lily propped herself up on one elbow. 'This is *something*, right? Us. All of this.'

It's everything, Mort wanted to say. *It's everything, and that terrifies me more than you could imagine.*

But he could feel the words sticking in his throat. All he managed was a nod.

'I think,' he managed finally, 'that the switcheroo knew what it was doing when it brought us together.'

'Hmm,' said Lily thoughtfully. 'I like that.'

She lay back down. Between the night-time wind rustling around the tent, the distant twanging of the folk band still intrepidly earning their overtime, and Lily's calm, measured breathing, he felt himself drifting off to sleep.

But it was not to be.

'Mort, are you in there?'

A blue-rinsed head adorned with a familiar pair of cat's-eye glasses and painfully dangly earrings poked through the tent door. At least Reba had the good form to pretend to cover her eyes.

'We've got a body,' came Reba's sing-song voice. 'I know, it's like my wedding night all over again. But with less weed.'

Mort sighed. Could the town of Mirage-by-the-Sea, which prided itself on its healthy ocean air and active lifestyle, go a single day without someone heading off into the unseen realm?

'Oh wow, speaking of bodies.' Reba gave Lily a cheerful wave. 'Told you the debauchery boxes would come in handy, didn't I? There'll be plenty of time to bump uglies later. For now, there's a corpse out there with your name on it. Not literally. I know you're not a serial killer. Although you never know. I knew this lovely Australian gent back in Brooklyn – turned out he'd been chopping up people in a coffee roaster. Anyway, it's one of the marketing team. Happens all the time with these corporate types. Too much cocaine, too much stress, a minor fist fight and bam, you've got a brain bleed. I'll wait out here, shall I?'

She did, but she didn't stop talking.

Mort threw his trousers on. He had to get moving before Reba inspired some additional violence.

Tell it to the Big Guy Up North

Lily

It was hard to top a wedding involving a runaway bride, some hot sex and a late-night death, but the Christmas in July wedding was apparently going to do its best. The off-season holly jolly festivities kicked off with a text message bearing the worst two words in the history of the English language: *Santa's sick*. Followed by two of the worst emojis in the emoji language: the green puking face and the poop.

Lily, who'd arrived back home from her glamping expedition, checked to see whether Venus was around (no, she was already sipping gimlets in the sky) then immediately got Santa on a video call.

Santa, unfortunately, very much resembled the first emoji that he'd texted, right down to the shade of green. He could've played Elphaba in *Wicked*.

Lily grimaced. Her ratio of successful to disaster weddings was skewing in the direction it absolutely shouldn't. Maybe all of her achievements to date were mere beginner's luck. Maybe Mom had been right about a small business being something that sucked the life out of you. (*'But worth it!'*)

'What do you mean, Santa's sick?' she asked, hoping the

sheen covering his face was a filter. 'What's going on? Can I have Roddy DoorDash you some Pepto?'

Santa puffed his bearded cheeks in an expression that triggered Lily's sympathetic retching response. She clapped a hand over her mouth. This was not good.

'I bought some raw oysters from the side of the road, and now I'm a full-on bubble guts. Oh God, I've gotta . . .'

Santa dropped the phone, leaving Lily cringing to a soundtrack of hasty footsteps and—

She rang off. No need to subject her ears to that. She could extrapolate without being a witness.

But now what? How was she going to pull off a Christmas-themed wedding when the star of the show was getting up close and personal with the porcelain throne instead of the sleigh he'd promised?

Lily frowned, trying to think of the gents she knew who could pass as Santa. The Grief Guys were already on table duty, and Jorge and Roddy were both at work – Roddy had hurried by earlier with some birthday balloons, and Jorge was outside right now watering a flower basket. (Waving, she hurried out with a slice of cake for him.) Where were the potbellied, white-bearded dudes of the village when she needed them? And who would willingly suffer the indignity of dressing up in head-to-toe red velvet and donning a pom-pommed hat just because Lily asked?

Gentle piano notes sifted through the grille that separated the two Eternal Elegances.

Mort. Mort loved velvet. And she'd seen him sporting stubble a few times. Plus Lily had an excellent selection of wedding cake samples to share with him. And also, if it came to it, her body. How could he possibly say no?

'No,' said Mort immediately, taking in the Santa outfit draped over Lily's arm. 'It is far too early in our relationship to reveal that you're a furry.'

Relationship, hmm? So they were on the same page there (and also about furries, apparently). But that whole discussion would have to wait because procuring a Santa was the priority right now.

'*Please*,' begged Lily. 'It's an emergency. Santa's stuck down a white porcelain chimney and the wedding is in an hour. And I *know* your dead can wait. Pretty please with a pom-pom on top?'

She waggled the pom-pom on the Santa hat.

Mort sighed. 'You can't ask Gramps? He's more Santa age-appropriate than I am.'

'They specifically asked for a sexy Santa.'

Mort gave another sigh. This one was so deep that Lily worried he might be at risk of hypoxemia.

'I do have a pretty grisly reconstruction job I'd rather avoid if at all possible. Not the toothpaste marketer – a bear mauling thing. And I kind of want to see how the whole seating situation turned out.'

'That's going to be the absolute highlight of the day.'

A third sigh, but this one a sigh of resignation. 'All right. Santa me up.'

Lily clapped her hands together in joy. 'You're going to make a fab Santa. Just don't eat any raw oysters before the reception.'

'Noted. Let me go transform into everyone's favourite home invader.'

Mort slid the formerly black (and now pink-streaked) pocket door to his office closed so he could change. Lily sat patiently in one of the plush chairs by the front door, flipping through the Eternal Elegance (Funeral Edition) guest book that lived on a coffee table that was for some reason decorated with a map of Ibiza. Was that new?

The guest book had been partially switcherooed: it was half-bound in black leather and crafted from stern off-white paper that guests had filled with morose notes about grief, loss, life after death and the occasional sad face or commentary on the thickness of the toilet paper provided in the funeral home's bathrooms. But halfway through, the album started to take on a rainbow tinge, with fingers of pink and yellow peeking through the pages. Even the ribbon that marked the current page was imbued with a freshly vibrant tint: its black satin transitioned to pink lace hearts.

Lily smiled as she flicked through the pages in the latter half of the book. The handwriting had become less stilted and cramped, with guests writing freewheeling poems and missives and drawing little sketches in honour of their loved ones. Someone had even stuck googly eyes to a Polaroid depicting a (presumably) dead relative that they'd glued in. All right, so the switcheroo was not without its problems. Last week Pickleball Candice had locked herself in the library bathroom because she'd decided that the shelves were going to topple on her and squash her, and Derrick and Fran were on the rocks over the whole resurrection cult thing. And Lily had spoken with the local volunteer neighbourhood watch more times than seemed reasonable. (Fortunately the neighbourhood watch was mostly one old guy on a golf cart.) But it wasn't all bad. Mort was coming out of his grumpy shell, and the village's grieving populace seemed to have a healthier outlet for their grief. The Grief Guys even had a logo!

But what about after Lily's lease was up? What then? What would happen with the switcheroo? With the business? With Mort? Would they take things long distance, like Lily's friendship with Annika? Or would they take a leaf out of Reba's book and just fondly remember what had been?

The thought of that made Lily's heart ache. Because that was the basis of all grief, wasn't it: being forced to close the book on something you weren't ready to let go of.

The door to Mort's office opened, breaking into Lily's thoughts – and how! Cackling in delight, Lily dramatically clasped her hands over her heart.

'Damn, Santa's ready to sleigh.'

Mort scowled beneath the enormous white beard he'd affixed to his extremely unSanta-ish jawline, but generously struck a fetching pose in his velvety suit. His shiny Oxfords didn't quite fit the whole Santa vibe, but so long as he kept a sack of gifts at his feet, he'd be fine.

'All we need is . . .' Lily grabbed one of the throw pillows off the chair she'd been sitting on and shoved it up under his shirt, adjusting the pillow so Mort sported a chunky, squishy Santa belly.

'Oh, I could rest my head on that,' said Lily, giving the pillow a squeeze.

'Absolutely not,' said Mort, glowering.

Lily was not about to be dissuaded. 'Please can we take a photo in the photo booth? For posterity's sake?'

'Absolutely not,' repeated Mort.

'Absolutely yes,' corrected Lily, guiding him towards the back viewing room, where the photo booth sat waiting to capture Santa Mort for the viewing pleasure of generations to come. At least, that was the goal, thought Lily, as she pushed Mort inside and pulled the curtain into place.

Well, maybe not the photos with said Santa in various states of undress.

A Frosty Reception

Mort

'You've got some lipstick on your beard,' whispered Lily, as she settled Mort into position on the sleigh.

Fortunately the beard was robust enough that it hid the blush creeping over Mort's cheeks. Although that might have been an allergic reaction to the extreme amounts of glue they'd used to re-secure said beard after things had got a little carried away in the photo booth. Not that Mort minded. He was perfectly happy to reprise the events of the previous night without someone barging in screaming about a corpse. That, and he was delighted to know that Lily hadn't regretted the whole debacle – that she hadn't run off the way she'd told him that she'd always done in the past. That she still felt comfortable enough to show up on his doorstep. Even if it had been with a Santa costume in hand.

Even if their days together would, a few months from now, come to an end. It was only a matter of time before Angela pushed the applications for next year's discounted small business opportunity live.

'Presents under the tree!' called Lily, as the guests filed in wearing their Christmas best. Ugly sweaters assaulted the eye; Rudolph earrings flashed on and off in stretched earlobes, and a few grinches made finger guns at each other.

'Now, if you have any requests for the special couple, hop up on Santa's lap and let him know. He'll write them down in his special notebook for you.'

Mort waved gallantly from his sleigh – ugh, these Santa gloves were making his hands itchy – then pointed to the huge red leather-bound Naughty & Nice guestbook that Tink had prepared for the wedding.

'Ho, ho, ho!' called Mort, waving at the gathering line of guests. A buxom older woman with impressively teased hair teetered up on majestically tall heels. Mort was astonished that, given her extremely high centre of gravity, she didn't topple head-first into the stack of presents.

'Ho, ho, ho!' he cried, as she squeezed herself onto the padded bench seat of the sleigh.

'That I am. I'm Cousin Nolene, by the way,' simpered Cousin Nolene, with a lascivious wink, and then a wiggle that planted her firmly in Mort's lap, which was very much against the rules for comportment that Lily and Tink had outlined on the chalkboard in front of the sleigh. Alas, Lily was adding candy cane toppers to the cocktail pyramid, and Tink was busy placing lyric booklets on the pews. There was no one to rescue poor Mort.

Cousin Nolene flicked her hair, whacking Mort in the face with a lacquered bevy of fake curls. She smelt alarmingly of cucumbers and elderberries, as though she'd steeped herself in a fortifying gin bath for an hour or so before the wedding.

'*So*, Santa, baby.' She sang it like the carol. Well, like the carol, but slurred. 'What do I need to do to become your Mrs Claus?'

Mort swallowed. What on earth had Lily got him into?

'I, um, already have a Mrs Claus,' he said, pointing to Lily in the velvety costume that twinned his. Well, not quite twinned – it was a lot shorter and a lot more form-fitting, and didn't involve an itchy beard. But he felt a flash of pride at the fact that they were each one half of an iconic couple, that Lily wanted to be visually connected to him.

And physically.

Ahem, Mort.

As if reading his thoughts, Lily winked across the room at him, making Mort blush the colour of his velvet suit.

'How about a *mistress* Claus?' purred Cousin Nolene.

'So. What note would you like me to pop down for the happy couple?' Mort waved his snowdome pen, trying to get this awkward situation back on track.

'How about my phone number?' simpered Cousin Nolene, wiggling in Mort's lap. She trailed a fingertip over Mort's shoulder.

'Um,' said Mort. 'Santa is very careful about data privacy.'

'I understand.' Cousin Nolene gripped Mort's bicep. 'Wow, so *strong*. It must be from all the toys you build in that workshop of yours.'

'Oh, the elves are in charge of that,' said Mort. 'I mostly handle . . . logistics.'

'Logistics can be sexy,' purred Cousin Nolene, dropping her hand and giving Mort an alarming leg squeeze. An inch higher and he'd be singing like a castrato. 'So, you're saying that if I give you directions to the powder room down the hall, you'd be able to find me?'

'Um, yes. Let's give that a try.'

'I'll be waiting with your Kris Kringle,' she breathed, sliding off his lap and trip-trapping away through the reception area.

Mort exhaled in relief, then turned an alarmed gaze on the gathering crowd. Dozens of costumed people bobbed along to 'Rocking Around the Christmas Tree' as they waited for their moment with Santa: groups of kids dressed as elves; a couple dressed as sexy reindeer; someone dolled up as a menorah; an out-of-place werewolf who'd apparently got their dress codes mixed up. It was going to be a long evening.

He'd managed to smile and chuckle his way through half a dozen guests when an elderly, dramatically dressed sugarplum fairy (Mort guessed) hauled herself up the ramp towards the sled using a rickety walking frame with disco-ball-covered tennis ball feet on the bottom.

'Ho, ho, ho!' he called, reaching out a hand to help her up onto the sleigh.

'Don't touch me,' she snapped. 'A handsy Santa is the last thing I need. Haven't you heard of personal space?'

'I'm sorry,' Mort said as politely as he could. *Be like Lily. Be like Lily,* he thought. 'I'm used to working around elves. The South Pole has different personal space norms.'

'Bah. You're no Santa. Santa's jolly. You're morose.'

Is that any fucking surprise? Mort wanted to say. But Lily wouldn't do that. Lily would make a joke, or she'd offer the old biddy a mint. Or she'd use her natural charm to somehow shift this woman's mood from grump to giggly.

'So, how would you like me to sign your guest book note?' asked Mort, opening the Naughty & Nice book. Tink had done a fabulous job with it, as always: the entire thing was handbound, with tooled leather and debossing, and a little ribbon bookmark topped with a bell.

'Just Jemimah,' snapped the old woman. '*Not* Gemma. Or Genevieve. Jemimah, like the Puddle-Duck, but with an h on the end, although you're too young to know. I bet you grew up on screens. Like my third husband, and the one after him. Not husband . . . more . . . beau. Full of drama, that one. The whole family was against it from the start.'

Mort's snowdome pen skipped. This was Aunt Jemimah of

the seating chart fame. The one they'd decided to rotate from table to table every ten minutes to avoid the inevitable fist fights, or in the case of Sissy Chalmers, who had a documented history of such behaviour, someone being glassed in the face. The Grief Guys had been enlisted to distract Aunt Jemimah with hors d'oeuvres and photo opportunities and the travelling spring of 'kisstletoe' that was going around so that she'd never actually take a seat at any time during the night, and therefore couldn't raise hell.

'So, Aunt Jemimah, what wish would you like to make on behalf of the happy couple?'

But Aunt Jemimah had gone very still. She stiffened next to Mort, clutching at her heart. Then she toppled into him, the way he'd worried that Cousin Nolene might. Although, alas, Aunt Jemimah lacked any padding, making it a very bony fall.

Now what? Pretending to scribble a lengthy note in the Nighty & Nice book, Mort glanced around the room for Lily, who was helping prop up a giant blow-up snowman that had sprung a leak. The Grief Guys rushed in with tape and a bicycle pump.

'Lily,' whispered Mort, when she glanced his way. He waved his beard like a flag on a ship. 'Lily! Aunt Jemimah. She's . . . carked it.'

Lily hurried over, the flared skirt of her Mrs Claus outfit swishing. 'She's what now? But we put all that work into the logistics for tonight.'

'What do I do with her?' he whispered.

Lily handed out candy canes to a couple of kids and sent them on their way. 'I mean . . . you're the corpse guy.'

'I'm not a corpse guy! I'm a funeral director.'

'But there's quite a bit of overlap, no? Just . . . haul her out the back and put her in the hearse.'

'But we dressed up the hearse as a sleigh,' Mort reminded her. 'There are twelve papier-mâché reindeer attached to it, all of them with remote-controlled cars – courtesy of Stribley's grandson Hunter – attached to their cloven hoofs, and all of them requiring the assistance of the Grief Guys with their remote controls. So moving it is going to be a joint effort.'

'Can I just put her in the Miata? She's small. She'd fit.'

'Absolutely not,' said Mort.

Lily eyed the giant empty moving boxes she and Mort had so carefully gift-wrapped the night before.

'The fridge box,' she whispered. 'It'll hold her until we're done. Will she be okay for a few hours?'

Mort grimaced. 'How low does the AC go in here?'

Lily produced her phone and pulled up an HVAC app. 'We can get close to freezing. I mean, this *is* a Christmas-themed wedding. People are dressed for the snow. And once they get dancing they won't mind if the ambient temperature's a bit nipply.'

'A bit . . . what?'

'I'll show you later.' Lily grinned, gesturing at her bodice. She adjusted the Naughty & Nice book so that it covered Mort's trousers. 'There. Just in case it gets a bit tenty, too.'

'I'm not . . . aroused!' hissed Mort, although he was a little, having at last figured out what *nipply* meant. 'There's a dead woman sitting next to me!'

'Not for long,' said Lily. 'Here. The wedding party's about to make their entrance. That'll be perfect timing. The choir's ready, and everyone's pretty jolly on eggnog, so you should be able to jam her in there without anyone noticing. Plus you've got the ice sculptures in front of you for plausible deniability.'

'They're coming,' said Duggo, hurrying past with Sausage (who wore a fetching reindeer costume complete with antlers).

'Lyric booklets have been distributed,' whispered Tink, who was dressed in her usual polka dots, but festive. 'Is Aunt Jemimah all right? She looks almost . . . personable.'

'She's fine,' Mort reassured her. 'Just resting her eyes.'

'And, action,' called Lily into her walkie-talkie. The choirmaster gave a nod.

Sleigh bells started shaking; the soloist out front gave a spin of tinsel and string lights. Lily gave Mort the thumbs up.

The choir conductor cued everyone in on their note, then punched the air, rather alarmingly. The choir launched into a dramatic burst of harmony familiar to anyone who has watched a period film battle scene or a beer ad.

'That's not . . . "O, Holy Night",' whispered Lily, alarmed. 'This is far more ominous.'

'It's "O Fortuna" from the *Carmina Burana*,' said Mort, who personally thought it was a better choice.

The wedding-goers were looking around awkwardly, trying to figure out whether they'd all somehow shown up to the wrong event. Some flipped through the pages of the Christmas-tree-shaped carol booklets, trying to figure out where exactly in 'O, Holy Night' this dramatic interlude came from.

The choir reached fever pitch. Someone had brought in a set of timpani and was bashing the living hell out of it. Fire seemed to spurt from the candles planted in the wreaths hung about the room, and the snowy chandeliers flashed.

'Is this a switcheroo thing?' whispered Lily. 'Or did the choral director just google songs that started with O?'

Mort grimaced. 'Or worse, there's a conductor in the crowd the choral director wants to impress, and now is the perfect opportunity.'

Lily groaned. 'Of course. Dr Gardess – the bald one in the ugly sweater next to the woman dressed like a candy cane.'

Lily scribbled a note and hurried over to Dr Gardess. 'Excuse me, Dr Gardess? Could you sign this for me? It's not legally binding. Also, *wow* that is a fetching sweater. An adornment of pom-poms could be a new collective noun.'

Dr Gardess, nodding along to the choir, scribbled his signature. Then pulled out a cigarette lighter and a wax seal and sealed the note with an elaborate stamp bearing something that looked to Lily's untrained eye awfully like a masonic symbol. This could explain a lot.

Lily hurried over to the choir director, who turned to her, eyes flickering with the reflection of the candles. His temple thrummed in time with the timpani.

'Um, sorry to interrupt, but Dr Gardess wanted you to have this.'

She passed the choir director the note, who thumbed it open and read it while flinging his free hand up and down in time with the seemingly endless crescendos of the choir. The walls shook alarmingly.

'He wants to talk about a residency!' The choir director's eyes lit up (not with flames this time). 'I knew it! My dreams are coming to rest upon the balcony of wonderment!'

'Um, sure,' said Lily. 'Given that's the case, how about we return to our regular programming?'

The timpani players dropped their sticks and grabbed up some sleigh bells instead. The unmistakable notes to 'All I Want for Christmas is You' rang out, a cappella.

'Another wedding saved,' whispered Lily, as she returned to Mort's side, ready for the ceremony.

'Except for the corpse in the decorative fridge box,' he noted drolly. Still, he was impressed with Lily's problem-solving skills; nothing, no matter how ridiculous, seemed to faze her. It was hard not to be struck by a woman who could dispose of a body with a smile on her face.

The groom, in a delightfully tailored *Elf* costume with a gingerbread man boutonniere, took his place in front of the dramatic wedding arch composed of snowy baubles and guttering lanterns, the throughline of which was tied together with tinsel and string lights. A finger in his ear to confirm that he still had eardrums after the timpani drum break, he kept a close watch on the doors.

'Hit the smoke machine,' whispered Lily into her walkie-talkie. The Grief Guys started up the machine, and the floor grew white and misty with the clouding smoke. Cousin Atticus huffed heavily on his inhaler in between reminders to everyone around him that he had a severe case of mild asthma.

'Ooh, smoke. It's like being in a pub in the Eighties,' said Grandma Darla, who'd been a bingo caller back in the day and was apparently nostalgic for a nice cancer-causing ambient smell.

The tinsel-wrapped doors to the venue swung open. The choir, bless them, remained true to the requested programming, and continued to hum Mariah Carey on repeat as Christmas tradition demanded.

A murmur of approval went up as the bride made her entrance on the arm of her father. She was clad in an off-the-shoulder red velvet number with white fur trim and a fluffy white pillbox hat with string lights wrapped around it. Ornaments swung from her snowy train, clinking and gleaming as she walked.

'I found those in Then Again,' whispered Lily. 'Tink helped me sew them on.'

Mort, in spite of his inherent lack of festive joy, felt his heart swell (romantically, not dangerously). The bride looked so joyful and excited as she minced down the aisle on her stepfather's arm. Her smile was as high-wattage as the lights in her hat, and tears shimmered in her eyes around the glitter that also shimmered in her eyes.

Maybe there was something to this matrimony business after all.

'I'm going to have so much glitter to clean up,' whispered Lily. 'You'll be finding it on my corpse when you embalm me. Which is probably your thing.'

'Wow, sexy. I love it when you talk necrophiliac to me,' said Mort drily.

Lily winked. 'Death is but a small inconvenience.'

'Shut it, Santa and Santa's Little Helper,' shushed Great-Aunt Adeline, a tad judgementally for a woman whom Mort had learned had had affairs with no fewer than three of the great-uncles and was therefore destined for an evening on table 8, the table for extramarital mischief makers. (Lily and Mort had eventually decided on a sort of Dante's Inferno approach to seating arrangements, and had grouped people together according to their particular proclivity for a specific type of awfulness.)

But still, Mort and Lily shushed, Mort clapping his false beard over his mouth in a way that made Lily giggle again.

This invited a fresh round of shushing.

'We should've put her on table 12 with the suspected murderers,' whispered Lily, hiding herself behind her Christmas-tree-shaped songbook.

Mort bit back a laugh.

The bride had reached the altar now. As she reached for her soon-to-be husband's hands, the best man stepped forward with a snowdome, which he opened to reveal the rings.

'Nice touch,' said Mort approvingly. 'Almost as good as the goths with their skull.'

The starry-eyed couple stumbled through their vows, which were an odd mishmash of the traditional lines and tortured Christmas metaphors.

'Do you, Rina Morgan,' said the celebrant, who was dressed as Olaf from *Frozen*, 'take this Elf to be your husband, in naughtiness and niceness, in snow and sunshine, and agree to follow him down the chimney of life?'

'Ho-ho-ho,' whispered the bride, barely able to contain her grin.

'And do you, Emmett Smiley, take this snowy bride to be your wife, from North Pole to South, in cookies and milk, and let her be the Rudolph that guides your way?'

'Ho-ho-ho,' assented Emmett.

Mort wasn't entirely sure these vows were legally binding, but he also wasn't sure he entirely cared. Lily was right about weddings: they offered as many ways to show your love and joy as there were people in the world.

Olaf's carrot nose waggled as he said: 'I now pronounce you Elf and Snowy Wife. You may kiss Mrs Claus.'

The celebrant held up a sprig of mistletoe.

'You know what to do.'

The newlyweds embraced passionately, and Lily joined in with the chorus of whoops and cheers and *ho-ho-hos* that rose up from the crowd.

She nudged Mort with her velvet-clad elbow. 'Go on, you old grump. Don't pretend you're not feeling the love.'

Mort was indeed feeling the love. But it was directed elsewhere. Where was that roving sprig of mistletoe when he needed it?

'Ho-ho-ho,' he managed, a bit croakily.

The grin Lily shot him felt like a stun gun, and he staggered slightly.

'There you go. The mark of a man unused to expressing emotion, huh? Bowls you over the first time.'

At the altar, the newly married couple turned to the rows

packed with their friends and families. It was time to head to the sleigh-hearse and be transported off to the reception venue.

The choir broke into an a cappella version of WHAM!'s 'Last Christmas', which was, as Lily put it, 'quite the bop'.

Hand in hand, Rina and Emmett made their way back down the aisle, which was Lily's cue to . . .

'Release the confetti!' she shouted.

Reaching into the red velvet stockings draped over the backs of their seats, the guests threw handfuls of confetti over the happy couple and the bridal party that followed. But instead of the paper snowflakes and pine needles that Lily had worked so hard to manually holepunch and package, the confetti was a weird, dreary grey that clung to the wedding party's beautiful outfits like ash from a bushfire.

The bride's blonde hair was coated grey beneath her snowy pillbox cap, and the makeup that had taken a team of three big-lashed makeup artists several hours to apply had taken on a wan vibe.

She looked less like a sexy snow queen and more like one of those street performers who paint themselves grey and pretend to be a statue.

'Something's wrong,' whispered the mother of the bride, who was outfitted in a tiered green frock ornamented with bows and baubles. 'It's meant to be Christmas tinsel. Glittery stars and trees and crushed up candy canes. Not . . .'

Lily swallowed.

So did Mort. Oh no. Not now. He had an awful feeling she knew what exactly the guests had sprinkled all over the wedding party, and it wasn't festive spirit.

'Is that . . . a bone shard?' said the maid of honour, who'd just picked something white and sharp from the snowy bobble of her Santa hat. She pulled a pair of reading glasses from the pocket of her velvet dress and squinted at the shard.

It's beginning to feel a lot like . . . corpsemas.

The flower girl giggled, holding up a tooth. 'Mama, look what I got! Santa read my letter!'

Her horrified mother swept in before the flower girl could jam the tooth between the gap in her own gummy smile. 'Luna! Drop it! Drop it right now!'

She turned on Mort. 'Santa! How *could* you!'

'Ashes!' screamed Rina, spitting. She scoured at her tongue with her velvety train; ornaments flew all over, shattering on the fake-snow-covered floor. 'I've got ashes in my mouth! IN MY WEDDING HAIR!'

She flung off her pillbox cap, short-circuiting the string lights and sparking a small fire that Mort quickly doused with a few measured stomps.

Lily stepped forward. She grabbed a set of sleigh bells from one of the choir members and shook them frantically. 'It's just . . . day-old snow, everyone. Part of the festive experience. No need to worry.'

Mort was holding a bone shard. 'Quite a bit to worry about, really. Judging from this, I think the crematorium's out of order.'

'The *what?*' bellowed Great-Grandma Zinnia. 'The ice-cream parlour's out of order? What kind of Christmas party is it without ice-cream and pudding?'

Lily shoved the photographer forward. 'Quick, do something!'

The photographer waved their camera around. 'Everyone, group shot! Say . . . CONFETTI!'

Ashes, Ashes, We all Fall Down

Mort

'*Confetti*!' came the howl through the funeral parlour's mail slot.

Mort, who was standing in front of the viewing room mirror trying in vain to unglue his Santa beard, was not particularly in the mood for visitors. Trying to figure out precisely where he and Lily stood while being decked out in head-to-toe velvet and ducking the determined advances of a bevy of elderly relatives had depleted his social battery entirely. And now he had the added punishment of homework: he had Aunt Jemimah's body to deal with and a whole set of funeral preparations to handle. At least her entire family was in the area – although judging from the whole seating debacle, it would be a sparely attended funeral. Perhaps Mort could advertise grave-spitting as part of the festivities.

The person at the door was not going anywhere.

Mort stooped to open the mail flap.

'Can you come back during office hours?' he called through the flap. 'I'm . . . dealing with a particularly difficult reconstruction job.'

It wasn't precisely a lie; it was going to take a good deal of effort to return his face to its normal, Santa-beard-free state.

No dice. The door swung with nose-breaking alacrity as Mr

Pompo, whose wife's funeral Mort had quietly handled earlier that week, shouldered his way into the funeral parlour. Mort leapt back just in time to avoid a Mr Potato Head situation.

Mr Pompo had the windswept look of someone who'd embarked upon a stroll along the beach, thinking it would be a tranquil, picturesque thing like in the movies, and not a situation where the ocean breeze tried to rip your head off. The man's wig/toupee/curled-up possum had been scattered to the four winds, holding fast only due to the strength of the super-strong glue some enterprising barber had employed in his work. (Apparently the same glue had been used on Mort's Santa beard.) Mr Pompo's clothes were similarly buffeted: his tie had been tossed over his shoulder like, as the ditty went, the ears of a regimental soldier, and his shoes poured sand over the carpet with each step. Seagrass sprouted from his breast pocket.

He looked as though he'd been cast into the ocean and then spat back out again by Poseidon, who was apparently picky when it came to his meals.

But most alarming of all was the glitter.

Mr Pompo, unkempt, verklempt and all the other words ending in -empt, was delightfully dusted in bits of shimmery foil and tiny paper cut-outs. The exact same bits of shimmery foil and tiny paper cut-outs that Mort had pored over at Lily's shop on his last visit, marvelling at how confetti had evolved dramatically from the traditional rice and seeds that he remembered hurling with glee during the quiet, understated weddings of his childhood.

He braced himself for what was to come.

Mr Pompo hefted a funeral urn in one hand. Mort knew the urn well: it was the second-cheapest one the funeral home sold, and therefore the most popular. (The cheapest was a Mason jar, which performed at quite a solid clip as well, especially among the homesteading types.)

'We just scattered rainbow and unicorn confetti off the cliffs and into the ocean.'

Mort blinked. How did one respond to that? 'Sounds like a fitting send-off for a sunny, creative individual.'

Mr Pompo's thick eyebrows abruptly connected in the middle, as though someone had pulled a drawstring behind his head. 'It was *Dulce's* send-off! There was nothing sunny and creative about her! She was mean as Greenwich Mean Time. Bitter as Angostura bitters! She'd be livid at the thought of her send-off being all sunshine and rainbows.'

The Mort of a few months ago would have been inclined to agree. But Mort had spent so much time recently celebrating milestones of all types – including the wayward funerals courtesy of the switcheroo – that he wasn't now so sure that people wanted their final moments to be ones of doom and gloom.

'Are you sure?' he asked gently. 'Are you sure she'd be upset?'

'Of course! Dulce never asked for frippery and froufrou. She was a simple woman. Utilitarian. Never asked for anything.'

Mort thought about what he knew about Dulce, which wasn't much: she'd been a nurse, then a mom, then a nurse and a mom. She dressed austerely, bought cleaning supplies in bulk, wrote letters to the *Mirage Daily Mirror*, and walked the length of the promenade every day.

But she *had* always worn lipstick. Every single time Mort had crossed paths with her, her lips had been freshly tinted pink.

Perhaps Mr Pompo was wrong about Dulce. Perhaps she'd wanted it all but just kept it inside, like Lily had a habit of doing. Mort thought of all the times that he'd caught her staring off at the *We're Getting Hitched!* neon sign on her wall. Of all the times he'd asked her how she was doing, and there'd been a tinge of sadness behind the 'great!' she always responded with. Of the way she threw herself into making other people happy, while eating a dinner of mac 'n' cheese, or skipping showings at Rerunning Up That Hill so that she could work on seating plans instead. Everything she did was for someone else. In fact, the only time she ever asked Mort for anything was when it would benefit another. Like how she'd explicitly invited him to Tink's birthday – which she'd spent all of her spare, non-wedding time planning.

Maybe Lily needed someone to throw confetti on her behalf. To remind her that *she* was the sunshine in their lives. That she was worth celebrating as well.

But first, he had to head to the urn room to check that each vessel held the remains of a beloved family member, and not an explosion of tinfoil and glitter.

Mort sighed as he wrote Mr Pompo a refund and promised to give him a call if he happened across Dulce's wayward ashes.

Gramps hadn't been wrong. Death was never boring. And maybe, he thought, the notion crossing his mind before he had time to question it, maybe marriage wasn't either.

Wouldn't Be Caught Dead

Lily

Lily was so wrapped up in putting together a Typeface-Spotting bingo card for Tink's birthday party (which was somehow tonight) that she didn't register that the doorbell was blasting 'Highway to Hell' until she'd worked her way all the way down to Wingdings.

'So, where does a girl go to satisfy her appetite for sugared almonds around here?' came a warm, drawling voice, one seasoned with the spray of the ocean and the long days out in the sun.

A familiar cheerful face popped up over Lily's desk: one with the same bright blue eyes and high cheekbones as Lily, but framed by darker curls and made all the more striking by a bold Roman nose that Tessa always proudly said entered the room before she did in order to sniff out any nonsense.

'Tessa!' Lily's swivel chair made three solid rotations as she leapt up to embrace the cousin she hadn't seen since their mutual best friend's wedding, the one that had inspired this whole start-a-wedding-planning-business dream in the first place. 'What are you doing here?'

Tessa obligingly let her cousin tilt her from side to side for a solid thirty seconds before she prised Lily's arms away. She was wearing gloves – a bit odd, given the warm weather, but Tessa had always been a fashionista.

'Second time's the charm. I went in next door first. Did you know there's a *funeral parlour* right there? The poodles had me absolutely confused. Who puts daisy-chain garlands on a mortuary poodle? And then there was this *guy*. Hot, but weird, a bit like . . . did you ever watch *Black Books*? He was like Bernard, but if Bernard had grown up in the Addams family.'

'Ah. Mort,' explained Lily, mentally adding *Black Books* to her to-watch list.

Tessa was scandalised. '*Mort*? Like in *the Sims*? Cruel world. The courts should've stepped in.'

Lily smiled as she thought back over her conversation with Mort about nominative determinism, and how she should technically be a florist – although wedding planner was at least florist adjacent.

At least I wasn't an executioner's assistant, Mort had said. *Or Death himself.*

'Lily?'

'Mm?'

While Lily had been daydreaming, Tessa had been strolling the length of the shop, nudging bud jars and stopping to look at the collection of framed chalkboards on the fireplace mantel. Her gaze lingered on the photo booth printing of Lily and Mort pinned to a photo board filled with snaps from the weddings Lily had recently worked on. Or maybe she was looking at the photo of Lily and Mort laughing as the crows flew overhead that Gracie had captured at Venus's wedding. All right, so perhaps there were more photos of Lily and Mort than of her actual clients, but she hadn't worked on *that* many weddings, had she? She had to fill the space with something.

'I have to be back home in a few hours, but I have time for a coffee. Is there a good place?' asked Tessa.

Lily yawned, the late nights of table arrangement organisation and thank-you-card writing making themselves known. 'I thought you'd never ask.'

She led her cousin out onto the picture-perfect promenade, with its vibrant bushes and shimmering glass ornaments. The sun splashed over the koi-filled stream, and a gentle breeze nudged the wind chimes into a tinkling musical cadence.

'This place is dreamy,' said Tessa, as they passed The Naked Bookshop and a pop-up doughnut cart called Forget-me-Nuts. 'I can't believe it's only an hour and a half from the city. It feels like another planet. No smog. No people. No traffic.'

'The no cars takes some getting used to, but I like it.' Lily led Tessa around the central roundabout – what Mort called *the swirl* – and off to the left branch of the path, where The Hot Pot hugged a curved corner, all thatched roof and ivy-smothered walls. Out the front, couples filled their cups from tall metal teapots, and parents furtively dabbed at the messes their small children had made. A familiar terrier with a brown eye patch wagged his stubby tail as they approached, then rolled over, showing his spotty belly.

'Hey, Jenkins,' Lily greeted him, giving him a belly rub. The dog flipped back over and gave a solid shake, as though drying off after an imaginary shower.

'The Hot Pot does incredible drinks – and pastries,' she explained, as Jenkins trotted off towards a group of students, demanding more belly scratches. (They happily obliged.) 'If you can imagine it, they can make it. I swear there's a witch back there mixing everything up in a cauldron.'

'Do they do Turkish delight?' asked Tessa with a grin. As kids they'd dived into every wardrobe they could find, looking for the fantastical worlds that surely existed behind all the winter coats and mothbally Gore-Tex. They'd even tried making their own Turkish delight, but they'd ended up with rose-smelling toffee. It had been a costly exercise for the Tooth Fairy.

'Can't hurt to ask,' said Lily, pushing open the door to the coffee shop.

'Heya, Lils!' called Dierdre, who today was clad in a rockabilly dress with skulls and roses on it. 'We missed you at romance book club. And we had a *spicy* one, let me tell you.'

Dierdre shoved a ratty paperback across the counter for Lily.

'Your homework. I highly recommend reading it in public if you want to scandalise the HOA. New friend?'

'My cousin Tessa, visiting from La Jolla,' explained Lily.

'Ooh, I love that flamingo-themed pastry shop on that corner right before you get into the downtown area. Magical. What's your potion, Tessa?'

Tessa ordered an extravagant drink with more ingredients than the local bodega held on its shelves. Lily went for the Flower Garden tea blend, mostly because she loved seeing what kind of oddly shaped teapot would appear on her table, complete with ornate tea strainer. According to Mort, Dierdre had inherited the collection from a late aunt, who'd made the mistake early on in her life of telling people she liked teapots. She'd subsequently received a teapot for every birthday, anniversary and life milestone until her death. Her ashes currently lived in a custom teapot with a stopper in the spout.

The ancient wooden floors creaked and complained as Lily led Tessa through the cosy rooms of the shop and into her favourite spot: a pink room with stained glass windows and plants filling every inch of the railing that encircled the room. Coffee table books about food and spices were stacked on each tiled tabletop; candles glowed in vintage teacups.

'Ooh, it's like if a fairy built a greenhouse!' said Tessa. 'I can see why you love it here.'

Lily held her hand over the tea candle flame, enjoying its warmth.

'I really do,' she admitted. 'Although I do miss giant grocery stores and same-day delivery. And there are some . . . quirks I'm still wrapping my head around.'

'Like your hot next door neighbour?'

Lily flushed.

'Ah, I *knew* it. I saw the look on your face when I mentioned him before. And the photos. So many photos. Spill.'

'There's not much to spill.' Actually, there was an astonishing amount to spill, but most of it would make Lily sound, as Ambrose's budgie would say, 'off her cracker'. Tessa's days of magic and mystery were long behind her – once she'd turned thirteen, she'd been all about that Susan Pevensie life, reading magazines and decrying her former crush on Mr Tumnus. Lily wasn't sure she'd want to hear about the way her business had become magically entwined with the one next door, giving every wedding a lovely dousing of death, and vice versa. Lily was becoming used to the quirks of the spell by now, and was getting good at anticipating when a cake smash might involve a jar of ashes or when the Eighties cover band might decide that 'Ave Maria' was a better pick than Blondie's 'Maria'. It was a fun puzzle sometimes, but also, a sword of Damocles at others.

'We've kissed,' she blurted instead. Kissing the messy-haired hot undertaker next door was information that seemed safe enough to volunteer.

Dierdre popped up at that moment, setting down Tessa's enormous drink – it was served in a sundae glass – and Lily's pot of tea (shaped like a mushroom with a chipmunk peering out of one side). Lily wasn't sure if Dierdre had overheard her remark, although the faint smile on her red-painted lips suggested she had.

'Look at you,' said Tessa approvingly, sipping at her triple-vanilla iced latte cinnamon swirl something-or-other. 'Maybe you can buy his and hers funeral plots. Together forever.'

Lily toyed with the mushroom cap lid of the teapot. 'Maybe. I'm not sure Mort's that kind of guy. The whole being surrounded by death thing shapes your attitude towards relationships in weird and woe-derful ways.'

'I see what you did there. Well speaking of love . . .'

Tessa removed her gloves, then fluffed her hair – she had the kind of curls that Lily's own hair aspired to, but lacked the follow-through to achieve – and retouched her lipstick. As she did, an enormous diamond flashed on her finger, almost blinding Lily.

'Ow! You just performed Lasik on me with that thing!' Dropping the teapot lid with a clatter, Lily grabbed her cousin's hand, gazing with wide (if half blinded) eyes at the beautifully cut stone.

'I thought you'd never notice,' said Tessa. 'I put it up on Facebook – I thought for sure my mom would've told you all about it. And I did drop a few hints through text.'

Lily butted her palm to her forehead, finally understanding Mom's persistent questioning about checking her Facebook and Tessa's cryptic emoji string from the other night. So her cousin hadn't just had a case of the butt dials.

'I'm so sorry,' said Lily, feeling terrible for not responding. 'I've been absolutely overrun managing the business. You wouldn't believe how wild this industry is. I need danger pay.'

'It's fine. I wondered if maybe you were a bit wedding-shy, being the last one standing and all. But. With your career change and your five-star rating on Google – well, except for that really weird one about the ashes that I assume was meant for the funeral home next door – I wanted to ask if you'd do me the honour of planning the wedding.'

Lily sipped at her tea, scalding her tongue. She waved her hand frantically in front of her mouth, pretending that her skin wasn't sloughing off.

Tessa mistook Lily's pain for enthusiasm, her eyes brightening. She pulled out her phone and pulled up a photo collage, pushing it into Lily's hands. 'Oh, I'm so glad! Here's what I'm thinking. I want *super* classic. White dress, white veil, six-tiered wedding cake, doves, Enya, the whole lot. The opposite of my parents' wedding, because looking back over those photos gives me the hives. They should've just put an embargo on any and all Nineties weddings. Except the music – I could get down to some Ace of Base. Anyway, nothing edgy, nothing trendy, just *classic*. Like if Barbie got married, only without all the pink. I'll pay your full fee, of course – I wouldn't expect a hook-up type thing where you put in months of work and get a thank you on my Instagram or whatever.'

Lily swallowed. Between the very laissez-faire approach that Venus took to paying her bills (a problem given all the returns that Lily was fronting) and the money she'd been spending on ads, her bank account was gasping for air. She could seriously do with the commission. But Tessa was her cousin. They'd known each other their whole lives, and Lily knew for a fact that Tessa did not do surprises. If Lily planned her wedding and the cake collapsed into a maggoty mess or the dove release turned into a murder of crows, her cousin would never forgive her. Lily had worked so hard to overcome their tiff in ninth grade, when Lily, who at the time had decided she was an aspiring hairdresser, had helped Tessa bleach her hair using household bleach. It had taken a year for Tessa to forgive her (and to grow her hair back). She didn't want to risk losing her cousin again.

'Can I . . . think about it?' she asked, her voice thick in her throat.

Tessa pulled her phone back, frowning. She was clearly hurt. 'Sure, I suppose.'

She sipped from her drink.

'Is it that you don't like Adam? That you don't think it'll last?'

'No, no, Adam's great,' said Lily. Where had that come from? 'You two are meant to be together. I mean, you've been together since college.'

'Yeah, we have.' Tessa twirled her straw in her cup. 'When you know, you know.'

Something was going on here, and Lily wasn't quite sure what.

'It's not anything like that,' said Lily. 'It's just that I don't know if I can do your wedding justice. Everything I've been working on recently has been a bit . . . off kilter.'

'I get it.' Tessa nibbled primly at the coconut-creme cronut that Dierdre had dropped off at their table. 'I've never been cool enough for you. Of course you don't want my wedding in your portfolio.'

Lily wished she'd ordered a tequila instead of a tea. Everything she said was making things worse.

Then she took a deep breath. Against all her better judgement, she said, 'I'd love to do it. Count me in.'

'Really?' Tessa squealed with joy.

'Really,' said Lily, desperately hoping that the switcheroo had a limited radius that wouldn't extend to La Jolla, or that she and Mort would have figured out how to reverse the spell before the wedding date, or that Tessa would be uncharacteristically charitable should the event take a deathly turn.

Tessa's phone alarm chimed. 'Ugh, I'd better be getting back,' she said, pulling up Google Maps on her phone. Red squiggles filled its screen. 'Traffic is already backing up.'

Then she frowned. 'Is your lip okay, Lils? You're looking a bit bee-stung.'

Right as Tessa said it, a tingling started up in Lily's lip. Lily's eyes widened.

Oh no, the tropical lip balm that Venus had dropped during their first meeting, and which Esmeralda had batted out from behind a chair just that morning. Against all of Lily's better judgement, she'd tried it – just a fingertip's worth – because how could you not? Nothing so expensive and so limited edition would ever grace Lily's makeup cabinet. She'd fully intended to send it off to the world-renowned team at UC Davis so that they could use it to clone whatever now-extinct plants had gone into its production. But now she'd been cursed for her dishonesty.

Hastily seeing Tessa off with a hug and a promise of a personalised wedding mood board, Lily raced back to her shop, slamming the door and turning over the 'open to love' sign so that no hapless visitors would come in for cake and a chitchat.

She hurried upstairs, her lip aching from the swelling. Where was her tube of Lysine? She scrabbled around in her dresser for it, hoping to reverse the cruel spell of herpes simplex 1 which, unlike the switcheroo, had absolutely no positives. Aha! Victory. Lily lunged for the tube, uncapping it. But why was it blush red?

Oh no. It had turned into a tube of mortuary makeup.

And now it was too late. In mere moments, the tingle had turned into a swollen lip that had seemed mildly bee-stung, perhaps the result of a generous dose of lip filler or something similarly glam. And then. And *then*. The swelling had pustulated. Was there a worse word – or concept – in the English language than pustulation?

Lily sobbed. Her poor lip had gone through the kind of grisly

335

practical effects transformation you might see in an Eighties horror movie.

And now she was a monster. A freak. She simply could not show her face in public for the foreseeable future, or even the future beyond that, if such a future even existed.

Lily went to close the upstairs Venetian blinds with the fluffy pom-pom tassel, but they'd been switcherooed with dramatic wooden shutters that looked like something stolen from a medieval dungeon by very committed ren faire fans.

Draping a towel over her hideous face, she slammed the shutters closed as though she were the resident of a plague house. Although was there much difference, really? A cold sore was a pustule was a bubo, as far as she was concerned.

She texted Angela. *Babe, I'm so sorry. Cold sore. I hope Tink's birthday is a blast. I'll have Roddy drop off the stuff for tonight.*

Angela texted back a string of sympathetic emojis. She knew the pain. Everyone knew the pain. Basically everyone in the world got cold sores. But no one wanted to admit that they, personally, did.

Lily replied with a fainting gif and then sadly made her way over to what was likely to become her deathbed. What a way to go out. What a way to see the bright spark of her life fizzle into sheer nothingness. Oh, the pathos of it all.

Always the Death of the Party

Mort

Parties were not Mort's preferred way to spend his time. They were associated with drink-driving incidents, roof-diving accidents, and bathtub drownings, and there was always the risk of a freak encounter that sent someone stumbling through a glass coffee table. To their *death*. And then there was the whole social side of things, which was almost as terrifying as facing the increased possibility of one's demise.

But of all the party types in the world (and it was a highly complex taxonomic landscape), birthday parties were ones that Mort could get behind. After all, birthday parties were a celebration of not dying. A whole 365 days – occasionally a whopping 366 – spent moving through life without Death stopping by to give you a jab with his scythe. And that was no mean feat. Mort, who'd seen peanut butter choking deaths, stairway stumble deaths, slipped in the shower deaths and shoelace caught in a bike pedal deaths, just to name a few, knew just how closely the skeletal dude in the black cloak watched the world's human residents.

Besides, Mort liked Angela and Tink, who were delightful fixtures around Mirage-by-the-Sea, Angela judiciously checking in with the town's business owners on a weekly basis to see who might be willing to buy, sell or rent their current property (real estate was a tough gig), and Tink with her letterpress setup, which had a rattle and grime to it that appealed to Mort's sensibilities.

And most importantly, Lily was going to be there. For weeks she'd been talking about the magnificent printing-press-themed shindig she'd been planning – they'd had several conversations through their joint grille about whether a game called I Shot the Serif would be too obscure, and just what should go into a Gutenberg cocktail. Best of all, since it was a birthday party and not a wedding, it was presumably safe from the switcheroo.

And besides, Mort rather wanted to discuss the events of a few nights earlier, which in the whirlwind of subsequent deaths and marriages neither of them had had a chance to comment upon properly. Lily had hinted at wanting a future with him that night, and she'd been quite happy playing the role of Mrs Claus at the Christmas in July wedding, but today she'd been strangely quiet, which worried him. Lily wasn't the quiet type. She embodied extraversion. She was the epitome of the bubbly blonde, whereas when Mort came to bubbles, well, he put the 'tension' in surface tension.

Lily hadn't even responded when Mort had called through the grille to inform her that the tamale lady was out on the promenade. The shutters (when had she put in shutters?) on her upstairs apartment had been slammed shut, which thankfully put to rest the fleeting idea Mort had had about serenading her from his balcony. (It was for the best.) And the doors to the wedding boutique were firmly shut. Lily never closed her doors during the day – she wanted her space to be as welcoming as possible to anyone who might be passing by. It wasn't even necessarily that she wanted to host their weddings.

She genuinely loved chatting to people. In the few months she'd lived in Mirage-by-the-Sea, she'd made more friends than Mort had managed to make during his whole life.

Had she realised she'd made a terrible mistake in sleeping with Mort? Had she looked at the dwindling hourglass of her lease and realised that it wasn't worth getting involved in something that came with a built-in time limit? Or was something else at play?

All of this was running through Mort's head as he arrived at Angela and Tink's place, which was one-third of a storybook cottage that had been transformed from a house into apartments around the time that Airbnb had gone public. And which had been transformed again by Lily's very maximalist eye. Screen-printed signs swung gently from the olive trees in the front yard. Bobbing foil balloons reminded people to 'Remind their Ps and Qs'. And the soundtrack . . . was that the Editors?

'Mort! Mort's at a social gathering!' cried Angela, pointing with a beer.

A cluster of locals, vaguely familiar vacationers and total strangers descended upon him in precisely the way Mort tried to avoid. He was a wheat stalk during a locust plague.

'Happy birthday, Tink,' said Mort, thrusting the pre-need he'd thoughtfully printed out on colourful stationery in her direction. He'd even tied it off with a bow, which truly went above and beyond. And on Reba's extensive online shop (which a tipsy Reba had shown him at length while Lily had been running about trying to rescue Venus's disastrous hippie wedding) he'd found an excellent, extremely colourful greeting card that summed up the occasion perfectly: *Congratulations: you lived to die some other year.*

Tink, emotive in a dress patterned with punctuation marks, raised an eyebrow. 'Nice card. Usually people just give my own cards to me, but look at you. Breaking out of the circular economy trap.'

'It's one of Reba's. I couldn't pass it up.'

Tink flipped over the card, thumbing the Dyer on the Mountain brand logo – a mashup of Grateful Dead elements tweaked just enough to avoid a copyright suit. 'Ah, Reba. She's got the hippie market sewn up, but I'm chasing her.'

'She'll die eventually,' said Mort, deadpan. 'Lily's done a great job. I love the Kern-it the Frog mascot,' he said appreciatively, glancing about at the decor, mostly as a way to sneakily look around for Lily. Then, in as nonchalant a tone as he could manage, he added, 'Is she around?'

Tink made an awful face – for such a pretty person, she was excellent at awful faces. 'She can't make it. She's deathly sick. Deathly.'

Mort's heart seemed to skip a beat. Deathly? Lily was on her *deathbed*? And Mort was here, at a *party* of all things.

'It's bad. She said bubonic. You don't want to go over there.'

Mort could feel the sweat starting to bead against his suit collar. He pulled out his phone, pretending to read a solemn text message.

'I wish I could stay, but . . . death calls.'

'Ugh, you can't even stay for the Celebrity Fontheads game?' Tink brandished a series of paper headbangs with typeface names on them. Wow, Lily really went all in on this stuff. 'Death is always calling. It's the worst.'

'It really is,' agreed Mort.

'Who is it this time?'

'Mrs . . . Helvetica,' said Mort evasively.

Tink folded her arms. 'Helvetica, huh. Is this a bonus murder mystery party element cooked up by the absent Lily?'

'Happy birthday, Tink. Gotta go.'

Hurrying out the door, Mort grabbed a scooter from the side of the promenade and rode it at top speed back towards Eternal Elegance (Wedding Edition). Helmet be damned. Safety be damned. If he cracked open his skull or bruised his tailbone, so be it. What was the point of anything without Lily, delightful, silly, sunshiny Lily in his life?

Mort rounded the familiar curves and twists of the promenade, almost taking out a corgi-toting couple setting up a tripod for the internet likes, and actually taking out a garden bed of ornamental thyme. Sorry, bees. Well, not really. Pollination was the last thing on Mort's mind right now. Oh no, now that brought to mind *My Girl*, the movie that had traumatised a generation of kids.

Lily was *dying*. She needed him. She wasn't just his neighbour. She was his business partner. His . . . partner. His other half. His joy in this bizarre, confused world. And whatever happened – and goodness, so much *had happened* – he wanted to laugh through it all with her. Because that's what they did. They chuckled over smashed wedding plates and corpse brides and confetti debacles and vow disasters. Because sometimes it was funny when a bunch of people got it into their heads that shovelling dirt on someone was a good idea. Or when the photographer insisted on waxy black-and-white photos with a corpse-like vibe. Or when the photo booth . . . well . . . all sorts of things happened in a photo booth.

He dumped the scooter by a planter filled with poppies and pomegranates and hurried up the colourful pathway to Lily's shop. The Polaroids of Lily's most recent clients smiled out at him from the photo board near the bay window. Mort did a double take. Hang on. Hadn't there only been *four* weddings? Who was that fifth couple?

He leaned in, then clocked who it was right away. It was the two of them, first in the apparently perpetually resident photo booth at the funeral home, and then at Venus's wedding during the disastrous crow flight. Mort wondered when Lily had pinned the pictures up – right after they'd been taken? Or perhaps one of the other times, one of hopefully the many other times, that she'd been thinking of him. Of them.

'Lily!' he shouted, fists banging at the stained-glass door like a restrained Stanley Kowalski. 'Let me in!'

Silence.

Mort tried again, to no avail. He stood back, trying to see whether there was movement upstairs, but the massive mediaeval shutters hid all evidence. He squinted – was there a light coming out from one of them? All of the worst possible scenarios ran through Mort's head like an aeroplane safety film. Maybe Lily was trapped upstairs. Perhaps she was so sick that she was unable to get out of bed. Or worse, she'd fallen out of bed and couldn't get back up.

Then, Mort caught sight of two familiar glowing mismatched eyes. Esmeralda, up on his balcony. Regarding him haughtily, she nimbly leapt from his balcony to Lily's, then sat there, quite impressed with herself, licking a paw.

Mort sighed.

'This is what it's going to take, isn't it, Esme?'

Mort let himself into the funeral home, trying not to think of the last time Lily had been here. Of her easy laugh. Her astonishing facility for jigsaw puzzles. The lean length of her thigh . . .

Not now. Hurrying upstairs to his living quarters, Mort shoved open the balcony doors, letting the evening's breeze rush at his face. He stepped up to the wrought-iron perimeter, which had for months now been entwined with the balcony for Lily's place, the funeral home's black skull and bat motif melding seamlessly with the pink roses and gerberas of the wedding planner. Two lengths of the twisted iron ran between the twin balcony areas. Mort's breath caught as he thought about the danger involved in climbing from one to the other. Esmeralda had made it look so easy, but cats had a preternatural ability to land on their feet. Not only that, but they had a bonus eight lives in the event that they misjudged a jump. Mort did not have this (possibly apocryphal) benefit to his name.

Mort jammed the toe of his Oxford into the railing, then pushed himself upwards, balancing his other foot on the top of the railing. He felt like the world's most uncoordinated Batman.

Now what?

Forwards. The only way out was forwards. Well, and down, but he wasn't going to think about that.

Mort leaned forward, stretching out a hand to catch at the railing on Lily's balcony. Ouch, a rose thorn. Wincing, he walked his hand to one side, reaching forward with the other.

Now he just had his feet to deal with.

But as much as he tried to will himself to pull a foot forward, his body simply wouldn't do it. *Do you want to fall to your death, you dingdong?* it was saying. In between internal screams.

He was stuck. Horribly stuck. In a position that did not look unlike the Hungry Caterpillar. Horrific flashbacks of childhood Twister games ran through his head. (People had *died* playing Twister. And many more had thrown out their backs.)

'Esmeralda, get help,' whispered Mort.

Esmeralda gave him a slinky look, then launched a leg over her head and started washing her butt.

But then, disaster. Mort's foot slipped, and he fell forward, his body stretched out between the two railings like some poor prisoner on a torture chamber rack. A family of doves indignantly burst up, flapping at his face and creating a commotion that threatened Mort's balance quite significantly.

Mort might have howled, just a bit.

The shutters flew open, revealing Lily, clad in a . . . motorcycle helmet.

Lily flipped up the visor of said helmet, revealing concerned but also extremely amused eyes.

'Mort! What on earth are you doing? Are you finally participating in the planking trend of 2011?'

'You're alive!' gasped Mort, almost relaxing his grasp in his relief.

'Oh shit, don't fall!' Lily reached for his hand. 'Do you trust me?' she asked.

Mort swallowed. The ground below was vertiginously far away. 'I trust you.'

'Then grab my arm.' Lily's nails gleamed as she slid her hand down his wrist until her fingers clasped around the meat of his forearm. Mort wrapped his fingers around her arm, gingerly, afraid he'd break her. 'Oh come *on*, Mort. I get my calcium. You're not going to snap my bones.'

Mort increased his grip.

'There's a guy who's eaten his Cheerios.' Grip tight on his arm, Lily lunged forward to wrap her arm around his chest. 'On the count of three, I'm going to pull you towards me, like I'm dragging a puppy from the mouth of an alligator.'

'That doesn't make me feel better.'

'I could let you fall to your death?'

'We're not doing that. Three it is.'

Lily's eyes sparkled from within her motorbike helmet. Why on earth was she wearing that? Was she planning a trip down the highway? Was she *leaving*? The very thought made Mort's stomach clench. Well, it would've clenched, had he not been stretched to the full extent of his height.

'One. Two. *Three.*'

Lily hauled, and Mort unlatched his shoes from the other balcony. With an awkward, bruising slither, he landed on the rose-patterned tiling of Lily's terrace, crumpling like a dead spider. But not dead. Not dead at all, he thought, staring up at Lily's bright blue eyes, which were crinkled at their corners the way they always were when he'd done something silly, which apparently was often.

'Mort. Tell me this instant why you were auditioning for Cirque du Soleil on my terrace.'

'I thought you were dying,' gasped Mort, who was winded both physically and spiritually. 'Angela and Tink said that you were on your deathbed. That this was a plague house. They started singing "Ring a Ring a Rosie".'

Lily covered her eyes with her hands. Then, splaying her fingers slightly, she peeked through them.

'Mort,' she said through her helmet. 'It's just a cold sore. Not deadly. Not even debilitating. Just . . . gross.'

Mort groaned. 'I climbed a balcony to rescue you from a cold sore?'

Lily chuckled. 'Mort, my love, nothing can rescue me from the clutches of HSV1. We just need to wait for time to work her magic. Now, do you want a cup of tea?'

'Will you take off the helmet?' he asked curiously.

'Never,' she said, putting down the visor.

Say Yes to the Hearse

Lily

It was a week until Lily was ready to emerge from the plague house, and by then she was dying for social interaction. She'd had to turn away her usual cake-seeking visitors, and she'd been strictly camera off during her client calls (and even with Mom, who could go on for hours about cold sore remedies if you gave her the chance). At least she'd been able to chitchat with Mort through the grille, which was crucial, given that the two of them had big plans together. Big plans for Gramps's place, at least. After extensive discussions with all involved (and some mood boarding on Lily's part), the Gramps housing situation had been sorted. The solution? Roommates.

'The Grief Guys,' Lily had exclaimed triumphantly, waggling her chair back and forth in front of the grille. 'They'd be the perfect roommates.'

There'd been a pause as Mort had considered this. 'There *are* three spare bedrooms,' he'd mused. 'And plenty of room for Sausage.'

'And Gramps would have a plumber and a quasi-electrician under one roof. Plus whatever Duggo does.'

'Cooks a mean spaghetti, apparently,' came Mort's voice.

'And they all want the company, right? It's perfect.'

It *was* perfect. Lily was more proud of the idea than she'd been of any of the highly elaborate weddings she'd cooked up over the past year.

While Lily had been cooped up, Mort had set the ball rolling. When not hosting a wake or a graveside vigil, he'd spent the week helping transport the Grief Guys' furniture up to Gramps's in the hearse. (Apparently a hearse with roof racks and a couch on top was a sight to behold, and had caused quite the chatter on the Nextdoor group.)

'Lily, are you decent?' asked Mort. 'If so, can I get your help?'

Lily looked up from the endless stack of apology cards she'd been writing to Venus's guests (and which she'd been pairing with the various gifts that had to be returned). She touched gently at her lip, which finally felt human again, then glanced down at her outfit: pink linen trousers and a sheer chiffon top with daisies embroidered on it. She was more than decent – she looked fabulous.

'Do I need to wear sensible shoes?' she called.

'I would never ask that of you,' promised Mort.

'Well then, let's do it.'

'I'll meet you at the hearse in five.'

Wearing her favourite heeled sneakers (yellow, with a rainbow decal), Lily trotted down the laneway that led to the parking lot. It was a perfect evening, the way it always was in Mirage-by-the-Sea: luminous where the waning sun met the twinkling fairy lights, fragrant with flower baskets and baking, the air gently nudged by a mischievous ocean breeze. Lily couldn't help but grin. She *loved* it here, the way she'd never loved living anywhere before. The quaint shops, the warmly eccentric people, the sheer beauty of the place.

And Mort. Of course, Mort.

Just this morning she'd received a text from Angela about her lease, and for the first time she hadn't felt that weird itchy flight response that told her that it was time to move on for the next thing.

I'd love to stay, if you'll have me, she'd texted back. *But what about the next business?*

Leave it to me, Angela had responded cryptically.

Speaking of Mort . . . There he was, leaning against the hearse in a way so sexy that it seemed improper. The Funeral Board could have his head for that, surely.

As she approached, Mort broke into a grin of his own – that slightly shy grin that set his whole face alight. He produced a bouquet of wildflowers tied with a twine bow.

'For you,' he said gently.

'You needed some help carrying these, huh?' Lily took them and buried her face in them, admiring their heady mix of colours and textures and aromas. 'I guess you've been slacking on the gym.'

'Wrong. Flower picking works the small muscles you never knew you had.' Mort opened her door for her. 'Anyway, I needed your help as my date tonight.'

Lily smacked him with the flowers. 'Your date?'

Mort raised an eyebrow. 'That was before I knew you were abusive.'

Chuckling, Lily climbed into her seat and – before Mort could say anything about car accident statistics – buckled up. 'Sorry, I was just surprised. I would love to be your date. Depending on the destination. And what kind of food is involved.'

Checking that the fuel gauge showed a full tank and that the oil level was more than acceptable, Mort pulled the hearse out of its spot at his usual excruciatingly slow pace. 'A picnic under the stars. All the way up there.'

He pointed to the topmost point of the rolling hills that surrounded the picturesque town centre.

'Solid views,' said Lily with a whistle.

The hearse cruised around the windy roads, pulling over at the occasional turnout to let the traffic gathering behind them pass. Lily kept count of the sheep and cows they spotted, being sure to make the appropriate animal sound with each sighting.

But then on a particularly sharp incline, something under the hearse started to rattle. An alert on the dashboard dinged.

'Is our popcorn ready?' asked Lily.

'The check engine light,' said Mort, frowning. 'But I just had her serviced. You can even check the log book.'

Lily opened the glove box and pulled out a tidy log book in which Mort had diligently recorded every piece of maintenance that had been done on the hearse in the past . . . well, since ever. It was a much more impressive testament to car ownership than Lily's haphazard set of receipts, which were jammed down the side of the door and had to be dug through every time her mechanic asked her about her car's chequered past.

More rattling, then another ding. Then another.

'Is it the switcheroo?' asked Lily. 'Is the hearse becoming a pumpkin or something?'

'I think it's just . . . dying,' said Mort, with a sigh. 'As all things do.'

Lily couldn't help but laugh. 'Well, you're never not on brand.'

'Very funny.' Frowning as the entire dash console glowed red, Mort pulled over.

He popped the hood, then walked a lap around the car. As he got to the doors at the back, he folded his arms.

'Well, I've found the source of the rattling,' he said, holding up a set of tin cans, the type that newlyweds might hitch to their car. 'I think one of them got stuck underneath and broke something.'

'So now what?' asked Lily. She checked her phone – no signal.

'It's just us and an overnight wait for roadside assistance.'

'We should've taken the Miata,' teased Lily. 'She's reliable. Still going strong, 200,000 miles in.'

'That's a warning sign in and of itself. A car with that many miles is at the end of its mechanical life.'

Lily huffed. 'I'm glad poor Lucille isn't here to hear you say that.'

'Lucille would still be at the bottom of the hill,' pointed out Mort.

'At least we picked a nice place to get murdered by a hitchhiker,' observed Lily.

Despite the irony in her tone, she spoke the truth: they'd broken down by the side of a wildflower-studded field, high up on a winding road that offered glimpses of the slow-moving ocean and the twinkling lights of the town and the estates that spilled out from it in every direction. The air was a scarf of scents and sounds: the citrusy scents of yerba buena and wild roses mixed with the hum of crickets and the wind over the hills.

She checked the time on the dash. 'So, how much longer do we have until someone comes for us?'

'From my knowledge of the hours that Tow Truck Trent keeps, about eight hours,' said Mort. 'He'll be at bingo, then in bed, then walking his dog. Promise me you're not going to keep asking.'

'I promise,' said Lily. She grabbed his hand. 'I mean, if you're saying we have time . . .'

She pulled him around to the back of the hearse, yanking open the doors and dragging him in after her.

Mort blushed. 'About the bunk bed mattresses,' he began.

'What bunk bed mattresses?'

'The ones from the switcheroo. I thought it couldn't hurt to have something comfortable to lie on.'

'Ah, lie on,' said Lily knowingly. 'But there are no mattresses. There's only one . . .'

Mort sighed. 'Coffin. There's only one coffin.'

The switcheroo had struck again.

'It's a double coffin, at least?' said Lily, poking at it. 'To be fair, the lining's really soft. And the padding is quite solid. Ooh, and it has drop-down sides.' She demonstrated. 'It's like a futon coffin. A coff-on. A fut-in.'

'You know your tombstone is going to list your terrible sense of humour as your cause of death.'

'I can think of worse ways to go out.' Lily climbed into the back of the hearse, musing, 'I like the sunroof up the top. You can see the stars from here. All of them. No wonder Desdemona was all about this thing. Come have a look.'

Mort grumblingly followed after her, crawling across the thick mountain of velvet blankets and pillows. He lay down on his back next to her, taking in the starry night sky.

'All right, that's a solid view,' he said. He turned to face her, his dark eyes boring into hers. 'We should eat the picnic stuff while the salmonella risk is low . . .'

'Oh shut up and kiss me,' said Lily.

'But there's soft cheese,' protested Mort.

'Nope. No food poisoning talk. Only kissing.'

Begrudgingly setting aside his safe food storage concerns, Mort leaned in, the faint hint of cedar that always followed him enveloping her. His lips were gentle against hers, then firm as she pulled him in, knotting her fingers in his dark, messy hair. Their timing was mismatched at first – it always was when you were learning someone new – but there was something about that slight clumsiness that made Lily's heart swell. There was no erasing their respective oddnesses, their imperfections, and frankly she had no desire to.

All right, so they were an unusual combination, but they . . . gelled. And for all the weirdness that the past few months had thrown at them, they'd somehow only grown closer. Under all those doom-and-gloom trappings, Mort was as sunny as she was: always willing to help out or lend a hand. He was funny, in his sharp, dark way, and something about him made Lily feel . . . at rest. (Not in a dead way.)

'Earth to Lily,' said Mort, pulling back to regard her. There was a flush to his usually fair cheeks, and Lily momentarily felt all-powerful – there was something to be said for being able to affect another human in such a way.

Well and in other ways, too, she thought, as she scooted backwards onto the plush softness of the coffin's interior, pulling him towards her.

'Sorry,' she said. 'Just thinking about furniture definitions. Does this really count as a coffin? It's more of a sectional, if you ask me.'

Mort shook his head. 'Oh to be so poorly versed in basic furniture types. Did you not read the IKEA catalogue as a kid?'

'Of course!' Lily pretended to be offended. She raised an eyebrow and sucked suggestively on her finger. 'I had two Billys in my room. Scandalous.'

Mort, to his credit, did not roll his eyes. 'All right, all of your sins are absolved.'

'I thought you were a funeral planner, not a priest?'

'It's a multifaceted role.'

'How multifaceted are we talking?' murmured Lily, drawing him close and drinking in the scent of him, the heat of him. She loosened his already shambolic tie, then set to work on the stiff buttons of his black shirt.

Mort let her work, watching her from beneath heavy eyelids. His hands slid the length of her body, catching on her waist, then holding there for a moment as though in awe of her form. The feeling went both ways: she was fascinated by the strength that hid beneath his trim, formal clothes – the bulge of his forearms that occasionally peeked out from behind his rolled-up sleeves, the shape of his chest. In his lifelong effort to outrun death, Mort had become quite the gymbro. But in a Mort way, not in a posing on the internet way.

His shirt finally unbuttoned, the black fabric sliding aside to reveal a taut stomach and well-muscled obliques, Mort was the sexiest harbinger of death Lily had ever seen (and she'd watched *Meet Joe Black* several times). She pushed him back onto the silken lining of the coffin, pinning him there with the palm of her hand as she straddled him. The moonlight streamed in through the sunroof of the hearse, cloaking her in a gentle white light that ran the length of her arms, hands, fingers, drawing a connecting line between the bright pink of her fingernails and Mort's skin.

'I think that's the sexiest anyone has ever looked,' Mort breathed, his eyes shining from where the moonlight struck them.

Lily grinned. 'The sexiest anyone has ever looked *yet*.'

She drew her shirt over her head, dropping it in a puddle of pink lace to Mort's left.

Abdominal muscles straining, he rose up to cup his hands around the frills of her bra – the one with the layers of varyingly pink satin, the one with the straps so thin she feared doing any kind of energetic movement in them. The one that had made the woman in the bra shop nod approvingly and say, 'Yes, yes, that's the one.' (Then, in an undertone, '*lucky bitch*.') The one that she'd almost tossed aside this morning in favour of her less sexy but more comfy grandma bra. *Good job, past Lily. Your pride continues to treat you well.*

Mort's thumbs traced her bra, then the soft skin of the tops of her breasts. Lily fought the urge to swoon.

'May I?' he whispered, his breath hot against her neck as he reached behind her back to unhook the bra. His fingers were electric against her skin . . . for what felt like several minutes. 'Holy fuck, did you get this from the straitjacket department of the upstairs section of the local hospital?'

Lily grinned. 'Behold, a deep, feminine magic.'

Returning Mort's hands to her breasts, she reached a hand behind her back, then with a quick pinch of thumb and forefinger released the lacy fabric. The bra dropped, and Mort's hands caught the softness of her breasts, holding them gently as he devoured her, his mouth exploring one nipple, then the other.

Her body pressed close to his, she leaned forward, pushing him back down on his back, where he lay, his eyes drinking her in. Lily had never felt so beautiful, so *wanted*.

'You're stunning,' whispered Mort. 'The kind of woman I'd write poems about.'

'But promise me you don't write poetry.'

'I don't write poetry.'

'Oh thank God.'

Her hands found the button of his trousers, then the zip, and momentarily there was just a thin barrier of fabric between him and her searching fingers.

Mort swallowed as she teased him through the fabric, then dragged down the trousers together with his boxers, releasing him.

'Now you're just being cruel,' he murmured.

Raising an eyebrow, Lily curled her fingers around him and stroked his length. Damn, he felt good in her hand. So strong, so sure, so *ready*.

'Still being cruel?' she asked innocently.

'So cruel.'

'I have my flaws, I suppose.' She dipped down, touching her lips to him, running her tongue around his tip and testing the saltiness of him.

Mort swore.

'That bad, huh?' she said, before covering him with her mouth, until her lips met where her fingers were curled around his base.

Mort had a few choice additions for the swear jar.

Lily found a rhythm, enjoying the strength of him, enjoying the strain of his legs and the urgent grasping of his fingers against her shoulders.

'Come this way,' he said finally, drawing her back up, higher and higher, until he faced the skirt that just this morning she'd decided was too much (or rather, not enough), before saying fuck it and pulling it on anyway. His fingers found the edges of the skirt hem, dragging it up until he revealed the wisp of lace essential to preventing an underwear line – comfort be damned – which he pulled aside, finding her slickness with his fingers and opening her gently, yet hungrily. He slid a finger into her, then another, and Lily could feel her muscles clench. Fuck, she wanted him so badly.

Mort rose up to his knees, following his fingers with his mouth. As his tongue found her, probing her, worshipping her, exploring electric circles around her clitoris, Lily groaned in ecstasy.

'Now who's cruel,' she murmured, her hands knotted in his hair as she pulled him closer to her.

All she wanted was for him to be inside her.

Like this, for now, but then . . .

Momentarily, she pushed him back down, straddling him and rubbing her wetness against his length. His dark gaze on hers, Mort held her hips to him, grinding cruelly against her.

Now it was Lily's turn for a display of abdominal prowess. Still straddling him, she reached across to her handbag, pulling out one of the condoms she'd swiped from the leftover debauchery baskets from Venus's wedding. (Apparently wealth did trickle down, in its own way.)

Fingers teasing, she rolled the condom on, then arched her hips forward, positioning herself so that Mort could enter her. He did, easily: Lily accepted him impatiently, rolling her hips so that she could sheathe his entire length.

'You take me so well,' he whispered, his voice low and urgent, layered with animal desire.

'Like this?' murmured Lily, grinding her hips even deeper, so that there was no space between the two of them. No room for anything else but the heat of their bodies and the shared, starving look in their eyes.

Mort reached to clasp her thighs, his hands slowly shifting around to her butt, then the small of her back, pulling her into him over and over. Lily bit her lip, focused on the pleasure of him inside her, the slight ache of it where he filled her.

As they moved together, she could feel the waves of pleasure building in her, travelling up through her body, then into her neck, face, hair – all of it tingling as her rhythm grew more determined and her breath grew more ragged. Her finger found her clitoris, and she could feel her entire body fizz from the pleasure.

'Are you going to come for me?' whispered Mort, his eyes daring her to let herself go entirely.

Lily was holding on to her orgasm, revelling in the feeling of the connectedness of their two bodies, not wanting the pleasure to stop. But the cliff edge was coming, and sooner or later she'd have to back away – or let herself go. Finally, she relinquished, letting Mort take her over the edge with a final stroke and the touch of her own hand.

Her muscles clenching over and over as she carried herself downwards and back to earth, she leaned into his neck, her teeth grazing the stubbled skin as she coasted back to reality. Mort followed, his hips rising to hers as he found his own release. Lily could feel the pressure of him inside her as he held her close, and she nipped and kissed at him until his shudders subsided.

'Wow, we might get a noise complaint after that,' murmured Lily, scooting aside and settling into the crook of Mort's arm. He was sheened with sweat, as was she, and she loved how he glimmered faintly under the lighting of the moon.

'I'm sure the great outdoors has heard worse,' Mort pointed out, his voice hoarse.

'I mean, I can do worse, if you'd like,' said Lily, eyes sparkling. Her hand traced his hips, then his length, and Mort closed his eyes, remembering, anticipating.

'I would love to see what your idea of "worse" is,' he said, kissing her forehead in that gentle way he always did. The way that made her feel safe, and wanted, and loved.

'Oh, your poor little heart couldn't bear it,' Lily teased. 'We'll have to work up to it.'

Mort chuckled. 'I think I can manage that. Just so long as you give me a little time to recover.'

A banging noise woke Lily from her slumber. Wiping the dried drool from her cheek, she reached for her phone, but it was flat. That last eleven per cent of battery didn't go far these days.

It was still dark, but there was a tinge of dawn to the edge of the world, and the stars were fading into the velvety sky. The moon had set sail, travelling from one end of the sunroof to the other, and was now making a beeline for the forest.

The banging sound again.

Lily prodded Mort, then upgraded her prodding into a solid elbowing. 'Mort. Mort! There's a serial killer outside. He's mistaken me for Pickleball Candice! Please, I'm too young to die! I haven't completed my pre-need! I don't even know if I want a casket or a cremation!'

Mort blinked, groggily sitting up. 'Don't be silly. If he chops you up into a million pieces, you won't have to worry about either. It'll be a natural burial for you. Or a vat of acid.'

'That actually doesn't help me feel better. Oh crap, was that a chainsaw?'

A flashlight danced over the hearse, brightening the spaces where the window tint didn't quite cover.

Lily pulled her shirt on. If a serial killer was going to pull her out of the car and drag her off into the woods, she was at least going to have the buffer of a thin layer of cotton. (When you were dealing with pine needles and rocks, every bit of protection counted.)

'Hang on,' said Lily. 'Does the sky usually strobe red and blue like that?'

'Only after an intense orgasm,' said Mort. 'Or . . .'

'Aliens?' suggested Lily, who had a solid collection of Roswell T-shirts she cycled through when she hit the jogging trails.

'We'll see. On the count of three,' said Mort, hands on the hearse's back doors. When Lily nodded that she was decent, he shoved the doors open.

Lily dug in her bag and brandished a wooden cross left over from Desdemona and Ambrose's wedding.

'Um, excuse me, folks, sorry to bother you.' A cop so young that Lily suspected he still had a parental curfew stood there, nervously running a string of garlic between his fingers. All right, so probably not a serial killer. Well, maybe. Hopefully not.

'We're not vampires,' Lily assured him. 'We're waiting for a tow truck.'

Mort lifted his collar, hiding the evidence her lips had left against his neck.

The cop tucked the garlic into his pocket. 'Good to know. Can I help you folks out? I've got some jumper cables, and some extra oil in the back. Just saying, you're causing a bit of a traffic delay here, what with the whole late-night funeral procession thing and all.'

The cop pointed down the road, where about a hundred cars idled patiently, pulled over to the side of the road, as was the norm when they encountered a hearse on its way to a funeral.

Mort, buttoning his shirt, swore softly.

'How long have they been waiting?' asked Lily curiously.

'How long have you been here?' countered the cop.

'Um,' said Lily.

'I see.' The cop cleared his throat. 'Let me grab my tools and see if I can get you moving.'

'Sounds good,' said Lily, giving Mort a slap on the butt – and inspiring the car at the front of the queue to flash its high beams. 'Come on, let's get this peep show on the road.'

Gone to a Better Place

Mort

It was move-in day at Gramps's place. Mort squeezed Lily's hand before ushering the Grief Guys out of the back of the hearse. (Which had been carefully rid of any evidence of the previous night's travails.) There was a clattering of suitcases and hatboxes and the nails of Sausage, and then the motley group stared up at Gramps's Gothic fairy-tale cottage. Well, Gramps's not-as-Gothic-as-it-had-once-been fairy-tale cottage. Lily and Mort had spent every spare evening and weekend they had (which was not many, given the town's busy deaths and marriages schedule) filling the planters with vibrant flowers, repainting the house's front doors, and hanging wind chimes and local art to brighten up the place. The windows streamed with tie-dyed curtains repurposed from Venus's wedding, and horseshoes from the cowboys' wedding were nailed around the ornate front door, welcoming the visitors in a display of good luck and cheer. New letterboxes had been set up along the front garden bed, and a variety of chairs and tables and lawn games dotted the lawn invitingly.

Their handiwork was on full, bright display – and so too was Gramps.

'Welcome to the Old Codgers' home,' cried Gramps, flinging

open the heavy front door. Lily grinned; over his usual black, he'd thrown on the tie-dyed scarf that Lily had commissioned from Reba before the old hippie had departed for Tie-Dyepalooza, an annual event that drew the nation's entire hippie population in one colourful, weed-filled extravaganza.

The Grief Guys followed Mort up the stone steps, Duggo pausing to pat one of the gargoyles on the head. Sausage planted his paws and growled jealously until Duggo gave him a scratch behind the ears.

'It's all right, boy. It's just a stone monster making a face.'

'It wards off bad spirits,' explained Mort.

'So does Sausage. And he's a lot cuter,' said Duggo, sneaking the fat dog a treat.

'You might be right there,' said Gramps. 'Come in, come in, *roommates*.'

The Grief Guys followed him into the dim hallway, which Mort was now seeing through their eyes – and perhaps Lily's as well. He'd been so used to the heavy fabrics and dim lighting – it was just a part of life. But now, after being surrounded by bright floral bouquets and sequinned fabrics and colourful stationery, he couldn't imagine the house any other way.

'Avert your eyes,' said Lily, yanking back a set of curtains so that light streamed into the living room. Mort was stupefied: he'd never even noticed that the huge area rug had a pattern.

The Grief Guys followed Gramps around the house as he gave them the official tour: the drawing room, the library, the jigsaw puzzle collection.

'And of course, your rooms,' he added proudly.

Lily smiled as each of the Grief Guys went to their respective rooms – which Lily, with some help from Tink, had marked with handmade signs. Opening the door to his room, Orson clapped his hands over his mouth.

'It's so homely and cosy,' he exclaimed. 'Like my place, but condensed. And cleaner.'

Stribley wiped away a tear as he saw how Mort and Lily had set up his room with all the things that Mort had noted as being important to him during their Grief Guy chats.

'Where did you get all these records?' he whispered. 'It's like my old studio setup in here.'

'And mine has all the Amtrak maps, oh, and a world coin collection! And the Luke Skywalker figurine I've been carting around my whole life. It even has a bed for Sausage!' exclaimed Duggo. 'Even though he insists on sleeping at my feet. I hope that's all right.'

'Of course it's all right,' said Gramps. 'Happy sausage dog, happy life.'

'We even brought over a copy of the ice-breaker game,' said Mort, hoisting up the *Dirty Laundry* box. 'Although something tells me that you lot aren't going to need it.'

'Ice-breakers,' snorted Gramps. 'With all the work they've done over here the past few months, these lads are my best friends. Besides, what does an ice-breaker game have to offer that a jigsaw puzzle doesn't?'

'Just so long as you start with the edge pieces,' agreed Orson. 'Any other way is anarchy.'

Lily chuckled, and Mort wrapped an arm around her.

Anarchy wasn't so bad. After all, as Mort had learned since the switcheroo, sometimes the world needed some shaking up.

An Indecently Affluent Proposal

Lily

It was the helicopter rotors that belied Venus's presence: the sky boiled with the sound of a million leaf blowers, and skirts and parasols within a mile radius flapped and turned inside out. Lily, who'd been watering the ever-growing collection of plants outside her shop while waiting for a local caving destination to call her back regarding a below-ground wedding for two avid spelunkers, watched as the town's semi-tame peacock population hurried off in a profusion of tail feathers.

A knot of picnic-goers quickly packed up and rushed their tablecloth and basket over to the shelter of one of the laneways, which to be fair, with their cushioned benches and tables, were more than ideal for tea and baked goods.

As Venus floated down the promenade, borne upon the currents of wealth and possibly a small hoverboard, Lily waved with the watering can she'd been using to give the bougainvillea outside her shop a drink.

'Hi, Venus!'

'Lily, darling,' Venus purred, darting in like a hummingbird for some air kisses. 'How's marrying life treating you?'

'Couldn't be better,' said Lily, dusting down her yellow

gingham skirt. She held out a hand, inviting Venus inside the shop. 'So, how are things with Desmond? Did you talk?'

Venus shrugged. 'We did a Zoom with the boards. It was all amicably resolved by our lawyers. He's taken up with a plastics magnate in the interim. The stock prices are soaring. My mother's delighted. Did I tell you I got a lizard?'

Venus pulled up an image of a fat, dragon-like lizard with a frilled neck on her phone.

'He's Australian. His name is Bozo. Doesn't talk much, and has absolutely no business interests. It's the perfect partnership.' Venus glanced around approvingly. 'The shop is positively glowing. Look at that intention board – it's fizzing with energy.'

'I really think I've found my place here.' Lily smiled, glancing over at her treasure map. She'd visited every business in town, and met just about every local (and probably every tourist as well). And best of all, they'd all stopped by to see her and grab a reciprocal stamp. The only stamp that was missing was Mort's – but she figured the Chamber of Commerce would let it slide when she went to claim her hamper and hopefully successfully plead her case to stay on in town at the conclusion of her lease. If not in her little shop, then *somewhere*. Maybe one of the many empty apartments at Whispering Waters, where dying was the third-most popular activity, behind only bingo and arts and crafts.

Perching on one of the acrylic ghost chairs, Venus waved a hand. A bounty of gold clinked and jangled. 'About that. I have a proposal for you.'

Lily set down a cup of tea in front of Venus. On its saucer she placed the cursed lip balm that she'd decided needed to go back to its original owner. 'Are we talking a marriage proposal here, because . . .'

'Oh, no. Not like that.' Venus applied some of the lip balm, making Lily's lip tingle in nervous solidarity. 'I had a chat with Gracie Nivola, and I'm going to take a page out of her book: asexuality. Well, celibacy in my case, but the outcome is the same.' She clicked her fingers. 'A job. I'm talking about a job. A calling that you get paid for. More specifically, an opportunity where you help me wiggle my way out of sticky situations. Not all of them involving toothpaste, but some.'

Lily stirred her teacup.

'I saw how you brilliantly you wrote the apology notes,' said Venus. 'I was in no headspace to do it, and you came through. It was poetry! Magic! I only received a handful of cease-and-desist letters. That's good,' she added, for Lily wasn't sure. 'The only thing is that it would be a demanding job, and I'd need you on the ground with me. Or in the helicopter. Or the Bentley. Or the golf cart. Depending on the vibes of the day. You'd have to come with me back to LA I know you've got all this going on.' Venus gestured around at the shop. 'But you said you weren't sure about putting roots down here . . .'

Lily's teacup trembled in her hand. She *had* said that, hadn't she. But things were different now.

'And soon there'll be just the lease, and after that, nothing at all. The business, though darling, is new. Your family's back in La Jolla.'

'And Italy,' whispered Lily, who'd just been texting back and forth with Annika about her friend's new-found passion for Italian culture (i.e. Italian men). 'And Oregon.' (Mom was doing a month-long consulting stint up in Portland for a tech client, which she'd taken as an opportunity to ditch Mustard Rick.)

'Might as well be the moon. And let's face it: no Coachella

headliner is going to come out here, am I right? I'm just a toothpaste heiress, but I know a woman with potential when I see one, and you have potential. I can see it in your aura.'

Venus's opal rings flashed as she waggled her fingers dramatically.

Then she slid a piece of paper – in landscape format – across Lily's coffee table. 'Here's what I'm offering.'

Lily spilt tea in her lap. 'I think . . . you've misplaced the decimal point.'

Venus frowned. 'Oh, you're right.'

She scribbled a new number, moving the decimal point one place to the right.

If Lily hadn't already spilt her tea, she would've done so again. It was an absurd amount of money. So absurd that if Venus hadn't written out the full amount in words, she would have assumed that the other woman had failed third-grade maths. But Venus seemed completely sincere.

'I see you're already packing,' said Venus, eyeing the pink duffel bag Lily had kicked under her desk when they'd entered the shop. Lily might be a maximalist, but she didn't abide a mess. 'How about you come back with me on the helicopter, and I'll have my people pick up your things later. I'll even pay out the rest of your lease.'

From the other side of a grille came a sneeze, followed by some muttered swearing.

Venus cocked her head, then pointed towards the grate on the wall that divided the two Eternal Elegances.

Lily froze. How much of this conversation had Mort heard?

'Either you have ghosts, or an eavesdropper,' chided Venus. 'Shall we grab a coffee first? For old times' sake?'

Lily's mind was whirling from Venus's offer and what it represented. Financial security. Prestige. Amazing networking opportunities. A creative blank cheque to go with the literal blank cheques that Venus liked to throw around.

It was the kind of offer that no one in the right mind would turn down. Not unless they had a very specific reason not to.

Lily grabbed the pink duffel and slung it over her shoulder.

'A coffee sounds great,' she said.

A Matter of Love or Death

Mort

Mort had heard it all through the grille that separated the two Eternal Elegances. Of *course* Lily wasn't going to stay. Why would she, when she could take an astonishingly well-paying job with Venus, a role which presumably came with a lifetime of helicopter rides, hand-me-down sports cars and a subscription to each of the several dozen magazines that kept ending up on Mort's doorstep instead of Lily's?

Like this one coming through the letterbox flap right now: the latest edition of *The Gown*, featuring . . . hang on, featuring *Lily* on the front?

Mort flipped open the magazine to the cover story, which was a glowing review of Lily's business that spoke to her passion, ingenuity and ability to create a unique event around any theme, no matter how avant-garde. (And her singledom, but only twice, which seemed generous from what he'd overheard from the whole Coriana interview.)

Lily Ellis is a sunny addition to Mirage-by-the-Sea – and to the wedding world, concluded the article. *You'd be mad to let her pass you by.*

'It's Lily!' cried Stribley, who along with the other Grief Guys was seated in the parlour, eating cake and discussing

Gramps's incredible snoring volume. 'Oh, but she's a good one, isn't she?'

'The best,' said Mort slowly, staring down at the photo of Lily, all windswept curls and twinkling blue eyes.

He couldn't bear the thought of life without Lily. Of going a day without seeing her brilliant smile and her fantastically bright outfits and the endless array of costumes she kept on hand for the poodle statues. Of not being able to chat with her through the grille. Of her cheerful shop being overtaken by a dry cleaner or a dentist or a weed dispensary. (Although Angela, now that she didn't have Gramps's lodging to worry about, had mysteriously assured him she was working on this.)

'What are you doing, lad?' asked Orson incredulously, around a bite of tiered black funeral cake (a new local trend). 'Go on. Fight for her.'

'Not literally,' added Stribley, jabbing with his cake fork. 'Use your words.'

'But give your hair a once-over first.' Duggo proffered the dog brush he kept in his pocket.

Sausage wagged his tail, adding his two cents to the mix.

Mort swiped his hands through his hair and straightened his tie.

'At least you're wearing your best cufflinks,' pointed out Orson. Mort was: the coffin ones Lily called his 'coffcuffs', which she said were better, by a smidge, than the ones that Reba had given him at Venus's wedding, dubbing them the 'fisticuffs'. (These were an anti-capitalist set that involved a hand punching up. Reba had made them from the melted-down badge of a police officer.)

Squaring his shoulders, Mort shoved open the front door to Eternal Elegance. A woman in black stood there, trying in vain to mop at her smudgy eye makeup beneath the lace mourning veil she wore.

Mort sighed in exasperation. What was with all this death? Why was it so inconvenient? Why hadn't Gramps franchised this bloody place if it was in such high demand?

'Sorry, not now. Death can be patient, but love waits for no man. Here, run down to The Hot Pot and grab a cup of tea. That'll get you twenty per cent off.'

He thrust a coupon at the woman, then pausing only to rub the noses of the poodle statues for good luck, he hurried over to the pagoda, where Lily stood in head-to-toe yellow, clutching a pink duffel bag as though it held the meaning of life. A fluffy pink skateboarding buffalo keyring gleamed as it swung back and forth.

'Lily, you can't. Don't go.'

Lily turned in surprise. The peeping sun caught her eyes, highlighting the flecks of green that hid within the bright blue. Mort couldn't bear the thought of never looking into them again.

'Why not?' she said, sounding bewildered.

'Because I need you here, with me. We all do.'

Mort stepped forward, touching his hand to the warmth of her cheek. The soft skin took on an additional flush under his touch. Mort never wanted to break contact, not ever. He wanted to frame her face with his hands and kiss her until he felt dizzy from lack of oxygen, until he felt weak at the knees from the pounding of his heart.

All he wanted was Lily. Lily, who brightened every single moment – even the darkest ones. Who somehow understood his wayward sense of humour and who took his preoccupation with death in stride. Lily, who toted Esmeralda around on her hip and finished jigsaw puzzles with Gramps and who invented silly Gutenberg drinking games for her friends, and who happily introduced herself to every stranger making the winding trek around the heart of the village. Lily, who was so unflappably funny, and so intensely kind, and so thoughtful and creative and fiery and passionate. Lily, who was so perfectly Lily, and so perfect for Mort.

Mort wanted to sit with her through the end of every movie she'd never finished, to help her tend the garden beds out front she was so worried she'd kill, to stand by her side throwing every coin he could find into the fountain at the Spanish mission, that maybe, just maybe, might play a part in their future. He wanted to see it all through with her. Every damn moment.

Mort pulled the funeral home's treasure map stamp out from his back pocket.

'You give me life,' he said, the words catching in his throat. He'd never before spoken with more meaning, with more heart, and from the tiny crinkles at the corners of Lily's eyes he could see that she felt it as well.

And as she passed him her well-thumbed treasure map for him to add that final stamp, he added, earnestly, passionately: '*You make me feel alive.*'

And Many Happy Returns

Lily

Mort's words coursed through Lily like a spell. Every part of her, every *cell* – right down to all the mitochondria bits – felt electrified. Beside her, Esmerelda meowed quietly, the iridescent crystal in her collar catching the sun and spinning...spinning...

Clouds rolled in over the blue sky, deepening from fluffy white into a foggy grey and then the darker, weightier hue that meant a storm was imminent. They shimmered with the onset of lightning, then cracked open like an egg. Rain pelted down in a cross-stitch of colours, kicking up the musky smell of petrichor from the parched Spanish tiles and setting the hot pink bougainvillea bushes nodding.

Umbrellas and parasols were grabbed from the baskets outside each of the shops, adding a rainbow canopy to the picturesque street. Hummingbirds hovered, all shimmering greens and yellows in the threading rain. A small child jumped up and down in a puddle quickly accumulating in a dip in the tiled path that wound through the leafy neighbourhood. A theatre kid let loose with a rendition of 'Singin' in the Rain' as they spun around an ornate lamppost, narrowly avoiding a whack in the head from a hanging planter trailing with vibrant morning glory trumpets.

Everything about the moment felt like the opposite of the storm that had struck when hateful words had been uttered. This was a storm of love, an expression of adoration and vulnerability and togetherness that was so great it couldn't be contained within one person . . . but spilled over into the world at large. Which was exactly how Lily's own heart and soul felt right now.

Fighting a grin, she pressed her lips into the firmness of Mort's, tangling her fingers in his sodden hair and letting herself sink into his broad form. Pooling from the arms of the reaching fig trees and leaping from the fairy-tale shade cloths that ran from business to business, rain rattled over them, ensconcing them in a clear curtain of water. Making this moment theirs alone – even if, around them, dozens of visitors and townsfolk were singing, dancing, splashing, whooping.

All Lily wanted this second was to share every part of her life, every part of *herself*, with Mort. She wanted to ride cerulean bicycles down the bumpy trails to the ocean. Wanted to watch retro B-horror movies with him as they provided their own sardonic narration. Wanted to embark upon a jigsaw puzzle for the ages, divvying up their roles between edge pieces and central blobs of colour until it all came into focus.

Wanted to wake up with him every single morning for the rest of her life.

'But I'll be back in an hour,' she said. 'You can't wait that long?'

Mort gulped, swiping rain from his hair, which seemed to bear the marks of . . . styling? Had Mort *styled* his hair for her? 'But . . . the job offer. The coffee with Venus. The helicopter. I thought you were going. Leaving for good.'

Lily booped his nose, the way that only Lily could get away with.

'Leave you? And the business? And the village?' Lily shook out her wet curls. 'I love it here. I'm finally where I need to be. I was just going to join Angela and Tink at hot yoga – Angela said she had some news about the lease extension. But honestly, I'd rather be rain-damp than sweat-damp.'

Mort twirled one of her curls around his finger. 'You look perfect either way.'

Lily beamed.

'The roof!' came a cry from the crowd.

Lily broke from Mort's embrace to see a toddler dancing beneath the downpipe at the front of Eternal Elegance (Wedding Edition). Water overflowed from the gutters like a dramatic swirl of royal icing on a tiered wedding cake, pouring down the hand-painted shop façade. Rain sheeted over both sides of the windows.

'Really should've gone with a licensed and bonded roofer,' muttered Mort. He rubbed his forehead as he took in the trickle of water that was starting to pour into the funeral home.

Lily grimaced. 'But Timbo was so nice!' And he had been – he'd brought over wildflowers for Lily's bud vases and had even joined her in testing out the karaoke machine she'd purchased for the cowboy wedding.

'Lily, look . . .' Mort's fingers clasped around her own, and they looked on in awe as the decor of their businesses began to revert to their original colours . . . drip by drip, and then in a deluge of paint and dye. The black tinge that Lily had tried so hard to paint over faded, creeping from her building over to Mort's, where it deepened the white-bleached areas of the funeral parlour, returning it to its original deep black. The dog statues out the front turned from white toy poodles to dalmatians to the jet black greyhounds that Lily had marvelled at on her first day. The flower baskets outside her own doors brightened and bloomed, adding a profusion of colour to the charming façade, and the wrought iron of the balconies retreated to their original addresses. Even the weird mediaeval shutters that had emerged from Lily's apartment like strange mushrooms were shrinking back into normal window treatments, and the light from inside her apartment had taken on its original pinkish tinge.

And then there was Esmeralda. Always black and white, her bicolour markings swirled and surged, the white becoming ebony, and the black the whitest fluff. Her blue eye became brown, and her brown blue, and then she – and Lily absolutely wasn't imagining this – winked. Then, crystal gemstone on her collar flashing, she performed a slinky figure eight around their ankles and gave Mort's leg a solid nip.

'Fuck! Esme!' he grumbled, as he rubbed at his trouser leg.

Lily chuckled. Everything was set to rights.

Knock 'em Dead

Mort

Mort regarded the interior of the funeral parlour. It was, to put a fine point on it, in a fucking shambles of a state. Sure, the carpets were black again, and the drapes had shifted from chiffon to the kind of heavy velvet Dracula would choose for his wedding attire, and the Hello Kitty motif had disappeared from the bestselling coffin line-up, which was going to make the sales part of the job a little less formidable. (Although he'd probably lose the customers that one viral Buzzfeed article had sent his way.)

But things hadn't gone back to quite the way they had been. Obviously there was the water intrusion to deal with – the puddles were deep enough that Mort half expected a posse of three-year-olds wearing yellow raincoats to come in and jump around. But in the intervening few months since the switcheroo, Mort had been shuffling things around to accommodate the Lilification of everything: rugs had moved, chairs once deemed too bright had been taken out of storage, new paintings had gone up on the walls. And of course there were the designs that he and Lily had painted here and there to cover the worst of the resulting crossover decor. But now with things reverted back to their original design, these newer design elements seemed . . . odd. Higgledy-piggledy.

Mort's heart gave a pang. He'd come to appreciate the whimsy and colour that the switcheroo had brought into his life. His clients had as well – his greeting book had been filled with so many joyful notes about getting to send off loved ones in a way that prioritised celebration over grief. Even though Mort wouldn't miss *some* of the switcheroo's surprises – like people manhandling the corpses or hurling around bouquets – it seemed like a loss for everything to return things to the way they had been.

Esmeralda leapt elegantly up on the pianola, and Mort realised that not *everything* had changed.

The ancient organ that had claimed pride of place in the viewing room had apparently decided not to return. Instead, the rickety instrument that Lily and Mort had hauled into the funeral parlour remained, all ornate curls of wood and dramatic candelabra filled with floral candles from Eternal Elegance (Wedding Edition).

Ignoring the pooling water and fizzing lights, Mort ran his fingers over the keys. Ah, that middle C where the plastic veneer had snapped off to reveal the rough wood underneath – the wood that Lily had tagged with her name. The dead high E with its whimpering tone.

He pulled up the bench seat, tinkled out a quiet arpeggio. Then he launched into Lily's favourite Mendelssohn. Not the 'Wedding March'. But 'Fleecy Cloud', with its gentle melody and the name that made her smile every time.

The tender music had the same effect on Lily as rattling a tin of tuna did on Esmeralda. A mere few notes in, and . . .

'Are you playing my song?'

Lily's voice carried through the transom, the decorative grate that allowed them to eavesdrop on each other's lives. And oh, how they eavesdropped. Well, in the beginning. After that, they'd upgraded to full conversations through the decorative little grille. Lily always joked that she felt like a prisoner in isolation talking to the inmate in the cell next door. Not that Lily had ever been isolated from people in her life – except during the Great Cold Sore Scare.

'Your song? You're claiming it all to yourself?'

'I can compromise,' said Lily. 'You can have the last few bars.'

'Seems fair.'

'Or we could make it our song.' He could hear the smile in her voice.

He fumbled a note. It rang out in the mess that was his business. Which reminded him, he really had to deal with that. Not that electrocution was a worry – he was the only one on the premises who wasn't dead. Unless the switcheroo had messed with the bodies he had on ice again . . .

THUD.

Mort jumped. Were the zombie hordes upon him? Dammit, he shouldn't have let Lily tempt him into watching that Romero marathon.

Another THUD. It was coming from her side of the wall.

'Are you okay over there?' he called, as the chandelier above his head – back to dark Murano glass twisted like serpents – swung wildly back and forth like a spirit guide's pendulum.

'Chekhov's sledgehammer,' came the panting reply. 'Stand back.'

Plaster crumbled as the thudding continued. A decorative cornice smashed on the black-painted hardwoods.

Then Mort was staring at Lily's dust-smudged face. Plaster fragments tumbled down on her like glorious confetti, suspended in the light that poured through the stained-glass windows at the front of her shop. She looked as though she were wearing a bridal veil. Mort's heart hitched.

'Thank God that wasn't a load-bearing wall,' Lily said, hand propped on the sledgehammer.

'You didn't check?' Of course she hadn't. It wouldn't be life with Lily if it were governed by permits and applications and approvals processes.

Blonde curls flicked as Lily cocked her head thoughtfully. 'I crossed my fingers before I started. That has to count for something.'

'Pulling permits would count for something.'

But he didn't mean it, not really. He'd happily let the businesses crumble around him if it meant being close to Lily. Although he might need to invest in some hard hats and goggles.

'I don't want you on the other side of the wall,' she said, as Mort picked a flake of plaster from her hair. She smelled of apples and laundry detergent and the humid tang of sweat from her recent wall-smashing session.

She stared up at him, eyes crinkled at their edges the way she hated, but the way he loved so much. 'I want you here, with me. Us doing our thing, side by side. No barriers. No walls. Our businesses are two pieces in the same two-piece jigsaw puzzle . . . and so are we. Let's join it all up. For good.'

For good.

'But the lease,' he said.

Lily pulled out her phone. 'Angela just texted me. Derrick and Fran have reconciled, and the cult's done – Derrick's going back to the bodega biz. Next year's business is going into the old church instead. I can stay. Right here.'

Mort traced her dusty cheek, then wiped flecks of plaster from her hair. 'Till death do us part?'

'Or whatever do us part. Don't focus on what can come undone. Focus on what's *now*, what's right here. What's in front of us.'

Mort's heart thudded.

It felt spontaneous, unplanned, all the things that terrified Mort in the way that going outside without checking the weather did, even though – magical storm clouds aside – the weather was always the same here. But with Lily by his side, the risks felt . . . worth it.

Mort swept her curls off her shoulders, then gently put his hands to her waist. 'I have a suggestion.'

'So do I.' Lily took a deep breath. 'So, I'm going to plan my cousin Tessa's wedding. It's very traditional, very old-school, all that jazz. No switcheroo stuff. And I'm wondering, Mort?'

Mort knew that whatever she was about to ask, he was going to say yes to. He was slipping down that slope of pure, unfettered joy, one that meant possibility and delight and entire new photo albums that would collect on Gramps's shelves until one day they would pass over to Mort's shelves. Because that was the way things went. That was the deal. You loved, and you loved, until you simply couldn't anymore. And however it ended, because it always ended, it would be worth it. Look at Reba and Frank. Look at Angela and Tink. Look at all the bizarre, starry-eyed couples Lily had helped affirm their commitment to each other.

'Tell me, what are you wondering?' he said gently.

'Will you be my plus-one?'

As Mort kissed her, the funeral parlour doors swung open. It was Pickleball Candice, and in her hand she clutched a slip of paper – an *unsave the date*.

'Funeral's off, fuckers! I'm not going to die after all!'

Until We Meet Again

Lily

Life comes at you in weird, winding ways. So does love. And so does death. And the intersection of all three of these was how a hearse came to be racing down the highway towards La Jolla, a generous hamper from the Chamber of Commerce wedged in the passenger footwell and 'Born to Be Alive' blasting on the radio in spite of Mort's protestations. Although somewhat half-hearted protestations, Lily had to admit. He'd come a long way since his first dour tutting at her Bops of Lily playlist.

And so had she. Instead of running the moment that feelings started to pop up, or muting a number when thing got difficult, she was *here*.

Because, look, sometimes you don't know if it's a sure thing. Or if it'll last forever. Or even ten years, or five, or two. All you know is that you don't have always, and that what you have now is something that you want to chase all the way down Highway 1, the ocean sparkling on one side of you, and the eyes of the person you love sparkling on the other as they tried not to cringe at the *a-ha* song – and its accompanying karaoke – they knew was coming up.

Maybe Lily would be planning an event for the two of them one day. Or maybe they'd just settle into something comfortable and kind, connected by their work and proximity and their equally terrible sense of humour. Maybe it would end like the series finale of *Six Feet Under*, or maybe it would end with the extra plates repurposed from Venus's wedding being hurled, or maybe it would end with a tender smile and a box of belongings on the other's front steps. Everything ended, but that was the risk. That was the whole glorious risk: putting your whole self into something that might not work out in the end, but that meant that in the meantime you were building something new together that you couldn't build alone. That you were willing to put your heart and soul and Netflix password and that amazing yellow vintage couch you'd found thrifting together up as collateral. That anyone did this at all, knowing what could go wrong, and what probably would, was testament to the sheer, wild beauty of love.

Mort's slim fingers found Lily's knee, giving it the gentle squeeze he always did when they were on the road together. 'What are you grinning at over there?'

'The fact that "Take on Me" is coming up next, and I will hit that high note or die trying.'

'Well, if you do, I promise to give you the proper send-off.'

'Pom-pom-bestowed poodles, confetti cannons, cake smashing, Cossack dancing, the whole nine yards?'

Mort nodded seriously. 'The whole nine yards of sequinned fabric. Now warm up those lungs. We have a wedding to get to, and you never know who you're going to have to fight to catch that bouquet.'

Lily made a jabbing motion with her elbow, then blew on it like she'd just unleashed multiple rounds from a revolver.

'For you, babe, I will give my own cousin a whack in the ribs.'

'Not the one getting married, though.'

'No, the middle one with the snaggle tooth who used to steal my Polly Pockets.'

'That's my girl.'

Mort glanced down at the dashboard and frowned. Lily could see exactly what was going through his mind: *250 miles till empty*, said the fuel monitor.

'You have three-quarters of a tank,' said Lily calmly. 'You don't need to top up just yet.'

'But what if the zombies come?' said Mort. 'Imagine running out of gas at the end of the world.'

'Then we'll run,' said Lily. 'Hand in hand, we'll outrun every last zombie, every last mushroom cloud, every last gang of cannibals.'

Mort swallowed, then nodded.

Lily squeezed his hand.

Mort gunned the engine, and they cruised along the endless curve of the highway, so many glorious moments behind them, and so, so many more glorious ones ahead. Weddings, funerals, and everything that came before, after and between.

In Loving Acknowledgment . . .

In *Four Weddings and a Funeral Director*, Mort wonders at length what comes after the end, and it turns out that it's the acknowledgments. Because every story that departs my laptop and grows its bookish wings is helped along by a posse of wonderful people, and we wouldn't be here without them.

To my husband, Wes, every love story that I write lets me relive the experience of falling in love with you, and I'm reminded each time of how lucky I am. Thank you for indulging my constant muttering about plot and character and helping me brainstorm my way through the roadblocks of my own creation (and for giving me Premetheus – brilliant).

To little Leo and my good boy Samson, oh, it's a brighter, more wonderful world with the two of you by my side, even if it means I end up covered in chocolate smudges and dog hair. Leo, I can't tell you how much it makes my heart sing to see you creating your own books, just like Mum.

To my brilliant agent Joanna Rasheed, my goodness, you are a powerhouse (and a fabulous juggler). Thank you for helping herding all the career cats that I seem to be collecting – I'd be sobbing in a corner without you. And to Elizabeth Aaron at Ultra and Imogen Bovill at Abner Stein, thank you for handling the across-the-pond communication and making sure I get all my paperwork ducks in a row.

To my exceptional editors Amy Mae Baxter and Jess Zahra, I'm endlessly grateful for your guidance, insight, cheeky edits, and absolute willingness to let me turn the silliness up to eleven. Thank you for not batting an eye when I propose stuff like 'there's only one coffin'. Here's to the next ones!

To Helena Newton, copyeditor extraordinaire, thank you for keeping my wayward characters in check across two books, and for apprising me about the Nutbush's limited geographic distribution, devastating though that was. (Aussie readers, just substitute the Nutbush for Cotton Eye Joe in that one scene.) To Clare Wallis, thank you for fixing my typos.

To Jessie Whitehead and Emily Hall, thank you for doggedly pushing this book into brilliant readers' hands, and to the rest of the wonderful Avon team, thank you for helping transform my stories from a badly formatted Word Doc into a beautiful volume worthy of TikTok viraldom (and even better, sending wonderful books from other Avon authors my way to read)! I'm very lucky to have found the publishing home I have.

To Janelle Barone, thank you for your fabulous cover art, and thanks to the always superb Toby James for yet another brilliant design. If readers judge my books by their covers, they'll be in fine stead indeed. And to audiobook narrator Amelia March, thank you for giving Lily her voice!

To Sofia Shelley, Alice Lee, Svani Parekh, Erin Petti, Kate Farrell, Chris Modaffieri, Brenna Jeanneret, Breanna Wright and Linda Bennett, thank you for cheering me on as this book transformed from a strange little duckling into a truly bizarre swan (or perhaps a badly behaved goose). Like weddings and funerals, books are all about community, and I'm so glad you're part of mine.

And to the person reading this, please know that I am beyond delighted that you chose to join me on this fun, bighearted romp – I loved inhabiting this book, Mirage-by-the-Sea and its bonkers cast so much, and I hope that Lily and Mort and their mischief brought some sunshine to your life as well.

One new owner. One hot barista. And one seriously weird coffee shop . . .

A latte love, a grande nightmare...

THE LITTLE COFFEE SHOP OF TERRORS

HAZEL GRAVES

Adele is down on her luck. She's just failed her last musical theatre audition, and it now looks like the bright lights of Broadway are behind her for good. So, when the opportunity comes up to take over a Brooklyn coffee shop, things finally seem to be going her way.

The only issue is the coffee shop comes with strings attached in the form of one very grumpy (but roasting hot) barista, **Ben**. He's worked there for years and he's not about to move on just because there's a new owner in town.

But soon it's not only Ben who's smouldering, because strange things are happening with the old coffee roasting machine in the basement, with roaring flames and weird noises that seem to come from nowhere. She'd ask Ben for help, but he never seems to be around when there's a problem to fix. And to add to it all, now some of the regular customers are nowhere to be seen . . .

Trouble is brewing for Adele and, before she knows it, she's in a whole latte trouble . . .